GROUNDED

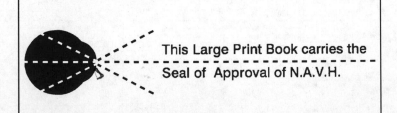

This Large Print Book carries the
Seal of Approval of N.A.V.H.

GROUNDED

NETA JACKSON
DAVE JACKSON

THORNDIKE PRESS
A part of Gale, Cengage Learning

GALE
CENGAGE Learning·

Detroit • New York • San Francisco • New Haven, Conn • Waterville, Maine • London

Copyright © 2013 by Dave Jackson and Neta Jackson.
Scripture quotations are taken from the following:
The Holy Bible, New International Version®. Copyright © 1973, 1978, 1984 by Biblica, Inc™. Used by permission of Zondervan. All rights reserved.
The Holy Bible, New Living Translation, copyright © 1996, 2004, 2007 by Tyndale House Foundation. Used by permission of Tyndale House Publishers, Inc., Carol Stream, Illinois 60188. All rights reserved.
The New King James Version®. Copyright © 1982 by Thomas Nelson, Inc. Used by permission. All rights reserved.
Poem beginning with "For food in a world" is by Manfred Wester. Copyright © 1985 by Gisela Wester.
Thorndike Press, a part of Gale, Cengage Learning.

LIBRARY OF CONGRESS CATALOGING-IN-PUBLICATION DATA

Jackson, Neta.
  Grounded / by Neta Jackson, Dave Jackson. — Large Print edition.
    pages cm. — (Windy City Neighbors Series ; #1) (Thorndike Press Large Print Christian Fiction)
  ISBN-13: 978-1-4104-5942-8 (hardcover)
  ISBN-10: 1-4104-5942-X (hardcover)
  1. Large type books. I. Title.
PS3560.A2415G76 2013
813'.54—dc23   2013012008

LT

Published in 2013 by arrangement with Worthy Publishing, a division of Worthy Media, Inc.

Printed in Mexico
1 2 3 4 5 6 7 17 16 15 14 13

GROUNDED

CHAPTER 1

The last note of her signature song hung in the cavernous space like the echo of a songbird . . . and Grace Meredith knew she'd "stuck it." Like those agile Olympic gymnasts on their flying dismounts from the uneven bars or balance beam. The final moment, a breathless hush . . . and then beyond the lights, applause thundering from the front-row seats clear up to the balcony.

In spite of the sore throat she'd been battling all week.

"Thank you," she called out over the applause. "Thank you so much. I love you! God loves you! And remember, you're worth the wait!"

With a smile, a wave, and a few kisses thrown to her excited fans, Grace backed off the stage of the huge Nashville auditorium, her royal-blue chiffon dress fluttering after her until the heavy, red stage curtains hid the audience from sight.

"Grace! That was awesome! They love 'You Are Special to Me.' " A young African American woman, clipboard and water bottle in hand, was the first to meet her backstage. "Here's your water . . . Do you want to go back to your dressing room before the meet and greet? . . . You should rest first . . . Here, this way."

Grace nodded, grateful for her assistant's firm grip on her elbow as they threaded their way over electrical cords, around ladders and props, and down the stairs to the dressing rooms. "Thanks, Sam," she breathed, sinking into the padded lounge chair. "I just need a few minutes." Hopefully, merchandise sales in the lobby were going well. It was going to be tight meeting all the expenses from this New Year, New You tour — her first independent tour — but sales of her new CD always seemed to skyrocket after that last song.

Sam poured a cup of hot tea from a thermos into a mug and handed it to her. Grace had been drinking honey-lemon tea and sucking Slippery Elm Lozenges like an addict just to keep her throat from giving out. She sipped the hot, sweet liquid, sighed, and closed her eyes.

Behind closed lids, she heard Sam — Samantha Curtis, five years her junior, recent graduate of Fisk University's music program, and Grace's personal assistant for the past three tours — answer a knock and send whoever it was away. Thank God for Sam. The adrenaline rush of the concert was quickly seeping out the bottom of her feet. If she stayed in the lounge chair much longer, she'd lose whatever energy she had left. But she couldn't stop yet. The meet and greet was important. She'd promised to be there . . .

Swinging her feet off the lounge chair, Grace sat up. "Uhhh, let's do it. Spritz me up, will you?"

Samantha frowned. "You don't need to rush. They can wait another five minutes . . . okay, okay." Grumbling under her breath, her assistant grabbed a hairbrush, gave Grace's long dark hair a quick brushing, and spritzed it with a styling gel. "Just one more sec," she murmured, freshening Grace's cheeks with a flick of powdered blush. "Okay, you're good to go."

Grace caught a glimpse of the two of them in the dressing room mirror as Sam ushered her out the door and smiled at the contrasts. Her own pale face and amber eyes, perked up with artfully applied eyeliner and peachy makeup, were framed by layered lengths of rich brunette hair creating a casual shag that hung past her shoulders. Samantha had honey-brown skin, large dark eyes, and tiny black twists all over her head. She looked "cute as a button," as Grace's mother would say.

But looks weren't the only differences between them. Samantha had the more outgoing personality, the chutzpah Grace wished she could muster in everyday life. Only when she walked onto the stage did Grace feel the certainty, the boldness, that enabled her to "sing her guts out" — as one reviewer had described her performance — and speak confidently to her thousands of young fans about the virtues of waiting till marriage for physical intimacy.

She was at home on the stage — *and* at the meet and greet time she always scheduled afterward. Like now, as twenty randomly selected fans gathered in a lounge to meet their favorite contemporary Christian music artist. Grace took time to speak to each one, asking about school or friends or favorite activities. And answering the inevitable question asked by her female fans, usually accompanied by self-conscious giggles: "Miss Grace, do you have a picture of your fiancé?" To which she happily showed a little "brag book" of photos of Roger Baldwin, the love of her life, including pictures of the two of them, laughing, holding hands — one of which also included Oreo, her black-and-white cat, cuddled in her arms. Prodded by starry-eyed teenagers, she would then make a show of modeling the silver princess-cut diamond engagement ring with tiny rubies Roger had slipped on her finger the previous year.

"I love your song!" . . . "Can my friend take our picture?" . . . "Are you going to sing at your own wedding?" Grace laughed at the fun questions, ready with easy banter.

But sometimes the comments got personal. "I want to be just like you," one teary girl whispered. "I'm going to wait to have sex until I get married too. Thank you."

Grace cleared her throat. That "just like you" thing always made her uncomfortable. She opened her mouth to say, "Oh, sweetheart, don't be like anybody else, just be yourself" — but the girl had already scurried away. Grace swallowed the words and turned to the next fan eagerly waving a CD for her to sign.

As the room emptied, Grace realized just how tired she was. It had been a particularly grueling tour — nearly four weeks through six southern states. Many of the concerts had been scheduled back to back, which meant traveling at night in a chartered tour bus with her small band of dedicated musicians, singing to packed houses four or five times a week — and that wasn't counting the Sunday morning performances in various churches. Touring had always been exhausting, but without the support of a record label, she was doing twice the work, and feeling every bit of it at the end of the day.

Hopefully the band had already broken down the set and was loading the tour bus so they could get on the road soon. They were heading for Memphis tonight, where she and Sam would be able to stay in a hotel. Just two more concerts left in her New Year, New You January tour, and then home to Chicago for a much-needed break.

And to see Roger. She could hardly wait.

Half an hour later, Grace collapsed on the queen-size bed in the private compartment at the back of the tour bus and took out her cell phone. Roger usually waited up for her call, though sometimes it went to voice mail and she had to wait till the next day for his return call. Like last night. There'd been no answer, and she hadn't heard from him today either. He must've had a busy day at work . . . though she wasn't sure why a financial consultant with a prestigious Chicago firm couldn't find ten minutes to return her call.

She tried to ignore the laughter and joking going on in the rest of the tour bus as the phone rang in her ear. The band was letting off some steam. They'd settle down as soon as the bus got on the highway —

"Hey there, Grace." Roger!

"Hi, honey! I'm so glad I got you tonight. Missed you last night."

"I know. Sorry about that. I had some international calls . . ."

Yeah, yeah. She knew the song and dance. It had to do with time differences in China and India and the Middle East or somewhere else on the other side of the world.

"I was hoping you'd return my call today." The moment she said it, Grace wished she could take it back. She didn't want to sound like a nag.

"Figured you'd be busy getting ready for tonight's concert, and I had back-to-back meetings today." He sounded matter-of-fact. "So how'd tonight's concert go? This was Nashville, right?"

Her tone softened as she told him about the wonderful auditorium the sponsoring churches had rented. "Some of the great Opryland stars have sung there," she said with a laugh. "I thought that would make me nervous, but it . . . I don't know, it in-

13

spired me. One of my best concerts, I think."

No response. "Roger? Are you still there?"

"Yes . . . sorry. Uh, that's great. Glad it was a good one."

Was she talking to the wall? Guess you had to be there. Which gave her an idea . . .

"Roger? I'd really like you to hear one of my concerts from this tour. I think it's my best tour yet — which is saying something, since it's the first one I've done on my own. Is there any chance you could fly to Memphis for the final concert on Saturday? I know it's short notice, but it's the weekend. If you came, we could fly back to Chicago together on Sunday. Memphis is Sam's hometown — she'd probably love the chance to stay a few extra days once the tour is done. It'd be just us —"

Beeping in her ear cut her off.

"Grace? Grace, I'm sorry. I'm getting a call from Beijing. I need to take it. Uh, look, we'll talk tomorrow night, okay? Sorry, darling, gotta go."

The line went dead. Grace held the phone out in front of her and just stared at it. *Argh.* Good thing she was going home this weekend. She and Roger needed some real time together, not these frustrating long-distance calls.

14

Sam woke her up at eight the next morning. "Don't know how you do it," Sam said, pushing the bus's room-darkening shades up to reveal the parking lot of the Embassy Suites Hotel. "We got in at four, and the band has already unloaded their equipment at the church. How do you sleep through all that?"

Grace didn't answer. It had taken her an hour to fall asleep and she still felt exhausted.

"I checked us in already," Sam went on, starting to gather articles of clothing tossed here and there. "Thought you'd rather shower and dress in your hotel room instead of here. I ordered breakfast to be sent up at nine, time to eat before sound checks at ten. Management said we could use the side door, go right up to our suite." She held up a burgundy velour lounging set — pants and top. "This okay for now?"

"Thanks." It came out as a croak.

"Uh-oh." Sam frowned. "We've got to take care of that voice. Two concerts to go before it can take a vacation. I'll fix a hot salt-water gargle . . ."

■ ■ ■ ■

By the time the taxi dropped them off at the church, Grace was feeling better after a steamy shower, gargle, and good breakfast. A church staff person met them at the front door and ushered the two women into the large sanctuary, where the band was tuning their instruments on the wide stage and Barry Fox, band manager and all-around sound technician, was standing at the back, hands on hips, hollering, "Move that amp more to the right . . . no, no, too far! Back six inches . . . okay!" He glanced at the two women. "Oh, hey, Grace . . . Sam. Not quite ready for sound checks. Give us fifteen, okay?"

"No hurry." Grace smiled at the fiftysomething band manager, already sporting a closely cropped salt-and-pepper beard to match his steel-gray hair. "You ever get those guys to sleep last night?"

Barry rolled his eyes. "Sometimes I feel like a glorified nanny to a bunch of twenty-somethings. But we got a few hours . . . you?"

"Not enough," Samantha butted in. "She's sleeping in the hotel tonight. And only once through both sets this afternoon. Her voice

16

is on the edge, and we don't want to push it over. Can we tell the guys to take the chord down at the end of 'Pure Heart' during practice instead of going up?"

Barry chuckled. "Be my guest." He gave Grace a playful poke as Sam hustled down the carpeted aisle toward the stage. "Now *she's* got the nanny thing down pat."

Grace laughed and dropped into a pew to wait until Barry was satisfied with amps, plugs, wires, lights, and tune-ups — all the mysterious details that had to be cared for before she stepped out on stage. How serendipitous that her Denver-based booking agency — Bongo Booking — had rounded up this gem of a garage band in Chicago, her hometown, and hired them to tour with her. No, that wasn't serendipity — it was a God-thing. Their sound and her voice had fit like the proverbial hand in glove, and the guys were fun to work with too.

She watched and listened, amused, as Petey, the saxophonist, shaved head glistening, jammed with red-headed Alex and his electric guitar. Hefty Reno, the keyboardist, was still pushing amplifiers around, while Nigel — ponytailed and tattooed — set up his drums, and Zach, the only African American in the band, sporting his "African

17

knots" hairstyle proudly, joined the jammers on his electric bass.

Her fingers itched to take out her cell and try Roger again before things got busy . . . but she resisted. No, he'd promised they'd talk tonight. Maybe he could still get a flight to Memphis tomorrow and take in her last concert.

"Grace! We're ready!" Barry called from the front.

She smiled to herself as she headed down the aisle. Tomorrow, hopefully, she'd sing for Roger too.

Chapter 2

Two nights in Memphis . . . that was a luxury, especially at the end of a tour. The concert had gone well that night, and Sam said CDs and T-shirts had brisk sales. Only one more concert. Grace slipped into her red-and-black silk pajamas and flopped backward onto the king-size bed in the hotel suite, arms flung out. Ahhh, no more nights on the tour bus. She could even sleep late while the guys moved all their equipment to the next venue — the Orpheum Theater, no less.

How Bongo Booking had managed to snag the Orpheum for this tour, she wasn't sure — though she'd done the Orpheum two years ago when she was on a multi-artist tour organized by her record label. It would be a strong ending for her New Year, New You tour.

Sam's sister and a cousin had come to the concert tonight, and she'd brought them to the meet and greet. Fun girls. Sam had asked for a couple hours off tomorrow to go see her mother and extended family . . . that should be possible. And if Roger was able to come early in the day, maybe they could have a light dinner together before the concert —

A knock at the bedroom door interrupted her thoughts. "You need anything else?" Sam asked as she peeked in. "Shawnika and Crystal are downstairs in the café — thought I might go down and hang out with them for a while if you don't need me."

Grace leaned up on her elbows. "I'm good. Go, have fun. I'm glad to get rid of you anyway" — she grinned slyly — "because I'm just about to call Roger."

Samantha rolled her eyes. "I am so out of here." The bedroom door started to close, and then pushed open again. "But I've got my cell with me if you —"

"Go!" Grace laughed, grabbing a pillow and throwing it toward the door. A moment later she heard the outer door close as well. *Good grief.* Sam meant well, took her job seriously, but there were times when Grace needed her privacy.

Retrieving the pillow, she propped herself up with several of its mates against the padded backrest of the hotel bed, and reached for her cell phone. Hitting a speed-dial number, she waited for the rings . . . one . . . two . . .

"Hi, Grace."

Grace smiled at Roger's voice. "Hi, yourself." She pulled one of the pillows close and hugged it. "You aren't still at work, are you? 'Cause I'm here all by my lonesome in this hotel room, wishing I was there with you." It was almost a purr.

"No, I'm home. Was expecting your call."

"I'm glad." Poor guy sounded a bit stressed. "You okay? Been thinking about you all day . . . sounds like you could use some time off. Did you have a chance to consider flying down here tomorrow to hear my last concert? It's at the Orpheum Theater. Classy place. I'd so love the band to meet you and —"

"I can't come tomorrow, Grace."

His abrupt turndown of her invitation caught her off guard. She waited for the explanation . . . *"Have to work all weekend"* or *"Not feeling so good"* or *"I broke my leg."* But nothing.

"That's it? Just 'I can't come'? Roger, it would mean a lot to me! If it's the expense, I'd be willing to buy the ticket. I'm really missing you and . . . and this has been my best tour yet. I'd love to share it with you.

21

It's . . . it's an important part of me that I want you to know."

"I know. That's just it . . ." It sounded as if he blew out a long breath. "Look, Grace. I didn't want to do this by phone. But this touring business isn't working for me. You're gone so much. I know, it's what concert artists do. It's your dream come true. But . . . it's not my dream. What kind of life is that for me? If we got married, I mean . . ."

Grace stopped breathing. *If* they got married? "Wha . . . what are you saying?"

She heard him clear his throat. "I've been doing a lot of thinking while you've been gone, and I . . . I just don't think we should keep up the pretense anymore. It's not working. We're living in two separate worlds. I need a woman who's *there* for me." He paused, but when she didn't respond, said, "I'm sorry, Grace. I know this is hard. It's hard for me too. But I think we should step back, call off the engagement for now . . ."

Roger's voice continued in her ear, but Grace had grown numb. *Pretense? . . . Call it off?* The words echoed in her head, but at the same time seemed unreal, mangled, like so much gobbledygook.

". . . talk about it more when you get home," Roger was saying. "I'll let you get

22

settled for a few days, and then maybe we can —"

But her hand had dropped to the bed. Her thumb pressed the Off button. She lay there, numb, for a long time, staring at the abstract painting on the wall. But then the tears came. Rolling over, she buried her face in the mound of pillows as painful sobs erupted from deep in her belly. *No . . . no . . . no . . .*

How long she lay there crying, Grace had no idea. Much later she heard the outer door to their suite open and close and the muffled sounds of her assistant moving around the other half of the suite, pulling out the daybed, water running in the bathroom. She tried to stifle the sobs, but soon she heard a quiet tap at her door and Sam's concerned whisper. "Grace? Are you okay?"

She didn't answer. But as sounds quieted in the other room, voices seemed to scream in her head . . .

You're worth the wait?! Ha-ha-ha-ha.

What are you going to say to those starry-eyed fans now?

You fool . . . you stupid fool . . . you plastered your engagement all over this tour and now . . . now he's left you hanging to flap in the wind . . .

CHAPTER 3

Grace stared at her reflection in the lighted mirror. Samantha had just spritzed the finishing touch to her artfully arranged long shag. Arched eyebrows. Thick, dark lashes. Just enough blush. Creamy peach lipstick. All complementing her smooth skin.

But beneath the perfect makeup, she felt frozen.

"I can't do it," she whispered.

Behind her in the mirror, Grace saw Samantha react. "*You can't?* . . . Grace! The opening band is doing their last number. You're on in five!"

"Sam, I . . . I just can't." Throwing down the powder brush she'd been using to take the shine off her nose, Grace buried her face in her hands.

Samantha pulled up a stool beside the swivel makeup chair and, hesitating only a nanosecond, put her arm around the other woman's shoulders. "Grace, what's wrong?"

Grace just shook her head, face hidden in her hands. How could she go out on stage after Roger's phone call last night?

She hadn't gotten much sleep, but when room service brought their breakfast at ten, she'd pulled herself together, said nothing about the phone call, and Samantha hadn't asked. By the light of day, it all seemed unreal. Roger had *dumped* her — just like that? This couldn't be happening.

She'd pushed it out of her head and coped by keeping busy — sending Sam out to get her outfits steam pressed for tonight, making sure her laptop was locked in the hotel safe, double-checking that her concert bag had all the things she usually needed. Sam had seemed a little miffed at that — she never forgot the two bottles of Evian, the Slippery Elm Lozenges, spritz, coconut hand cream, mouthwash, deodorant, Grace's favorite perfume, makeup kit, hairbrush and dryer, hand mirror, safety pins, Band-Aids . . . everything Grace might need.

Sam had seen her to the theater after lunch for the usual sound check and run-through, before taking off for a few hours to see family. Things had been a little rough between Grace and the band. She'd felt tense, irritable, and had taken more than the usual number of breaks. But she wasn't the only one who was exhausted, and everyone had chalked it up to this being the last concert on the tour. Barry Fox had said graciously, "No worries. You always pull through, Grace." He'd even kissed her on the cheek. "Go get 'em, girl."

Grace heard a voice crackle in the headset her assistant was wearing and Sam responded, "Okay." Half a second later Sam turned the swivel chair away from the mirror, took Grace's hands down from her face, and held them firmly in her own hands.

"Grace Meredith, look at me . . . *look* at me!"

Grace shook her head, staring down at their hands, fingers interlocked, brown and white. She wanted to hang on for dear life.

"Grace, I know you must be exhausted. But there are a thousand fans out there who came to hear their sweetheart sing tonight. A lot of them are teenagers confused about sex, wondering 'why wait?' when all they hear from every direction is 'why not do it?' They came tonight because you've taken a strong stand about the value of waiting until marriage. You're their role model . . . and if that's the message God's given you, he'll give you the strength to get out there and sing, no matter what you're goin' through right now."

Grace was startled. Sam sounded more like her mother than her assistant.

She looked up and locked on Sam's face. The firm grip on her hands and the steady gaze of Sam's dark brown eyes were having an effect. "You're . . . you're right, Sam. I've got to go out there for my fans . . ." She let herself be helped to her feet. "Do I look all right? My hair . . . finger-comb it again, would you? And water — I need some water."

"We've got one minute. You look great. Here's your water. Go . . . go!"

Yanking open the door, Samantha hustled Grace through the cavernous hallway, up the stairs, through the backstage area around props, stage sets, instrument cases, and snaking electrical cords — "Watch your step!" — and into the wings of the stage, the two of them hidden by the rich folds of the heavy curtains falling from the pulleys above.

Doug What's-his-name, the concert host, glanced their way from center stage and a relieved smile lit up his face. ". . . and here she is, all the way from the Windy City to the Home of the Blues . . . Grace Meredith!"

A roar of cheers, whistles, stomps, and

claps erupted from the unseen audience beyond the stage lights. Grace sucked in a quick breath.

"You can do this!" Sam hissed, gently pushing the small of Grace's back. Grace nodded, took another deep breath, and swept onto the stage.

On cue, the five-man band broke into the familiar swing of her opening number, an old favorite from her first CD. The black silk dress she was wearing — its hundreds of rhinestones up and down the sleeves and around the neck flashing and sparkling under the lights — made Grace feel as if she were floating across the stage. As she took the hand mike, everything else — the long tour, the exhaustion, her tender throat, the upsetting phone call — disappeared. Closing her eyes, she crooned the first words of her opening song as the audience erupted in another roar.

But it didn't last.

As Grace moved through her first set, she knew her voice sounded ragged at the edges. To compensate, she began avoiding the high notes, filling in with a muddy middle range. With Roger's phone call nibbling at the edges of her consciousness, she skipped several of her homey talks between songs,

which were usually light-hearted and personal anecdotes during the first set. She
always saved the more serious reflections
about life and love and relationships for the
final segment.

The break and intermission couldn't come
soon enough.

"It's all right, gonna be all right," Sam
encouraged, as Grace collapsed into the
padded chair in her dressing room.
"Here . . ." Sam handed her a steaming cup
of the honey-lemon tea. "You'll make it. Just
give your voice a rest. Last concert, remember?"

Yes, last concert. And Roger wasn't here.
Wouldn't come. Didn't want to come. *O
God, I can't do this!*

But she had to do it. She couldn't just not
show up for her last set. The blogging community — a community so easily tempted
by rumor — would be all over it before
morning. She couldn't afford that kind of
hit to her reputation.

After finishing her tea, Grace changed into
the gray-and-lavender dress with the fluttering handkerchief hem, freshened her
makeup . . . then got the two-minute warning. The break was over all too soon. Sam
kept whispering encouragement as they
stood just offstage behind the heavy red

curtain. "I'm prayin' for you, girl. Remember, 'I can do all things through Christ who strengthens me' —"

"Miss Curtis?"

A male voice behind them caused both Grace and Samantha to turn. One of the stagehands, wearing a headphone over a Redbirds baseball cap, stood awkwardly in the wings, looking at Sam. He gestured over his shoulder with his thumb. "Main office says you've got a phone call. Said you might want to take it in Miss Meredith's dressing room."

Sam shook her head. "I'm sorry, I can't take it now. Just get a message, okay?"

"Uh, office said it was urgent."

Sam looked distressed. "Grace, I'm sorry . . ."

Grace always felt more secure when she could look offstage and see her assistant standing there, smiling, sending an encouraging thumbs-up. Something she especially needed tonight. But taking a deep breath, she murmured, "You better take it. I'll be all right. Just keep those prayers going."

"Okay." Sam rolled her eyes. "Better not be my cousin Keisha, though. If it is, I'm gonna kill her. She's been raggin' on me 'cause I didn't get her free tickets to tonight's concert. The nerve of that girl!"

Grace watched her disappear behind the jumble of stage sets, feeling slightly abandoned. But the concert host was saying, "Welcome back, Grace Meredith!" accompanied by waves of applause, hoots, and whistles from the audience.

"I can do all things . . ."

She pasted on a smile. The show must go on.

The crowd rose to their feet as she sang the final line of her last number, "Others can see . . . you are special to me." Acknowledging the enthusiastic applause with a final wave and a smile, Grace left the stage. It was over. She'd made it. Hopefully most of the audience hadn't noticed the strain in her voice, though Barry and the band would've, for sure. But she'd even given her usual pep talks, about the importance of purity, of saving the gift of sex for marriage, telling her mostly young audience they were "worth the wait."

But she felt like a phony.

Worth the wait? Obviously Roger didn't think so. But why? Why? Had he somehow found out . . . no, impossible. They just needed time. Once she got home, they'd work it out . . . wouldn't they?

Once hidden behind the heavy red curtain,

she stopped. Her assistant was nowhere to be seen.

"Miss Meredith?" The stagehand in the Redbirds hat hustled over. "Miss Curtis asked me to tell you that she has a family emergency. Said she left you a note in your dressing room."

An emergency? That sounded ominous. Fighting disappointment that the woman she counted on to pick up the pieces after an exhausting concert had disappeared, Grace managed to make her way to her dressing room. There on the dressing table was a folded sheet of tablet paper, with something paper-clipped to it.

A copy of their e-ticket back to Chicago. Dated tomorrow. Passengers Grace Meredith and Samantha Curtis.

Grace unfolded the note. *Dear Grace,* she read. *Mama had a heart attack late this afternoon — and I just saw her a few hours ago! But they've taken her to the ER and my aunt begged me to come right away. I'm so sorry to leave you in the lurch, but I don't have a choice. I'll probably need to stay here in Memphis for a while. Here's the e-ticket. I'll call you as soon as I know anything. Take care. I know you did great tonight because God is good . . . all the time. Sam.*

CHAPTER 4

The next day, as the limo driver piled the teal-blue suitcases on the curb in front of Delta Airlines, Grace Meredith squinted at the sheet of paper she was holding — just as a gust of wind tore it out of her gloved hands. "Oh, no! That's my e-ticket! Catch it! Catch it!"

The uniformed driver shoved the last suitcase on top of the pile and darted after the paper as it skittered across the three slushy lanes of traffic trying to unload at Memphis International Airport. Tires skidded as the driver stiff-armed a taxi, which managed to stop just inches from running him down. It happened so fast, Grace hardly had time to cry out — but by the time she realized the man was safe and looked back to see where the wind had taken her flight itinerary . . . it was gone.

Just then the pile of suitcases on the curb toppled over, splaying over the sidewalk and earning her nasty looks from other passengers heading for the sliding doors into the terminal.

Grace stood rigid on the curb, clutching her wool coat tightly around her neck. Could anything else go wrong this horrible weekend? First, Roger's devastating phone call. Then Samantha had suddenly disappeared, right in the middle of the concert. Her assistant had to know she was a wreck, especially at the end of a grueling concert tour. She —

Good grief, what's the matter with you, Grace? You've let yourself get mighty spoiled, that's what. The note said the girl's mother had a heart attack, for pity's sake! But it didn't help that her throat was sore, her head ached, she'd slept badly again — if at all — and having to do everything herself this morning had made her late. She had less than an hour to get through security and make her plane!

"I'm sorry, miss. Couldn't catch it." The limo driver had reappeared and was snatching the wayward bags out of harm's way. "You want me to get a cart" — he glanced nervously at the limo, motor running at the curb — "or do you want to do curbside check-in?" He gestured hopefully toward the Delta employees in the small enclosure nearby. "It's faster."

"Yes, yes, curbside, please. I'm late as it is. But my e-ticket . . ." Anxiety threatened to bring the tears to the surface again.

"Don't worry, miss. They can pull it up on the computer. Just give them your name and destination."

Scurrying back and forth, the limo driver managed to get the two large and two smaller bags to the curbside check-in. "That's it. They'll take care of you."

"Thank you." Grace pulled her carry-on out of the line of bags. It had her medicines, toiletries, jewelry . . . had to keep that with her. She glanced at her watch — only fifty minutes till her plane was supposed to leave! But just that simple glance made her wince. The delicate silver watch with the tiny ruby birthstone had been a birthday gift from Roger, matching the silver engagement ring on her finger . . .

She suddenly realized the limo driver was still standing there.

Oh, for heaven's sake. The tip. Samantha always took care of that too. *You've become a spoiled brat, you know that, Grace Meredith?* Fumbling in her large leather purse, she opened her wallet. Nothing smaller than a twenty. She handed one of the bills to him.

"Thank you, miss! Have a good trip."

Touching his hat briefly, the man hurried back to the limo, got in, and pulled away.

Grace watched him go.

Now she had nobody.

"Miss? Miss? Do you have your ticket?" The curbside agent beckoned to her. And just like the driver had said, when she explained about the lost e-ticket, he simply looked her up on the computer, and in five minutes had all three of the checked bags on a cart tagged for Chicago. He handed her a boarding pass. Another tip. At least she didn't have to pay extra for the bags — first-class passengers were allowed three checked bags free. Thank God for small favors, like free upgrades thanks to frequent flyer miles. And once she got on the plane, maybe she could sleep a little. She might even drink a glass of complimentary wine to help her relax — one benefit of traveling without Sam, who no doubt would give her a disapproving look.

Grace headed through the doors, welcoming the blast of heated air as she came into the terminal. Was January always this cold in Memphis? She'd been there two days and it felt no different than Chicago. Glancing at her boarding pass — Concourse B, Gate 12 — she surveyed the bewildering array of signs. There . . . that way.

A disembodied voice announced over the PA, *"The security level today is Orange."* It was always Orange. Pulling the carry-on, Grace followed the line snaking its way back and forth toward security. Why was it going so slow? Her anxiety mounted again. Forty minutes now . . . thirty-five . . . thirty . . . finally! She hefted her carry-on bag onto the conveyer belt, shrugged off her heavy winter coat and loaded it into a plastic bin along with her purse, zipped off her knee-high leather boots and threw them into another bin. Ugh! She hated walking on dirty airport floors in just her stocking feet. But she lined up the bins on the conveyer belt and watched the first one follow her carry-on into the scanner.

"Next!"

A Transportation Security Administration agent was waving impatiently at her. That's when Grace noticed that it wasn't the usual walk-through metal detector, but one of those new body-scan machines. She'd seen pictures — it was like you were stark naked! Grace froze.

"Lady? You going through or not?" said the passenger in line behind her.

Grace gave her head a quick shake and stepped back, letting the man pass. No, no . . . she didn't want to have her picture taken stark naked. That was . . . so invasive! She glanced up and down the other security lines. They were even longer than the one she'd been in. If she went to the back of the line, she'd surely miss her plane! And her bag and personal belongings had already disappeared behind the rubber flaps of the conveyer belt.

"Uh, sir? Sir?" She stepped closer to the agent instructing people stepping into the scanner. "I . . . I don't want to go through that machine. Is there an alternative? My plane is going to leave in less than half an hour —"

"Opt out!" he called out loudly. "We have an opt out here!" He unhooked the retractable belt divider and beckoned to her to step around the scanner.

Relieved, Grace hurried around the machine. But her relief was short-lived when another agent met her and motioned toward a glass enclosure. "Excuse me, miss. Step this way, please." The voice was gravelly, no nonsense.

Grace looked up into small gray eyes and a reddish face. The TSA agent was big and burly, the buttons straining on the shirt that covered his belly. "What . . . what is this?"

"Standard procedure. You opt out, we need to do a physical check." The man took her arm and firmly led her toward a glass enclosure.

"But . . . my purse, my shoes . . ." Grace twisted her head and pointed back toward the scanner, which had burped out the two plastic bins with her things in them, along with the bags and bins of the people who'd been behind her.

"Someone will hold them for you. This way, please."

His grip was firm on her arm until she'd stepped inside the glass enclosure, then he left her alone. Glancing anxiously through the walls of the small enclosure, Grace saw another agent pawing through her suitcase — and a moment later he held up a pair of small scissors. "Sharp instrument," he called out before tossing them into a bin with other confiscated items.

Was that *it*? Samantha always brought a whole kit of miscellaneous items for every little emergency on tour: scissors, tweezers, nail clippers, bandages, foot pads, needles, thread, safety pins, markers, sticky notes, even matches — which, she supposed, her assistant usually packed in the checked luggage. Grace had thrown the kit in the carry-on that morning, "just in case" she needed something, not thinking about security restrictions.

She stepped toward the opening of the glass enclosure. "I can ex—"

"Lady, you need to wait." The burly agent appeared from somewhere and planted himself in her way. "Stand on those footprints."

"But —"

"On the yellow footprints, miss. And don't move. Someone will be with you shortly."

What? How dare they treat anyone like this! And for what silly reason? She felt like shouting, *"Just take the kit! Whatever! I don't care! Just let me go so I can make my plane!"*

Did she dare look at her watch? She was afraid to move. But out of the corner of her eye she caught sight of a large wall clock. Fifteen minutes! She'd never make it now!

"Body search in Unit Two!" the man yelled. "Female opt out!"

Body search? Were they talking about her? What did they mean? *O God, O God, I don't like this.*

"But . . . I'm going to miss my plane," she protested weakly to the man outside the enclosure.

"Look. You gotta wait for a female agent. Sorry."

"How long will that take?"

"No idea."

"But my flight's about to leave!"

40

She looked around, but no one else seemed to be coming. The man made a show of looking around too. Then he gave her a look that lingered a bit long.

"Fine. I'll get you to your plane on time." The man reached for a box and removed a pair of latex gloves, pulling them on with a snap.

But she winced as he stepped into the glass enclosure. Too close, too close.

"Okay, Miss, I'm going to pat down the breast area, then —"

"My breasts?" Grace felt heat rise to her face. "That's . . . that's not necessary."

"You want to make your plane? No talking. Now . . ."

Grace felt a firm hand on one shoulder, and then the other running fingers around first one breast, then the other. "Arms out to the side!" the agent said. Grace obeyed, but her breath was coming hard and fast. An old memory resurrected in her mind . . . that unwanted touch . . . panic bubbled in her chest.

She turned her head away — and saw people in the line staring at her. No one had a right to touch her like that! Not then . . . not now! She'd made a vow . . .

The agent's hands ran down her sides from armpit to waist, then around to her back, down her spine, along her ribs.

"Spread your legs," the man commanded from behind her.

Grace started to shake. She squeezed her eyes shut. Hot tears gathered behind her lids. *No, no!* This couldn't be happening! She never should have allowed this!

Just then she heard another voice. "Walker! *Stop.*"

Female. Grace cracked her eyelids. A black woman, hair pulled back tight into a knot at the nape of her neck, stood in the doorway of the enclosure, hands on her hips.

"Lady said she was in a hurry, has to catch her plane." The gravelly voice.

"Are you serious, Walker? Do you know how much trouble you're in right now?" the woman snapped. "I'll take over now."

The man shrugged, and eased his gut out of the doorway, and the woman stepped in. "Sorry about that, miss."

But it was too late. By now Grace was shaking almost uncontrollably. Hot tears blurred her vision. She put out a hand, feeling for the glass wall, trying to steady herself as the woman completed the pat down, up and down her legs, even her hips and crotch area.

"You may step out," the woman said.

Grace felt faint. The tears spilled down

her cheeks. The glass wall seemed to tilt. She tried to take a step, but the next moment she crumpled to the floor, right on top of the yellow footprints, gasping for breath as loud, uncontrolled sobs shook her whole body.

Never! Never! She'd made a vow she'd never let anyone touch her like that . . . ever again!

CHAPTER 5

The taxi headlights shone momentarily on
the sign that said No Outlet as it turned
into the darkened residential street on
Chicago's north side, then crept slowly
down the block and pulled to the curb in
front of a tidy brick bungalow. "This it,
missy?" asked the driver in a heavy accent
— Indian or Pakistani or something — peering at the numbers under the porch light.

Grace croaked something she hoped
sounded like yes and struggled to open the
backseat door. She was so tired she could
hardly function. A limo driver would have
hopped to and opened it for her, but by the
time her standby flight had finally landed at
O'Hare, well after midnight, the car Samantha had arranged from Lincoln Limo Service had long been deployed elsewhere. A
week earlier, Grace would've called Roger
to come pick her up, to hold her in his arms
while she poured out the humiliation she'd

44

suffered at the hands of the TSA . . . but she couldn't very well do that now.

Her brother in Arlington Heights, a suburb northwest of the airport, might've picked her up if she'd begged, but he drove for UPS and had to be at work by six a.m. It would really be out of his way to take her all the way to her neighborhood in north Chicago and back home again. Besides, he had a wife and two kids. Why ruin the night for him too?

When she finally managed to get out of the taxi, the driver had her bags out of the trunk and was dragging them up the short walk through two inches of snow. Grace followed, stepping carefully in her high-heeled boots, hoping there were no icy spots lurking beneath the unshoveled walk. That's just what she needed, a nasty spill only a few yards from her front door.

Fumbling with her key ring, Grace got the door open and the man pulled the bags inside, snowy wheels and all, right over the mail that had accumulated on the floor beneath the mail slot. Almost in a stupor, she handed him her business credit card but he shook his head. "Don't take credit. You got cash?"

Gritting her teeth, Grace pulled the last two twenties from her wallet. The man grunted and headed out to his cab. She shut the door and locked it, sliding the safety chain into place, then turned and leaned against it with a moan, as if making sure it stayed shut, keeping everything and everybody out.

O Lord, O Lord . . . what am I going to do?

The antique schoolhouse clock on the living room wall had stopped weeks ago, but her cell phone said 2:10. She needed sleep, though her stomach pinched with hunger. All she'd had to eat at the airport was a banana muffin and a large paper cup of tea while waiting long hours for her name to be called. Traveling standby, she'd had to ride in economy. They didn't even call it "coach" anymore. No perks. No hot meal. Not even peanuts.

Pushing away from the front door, Grace shrugged out of her wool coat, dropped it on the piano bench, and dragged the carry-on down the hall to her bedroom, half-hoping to see her black-and-white cat curled up on the end of the bed. But Oreo was still at Meeow Chicago, the premier boarding home for cats — the only place she ever left Oreo after that fiasco boarding him at the vet, where they'd basically kept him in a cage for six weeks. Never again!

Never, never again . . .

Never set foot in an airport again, either, that was for sure. In fact, *never* sounded like manna from heaven. Never make a fool of herself like she'd done Saturday night, hyping her purity message, telling hormone-crazy teenagers "you're worth waiting for," when obviously, Roger had decided *she* wasn't worth waiting for.

Maybe she should quit singing.

Never do another tour.

Why not? That was Roger's beef, wasn't it? That she was gone so much? At least, that was what he'd said. But was there more . . . things not said? Things she'd never talked about, but maybe —

Stop it, Grace. Couldn't think about that. Her throat was sore, her head ached. She was so tired . . .

Pushing aside the temptation to just crawl into bed, clothes and all, Grace stumbled into the bathroom. A hot shower . . . that's what she needed. Wash away the dirty feeling she'd had ever since that . . . that awful man had touched her. Places even Roger had never touched her.

The tears started once more.

Standing in the shower, breathing in the steam and letting hot water run over her head, plastering the long, thick strands of hair to her back, Grace felt her muscles start to relax for the first time in two days. She lathered her hair, then her whole body. But for some reason she kept her eyes closed, as if afraid to see herself naked . . . as if she were still standing in that glass cage, being stared at like an animal in a zoo.

She turned off the water, toweled herself dry, covered herself quickly in her cozy fleece robe, and padded to the kitchen to make a mug of lemon tea with honey to soothe her throat.

Finally crawling exhausted between the sheets under her mother's heirloom quilt, the mug of tea and honey only half drunk on the bedside table, Grace stared into the darkness. The silence of coming home alone was loud in her ears. No fans clamoring for her attention, wanting to share their life stories or asking for her autograph. No Samantha to check on her, making sure she had everything she needed. No call from Roger, whispering sweet nothings into her ear. Not even the comforting weight of Oreo, curled up on her feet.

She had never felt so utterly alone.

Music . . . what? Don't want music . . . want to sleep . . .

The muscular notes of "All Hail the Power of Jesus' Name" finally throbbed into

48

Grace's consciousness . . . *uhhh.* Her cell phone ringtone. Eyes still closed, she fumbled for the offending noise, pressed the Off button, and burrowed deeper under the quilt.

Hugging her pillow, she willed herself into oblivion again, but sleep didn't come. Her mouth felt dry and her throat was still sore. The room was light in spite of the closed venetian blinds. Rising up on one elbow, she blinked blearily at the digital alarm clock. 2:13. Two in the *afternoon?* Grace sat up. Oh no. She'd slept right around the clock! But she had to go get Oreo or it'd be another day before she could pick him up.

Sliding out of bed, Grace wearily pulled on her robe and slippers, shuffled out to the kitchen — stopping just long enough in the living room to wind the schoolhouse clock — and started coffee. She peeked over the café curtains covering half the kitchen window at the thermometer just outside. Twenty-two degrees and cloudy. She shivered in spite of herself and glanced up and down the street. No one about. *Monday . . .* Kids still in school. Everybody else at work.

Oh, wait . . . there was the old woman who lived in the two-flat across the street and one house down, strewing rock salt on her icy walk. Grace shook her head. The woman was too old to be doing that. She needed a yard-care service or something. The woman used to have somebody living on the second floor, but Grace hadn't seen anyone but the woman — what was her name? Polish-sounding something — for months. Maybe longer. For a while it'd looked as if somebody was renovating the second floor, but even that activity had stopped.

A *ding* behind her turned her from the window. Coffee. She probably should've made more lemon-and-honey tea, but she needed a jolt of caffeine. Pouring herself a fragrant cup, Grace wrapped both hands around it and walked back toward the bedroom to get her phone. Someone had called earlier. Better not be Roger. She didn't want to talk to him. Not yet anyway. The alert said she had voice mail. She clicked the button and held the phone to her ear . . .

"Hello, Grace? This is Samantha. Just wanted to know if you got home all right on yesterday. Again, I'm so sorry I had to leave, but my mother . . . you know. She's stable now but still in the hospital, and I'm going to stay here in Memphis until I know more. I'll keep you posted. Talk to you soon."

Well, that was good news. She'd call Sam

later, maybe tomorrow. There were two other voice mails — both from her parents. Her brother would expect a call too. Mark usually checked on her house once a week when she was gone, and he knew she was coming home yesterday. But Grace clicked the phone off and sank into the padded rocking chair in the bedroom. She didn't feel like talking to her assistant or anybody else. Her parents and Mark would probably ask about Roger . . . No, all she wanted to do was drink her coffee, get dressed, and go get Oreo. Everything else could wait. She didn't have another concert until —

Another concert? Nausea cramped her stomach. She couldn't face another concert. Her voice was shot anyway. When was it? Sometime in February, she remembered that much. Where was her Day-Timer?

Grace found her purse in the living room under the coat she'd thrown on the piano bench, dug out the Day-Timer, and paged through it. Was today really the first day of February? There it was — a concert for a sweetheart banquet at a large church in Milwaukee, just two weeks away.

Grace groaned. Roger had planned to go with her since it was only two hours away. They were going to drive and stay the weekend to celebrate Valentine's Day to-

51

gether with a winter walk along the lake-front and dinner at a romantic restaurant. It had seemed like a fun invitation at the time, but . . .

Not going to happen. She'd have to cancel.

Tomorrow. She'd call her booking agent tomorrow. Right now she needed to get dressed and go get her cat. The house was too empty.

CHAPTER 6

A loud rumble in Grace's ear roused her
from a deep sleep. Opening one eye, she
squinted at Oreo, cuddled up next to her
head on the pillow. "Hey, you," she murmured, reaching out a finger and touching
the cat's wet nose. Oreo was definitely taking advantage of the fact that she'd carried
him around like a stuffed toy ever since she
brought him home yesterday afternoon. And
he hadn't seemed to mind the Fancy Feast
Flaked Fish & Shrimp she'd picked up at
the grocery store on the way home either.
Scarfed it down and begged for more.

But daylight was peeking in through the
venetian blinds. At least she'd slept through
the night. Stretching, she pushed Oreo out
of her face and yawned . . . *uhhh,* that hurt.
Her throat was still sore. Maybe she should
see a doctor. Better make that call — and a
few others she needed to make — before
her voice totally went kaput.

Sliding out of the warm bed, Grace shivered as she pulled on her robe and stuffed her feet into her slippers. The heat should've come on by now. She shuffled out to the thermostat in the living room . . . what? Only fifty-nine degrees?

"Please don't tell me the furnace went out," she muttered as Oreo did impatient figure eights around her ankles. She'd have to call her brother — who no doubt would remind her how often he'd told her the thing needed replacing. But it might be evening before he'd be free — and by then the house would be freezing!

Ignoring the mail still on the rug beneath the slot in the front door, she pulled back the living room drapes from the large picture window at the front of the house. A curtain of swirling snowflakes filled her view. Oh dear . . . was this going to be a major storm? Grabbing the TV remote, Grace clicked Power and was relieved to see the screen leap to life. At least the electricity was on. She tried the Weather Channel . . . no, they were doing New York. She clicked through to Channel 9, Chicago's local station, and stood in the middle of the living room watching the morning news. Sports, interrupted by two minutes of commercials. She glanced at the schoolhouse clock . . . almost seven thirty. Tom Skilling should be doing weather any minute now . . . ah, there he was.

Whew. Only two inches expected today.

Oreo meowed pitifully. "Sorry, baby, gotta make a call first. Then I'll feed you." Grace hustled into her bedroom and found her phone . . . dead. She'd forgotten to charge it. She plugged in the phone and tapped her brother's speed-dial number.

"Hey, you're back." Mark's voice boomed in her ear.

"Yes, and my furnace is out," she croaked. "Sorry to ask but —"

"What? Can hardly understand you. What's wrong with your voice?"

"I have a sore throat! And the house is cold. Can you come check the furnace?"

"Uhhh . . ." There was a long pause. "Isn't there somebody on your block who could come over? I'm on the job already doing deliveries."

"I don't really know anybody on my block," she said a little too sharply. "I mean, not very well. Most of them have probably already left for work, anyway."

"Hang on a minute, Sis . . ." Grace heard traffic noises, loud honking, and Mark snarling, "What's your problem, buddy?" He finally came back on the phone. "What about Roger? Maybe he —"

"Can't call Roger. He's . . . traveling. Business." The lie came out a little too easily.

"Hmm. Do you have electricity? Gas?"

"Electricity, yes. I'll check the gas." Unplugging the charger, Grace scurried into the kitchen with the cord trailing, replugged the phone, and turned on a stove burner. Bright blue flames leaped into a perfect wreath. "Gas is on too."

"Okay, look . . . Maybe the pilot light on your furnace went out. You should check that first."

"Can you — ?"

"No, Sis, I can't. But I'll walk you through it, okay? . . . Hey, I gotta drop off a package. Hold on. I'll be back in two shakes . . ."

It took Grace thirty minutes lying on the chilly concrete floor in the basement laundry room, reaching beneath the furnace with a lighted match taped to the end of a kitchen skewer — it actually took seven matches — but she finally got the pilot relit. With Mark's help on the phone — still plugged in with an extension cord — she held down the button that let gas flow to the pilot light until it would burn on its own, and then turned everything back on.

The furnace purred.

She felt proud of herself. Next time she'd know what to do.

But it would still take another hour for the house to warm up, so Grace pulled on tights, sweatpants, a turtleneck, and a hooded sweatshirt before making some hot tea and scrambling two eggs for breakfast. *Ha.* If her fans could see her now . . .

Fans. She needed to call her agent and cancel that sweetheart banquet date. She eyed the cat, who was begging at her feet. "He's not going to be happy, Oreo," she said between bites of eggs and toast, "but I've got a good excuse, don't you think?" Her voice was starting to sound like fingernails dragging down a chalkboard.

Setting her plate down on the floor so Oreo could finish off the last tidbits of scrambled eggs, Grace picked up her phone, which had finally charged, scrolled down through her contact list, clicked on Bongo Booking Agency, and sipped her tea while the phone rang.

"Bongo Booking Agency, how may I direct your call?"

"Um, I need to speak with Walter Fowler." Walter was good at his job, very professional, and had been working the music scene for twenty years, ten of those with the Bongo Booking Agency in Denver, but he wasn't exactly the warm cozy sort.

"I'm sorry, I didn't quite catch that. Can you repeat?"

Grace took another sip of the hot tea to help clear her throat. "Wal-ter Fow-ler, please." She enunciated each syllable.

"Oh. Mr. Fowler is out of the office for the next few weeks. Jeff Newman is taking his calls. Who should I say is calling?"

Out? Argh! She vaguely remembered Fowler had said he'd be gone in February. An anniversary trip or something. But what was she going to do now? Tell a perfect stranger she wanted to cancel a concert? For all she knew, Jeff Somebody-or-other might be one of Bongo's bigwig agents who booked the really top CCM stars and had never heard of her.

"Um . . . Jeff who?" she stalled.

"Jeff Newman. Mr. Fowler's assistant. He's handling his calls."

Assistant. She didn't know Walter had an assistant. At least he didn't sound like a bigwig. But she was *not* going to do that concert, so . . . might as well face the music. She almost snickered at the pun. "Yes, thank you. Tell him Grace Meredith is calling."

A wall of sound suddenly poured into her ear, a Christian rock group she probably should recognize, but couldn't quite place.

She was just about to lower the volume when the wall of sound cut out and she heard, "Jeff Newman speaking. Is this Miss Meredith?"

Grace was startled. The voice was light-hearted. Friendly. Young. "Uh, yes. Grace Meredith. Mr. Fowler is my booking agent and . . ." She had to stop and clear her throat. "Please forgive me. I'm on the verge of losing my voice . . . can you hear me?"

"It's fine, Miss Meredith. But you don't sound so good. Are you all right?"

For some reason, the obvious concern in the voice on the other end of the line made her feel like crying. How stupid was that! But she might as well use the opening . . .

"Well, that's why I'm calling. I just returned from my New Year, New You tour, and —"

"Oh, sure! I heard about that tour. Sounded like a winner. But guess it was tough on your voice. Nasty time of year. Don't know how you do it."

He'd heard about her tour? "Uh, right. I wanted to talk to Mr. Fowler, because I need to cancel my next concert —"

"Hold on, give me a sec . . . right, I've got your schedule right here. That would be the sweetheart banquet booked by Living Hope, that megachurch in Milwaukee, week from next Saturday. That the one?"

This guy was really on the ball. "Yes." She knew she sounded raspy but she didn't try to clear it. "But my voice . . . I can't do it."

There was a pause on the other end. Then . . . "Miss Meredith, I understand. You sound like you could use a long rest. But that *is* almost two weeks away. Are you sure your voice won't have recovered by then? Our contracts require a doctor's certification if we have to cancel a concert. Otherwise, the agency — and ultimately you — will have to repay the advance *with* a penalty. And, I hate to say it, it's not so good for your rep."

Grace's shoulders sagged. She hadn't thought about the cost of canceling. Hadn't really had time to think it through — hadn't thought through much of anything the past few days, for that matter. Or prayed. Or asked God what to do. All she knew was that she couldn't do that sweetheart banquet, even if her voice did recover. "I'm . . . I'll be seeing a doctor. I'll send you certification."

She ended the call — and then felt bad that she hadn't even said good-bye or thanked him for his concern. But she was so close to tears again, she was afraid she'd end up blubbering if she didn't get off the phone.

Picking up her plate from the floor, Grace dumped the dishes in the sink and checked the thermostat. Sixty-four degrees and climbing. At least the furnace was working. She should call Mark back, let him know everything was okay . . . then she should call Samantha . . . no, first she better make that call to her doctor and get an appointment.

She left a message with the doctor's receptionist for a callback and had just stepped into the shower when she heard "All Hail the Power of Jesus' Name" from the bedroom. Wrapping a towel around her wet body, she hurried into the bedroom and snatched up the phone. "Hello? This is Grace Meredith."

"Grace? Good grief, you sound awful."

Roger.

CHAPTER 7

Grace stood in the middle of her bedroom clutching the cell phone in one hand and the towel in the other. She didn't want to talk to Roger.

But what if he was sorry? Didn't mean what he'd said. Wanted to make up.

"I've got laryngitis." It was the only thing she could think of to say in the moment.

"I can hear that. I . . . was just calling to see if you made it home all right from Memphis. And, well, it's been a few days. I thought we should talk some more about, you know, ending the engagement. But if your voice isn't —"

"No, I didn't."

A silent blip hung between them. She could just see the sudden frown on his handsome face — square jaw, strong chin, gray-blue eyes, dark-blond hair he wore in an Ivy League style, short on the sides, a bit longer and slightly spiked on top. Probably dressed in gray slacks, white dress shirt with sleeves rolled up, a silk necktie loosened at the collar — proper, conservative, just a tad casual. No doubt calling between meetings at the financial consulting firm in downtown Chicago where he was climbing the corporate ladder. The firm didn't take coffee breaks.

Roger finally spoke. "Uh, you didn't . . . what?"

"Didn't make it home all right." Her voice was barely above a whisper. "You asked if I made it home all right from Memphis."

"Oh." Another silent blip. "What happened? Are you okay?"

"I can't . . . can't t-talk about it right now." She was shivering now, still wet from the shower and only partially covered by the wrapped towel. "My furnace went out. House is c-c-cold. I was in the shower. This isn't a g-g-good time."

"Okay. Sure. Maybe we —"

She clicked Off and threw the phone on the bed. Why did she do that? She'd whined like a four-year-old. But it made her mad that he assumed everything was hunky-dory just because she'd answered the phone. And then he'd gone straight to wanting to talk more about ending the engagement.

Probably wanted his ring back.

She'd make him beg first.

Grace got back in the hot shower until her teeth stopped chattering, finally dried off, blow-dried her long hair, dressed in a pair of slim jeans and a clean turtleneck — and on impulse dug out the old flannel shirt she used to wear horseback riding back when she was a horse-crazy teenager. She'd taken a gazillion lessons at a riding stable just outside Indianapolis where she'd grown up and fantasized about owning her own horse one day. The horse never materialized, but the flannel shirt had survived high school, university, the move to Nashville, then back to Chicago, concerts and tours, and numerous wardrobe upgrades, even though it mostly hung in the closet. One flannel tie to the girl she used to be . . .

She felt rattled by Roger's phone call. Part of her had longed to hear from him, hoping he'd apologize for the late-night phone call last weekend, surprise her by meeting her at the airport, kiss and make up. After all, his main complaint was how often she was on the road. But . . . why now? It was the end of her New Year, New You tour and she didn't have another long tour until April. Just a few fly in, fly out dates, be gone three days max.

The other part of her wanted to scream

and slap his face. How could he dump her the night before her last concert, making a fool out of her "I'm worth waiting for" testimony? Couldn't he at least have waited till she got home, told her face-to-face?

The coward.

Argh! She needed to do something physical, let off some steam. She couldn't go for a walk. It was still snowing. Besides, her sore throat might be a virus. Better stay inside. She'd vacuum. The house needed a good cleaning.

Striding into the second bedroom where she stashed the vacuum cleaner, she slid open the closet doors — and froze.

Her wedding dress hung in the closet, encased in a zippered plastic bag, white, full, and delicate. She stared at it for a full minute, and then slowly lifted the padded hanger off the bar. It was her dream dress, the dress she'd gone shopping for a week after Roger had slipped the diamond-and-ruby ring on her finger, even though they hadn't set a wedding date yet. Hanging it on the hook on the back of the bedroom door, she slowly zipped open the protective bag and slid the brocade dress off its hanger.

The silver threads woven into the fabric shimmered in the natural light coming from the snowy world outside.

Holding the dress up to her body, Grace looked in the mirrored sliding doors of the closet. The first time she'd put on the dress, she'd felt like Cinderella in her magic ball gown. The dress had a curved sweetheart neckline, plunging just enough to look feminine and luscious, but not so low it wouldn't be appropriate for a church wedding . . . short, capped sleeves with lace trim . . . and an empire waistline outlined with a white silk ribbon, below which the dress fell in soft folds in front and gathered in back into a train that would trail several feet.

Grace stared at the reflection in the mirror.

More like Cinderella than she'd figured. The clock had struck midnight and the magic was gone. *Poof.*

With swift determination, she hung the dress back on its padded hanger, zipped up the plastic bag, and stuffed the dress back into the closet. Yanking out the vacuum cleaner, she jerked it into the carpeted hallway, plugged the cord into a socket, and when the power head roared to life, pushed it vigorously back and forth.

Why am I still in this tiny house? Two bedrooms. One bath. She'd bought it two years ago with some help from her parents when she'd decided to move back to the Midwest after ending her run with the record label in Nashville. A classic brick bungalow in a decent urban neighborhood. Quiet. On a dead-end street bounded by St. Mark's Memorial Cemetery. Closer to family.

At the time, it seemed a good investment, a good first home — modest, gave her time to take her career in a new direction with the independent tours and her purity message. CD sales had been better than expected, maybe enough to afford a newer house in one of the suburbs. But, she'd figured, why move when she was going to get married? She and Roger would choose a house together . . .

Grace pulled the vacuum into her bedroom. She still hadn't unpacked. The damp bath towel lay on the floor. She threw everything onto the unmade bed and tackled the rug.

Roger had certainly seemed like "The One" when she first met him two years ago at County Line Christian Fellowship, a large suburban church straddling the line between Cook and Dupage Counties. He had All-American college-football good looks, was a leader of the singles group and one of County Line's many up-and-coming profes-

67

sionals. She'd participated in many of the church's musical presentations, and he'd seemed mesmerized by her soprano voice, even pleased as her career picked up. Everyone said what a great couple they made, so well suited. No one was surprised when they'd announced their engagement last year.

Should I have seen it coming? Roger usually called me every night when I was on tour . . . but on this last tour, the calls have been more irregular . . .

Pulling the vacuum cleaner out of the bedroom and down the hall into the living room, she plugged it into another socket and set to work again.

. . . and now that I think about it, when we did talk, he seemed kind of distant when I tried to tell him about that night's concert, as if he was bored, or distracted. Something . . .

As she stooped to pick up the mail on the floor by the front door, the framed photo on the lamp table beside the couch caught her eye. A picture of her and Roger, cheek to cheek, smiling happily at their engagement party. Turning off the machine, she picked up the photo and stared at it wistfully for a long moment. Surely it couldn't be over. They had so much going for them! Both were mature adults with solid careers, a shared faith, mutual attraction. They were equally active in ministry, though in different spheres. She'd considered herself blessed to be engaged to one of County Line's most eligible single guys — something she didn't take for granted at the age of twenty-nine.

Who'd just dumped her.

Pressing her lips into a thin line, she stuck the photo out of sight in the walnut drop-front secretary desk, along with all the letters, junk mail, bank statements, and magazines her brother had picked up each time he'd come by to check on the house. She could've asked the post office to hold her mail, but with a mail slot, no one could see the mail piling up inside and she didn't have to go get it when she got home. The bank paid most of her regular bills automatically. Still. She should go through the mail soon to check her statements and make sure everything was up to date . . . *and* read her fan mail — the mail that Samantha usually answered so artfully. Precious letters. Letters that encouraged her and kept her going.

Well . . . tomorrow. She'd take care of the mail tomorrow.

Grace resumed vacuuming, but for some reason the glut of mail lured her. Maybe just one letter, something reassuring. Turning the vacuum cleaner off and dropping the wand, she opened the secretary and picked out a letter, one with the familiar Forward from the box she rented at Mail Boxes Etc. just for fan mail. Slitting the envelope with a letter opener from the walnut desk, she curled up on the velvety sectional couch and pulled out a sheet of thin-ruled notebook paper. Immediately Oreo appeared and hopped into her lap as she started reading . . .

Dear Miss Grace,

I love your CD! I was so excited when you came to Florida this month. My parents got tickets for me and a girlfriend for my birthday, which is January 5. It was my Sweet 16. They didn't know it, but it was God who told them to get those tickets. Because you see, my boyfriend has been asking me to have sex with him. Big time. Told me if I really loved him, I'd prove it by having sex. Well, I do love him. He is so cute! Like, he plays basketball and is really popular, and might even play for the NBA someday. He buys me all kinds of gifts, like a watch and the cutest stuffed tiger and for my birthday got me some really cool perfume. All the girls are jealous of me, and I don't want to lose him. So I've been thinking about the sex.

70

But when you talked about how you decided to wait till marriage to have sex, because "I'm worth it" — it really made me think. How if a boy really loves you, he won't want to put you at risk for getting pregnant or getting a disease or needing an abortion, stuff like that.

Grace flinched. She forced her eyes back to the letter.

Like, that's so true! One of my girlfriends got pregnant and had a baby, and she can't do fun stuff anymore or anything. And her boyfriend didn't hang around after that either. So when you told us you're engaged to a wonderful man who respects you, and it was "worth the wait" — well, I just want you to know I want to be like you! I'm going to —

With sudden fury, Grace balled up the letter and threw it across the room. Startled, Oreo jumped off her lap and crawled under the couch. Snatching a throw pillow, Grace sent it flying after the crumpled-up letter. Then she grabbed another one and hugged it tight against her chest as sobs shook her body and pent-up tears came fast and furious.

"O God, O God," she wailed, "I don't understand why all this is happening!" Roger's devastating phone call . . . Samantha's mother having a heart attack . . . the horrible TSA people violating her . . . her throat on fire . . . her career up for grabs . . .

Was God punishing her? She'd thought she'd earned his blessing with her passionate message about purity! Look at that letter! She took being a role model seriously. So why —

Rocking back and forth, crying, her throat raw, Grace almost missed the familiar ringtone of her cell phone. But pulling it out of her jeans pocket, she saw it was the doctor's callback and hastily reached for some tissues to mop her face.

Five minutes later, she wrote on her Day-Timer page for Wednesday, *2:00 Dr. Stacey,* then looked around and called out hoarsely, "Oreo? Kitty, kitty . . . you can come out now."

CHAPTER 8

Grace absently paged through a six-month-old copy of *National Geographic Traveler,* wondering how much longer before she could see the doctor. The receptionist had squeezed her in between Dr. Stacy's Wednesday appointments — otherwise there wasn't an opening until next week.

But Grace was starting to feel nervous. Even getting in today was cutting it close. The sweetheart banquet was only a week and a half away, and when she checked her e-mail that morning, the banquet coordinator at Living Hope Church had sent her an attached schedule of the program, the name of the person who would be her "armor bearer" for the evening (*She'll make sure you have everything you need!*), and asked if she had any special needs or requests. *We're so excited that you and your fiancé are coming,* the e-mail gushed, *and we're expecting a record turnout this year!*

Grace had stifled a groan. Her name was going to be mud when she canceled.

But Bongo Booking Agency had been copied on the e-mail, and Jeff Newman e-mailed her an hour later wondering if she had a doctor's certification yet. He really needed to confirm with Living Hope one way or the other, especially if he had to cancel.

Grace was starting to feel guilty about canceling — but she really wasn't feeling well. She'd woken up that morning feeling feverish and headachy and had taken her temperature, a hair shy of one hundred degrees. Nothing serious, but still.

"Miss Meredith?" A middle-aged nurse in a royal blue scrub jacket came to the door and eyed the five people in the waiting room. Grace gathered up her things. "This way."

Seated in the examination room, Grace patiently tried to answer questions as the nurse skimmed over the medical history forms she'd filled out half an hour ago. No, she hadn't realized she'd skipped her physical last year — she'd probably been away on tour . . . Yes, in general her health had been okay . . . Main complaint today was a sore throat, hoarseness, headaches, a low-grade temp . . . Stress? Well, yes, she'd just come off a four-week concert tour, which had been quite demanding.

The nurse took her blood pressure (a little high) . . . height (five-six) . . . weight (128, down seven pounds from the last weight they had for her) . . . then gave her a gown and told her to remove her clothes from the waist up. The doctor would be in shortly.

Grace quickly changed into the ugly gown and sat up on the padded table. It was another ten minutes before the knock on the door and Dr. Stacy entered. The internist was probably in her late forties or early fifties, slender, pale blonde hair graying, cut in a short bob. "Grace," she said warmly. "You've been avoiding me. Nurse Thomson says you're seven months overdue for a physical . . . let's see." She opened the chart. "I think we usually see you around your birthday in July. Right?" She cocked an eyebrow. "Someone like you, on the road a lot, needs to be proactive about your health."

Grace flushed. She felt like a seventh-grader caught skipping school by a benevolent principal. "I . . . I know. I'll make an appointment before I leave."

"Good." Dr. Stacy studied the forms Grace had filled out and the nurse's notes. "*Mm* . . . uh-huh . . ." She set them aside.

"Tell me what's going on."

Grace took a deep breath and told the doctor when the sore throat had started, then the laryngitis, now a low temp. And . . . she also needed a doctor's note that she was in no shape to sing, so that she could cancel her next concert a week from Saturday.

The doctor pursed her lips thoughtfully. "Grace, I'm your doctor. The things you've mentioned might indicate a viral infection. But I think there's more. Your weight is down, your blood pressure is up. You want to cancel your next concert. I'm guessing a good deal of stress and overuse of your voice has a lot to do with what's going on. What happens in this office is confidential, so let's get the whole story."

It took some gentle prodding, but Grace finally managed to get it all out: the breakup with her fiancé, a family emergency taking her assistant out of the picture, the humiliating experience going through security at the Memphis airport . . . on top of four weeks of travel and a packed concert schedule. By the time she finished, Grace was in tears.

Handing her a wad of tissues, Dr. Stacy nodded sympathetically. "Well. Statistically speaking, that's enough stress to go right off the chart. But let's take a look at what's going on in that throat . . ."

Grace blew her nose and tried to hold still as the doctor checked her ears, shined a light into her mouth, had her say, "Ahh-hhh," felt the glands in her neck, then used her stethoscope to listen to her chest, front and back. "*Mmm . . . mm-hm . . .* take a deep breath . . . another . . ."

Finally the doctor scooted her stool back. "Well, we definitely have an infection going on, probably viral, but I'm going to swab your throat for possible strep. If it's strep, I'll order an antibiotic. Otherwise, all you can do is take care of the symptoms and wait it out. Should be better in four to six days with a lot of liquids and rest. But —"

"But I think I really need to rest my voice." Grace heard the anxiety in her raspy voice. "Can you —"

"Hang on. I'm getting there. I also think you should be seen by a laryngologist. I can recommend a couple names —"

"A . . . who?"

"An otolaryngologist, a doctor who specializes in treating vocalists like yourself. I'll be glad to contact one on our list and say you need to be seen ASAP." The doctor turned to her computer and began using her mouse to scroll through several pages.

Grace swallowed, which hurt. "But will I have to wait to see the laryn— uh, however you pronounce it — before I can get a doctor's certification to cancel? It's really urgent that I get it right away."

Dr. Stacy was typing something into the computer. "As your primary, I'm writing a note to that effect since a few weeks resting your voice and recovering from the mega stress you're under can only be beneficial. But Grace," — she swung around on her stool and eyed Grace soberly — "for anything beyond the concert next week, you'll need to be evaluated by a specialist."

An hour later, Grace pulled her two-door Ford Focus into the garage behind her house. The alley hadn't been plowed, but enough cars had used the alley since yesterday's snowfall that two well-established ruts allowed her to make it into her garage with only a few skids around corners. As the automatic garage door shut behind her, Grace wearily gathered up all her things and headed out the side door, stepping carefully on the icy walk. She'd had to stop at an Osco Pharmacy to fill a couple of prescriptions, and the whole excursion had exhausted her. At least her strep test had come back negative. Still, she couldn't wait to get inside the house and crawl into bed for a nap.

But the ticking schoolhouse clock on the living room wall said almost four thirty. What she really needed to do was make an appointment with the laryngologist, and then fax the doctor's certification to that new guy, Jeff Newman, before the booking agency closed for the day. The sooner he got back to the church in Milwaukee, the better.

The specialist she called couldn't see her until next Monday. She wrote the appointment in her Day-Timer, faxed the certification letter to Bongo Booking, and finally, fortified with a couple of extra-strength pain relievers and a cup of hot chicken broth, collapsed on the sectional couch in the living room. Curling up in an afghan, she gazed out the front window at the fading blue twilight as she sipped the hot salty liquid. Yesterday's snowfall had stopped with the promised two inches — but that was two inches on top of her unshoveled walks. Most of the front walks on Beecham Street had been shoveled, except for hers and the two-flat on the other side of the street where the old lady lived. She knew better than to get out there herself, not with her voice shot and an upper respiratory infection. Her brother might be willing to come this weekend — but that was three days away. The longer she waited, the more packed down the snow would become as people walked on it. It was already an icy mess underneath.

Grace sighed. Should she hire a service? The guy directly across the street had a truck that said *Farid's Total Yard Service* with a phone number — and she thought she'd seen it with a plow last winter. But did a yard service do something as small as shoveling walks?

Maybe she could hire one of the older kids on the block to shovel and spread some rock salt. There were some kids at the other end of the block, but she didn't know them at all, and the interracial couple in the house next door, both professionals of some kind, didn't have any kids. They seemed like typical DINKS — Double-Income-No-Kids. The family on the north side of her, though — middle-aged, African American — had a couple of teenagers, nice kids as far as she knew. They might be a possibility — except she didn't have their phone number. Last name? JASPER was lettered on an oval house sign alongside their front door. Maybe if she saw someone outside . . .

Her cell phone rang somewhere. The ringtone was beginning to get on her nerves. *"All Hail the Power . . ."* What had she been thinking? Grace pried herself off the couch and followed the ring into the kitchen, where the phone danced on the kitchen table — then went silent. Too late. She checked Recent Calls . . . oh, dear. Samantha. She'd never called her assistant back! She tapped Redial . . .

"Hello, Sam here! Grace, is that you?"

"Yes. Sorry about not calling you. I've been kind of sick, lost my voice."

"Oh no! You sound terrible! Look, I'll text next time, okay? Save your voice. I just wanted to tell you they're going to discharge my mom from the hospital tomorrow, but I'm going to stay for a few more days, maybe a week, to help out here. That's okay, isn't it? No, wait, don't answer. Don't strain your voice. But if I remember right —"

Grace wandered back into the living room with the phone and wrapped herself up in the afghan again as Samantha chattered.

"— your next concert is that sweetheart banquet thing the day before Valentine's Day, and Roger's going with you, right? You said I didn't need to come along, so hopefully this will work out. But if you've got fan mail and stuff you want me to do, I'll try to catch up when I get back to Chicago next week. Is that okay?"

Grace felt too weary to say anything but a

raspy, "Fine." She'd explain it all later. Sam had enough to worry about.

But the sweetheart banquet was only the tip of the iceberg. What about the other concerts Bongo had booked for her? And the upcoming West Coast tour in late spring? Did Roger have *any* idea how embarrassing this was for her? She'd been sharing about their engagement with fans all over the country for the past year — it made a great *denouement* to her testimony about abstinence and waiting until marriage. And now she was supposed to show up on stage with a plastic smile and say, "Sorry. Just kidding. Our engagement's off. But I'm still worth waiting for!"

She had a sudden urge to call Roger and blister his ear with how he'd managed to ruin her personal life *and* her career with his cowardly breakup! Except . . . she couldn't muster the proper decibels of outrage even if she tried. She'd come off sounding like a whining two-year-old.

Well, she'd bide her time. The doc had told her to talk as little as possible, anyway. Shouldn't be hard since she lived alone . . . though she realized she'd gotten into the habit of talking constantly to Oreo. Resting her voice actually gave her a good excuse to *not* talk to Roger until she was good and ready. *Ha.* Doctor's orders.

Glancing out the window, Grace realized the daylight had faded, and light shone faintly through blinds and curtains in windows all up and down the street. Drawing her own living room drapes, she felt a pang of frustration. Not talking was going to be a pain in the neck if she wanted to find someone in the neighborhood to shovel those treacherous sidewalks.

CHAPTER 9

As she opened a can of cat food Saturday morning — Oreo heard the electric can opener and came running — Grace realized she was starting to feel better. Amazing what a few days of rest could do. She still didn't have much voice, but the soreness was mostly gone, as well as the fever and head-ache. She'd taken Samantha's advice and let phone calls go to voice mail the past few days, then she'd answered them with a text or e-mail. Except for Roger's two calls. Those she just left in voice mail.

Her spirit was starting to relax. Jeff New-man had e-mailed on Thursday to confirm he'd gotten the doctor's certification and canceled her appearance at the sweetheart banquet. The Living Hope folks were natu-rally disappointed, he said, but they under-stood and were concerned about her. *But we should talk about your other upcoming concerts. I think there are four single events before the West Coast tour. What's the doc say about your prognosis?*

She had e-mailed back: *Don't know yet. I see a laryngologist on Monday.* Ha — and spelled it right too. She didn't add that the medical issue was only a small part of her problem right now. Each day that went by, it got harder to imagine going onstage with her usual program of songs and purity message. New Year, New You? More like, Same Old, Same Old. Besides, most of the single concerts were out of state, but *no way* was she going to get on a plane, not if it meant having to go through security again!

As Oreo greedily gulped his breakfast, Grace poured another cup of coffee — she was sick of lemon-and-honey tea — and idly turned on her laptop. Another e-mail from Jeff Newman? This one was dated Friday. *Grace, I'm coming through Chicago on my way to Nashville next Tuesday. Any chance we could meet? I could arrange to spend the day in Chicago since my meetings in Nashville aren't until Wednesday. Be glad to rent a car and meet you wherever. Just tell me what works for you.*

Grace frowned. A face-to-face meeting with Jeff Newman? Why? Wasn't this guy just filling in for Mr. Fowler? She typed: *When is Walter Fowler getting back?* and hit

Reply. Not that she really wanted to talk to Fowler either. Her agent wasn't going to be happy when he got wind that she'd canceled a concert. At least today was Saturday. Newman might not get her reply until Monday.

She scrolled through more of her e-mails . . . deleted the inspirational Forwards she was supposed to send to ten others within ten minutes to get a blessing and the plea from a total stranger "stranded in England" who needed money . . . but read the fan mail before moving them to a folder for Samantha to answer when she got back. She was just about to shut down her laptop when a new e-mail popped in. From Newman. Good grief. What was he doing working on the weekend?

Grace, I'm so sorry. I thought you'd gotten an official notice from Fowler. Walter won't be back till the end of February, but he's asking me to take over some of his client load permanently. Including you. He thought we'd be a good team. Which is why I'd like to meet you in person. Of course, you have the final say in who your agent is, but I'd be honored to take over your booking. What do you say? Can we meet Tuesday?

Irritation rose like bile in her mouth. No, she hadn't gotten "an official notice" from her agent. What way was that to treat a client?! First her fiancé, now her agent —

Okay, okay, get a grip, Grace. She leaned her elbows on the kitchen table and pressed the tips of her fingers against her temples. It wasn't like she and Fowler had ever really clicked. Maybe this would be a good change. But . . . meet up with Jeff Newman? She'd have to think about that.

Grace closed the lid of her laptop. Maybe she'd know better once she'd seen the specialist on Monday. Fact was, she was going a little stir crazy, stuck in the house for the past week. What she really wanted to do was go for a walk. If she bundled up, why not? Would do her good. They probably kept the walkways well shoveled through the cemetery that bordered their dead-end street. She could walk there.

At times like this, Grace wished she had a dog. Her brothers had had a yellow Lab — okay, a Lab mixed with something else — when she was a kid. Lovable mutt. But a dog definitely wouldn't fit into her current lifestyle, not with all the travel she did. It was hard enough leaving Oreo so often, but at least it was easier to find care for a cat than for a dog.

Walking through St. Mark's Memorial

Cemetery felt good. The temperature hadn't even made it above freezing, but there was no wind and the noonday sun was out. Bundled up in a down vest and a hooded parka with a wool scarf wrapped around her face, she'd walked over to Ridge Avenue to enter the main gate. Just as she'd figured, the narrow paved road that wound around the various burial areas had been plowed and provided a good surface to stretch her legs away from traffic and city sidewalks.

A sign on the gate said No Dogs Allowed. Couldn't take a dog for a walk here even if she had one.

The peace and quiet of the cemetery, however, and the pristine beauty of the snow blanket covering the graves and topping the headstones made Grace smile. Gray-and-black chickadees flitted in and out of pine-tree branches, and in spring the bare maples and elms would come alive with fluttering leaves. She ought to walk here more often — an oasis of nature in the middle of the big city. And she definitely could use the exercise!

But she shouldn't stay out too long. Still fighting that virus. Turning back, Grace walked around the bottom of the cemetery till she got to Beecham. Her house was almost at the end of the dead-end street, two houses away from the "McMansion" that had been built last year facing the cul-de-sac at the far end, backed up against the cemetery. It was a pretty house, stone exterior with lots of beveled windows, but totally out of character — and size — for the rest of the neighborhood. And as far as she could tell — though admittedly she wasn't around much to know for sure — seemed like only one guy lived there. Why did a guy without a family need such a big house? Probably partied a lot. That would explain the extra cars that filled the cul-de-sac on weekends.

As Grace approached her brick bungalow, a small gray SUV pulled up and a black woman she recognized as her next-door neighbor got out, opened the back, and started to unload plastic bags. "Tavis! Tabitha!" she yelled. "Get out here and help with these groceries!"

The front door opened and a boy about twelve or thirteen hustled down the steps.

"Where's Tabitha?" The mother handed two bags to the boy, clad in a sweatshirt, unzipped, hood down. "And where's your gloves and your hat?"

"I'm goin' right back in," he protested and hustled inside with the bags.

Grace cleared her throat as she walked

toward the SUV. "Hello!" Good grief, she could barely hear herself. Grace got closer and tried again. "Hello?"

The woman looked up. "Uh, hello."

"I'm Grace Meredith." Grace pointed at her house. "I live next door." Her voice was still raspy, but better than she expected.

"Oh!" The woman gave a laugh. "Didn't recognize you all bundled up like that. Haven't seen you around lately. You been gone?" Without waiting for an answer, the woman again called toward the house. "Tavis! Tabitha! Get your sorry selves back out here!" She turned back to Grace. "Like pullin' teeth gettin' those kids to stick with somethin' longer than ten seconds."

"Yes . . . yes, I was away most of January. As you can tell from my unshoveled sidewalk. But that's what I wanted to —"

"*Tavis! Tabitha!* Don't make me come in there!" the mother yelled again. This time the boy appeared with a girl who looked to be about the same age. Grace stepped aside as the two young teens grabbed several bags each and hustled up the walk into the house.

The woman slammed the back of the SUV. "I'm sorry . . . you were saying? Oh, by the way, I'm Michelle Jasper." She held out a mittened hand.

Grace pulled her own gloved hand out of

her parka pocket and shook the offered mitten. She was starting to shiver. "As you can see, I didn't get the sidewalk in front of my house shoveled while I was gone, and I've been sick this week. So I was wondering —"

"Uh-huh. Sounds like you still oughta be in the bed." The woman picked up the last two bags of groceries from where she'd set them on the snow.

"I know . . . But I was wondering if one of your kids wanted to earn some money shoveling my walk. I'm way overdue getting it done."

Michelle Jasper paused and looked at her a moment. "Well, guess I could ask. Do you want Tavis — he's thirteen — or my older boy, Destin?"

"Uh, either one would be fine. Thanks." Grace smiled. "Well, guess I'll go back in. Tell them I'll pay twenty dollars."

The woman scoffed. "Good heavens! Don't do that! Make it ten at the most or they'll be spoiled, wanting more when other folks need a favor."

"Oh. Well, I had no idea what to pay. I just know it won't be easy. Some of it's packed down from people walking on it. But I have some rock salt for the icy patches."

"Fine. I'll send somebody over. Probably

91

Tavis. Destin will probably say he doesn't have time. Basketball and all that, you know. Junior year. That boy keeps busier than both his father an' me put together!" The woman nodded at Grace and headed up her own walk. "Well, better get inside . . ."

Yeah, me too.

But as Grace turned back toward her house, something caught her eye across the street. A For Sale sign in front of the old lady's two-flat. How long had *that* been there? And what did the bright yellow strip on top of the sign say? She wandered past her bungalow until she was directly across the street from the two-flat . . . *Foreclosure.* Oh, now, that was really too bad.

She was really shivering now. Once inside, Grace peeled off her layers, pulled off her boots, and turned on the teakettle, blowing on her numb fingers as it heated. The walk had felt good, but maybe wasn't the wisest thing. She hadn't felt really cold until she stood still to talk to the woman next door . . . Michelle. Michelle Jasper. And the kids were Tavis and Tabitha. Could be twins. And the older one . . . Dustin? Something like that.

The doorbell ding-donged. That was quick. She hoped the boy had brought his own shovel. If he didn't, she'd have to go out to the garage.

Oreo had run to the front door at the bell, curious as always. "Scoot," she said, moving the cat out of the way with her foot so she could open the front door.

But it wasn't Tavis.

A tall man stood on her stoop, shoulders hunched against the cold inside a long gray topcoat, red wool scarf tucked into the neck, wraparound sunglasses, no hat.

Roger.

"Hello, Grace."

Grace stared. Swallowed. "What are you doing here?"

Just then a black-and-white fur-ball darted out the door, around the man's shoes, and down the steps.

"Oreo! Catch the cat! He'll freeze out there!"

CHAPTER 10

Oreo seemed startled to find himself belly deep in wet snow. He stuck his tail up and let out a pitiful meow.

"I'll get him," Roger said, stepping gingerly down the steps, back-tracking in his footprints as if to save his shoes. "Stay there. You don't have any shoes on."

Grace ran for her boots, not at all confident Oreo would let Roger get near. The door was still open, letting in a wall of cold air. But as she pulled on her boots, she could hear Roger coaxing, "Here, kitty, kitty . . . come on now."

She ran out onto the stoop in time to see Roger creep toward the cat, who'd made it to the front sidewalk. But just as Roger grabbed for him, Oreo took off across the narrow parkway between sidewalk and street, bounding across the deeper snow.

Oh no! Grace started down the steps, grabbing the cold iron hand railing. *What if he runs out into the street! What if —*

"Got him!"

Grace jerked her head. The boy from next door — though he was now bundled up in a winter jacket, sweatshirt hood over his head — was slushing through the snow across her tiny front lawn, arms wrapped around the black-and-white cat.

She blew out a relieved breath as he came closer. "Oh, thank you! Tavis, isn't it? Here . . ." She held out her arms for the cat as the boy reached her stoop. "I'll get him inside and be right back. Did your mom ask you about shoveling my walk?" She was pushing her voice beyond its raspy whisper in order to be heard.

"Yeah." The boy pointed back the way he'd come. "I dropped the shovel back there when I saw the cat runnin' loose. I'll go get it."

Grace hustled back inside, shut Oreo in the guest bedroom, grabbed her parka, and headed outside again as she pulled it on. Tavis had already retrieved his shovel and was staring at Roger, who had come back up the steps and was stamping snow off his leather shoes on the mat just outside the front door.

"Ya still want me to shovel? Or is your husband gonna do it?" the boy said.

95

Grace stifled a laugh, which she was afraid would come out slightly hysterical. "Yes, I still want you to do it. He's just . . . a visitor." Ignoring Roger, she told Tavis she'd like him to shovel the sidewalk along the street, then up her short walk up to the door, plus the walkway from the back door to the garage. "You can forget the side for now."

"Okay. Ten bucks, right?" The boy snickered. "Tabitha is gonna be so pissed."

Grace winced at his language, but couldn't help grinning. "Your sister . . . how old is she?"

"Thirteen. Same as me. We're twins." He rolled his eyes. "Double trouble, my dad says." He squinted up at her. "Mama said you got laryngitis, so I'm not s'posed to make you talk much. But I gotta tell ya . . ." His eyes strayed to the sidewalks. "This ain't gonna be so easy."

"I know. Do what you can. There's a bag of rock salt in the garage. I think the side door is open."

A masculine throat-clearing made Grace turn around. Roger, eyes still hidden behind his sunglasses, cocked a thumb toward her open front door. "Can we, uh, go in?"

"Wait a moment." The chasing-the-cat episode had given Grace time to recover from her surprise at finding Roger at her doorstep. Squeezing past him, she turned in the open doorway and said, "Let's start over." She stepped back, closed the door in his face, took a slow, deep breath, and then reopened it. "Roger. What are you doing here?"

Roger shook his head and looked away for a moment. She imagined he'd just rolled his eyes. "Let's not play games, Grace. I'm *here* because you won't answer my phone calls. But we really need to talk. That's why I —"

"I'm not supposed to talk. I've got laryngitis." She let her voice croak all it wanted — which didn't take much after all the talking she'd done in the last thirty minutes.

"Grace. It's cold. Please let me come in."

Grace stood there one more nanosecond, then stepped aside so Roger could come in. Closing the door, she shed her parka and boots and stowed them in the coat closet. She could at least try to be civil. She didn't want to burn any bridges with Roger, in case this whole breakup was just a case of getting cold feet.

She turned. Roger had taken off his topcoat and laid it neatly over the back of a chair. The sunglasses had also disappeared, unveiling his blue-gray eyes. She steadied her gaze. "Would you like some coffee?"

"That'd be great."

"I'll be right back," she said, giving him a clear signal he wasn't supposed to follow her into the kitchen. She wanted to keep this formal. Civil but formal. Fortunately she still had enough hot coffee in the pot for two cups, which she carried back into the living room on a tray with packets of sweetener. Roger took two sugars in his coffee and always let it cool. She liked hers hot and black. The kind of little details a couple knows about each other.

She set the tray on the coffee table near where he'd seated himself in the chair that matched her sectional, let Oreo out of his prison, then curled up on the couch with her own cup. The cat jumped up on the couch and settled down beside her. Grace watched as her fiancé — now *ex* — took a few sips.

She spoke first. "Why, Roger?"

He slowly set the cup down. "I told you why, Grace. Your career, your travel schedule . . . it's just too much time apart. It's not working for me — and we're not even married yet. It would only get harder — especially if we wanted to start a family."

Start a family. They'd only talked about having kids once, and he'd said it was too

98

soon to decide something that big — how many, or when, or if . . .

"But we didn't even talk about it! You just made your own decision, *bam,* like that."

He shifted. "Not '*bam,* like that.' Never was happy with these long separations. You know how much I miss you when you're gone . . ."

"Then why didn't you call more often while I was on tour?"

Roger cleared his throat. "I'm trying to explain myself here, Grace. You see, thing is — while you were away this last tour, it finally hit me. It's not just that I miss you when you're gone. I realized that this isn't what I want in a marriage."

"You should have thought of that a year ago . . ."

"A year ago I didn't know what kind of toll your absence would take on me. On us."

"I thought you supported my career."

"I did. And I still do. But . . . I want someone who's here for me, someone who isn't gone half the time."

Silence hung between them. "But . . . why end the engagement without even talking about it? Maybe I could slow it down, do fewer concerts —"

"Really, Grace? You're a singer. This is your career, your . . . your ministry. And you're doing really well too. I can't ask you to give all that up."

Uh-huh. How noble.

She sat there for a long minute, absently stroking Oreo's neck fur behind his ears. Then, without really thinking, she said, "I've already got my wedding dress."

"You . . . what? Grace! We hadn't even set a date yet!"

"I know." It was a whisper.

Roger threw out his hands. "Grace. We can't go forward with a relationship that's not working just because you already bought a dress."

Grace stared at her lap. "I know. But I was that sure of us. I mean, engagements tend to do that to a girl. I've been sharing about us at my concerts, telling my fans that waiting until marriage to be intimate is worth it." *That I'm worth it,* she almost added, but didn't.

"Exactly!" Roger looked almost angry. "Telling people from one end of the country to the other! I have to say, I don't appreciate being the poster boy for your little abstinence campaign — like some trophy you've won."

Grace was stunned. "I thought you supported my message! I mean, even for us, early on we agreed on the biblical —"

"Yes, yes, of course. I'm not saying that abstinence isn't important and the right choice. But it's one thing to make that commitment for ourselves, quite another to make a big public deal out of our personal relationship. That's a lot of unwanted publicity, Grace, and I don't like it!"

She hardly knew what to say — and besides, her throat was starting to feel dry and sore from all this talking. She took a gulp of her coffee . . . *ugh,* lukewarm. "I . . . I need some water."

Roger seemed glad for the interruption. "I'll get it." He disappeared into the kitchen.

Tears threatened behind Grace's eyes, but she blinked them away. She wasn't going to cry in front of Roger. *O Lord, what's going on? I'm all confused!*

"Here." Roger was back with a glass of water. He sat down on the edge of the chair and leaned forward, elbows on his knees, fingers tented. "Look, Grace, I'm sorry about all this. I know it seems sudden — but it's better to step back now than wait till we're married and things aren't working out. Then we'd either be stuck or . . . or dealing with a painful divorce."

Stuck . . . divorce . . . How had they gone from being madly in love to this?

Had they ever been madly in love?

Did she love him that way? They lived in two different worlds — he in corporate finance, she on the Christian music circuit. Their lives mostly overlapped at church. Had they fallen in love? Or just fallen together . . .

"Do you have any idea how embarrassing this is going to be for me?" she blurted. "After telling people for almost a year that I'm engaged to be married, now I have to go public and tell them it's off. I can just hear the rumor mill starting, the gossip on the CCM blogs . . ."

Roger seemed to wince. "I'm sorry. Really. It's not my intention to embarrass you, Grace. I'd protect you from that if I could. But . . . that's really your doing. You're the one who took our engagement on tour. And now you need to make it right."

"Oh, me? Just me? You were going to go with me next week to that sweetheart banquet." She hated sounding like a petulant child, but it still came out.

"I'm sorry."

"I canceled the booking."

He looked surprised, but just said again, "I'm sorry. But I can see why —"

"And my voice," she admitted, wanting to keep this honest. "Doctor says I need to rest my voice. It was a good excuse."

He nodded, but they both sat there in silence. Wasn't there a lot more to say? After nearly two years of being a couple in everyone's mind?

"Uh, there is one more thing." Roger squirmed, as if uncomfortable. "We should probably decide about the, uh, ring . . ."

Grace slowly stretched out the fingers on her left hand. The square diamond with its baby rubies sparkled in the bright snow light coming in through the picture window. So this was it. The ring would come off. And it'd be over.

Except . . . *he* was the one breaking the engagement. What if she didn't give it back? But why would she keep it? Just for spite? She didn't have the heart for that. She'd accepted the ring as a symbol of accepting his proposal of marriage. Why would she want to keep the ring if he didn't want *her*?

No tears, Grace. "Here." Wiggling the delicate band over her knuckle until it finally slid off, she reached out and dropped it into his palm.

He let it lie in his palm for a brief moment, and then slowly closed his fingers over it. "That's probably best."

She undid the clasp on the watch. "Take the watch too. They match, practically a pair."

"No . . . no. You keep the watch. That was a gift. I want you to have it."

She loved the watch, the way it hugged her slender wrist, made her feel so elegant. But mostly what she'd loved about it had been the sentiment. *A gift from Roger.*

She shook her head and slid off the silver band. "No, they should stay together." She held out the watch and kept holding it between them until, reluctantly, he took it. She watched as he dug out the original velvet box from a pocket in his topcoat and slid the jewelry inside.

He stood. "Guess I should go."

She did not protest and stood up too, just as her cell phone rang. She glanced at the caller ID . . . Denise, her sister-in-law. Mark's wife. With a quick push of a button, she sent the call to voice mail. She'd call her back later.

Topcoat and sunglasses back on, Roger opened the front door, and then turned to her. "Coming to church tomorrow? I suppose we ought to tell the pastors."

County Line? The church where she had assumed they'd get married. She shook her head. "You can tell the pastors."

He shrugged. "Okay. But . . . I hope we can still be friends, Grace. Don't stay away from church just because of me." He leaned toward her as if he was going to kiss her on the cheek, but she turned her head aside.

"Good-bye, Roger."

As he walked toward his car, she started to shut the door, but was curious about Tavis. The boy was nowhere to be seen — but her front walk and the length of public sidewalk in front of her house had both been shoveled, though it was obvious there were patches of packed snow and ice that hadn't come up. She listened and heard a *scrape, scrape, scrape* from behind the house. Good. The boy was still working. Definitely earning his ten dollars.

Oreo stretched and yawned in a patch of sunlight on the couch, turned around twice, and then curled back up into a cozy ball. All was well in the cat's life. Grace just stood in the middle of her living room, feeling bereft. Roger was . . . gone. Her ring was gone — the watch too. Her dream of marriage and family . . . gone.

Where was God in all this? She thought she'd been doing what he'd called her to do, and that he'd been blessing her for her obedience.

She felt like screaming. *What are you doing to me, God?!* But her stupid voice had let her down too.

The front doorbell shook her out of her

depressing reverie.

Numbly she opened it. Tavis. "Hey, Miz Meredith. I'm done. Found the bag of rock salt in the garage like you said and scattered it on the walks front an' back. Don't know if it'll help much, but . . ." He shrugged and grinned.

"Thank you, Tavis. Hold on . . ." She went for her purse and came back with a ten. "I could use some help when it snows again if you're interested."

"Sure! Thanks." The boy waved and trotted off with his shovel.

She watched him go. For some reason, the very ordinariness of getting her walks shoveled seemed like a tiny glimmer of hope. One problem solved. Like a Voice whispering in her spirit, *"Just take it one day at a time, Grace. My grace is sufficient for you."*

"My grace is sufficient for you . . ." Her mind scrambled. What was the rest of that promise? *". . . for My strength is made perfect in weakness."*

She felt like the poster child for that verse.

She scooped up the cat, who protested being snatched from his nap. So now what? Just take the next step. Which was . . . the phone call from her sister-in-law. She should call her back.

CHAPTER 11

The only problem with driving to her brother's house in Arlington Heights, Grace mused as she nosed her Ford Focus through westbound traffic — surprisingly heavy for Sunday afternoon — was the lack of east-west freeways this far north in Chicago. Seemed like she barely got on the expressway going north, and she had to get off again on Lake Avenue, a four-lane with stoplights every half mile, and take it west all the way to the northwest suburb.

Still, it was nice of Denise and Mark to invite her for Sunday dinner. She needed some company, something to distract her. It'd be great to be with family. "Bring Roger too!" Denise had chirped. "We're practically on your way home from church."

County Line Christian Fellowship was even further west. She might've looked for a church closer to home a couple of years ago, except for Roger's involvement there.

Maybe now was the time . . .

"No, it'll just be me. I'm not going to County Line tomorrow. Did you say two o'clock?" She'd explain about Roger when she got there.

In spite of traffic, Grace pulled into the driveway of Mark and Denise's modest suburban home after just the usual forty-five-minute drive. Another familiar car sat in the driveway . . .

"Hey, hey, hey, there she is!" Large knuckles were knocking on her side window.

Grace opened her car door. "Dad! What are you doing here?" Climbing out of the car, she was enveloped in a big hug. "Nobody said anything about you guys coming too." Her raspy voice was muffled against his big shoulder.

"Gotta see our girl!" Her father, hatless, his thinning silver hair lifting slightly in the chilly breeze, held her at arm's length. "Still got that nasty laryngitis, don't you," he scolded. "We gotta get you inside." Grace barely had time to grab her purse and the bag with souvenirs she'd bought in Florida for her nephews before being hustled through the front door.

"Surprise!" Marcus and Luke, eight and five respectively, nearly bowled her over with hugs. "Grandma's here too!"

Indeed she was. Grace smiled at her mom, an attractive woman in her early sixties, still working as a librarian at one of the branch libraries in Indianapolis. Margaret Meredith had let her hair go silver and wore it in a short pageboy, softly framing her pleasant face. Hugs all around . . . Mark, so like their dad, a bit pudgy in the paunch but still good-looking with his dark brown hair and lopsided grin, his pretty wife, Denise, and the two boys, all mop-haired and big smiles — especially when she handed the boys the two wrapped packages, which they immediately ripped open to discover large rubber alligators she'd bought at Orlando's Nature Park.

"Wow. Thanks, Aunt Grace!"

"Yeah," echoed five-year-old Luke. He squinted up at her. "How come you're talking funny?"

She pointed a finger into her mouth, and then grinned as she tousled his hair. "Laryngitis. You oughta try it sometime."

Grace took her father's arm as Denise shooed them all toward the dining room. "How's the hardware store, Dad?"

"Oh, you know, hanging in there. Now if one of my offspring would just take over the business, I could retire . . ."

"Dad!" Mark rolled his eyes. "Don't start

that again. Sis, why don't you sit on that side with the boys, Mom and Dad over here . . ."

When they were seated, they all held hands around the dining room table and Mark eyed his father. "Dad? Will you — ?" And Paul Meredith launched into a "Sunday dinner prayer," as the grandkids called it, a bit long, thanking God they could all be together, asking God to bless Tim and Nellie and the kids — Grace's oldest brother's family — who lived too far away to be with them today, blessing this home, thanking God for Grace being back home from her tour, safe and sound . . .

Not so safe. Not so sound, she thought, biting her lip.

". . . and bless the hands that prepared this scrumptious meal. Amen!"

The next few minutes were a flurry of passing the pot roast and vegetables, the usual, "Aw, do I hafta eat carrots?" and Denise jumping up to get this and that she'd forgotten.

"So where's Roger?" Mark asked, heaping roasted potatoes on his plate. "Thought he wouldn't be letting you out of his sight after being gone a whole month."

Grace swallowed. She took a deep breath. "We broke up."

All noise and movement stopped. Food dishes were held in midair. Even Marcus and Luke stared up at her from either side. Grace was aware that all eyes went to the bare third finger of her left hand. She nodded.

"Oh, honey . . ." Her mother's face looked about to crumple. "You bought your wedding dress!"

"Please, Mom, don't." Grace smiled bravely. "It's all right. Maybe we can talk about it later. I'm supposed to be resting my voice, so why don't you all tell me what's been happening around here while I've been gone?"

It took a false start or two to get the conversation going again, but the chatter finally picked up about jobs and politics and weather, until Marcus announced he wanted to quit piano lessons and play drums in the elementary school band next year.

"Like heck," Mark muttered under his breath and everyone laughed. "You boys go play video games or something until it's time for dessert. We'll call you." It took only two seconds for them to disappear toward the den.

With the boys gone, all eyes turned back on Grace. "Okay." She laid her cloth napkin on the table. "I need to keep this short,

111

though. Still trying to get over this virus." As simply as she could, she told them about Roger's phone call the night before her last concert, Samantha's mother's heart attack, and coming home sick. She didn't say anything about the humiliating "pat down" at the Memphis airport, not in front of her parents. She'd never been able to talk to them about sexual stuff. And . . . some things were better left buried. "Then he showed up yesterday and took his ring back."

Mark threw up his hands. "Of all the nerve! He's nuts!"

She shrugged. "He said he couldn't handle the long separations when I'm on tour, and he didn't like our relationship being so public. Not what he wants in a wife."

Her mother reached across the table and touched her hand. "But, honey, it's not like you'd be doing that forever. I mean, you're almost thirty. Once you're married, you'll want to start a family, stay at home with the babies —"

"Now, Margaret . . ." Her father gave a warning shake of his head.

Her mother looked surprised. "Well, wouldn't she?"

Grace shook her head. "I don't know, Mom. We never talked about it. That's what's so weird. This seemed to come out of the blue. But then, late-night long-distance phone calls when I'm on tour aren't exactly ideal for keeping up with each other. Somehow I missed the clues. But . . . Roger was quite clear. The engagement's off."

Her brother's face was a thundercloud. "Probably has his eye on some other bimbo at that matchmaking factory out at County Line."

Grace made a wry face. "What do you mean, some *other* bimbo, dear brother?"

Mark turned red. "Oh, you know what I mean. How old is Roger . . . thirty-two? And doesn't he teach some college-age Sunday school class? Mature single guy . . . college girls on a manhunt . . . recipe for disaster."

Denise poked her husband. "I think you need to shut up, Mark."

Grace felt the tears start. She picked up her napkin and dabbed her eyes. "Yes, please. Don't start any gossip about Roger. I don't know what happened. Right now, you guys just need to understand that it's over. And I'm so glad you're my family. I —" It was no use. The tears spilled over. Her shoulders shook.

"Oh, sweetheart." Her father moved over to the seat vacated by Luke and wrapped his arms around her. She sobbed on his shoulder. "It's okay, it's going to be all right. You'll always be our Golden Girl. Go ahead and cry."

Golden Girl . . . Her father's words made her cry even harder. Not so golden. Not if they knew. But held against her father's chest, Grace's sobs gradually eased as the others quietly started to clear the table. Grace heard her mother's plaintive voice from the kitchen. "I just don't understand!"

And her brother's still angry voice: "Jerk has no idea he just lost the best fish in the sea."

As hard as it'd been to tell them she'd been dumped, the Sunday afternoon with family felt like a soothing balm for Grace's wounds. They built a fire in the family room fireplace, and Denise served hot cider with cinnamon sticks and peppermint ice cream as they played a cutthroat game of Scrabble — a Meredith tradition. But her parents had to leave around five, heading back to Indianapolis — a four-hour drive — and Grace said she'd better get going too. Mark followed her out to the car.

"If you want me to go punch his lights out, just say the word, Sis."

She shook her head with a sad smile.

"Thanks, Mark. I'll let you know."

"Hey, sorry I didn't get over to shovel your walks. Maybe I can drop by tomorrow. I'll look at my —"

"It's okay. I paid a neighbor kid to shovel. Did a pretty good job."

Her brother looked surprised. "Really? Thought you didn't know anybody."

"Well, I don't really. But I met the family next door, some of them anyway, and they seem real nice. Tavis shoveled the walks. He's a twin. Cute kid. Thirteen."

"Thirteen. Hmm, never did think of thirteen as a cute age. All that angst. Kind of dreading it."

She leaned over and kissed her brother on the cheek. "Marcus and Luke are going to be *fine*. But good luck with the drums."

She got in her car, waved good-bye, and backed out of the driveway.

Daylight was fading fast and traffic was still heavy going back toward Chicago, but she felt relieved. She'd dreaded telling her parents about the breakup. Her mom had been so excited about getting to be mother of the bride — a whole different role than the mother of the groom she'd been at Tim's and Mark's weddings. And she knew her parents were a little anxious that she was almost thirty and not yet married. Tim had gotten married right out of college and he and Nellie had pre-teens already as well as a surprise baby, who was now three — all girls. They lived in Colorado Springs and she didn't get to see her nieces very often. At least she had Mark and Denise and the boys nearby. Family. What a gift.

But . . . there was a lot she hadn't told them. She just felt so weary. There'd be time to tell them about canceling the sweetheart banquet in Milwaukee next weekend — surely they'd understand *that*. She did tell them she had an appointment with a throat specialist tomorrow. After that, maybe she'd need their counsel — and surely their prayers — about what to do about her upcoming bookings and the West Coast tour this spring. And the switch in her booking agent . . .

Oh. She still hadn't called Jeff Newman back about him stopping over in Chicago to see her on Tuesday! Guess she couldn't put that off any longer. Why not meet the guy . . . she'd give him a tentative okay, and let him know for sure after her doctor's appointment tomorrow.

CHAPTER 12

Grace stood at her kitchen window Tuesday morning, wondering why she hadn't heard from Jeff Newman. It had started snowing during the night and was still falling lightly and getting foggy. His plane was probably late.

Why was she so nervous? It wasn't like she had to convince him to take her on as a client. She was already well established with the agency, and Newman had said the switch was simply a client overload for her agent. But was he experienced? He'd sounded a lot younger than Fowler.

Regardless, he wasn't going to be happy when she told him the otolaryngologist had strongly recommended a monthlong rest of her voice and treatments by a speech therapist to restrengthen her vocal chords. Besides the viral infection that had inflamed her throat, he'd said overuse, vocal fatigue, and stress were responsible for her loss of voice. The specialist had been very thorough, not only doing a medical workup and vocal history, but performing several tests, including an endoscopy — she hadn't been able to eat or drink anything for ten hours prior to her appointment — and something called a "nasal fiber-optic laryngoscopy," both of which required enough twilight anesthesia that they'd advised her not to drive, so she'd taken a taxi both ways.

So much for Monday.

Well, it was what it was. At least she had good medical reasons for a sabbatical. Maybe she'd be ready to resume doing concerts again after a few weeks of rest. And surely Bongo Booking had run into these types of problems before with other clients, since — according to the specialist — voice disorders were as common among singers as tennis elbow and knee injuries were to athletes.

Bongo Booking . . .

Grace couldn't help a small grin as she turned from the window and headed into the living room to get an update on the weather. Strange name for an agency that specialized in booking contemporary Christian music artists. Go figure. But at least "Bongo" got attention and a place near the front of the alphabet in listings.

The TV screen leaped to life as she pressed the remote. *Oprah.* Was she still on? She'd heard rumors the diva was moving her show to LA. Well, whatever the hot topic was, the show would be over soon. It was almost ten. According to the flight schedule Newman had e-mailed her, he was supposed to land at O'Hare around nine thirty, pick up a rental car, and drive to her house. He'd suggested meeting here so she wouldn't have to go out. Thoughtful of him. His last e-mail said the agency had lined up the rental car and a couple of other business appointments for him as long as he was in Chicago . . . *Wait. What's this?*

A weather warning was running across the bottom of the screen. *Heavy snow accumulation possible by evening rush hour.* Ugh. Now she was doubly glad she didn't have to drive anywhere.

But waiting was hard. She'd cleaned the house . . . had the makings for a simple Thai salad and pita bread lunch . . . answered a few e-mails . . . and changed outfits twice. Should she go homey, with jeans and bulky sweater? Business casual pantsuit? Long winter skirt and tall boots? Her phone finally rang at 10:25. It took her a moment to recognize it. She'd reset the ringtone to a simple pleasant guitar strum — for now, anyway. The caller ID said Jeff Newman.

"Grace! So sorry to keep you waiting. Air traffic was backed up because of weather and my plane just landed."

"That's okay. I figured as much. Glad you made it down safely."

"Oh, yeah. God's got us covered, right? Anyway, no checked baggage so I'm on my way to pick up the rental car. I've got GPS on my phone, so I should be able to find you. Let's see . . . it's going to be eleven thirty at the earliest. Still okay for you?"

"Fine." Not like she was going anywhere. "See you then."

It was noon before the doorbell rang. She'd changed again, deciding on business casual: black slacks over ankle boots, feminine white blouse, belted corduroy cranberry jacket, and her makeup had a soft-rosy glow. After a week of slopping around in slippers, hair in a ponytail or clip, and no makeup, it felt good to spruce up a bit.

Grace took a deep breath and opened the door. A gust of wind blew a swirl of snow inside. A man stood on her stoop, hatless, his shoulders hunched inside a leather jacket with the collar up, a leather messenger bag hanging from one shoulder. Snowflakes had already layered on his dark hair, but a red scarf was wrapped around his face and ears. "Grace Meredith," said a muffled voice.

She pulled the door open wider, remembering to keep an eye out for her four-legged escape artist. "And you must be Jeff Newman."

The man stepped in and she shut the door as he stamped snow off his shoes on the wide mat just inside. Unwinding the scarf, he shook his head and ran a hand over dark curly hair to rid it of the wet snowflakes. "Whew. Thanks. It's getting nasty out there. Again, apologies for being late. But the traffic!"

"I'm sure. May I take your coat?"

He shrugged off the leather jacket and handed it to her along with the scarf and a chuckle. "Not really dressed for this. I was thinking Nashville weather."

As Grace hung his jacket in the coat closet, she heard him say, "Great little house. I've always loved these Chicago bungalows."

She turned. Jeff Newman stood in the middle of the living room, slightly taller than average height, wearing charcoal slacks and a pale blue dress shirt, open-necked at the collar, no tie. His eyes were dark brown, framed by dark lashes and eyebrows. A dark shadow of a beard — deliberate? — outlined his jaw.

Grace was momentarily flustered. Hadn't expected him to be so darn good-looking. "Uh . . . please sit. Would you like coffee? Or . . . it's already noon. Are you hungry? I've got lunch." She felt like she was babbling, her voice scratchy.

He grinned, swung the messenger bag off his shoulder, and sat down on the couch, arms spread along the back. "Coffee's good for now. Black is fine."

Black is fine. Well, one thing they had in common.

While she set up a tray in the kitchen, she heard, "Hey there, buddy. What's your name?" A chuckle. "Got some attitude there."

She hurried back in with the tray. Oreo was up on the couch, giving this strange new person the once-over. "Oreo . . . scat! Sorry about the cat. I'll put him away."

Jeff reached out and let the cat sniff his hand. "Hey, no problem. I like cats. What'd you call him? Oreo? Cute name for a tuxedo cat."

"He'll get cat hair all over you. C'mon, you." She picked up the cat, deposited him in the guest bedroom, and shut the door. *Good. He likes cats.*

Her guest seemed in no hurry to talk business. He asked how long she'd been in Chicago . . . did she have family in the area? . . . where had she grown up? . . . what did she enjoy doing when she wasn't touring? . . . horseback riding — really? He'd never have guessed! . . .

Jeff seemed so laid-back and friendly, Grace found herself slipping off her ankle boots and curling up on the overstuffed chair, coffee cup in hand. But he suddenly looked stricken. "Here I am, asking all these questions and making you talk, when you're trying to get over a case of laryngitis! Turnabout's fair play. Your turn to ask questions. As I understand it, Bongo is not only doing your booking, but helping with career management. So you deserve to know who's taking on your career if I'm going to be your agent."

This wasn't what Grace had expected at all. Nothing like her previous conversations with Walter Fowler, which had been cordial, but *all* business. "Um, tell you what, why don't we take a break and have lunch. I'm sure you're hungry by now." Picking up the coffee tray, she headed for the kitchen. "It won't take long," she called back over her shoulder.

But to her consternation, he was right

behind her. "Let me help. I can set the table. Kitchen table okay?"

Well, okay. She'd been thinking about using the dining room table, but it was too big for two people. Pointing out where to get plates and silverware, Grace rummaged in the refrigerator for ingredients she'd already prepared for her Thai beef salad and tossed them together with the lime-cilantro vinaigrette. Salad divided between two plates, pita bread halves in the toaster, ice in the water glasses . . .

Jeff pulled out a chair for her. "That was quick. Looks fantastic too." He laughed self-consciously as he sat down. "Usually we take our clients out for lunch. I'm afraid I'm imposing on your hospitality." Before Grace had time to protest that his willingness to meet her at home was a gift, he raised one of those intriguing eyebrows. "May I do the honors and ask the blessing?"

Grace quickly ducked her head, more to hide the sudden flush in her cheeks than reverence. What was with this guy? In one hour he'd completely disarmed her, and now he was giving thanks for their lunch, sitting at the kitchen table like old friends.

"You eat," he encouraged a moment later, picking up his own fork. "I'll give you the fifty-cent version of Jeff Newman for now, and then we can talk business. I don't want to monopolize your time. Let's see . . ."

Grace toyed with her salad as she listened. He had grown up on the West Coast, was a preacher's kid, played bass guitar in a garage band in high school, followed all the CCM bands and most of the pop bands too — a major source of tension with his strict parents, his father especially. " 'You call that music? Just noise, son, just noise!' " Jeff furrowed his eyebrows darkly and shook a finger as he mimicked his father. He'd graduated from university with a degree in business — but a secretive minor in music — and shocked his parents no end by marrying a college girl he'd only known six months . . .

Married . . . well, of course. But he had no ring on his finger.

"Unfortunately," he shrugged, "she'd said yes to me on the rebound from another relationship, and wanted out of the marriage before we even celebrated our first anniversary." He looked chagrined. "That's when I decided to grow up and take things a bit slower. My parents and I have met somewhere in the middle, learning to listen to each other and respect our differences. That was five years ago. Finally realized I wasn't performance material, but I could use my head for business in the music world. Got my master's degree in business" — the left corner of his mouth tipped in a grin — "and Bongo hired me two years ago. I've loved getting a chance to personally relate to a lot of the CCM bands and singers. And . . . here I am."

Grace absently tucked a strand of layered hair behind her ear. The men she knew weren't usually that honest about their failures, their fits and starts. She hardly knew what to say. She pointed at his salad plate with her fork. "You better eat."

They finished their meal with small talk, and then she cleared the plates. "I'll make some more coffee. Half decaf okay?"

They took the fresh coffee back to the living room. The ticking schoolhouse clock said two o'clock already. Oreo was meowing and scratching at the guest room door so Grace let him out, and he settled down in her lap.

Jeff peered outside the picture window as he resumed his seat on the couch. "Hmm. Still snowing. I should probably leave in the next hour or so. I've got a four-thirty appointment downtown and an eight o'clock flight to Nashville. Better give myself some extra time." He reached for his leather messenger bag and pulled out an official-looking red plastic folder. "And we've still got some business to discuss." He opened the folder and studied it briefly. "The sweetheart banquet aside — which has been canceled because of your doctor's certification — you are currently booked for four fly in, fly out concerts between now and the West Coast tour in late April and May. Let's see . . . a megachurch in Norfolk, Virginia . . . another in Houston . . . and then two college venues — Greenville in downstate Illinois and Cincinnati Christian University." He looked up. "But you had another doctor's appointment yesterday . . ." Both eyebrows arched like a question.

Greenville . . . the little college with the big CCM program. Her alma mater. Grace realized the hand that held her coffee cup was shaking. She set the cup down on the coffee table, took a deep breath, and tried to keep her voice steady. The otolaryngologist was recommending at least a month of total voice rest — no singing, no concerts — with treatments by a voice therapist. She tried to explain the medical reasons as succinctly as possible.

"A *month.*" Jeff Newman frowned and glanced again at the red plastic folder. "That would mean canceling Norfolk and Hous-

127

ton." His eyes lifted and looked at her soberly. "You're sure? Those two are the biggest venues of the four. I'm sure the promoters will understand, considering the health concerns, but this could be a bump in your career, right at a time when your popularity is on the rise. These concerts have been on the books for a year."

To her dismay, Grace's eyes filled with tears and she had to grope in her jacket pocket for a tissue. She pressed the tissue to her eyes, hoping she wasn't smudging her mascara, and then blew her nose.

"Hey. I'm sorry. That was thoughtless." Jeff's voice was contrite. "Of course you need to follow doctor's orders! Yes, it's a bump in the road, but these things happen. Family emergencies, illness, death in the family — life isn't predictable. Just leave it to me." She heard a soft chuckle. "My mother used to tell me I could sweet-talk my way out of anything. One of my hidden gifts as a music agent."

They talked a while more. Jeff promised to keep in touch with her about his contacts with her bookings. Said how much he appreciated getting to meet her in person, getting to know her a little bit in her own "habitat." He also assured her she still had the option of saying yea or nay to his reassignment as her agent.

But he finally rose. "I better get going. Since moving to Denver two years ago, I've gotten indoctrinated in the science of driving in snow. Can't say it comes naturally, though." He waggled his eyebrows and grinned. "Better say a prayer for me."

Grace got his leather jacket and scarf and saw him to the door. Their good-bye was brief and cordial, and Jeff ducked down the steps, plowing his way through at least eight or ten inches of snow covering her once-shoveled walks.

Shutting the door and locking it, she went to the window and peered out. He must've parked down the block a way, because between falling snow and fog, she couldn't see him. She breathed that prayer he'd asked for, then just stood there, watching the falling snow.

The meeting wasn't what she'd expected, but she had to admit Newman seemed like a really nice guy. It'd certainly be a change from dealing with Fowler. More personable. She liked that. And it'd gone better than she'd expected. She'd been able to focus on the medical and physical reasons for taking a sabbatical and didn't have to get into her nightmare with the TSA or her broken engagement as the critical reasons she *really* needed some time to recoup: to rethink what she was doing with her career, and to evaluate what was next for her sans Roger.

Roger. Strange that Jeff hadn't said anything about her engagement. It was public knowledge, had even become part of her testimony. Surely Fowler had told his assistant.

But not a word. Odd.

Oreo was pacing on the back of the couch, meowing at her. "It's not time for you to eat, silly cat," she scolded, coming away from the window and heading for the kitchen. "But if you want to supervise the dishwashing, come on."

Grace put on some hot water for tea — coffee didn't have quite the same soothing effect on her throat as honey-lemon tea — and drew a sink full of hot sudsy water. Could've put the lunch dishes in the dishwasher, but she felt like doing the few dishes by hand. The hot soapy water was relaxing, made her feel domestic — after all, she had a whole month ahead of her to be *home.* Didn't have to travel, didn't have to put on her public persona. She could just be Grace. Wear her flannel shirt. Get some things done around the house she'd always wanted to do. She'd have time to think, time to pray.

Pray . . . Grace absently rinsed the last

dish and put it in the drainer. Not sure she and God were on the best speaking terms right now. Was she mad at God for things falling apart in her life? Well, yeah. Or . . . maybe God was mad at *her.* Felt like it. Maybe God had a long memory and now it was pay-up time. That wasn't what she'd been taught, of course. Confession resulted in forgiveness. She knew that. Believed it. Not that she'd actually ever confessed to anyone. But she'd confessed to God, one-on-one . . . surely that mattered.

She'd been having a hard time praying since she got home. Even though she definitely had some things she needed to decide in the next few weeks. Stuff that needed a lot of prayer. Canceling the next few bookings only gave her breathing room. What then? Go back on the concert circuit? Doing what? She needed a new program, a new —

Ding-dong. Ding-dong.

The doorbell cut into her thoughts. Oreo leaped off the kitchen stool and streaked toward the living room. Quickly drying her hands, Grace followed. She glanced at the wall clock. Three thirty. Kids would be coming home from school. Maybe it was the boy, Tavis, wanting to know if she wanted her walks shoveled. Well, yes, once the snow stopped.

Unlocking the door, she pulled it open, ready to tell him to come back tomorrow.

Jeff Newman stood on the stoop, shoulders hunched inside his leather jacket, the red scarf wrapped around his face and ears, snow layering on his curly hair.

"Uh, I'm stuck." He jerked a thumb over his shoulder. "And there must've been a fender bender at the end of the block, 'cause there are a bunch of cars every which way blocking the intersection. Can I, uh, come in?"

CHAPTER 13

Grace swallowed her shock. "Of course!" She stepped back and then shut the door behind him.

The Bongo agent stomped the snow off his shoes and unwrapped the red scarf before shedding his jacket. "I'm sorry about this, Grace. I should've realized the weather would be a problem. Uh, I need to make some calls . . . and do you have a phone directory? I might need a tow truck to pull me out."

She nodded, found the Yellow Pages, and then took his leather jacket and red scarf into the kitchen to drip. His shoes and pant legs — they must be soaked too.

Still in the kitchen, Grace braced herself against the kitchen counter and took several deep breaths. She'd prepared herself for their meeting, and it had gone well — but it was supposed to be over. She'd been looking forward to some quiet time to process what they'd talked about, make her decision about switching agents from Fowler to Newman — a no-brainer, really — and start thinking about the implications of taking a monthlong sabbatical.

But now Jeff Newman was back in her house — stuck, he said.

She could hear him on his phone in the living room, probably calling his next appointment or the rental-car people. Or calling for a tow — that'd be the best. If a tow truck could come out, it could move those other cars, then get him unstuck, and he'd be on his way. Might be an hour or two at the most.

But she felt awkward. She didn't want to go back to the living room and eavesdrop. Didn't want to be stuck in the kitchen either. But she could busy herself drying the dishes and putting them away, reheating the tea water, and making her tea. She'd make him a cup too. Something hot to drink. He had to be chilled after his foray into the snow outside.

Jeff was sitting on the edge of the couch, phone to his ear, phonebook splayed open on the coffee table when she came in with the tea. He acknowledged her with a brief smile as she placed the mug on the coffee table in front of him. ". . . All right, all right . . . yes, put my name on the list . . . you got the address? . . . Yeah, I'll let you know if I get it out." He flipped his cell phone closed and threw out his hands. "I can't believe this! I've called three tow companies, and all three said all their trucks are out on calls already and it might be tomorrow before they can get to me!"

Grace stared. *Tomorrow?*

Jeff shook his head in resignation. "Well, it's obvious I'm not going to make that four-thirty appointment. I'd better call . . ." He flipped his phone open again and punched a few buttons.

That's when Grace noticed his bare feet. He'd taken his wet shoes and socks off and put them on the mat by the door. Well, she could do something about cold feet. Heading down the hall to her bedroom, she rummaged in her dresser drawer for a pair of thick athletic socks. Might be a tad small, but at least they were dry.

Grabbing a small towel from the bathroom, she took her offerings back into the living room. He was still on the phone. She put the towel and socks on the coffee table and pointed to his feet. He gave her a nod of thanks as he explained his situation to someone on the other end.

Grace was tempted to turn on the TV to

get a weather update, but Jeff no sooner ended one call and pulled on the socks, than he made another. Retrieving her laptop from the bedroom, she set it up on the kitchen table and checked the weather online. Oh, brother. Looked like the snow would continue well into the night, with at least twelve inches accumulation.

She sucked in a deep breath and blew it out. *O-kaay.* If Jeff couldn't get his rental car out of its parking space . . . she was looking at having company for the next twelve to fourteen hours at least.

Overnight.

"Grace?"

She jumped at the sound of his voice. Jeff Newman was standing in the doorway of the kitchen, phone in one hand, scratching the back of his head with the other. He looked incredibly sheepish. Or frustrated. Some of both.

"I'm really sorry about this. I thought I'd left enough room to get out of my parking space, even with the snow, but a couple of cars parked after me and boxed me in. On top of that the tires started spinning, digging a rut. I had to quit before it got worse. But even if I get out, there's that mess at the end of the street . . ."

Grace just nodded. "Uh-huh," she said finally.

"Look," Jeff said, sliding his phone into his pocket. "I'll go back out and see if I can find someone who knows whose cars are boxing me in. Maybe if we get one car moved, we could get mine out." He gave her a questioning glance. "Uh . . . any chance you'd recognize the cars? Know who they belong to?"

She shook her head. "I'm sorry. With all my travel, I'm not home enough to know the people on the street very well, much less whose car is whose."

"Oh. Okay. Well . . . I've got a carry-on bag in the car with a change of clothes. Got a pair of gym shoes in there. Think I'll change first and then knock on doors . . . Oh, thanks for hanging up my jacket." He took it off the back of the kitchen chair where she'd hung it and went for his shoes by the front door.

He was back in five minutes. "Got a place I can change?" Grace showed him to the guest room, but the moment he closed the door she rued her decision. Hopefully he wouldn't open the closet door and see her wedding dress hanging there —

Grace! What's the matter with you? So what if he sees the wedding dress. At some point he'd have to know her wedding plans were on the rocks — unless he really was clueless that she'd been engaged. Either way . . . so what? Her personal life was her business, and it was only his business to the extent that it impacted her career — which, she had to admit, it did. But only in the short term. She would find a way to spin her concert message so it made sense. Or change it all together . . .

She heard the guest-room door open and Jeff appeared in the living room in jeans, denim shirt, navy fleece vest, and gym shoes. He was holding her thick socks. "Here . . . thanks. I had a pair in my bag. And, hate to ask, but —" He also held out the charcoal slacks he'd been wearing. "— do you have a dryer I can toss these into? These pants are pretty damp."

Grace laughed. He looked even more boyish now. "I do. Here, I'll take them. You go see what's what about the car. But you know you're just going to get those dry clothes wet pushing cars around."

He grinned. "Well, at least I can throw the gym shoes in the dryer. Don't try it with my leather ones."

Adding the soggy pair of socks he'd taken off earlier to her armload, she headed for the clothes dryer in the basement, even as she heard the front door open and close.

With Jeff's slacks and socks tumbling cheerfully on Warm, Grace decided to change out of her own business casual and get into some jeans. And she might as well gather up her dirty laundry and start a load to kill time until he got back with a report about the car situation. While she was in the basement loading the washer, she heard her ringtone going off faintly somewhere — where in the world had she left her phone? — but decided to let it go until she got back upstairs.

But once back on the first floor, she couldn't find the phone. Not in the kitchen . . . not in the living room . . . *ack!* This was awful. She needed her phone. Then, miraculously she heard the strumming guitar again. Following the sound, she found her cell phone at the bottom of the laundry hamper. Good grief.

She had two voice-mail messages. One from her parents and one from her brother. Probably just concerned, wondering if she was okay. But she didn't want to call them back right now — not with Jeff Newman coming back in soon. She wasn't quite ready to try to explain what he was doing here. She'd just send a quick text to both of them, let them know she was hunky-dory, and she'd call later.

Besides, it was already five o'clock. She ought to think about fixing something for supper. For two.

She was casing the refrigerator, trying to figure out what kind of meal to throw together, when Jeff came back in, stomping his feet on the doormat and shrugging off his jacket. "No luck. Nobody's out shoveling because it's still coming down. I did knock on a few doors, but nobody seems to know whose cars are boxing me in. One guy, Jewish fellow I think, had those curly sideburn things —" Jeff circled his forefinger near his ear. "— said sometimes people in the next block park in this one since it's not as crowded." He held up his damp jacket. "Where do you want this? Kitchen again?"

She nodded and led him into the kitchen, where he draped the jacket on the back of a chair and sat down to take off his gym shoes, now also wet.

"What about the fender bender at the corner?"

Jeff shrugged. "Still a bottleneck. More than a fender bender, because there's a cop car there, and at least one of the cars is pretty banged up. Looks like a third car slid into the first two. Cars coming down that street are having to back up and go around some other way. Cop said they're waiting for a tow to clear out the cars." He snorted. "Yeah, right. Good luck."

Grace held up a bag of tortilla chips and a can of refried beans. "You okay with nachos? I think I've got all the makings to make it a main dish."

"You've already fed me once today . . . look. Let me call the towing company again, and see if they can still come out tonight. If so, maybe I can return the car and get a hotel out by the airport. I'm going to miss my flight anyway, might as well get out there, see if I can get standby."

She opened the can with the electric can opener. "Fine. But in the meantime, we're going to eat. All we had for lunch was salad, and I, for one, am getting hungry. Go make your call. Nachos coming up."

By the time Grace heated the refried beans and set out the makings for do-it-yourself nachos, Jeff had once again tried the three original towing companies plus a few others from the Yellow Pages. "Can't believe it," he said, sinking into a chair at the kitchen table. "I either got a busy signal, or my call went to voice mail, or no one answered. Now I *am* hungry." He surveyed the outlay of tortilla chips, bubbling refried beans, grated cheese, chopped tomatoes, sliced green onions, sliced black olives, and jars of sliced jalapeños and chunky salsa in the middle of the table. "That looks great . . . uh, you go first."

"Okay." Grace piled cheese on a layer of tortilla chips, zapped her plate in the microwave until the cheese melted, and then added the other condiments. "Go for it," she grinned.

Her phone rang again as her accidental supper guest started his own pile. She pulled the phone out of her jeans pocket and glanced at the caller ID . . . what? *Roger!* "Uh, excuse me a moment," she said and took the phone all the way into the bathroom. If she didn't answer, he might show up at the door like he had last weekend. That would not be cool. Not tonight.

"Hello?"

"Grace! So glad you answered. Are you okay? This is turning into quite a storm."

"Uh-huh, I'm fine. Everything's good."

"Your voice sounds better."

"Yeah, thanks. Getting there."

"Well, don't try to go out. It's a madhouse on the tollways. I left my car at work and took public transportation. Even that's crawling."

"Smart." But she felt annoyed. What made him think he could tell her what to do? He'd butted out of her life. Let him stay there.

"You need anything?"

"No, I'm good."

Silence stretched on the other end, but she didn't try to fill it.

"Well, okay. I just wanted to check, make sure you were all right."

"Well, I'm fine. Thanks for checking." She hung up first. But she stood still in the bathroom for a few moments. Hearing his familiar voice, his concern for her, touched something. She'd kept her answers short, no more than necessary to be polite . . . but it had been all she could do to not fall into the cozy chitchat that had characterized their phone calls so many times in the past.

He still cared. Why else would he call to check on her?

Shaking off those thoughts, Grace strode back into the kitchen, where Jeff was lofting a loaded tortilla chip from the plate and into his mouth. " 'Ou caug' me," he mumbled, mouth full, grinning. He sucked stringy cheese off his fingers, chewed, and swallowed. "Everything okay?" He made a "phone" out of his thumb and little finger and held it to his ear.

She nodded, sticking her plate back into the microwave for half a minute. "Uh-huh. Just a friend, making sure I'm okay."

Jeff regarded her as she sat back down. " 'Friend' . . . as in, your fiancé?"

Grace caught her breath. Where did *that* come from? She finally blinked. "Why do you ask?"

He shrugged. "Fowler told me you were engaged. And I saw some of your recent New Year, New You shows — amazing what you can find on YouTube — trying to get up to speed before we met. You talked freely about your engagement to . . . Roger? Is that his name? But have to admit I'm a little confused. You haven't said anything about your fiancé all day. And then I realized" — his eyes dropped to her left hand — "no ring. I just wondered . . ."

Well, there it was. The elephant in the room. She looked down at her plate of uneaten nachos. "The engagement's off. That's why I'm not wearing the ring." Was that enough? "It only happened a week ago," she added, her voice suddenly husky. "It's . . . hard for me to talk about."

Jeff seemed taken aback. He spread his hands out contritely. "Grace, I am so sorry. I shouldn't have said anything. It was just, you know, so public, but today . . ."

Argh! Those darn tears. Grace fished for another tissue and dabbed at her eyes. "It's all right," she whispered. "I . . . I should have said something."

Jeff cleared his throat and stood up. "Look, I think I should get going. You've been kind to put up with me, but . . . the weather's not your fault, my rental car being stuck isn't your fault. I should go." He picked up his dishes and set them on the counter. "Thanks for supper. But, uh, if I can get my slacks from your dryer, maybe I can call a taxi to take me to a hotel and sort out this rental-car thing tomorrow. Unless you know of a motel or hotel within walking distance."

Grace blew her nose and frowned as he pulled on the leather jacket that had been hanging on the back of his chair. "Wait. Just . . . sit down a minute, will you?" She needed to get herself together.

He hesitated a moment, but sat down again.

She sucked in a deep breath and blew it out. "There are no motels or hotels within walking distance around here, so scratch that. And given the state of the roads until the snowplows get out there, even getting a taxi is going to be a gamble. So don't do anything stupid."

"Stupid?" he repeated, with a slight laugh.

Which sparked an embarrassed giggle. "Okay, I meant, don't do anything rash."

Did she know where she was going with this? There was only one option that made any sense. "You need to wait for the tow truck, and I've got a guest room. So just take off that jacket and wait this thing out. And those . . ." She pointed at the wet gym shoes he'd taken off. "Take them down to the basement and throw them in the dryer so you'll have at least one pair of dry shoes the next time you go out — dry for five minutes, anyway." She gave a little snort. "You know you're playing Russian roulette with your clothes."

Jeff reached for the gym shoes with a resigned grin. "Yes, ma'am. If you're sure about the guest room. So, where do I register for Hotel Meredith?"

"Ha. This is a bare-bones operation. No complimentary robe, no chocolate on the pillow, wait your turn for the bathroom." Now that she'd accepted the inevitable, offering hospitality to a business associate stuck in the storm didn't seem like such a big deal after all. "But we do offer entertainment — how about a game of Scrabble? But I'm warning you: the Merediths take no prisoners."

CHAPTER 14

*Shouts . . . an engine being gunned . . .
BANG! . . . metal hitting concrete . . .*

Grace sat up with a start. Daylight filled
the bedroom. What was all that noise? Better be the city snowplows clearing Beecham
Street.

She threw back the covers and headed for
the hall in bare feet and nightshirt — but
stopped short. *Wait.* She wasn't alone in the
house. Jeff Newman had spent the night and
was hopefully still asleep in the guest room.
They'd played Scrabble till almost midnight.

Pulling on a pair of sweatpants and a
sweatshirt — at least long enough to find
out what all the commotion was outside —
Grace once more headed out of her bedroom. Was that coffee she smelled?

She glanced at the schoolhouse clock as
she came into the living room. Nine thirty?
How could she have slept so late? Only then
did she realize her guest was standing at the

front window of the living room, drapes pulled back, coffee cup in hand. "Oh — good morning. You're up." Her first words of the day came out hoarse. Not surprising. All that laughing and talking last night.

He turned. Dressed in the same clothes as last night: jeans, denim shirt, and navy fleece vest. She had no idea what he'd slept in, since she hadn't had anything to offer him —

Don't go there, Grace.

"Good morning yourself." He tipped his head toward the window. "Something's going on across the street, but can't figure out what. Did you hear the siren a while ago?"

"No." Curious, Grace joined him at the picture window, suddenly conscious that she hadn't brushed her hair or put on any makeup. "Just some shouting and someone gunning their engine." She peered through the window. It had stopped snowing and blowing, but a foot of fresh snow covered everything. *Everything* — lawns, sidewalks, roofs, cars, the street. No city snowplows had come up Beecham yet —

"Whoa!" Jeff nearly spilled his coffee. "What is that guy doing?"

"Where . . . oh!"

From the direction of the cul-de-sac at the end of the street, she again heard an engine being gunned, and suddenly a large green pickup truck came roaring down the sidewalk across the street, plow affixed to the front, sending a large spray of snow over parked cars on that side. She gasped. "He's . . . he's plowing the sidewalk!"

Jeff snorted. "You think? Using a plow for a sidewalk is like cleaning your teeth with a rototiller. Uh-oh . . . there go a couple of bushes. Who *is* that guy? Do you recognize the truck?"

She nodded. "It belongs to the guy directly across the street — Middle Eastern family, Iraqi maybe? He's got a yard service." Her eyes followed the truck as it growled its way down the block, and then focused her gaze across the street at the two-flat one building over. A woman in a headscarf that showed only her face stood in the open front door, looking anxiously after the truck that was now halfway down the block. "That's his wife, I think, over there at the two-flat — except that's not their house. The two-flat belongs to an elderly lady . . ." Grace frowned. "Wonder what that's about?"

A few other people came out of their houses at the commotion. One man hollered after the big pickup, throwing up his hands at his ruined bushes. For half a minute there was a lull as the truck turned around down by the corner . . . and then it roared back up the sidewalk again, clearing a wide path. People jumped. "Is the guy nuts?" Jeff asked — but at that moment they both heard intermittent blasts from a siren and saw an ambulance following behind the truck, skidding to a stop in front of the two-flat.

Grace caught her breath. "Oh no! Must be the old lady." Almost forgetting Jeff standing beside her, she watched as paramedics jumped out of the ambulance, one disappearing inside the house accompanied by the woman in the headscarf as two others unloaded a gurney. They had trouble wheeling it up the unshoveled walk and finally picked it up, hefting it on their shoulders as they waded through the deep snow.

"Hey, where's your shovel?" Jeff said suddenly. He grabbed his gym shoes, now dry and sitting by the front door, stuffed his feet inside, and reached for his jacket. "They're going to need that walk shoveled when they come out."

A few minutes later, Grace watched as Jeff slogged his way across the street, red scarf wrapped around his ears, shovel in hand. Another man — it was hard to tell who it was all bundled up in a parka — also showed up with a shovel, and set to work. Then the driver of the pickup joined them. They'd only cleared the steps and a few feet of snow on the front walk of the two-flat when the paramedics came out the front door again, someone swathed in blankets now strapped to the gurney, carefully lifting their burden down the front steps. Jeff and the other men dropped their shovels and, together with the three paramedics, helped lift the gurney up over the snow to the area cleared by the pickup plow where the ambulance was idling.

Once the gurney was loaded, the back doors of the ambulance slammed shut, and the ambulance began backing up the way it had come, the siren pumping short warnings as it slowly disappeared from Grace's sight. After a minute or two, she heard the regular siren begin to wail and then slowly fade into the distance.

She breathed a quickie prayer they'd found Mrs. What's-her-name in time — though she had a momentary doubt God would pay any attention to her prayer, since she'd basically gone AWOL in the prayer department. She watched at the window as Jeff stood talking to the other two men a few minutes; then he shook their hands and started back toward the house.

Grace opened the door before Jeff had time to ring the doorbell, and he came in stomping snow off his gym shoes and brushing off his jeans. "Looks like it's their turn for another go in the dryer," she said wryly.

"No, it's okay — but this *is* the last time I come to Chicago without a pair of mukluks unless it's July." He pried off his wet gym shoes and flopped onto the couch, frowning. He seemed distracted.

"Did you find out what happened?" Grace curled up on the nearby chair.

"Yeah. The old lady fell down the basement stairs, broke her hip or something."

Grace gasped. "Oh, the poor thing! This morning?"

Jeff shrugged. "They're not sure when. Guess she was pretty incoherent when they found her."

"Found her? Who?"

"Not sure I got the whole story, but the guy who plowed the sidewalk so the ambulance could get through — the end of your street is still blocked by cars — said his son was throwing snowballs this morning and broke one of the basement windows in the two-flat, That's when they heard the old lady calling for help down there."

Grace was wide-eyed. "You're kidding. What if . . . oh, dear." The old lady lived alone. What if the kid hadn't thrown that snowball? She shuddered. It was too awful to think about.

"Krakowski," he said.

"What?"

"The old lady's name. That's what Farid said."

Krakowski . . . Didn't even sound familiar. "And the other man who helped?" she asked to cover the awkwardness she felt. These were her neighbors, after all.

"Jared Jasper he said." Jeff jerked a thumb. "Came from the house next door. He was supposed to be at work at O'Hare — air traffic controller he said — but the airport's shut down. Good thing, I guess. He couldn't get his car out either."

"Oh." She nodded. "Must be the twins' father."

Jeff's phone rang. He dug it out of his jeans pocket. "Newman here . . . Yeah, yeah, that's great . . . Thanks. I'll be there." He clicked off and grinned at Grace. "North Side Towing. Said they'd be here in the next thirty to sixty minutes. Guess the police called them to clear the cars blocking the intersection. Said they'd get me out too." He stood and began gathering his things. "I will finally be out of your hair."

Grace felt a twinge of disappointment.

Yesterday she hadn't wanted him to stay — but now his leaving felt too soon. She'd hoped for a little more time to visit, but she'd overslept, and then gotten distracted by the drama across the street. "It's been no trouble, really! But you need some breakfast before you go. Sorry it's so late." She headed for the kitchen. "Scrambled okay?"

"Sure," he called after her. "But don't go to any extra work for me. You've already fed me twice. Three times if you count all that popcorn we ate last night."

Pouring a cup of the ready-made coffee, Grace grinned to herself as she whisked eggs, poured two glasses of orange juice, and stuck two slices of whole wheat bread into the toaster. *All that popcorn.* And hot chocolate. And peanuts. Munching away to break the intensity of a cutthroat Scrabble game. She'd won — but just barely. And he'd demanded a rematch. Which she also won, but again just barely.

But it was fun. She'd laughed a lot. The Scrabble and easy conversation had taken her mind off her laryngitis and the awful experience at the airport and the canceled concerts . . . and even her broken engagement.

"Breakfast is ready!" she called a few

minutes later, dishing up the eggs.

"On the phone. Be there in a minute!"

It was more like three minutes, but Jeff finally slipped into a chair at the kitchen table. "Sorry. I was talking to the office, asking if they wanted to reschedule my meeting with the client in Nashville, or if I should just come back to Denver. Found out they'd already rescheduled with the client for tomorrow, so guess I go out to the airport and take the first standby to Nashville I can get."

She passed him the eggs. "Ouch. My guess is O'Hare will be pretty backed up after all the canceled flights yesterday. You might have a long wait. . . . Um, do you want to 'do the honors' again?"

"Sure." He bowed his head and prayed another brief and simple blessing over the food, though this time he added, ". . . and bless Grace Meredith for her hospitality above and beyond the call of duty. Restore her voice to full health, so she can continue to bless others with her gift of music. Amen."

She looked up and smiled at him. "Thank you. That was nice."

"Meant it. You've been a trouper."

"You're the one who's been inconvenienced."

He chuckled. "Don't feel too sorry for me. Cathy — she's our receptionist at Bongo, real nice girl, got married last year — said her cousin is coming to town in a couple days and she's lining up a weekend of skiing for the four of us. Cathy thinks I need to redeem my snow experience in Chicago."

Grace looked down at her plate. *A weekend of skiing . . . with "Cathy's cousin."* Jeff forked in a mouthful of scrambles. "Never been skiing. That was next on my bucket list, now that I live in Colorado. Something to look forward to when I get back. Though" — he made a face — "not my choice for a blind date. I'm likely to make a fool of myself on the slopes. Better pray for me . . . *mmm,* these eggs are good. Mind if I finish up the rest in that bowl?"

Feeling flustered, Grace handed him the serving bowl, but got up abruptly to stick another couple slices of bread into the toaster, her back to Jeff.

She should have just said, "Sure, I'll pray for you," but something stopped her. Something a little bit like jealousy.

That didn't make any sense at all.

She buttered the toast and handed one to Jeff, hoping he couldn't see through her forced smile.

CHAPTER 15

Grace sat cross-legged on the couch, staring at nothing in particular while Oreo kneaded his paws on her lap and purred up a storm, as if saying, *"Finally! Some attention!"* But if Oreo was getting any attention, it was by default. Grace's mind was elsewhere.

Good thing Jeff Newman was gone. Having a houseguest made her talk too much, and the doctor said she was supposed to avoid all "nonessential talking" — a directive she'd basically ignored while he was here. What else did the doc say? . . . Oh yeah, drink lots of liquids and use a vaporizer at night — which she'd also forgotten after their late-evening battle-of-the-Scrabble-board.

And another thing. She was glad he'd left because . . . she felt confused. Why did she have such a reaction to him saying he was going skiing with a date this weekend? He was just her agent, for pity's sake! The guy

157

was single, good-looking, personable — so of course he'd be dating. It was no business of hers.

Except that she'd enjoyed being with him. A lot. Enjoyed being in the company of a guy who seemed to like and respect her, which was no small thing in light of her recent experiences.

"Grow up, Grace!" she muttered aloud. "You're acting like a fickle teenager." She knew as well as anybody that when a girl gets rejected, it's tempting to fall for the first guy who gives her a second glance, trying to prove she's still desirable. She'd counseled a teen or two on that very subject. The break with Roger was barely a week old. Deep down she hadn't given up hope that they might find a way back to each other.

Maybe it was a bad idea for Newman to be her agent — except she'd already told him last night the switch was fine with her, and she was looking forward to working with him. To change her mind now would raise awkward questions — like *why.* So she was stuck with Jeff Newman. It was unlikely she'd see him again anytime soon, and even more unlikely he'd ever get stranded at her house again in a snowstorm. Soon, their unusual, yet entirely enjoyable, experience would sort itself out into a proper business-like arrangement —

Ding-dong-ding-dong-ding-dong!

The front doorbell rang urgently. For two panicky seconds, Grace's heart felt as if it stopped altogether. She hadn't actually gone out to check if his rental car was gone, but Jeff had left at least an hour ago. Surely he wasn't back *again.*

Dumping Oreo off her lap, she tiptoed to the door and peeked through the security peephole. A young brown face surrounded by the fake fur of a parka hood bounced on the other side of the door.

Her heart quit racing.

She unlocked the door and pulled it open. "Hey there, Tavis," came out in a croak. Ugh. She definitely needed to rest her voice. She was supposed to see the voice therapist tomorrow.

"Hi, Miz Meredith. You want your walk shoveled?" The boy pointed to the shovel that Jeff had left leaning beside the front door. "Or is that guy who's stayin' with you gonna do it? He an' my dad were shovelin' over at the old lady's house, but just thought I'd ask."

Grace cringed. What if it got out that a man had stayed overnight at her house? Gossip like that sometimes went viral . . .

159

her career would be toast! What if —

Calm down, Grace. Nip it in the bud. "Oh, no, he's gone. My agent was here for a business meeting and got stranded by the storm. But the towing company got his car out and he's on his way to Nashville." *Stop it, Grace.* The kid didn't need to know all that. She willed a smile. "So, yes, I definitely need my walk shoveled, if you're up to it."

The dark brown eyes glittered. "Well, gotta tell ya, I'm gonna have to charge more this time. That's a lotta snow. Gonna take me a long time."

"Hey, Tavis!" a girlish voice yelled. "You were s'posed to wait for me!" Another junior high–size figure waded through the deep snow toward her stoop.

Tavis rolled his eyes. "My sister — she wants to help shovel too."

Now Grace's smile was genuine. "*That* is a great idea. Except I only have one shovel. Do you have another one?"

Tavis's twin popped up beside him on the stoop. "Hiya, Miz Meredith. My mom says she met you. I'm Tabitha." A mittened hand shot out and Grace shook it, though she was starting to shiver standing in the open doorway with no coat.

"I'm happy to meet you, Tabitha. Tell you kids what — I'll make it fifteen bucks each

160

if you get the sidewalk out there and my front and back walks shoveled. If you can't do it all — I know it's a big job — I'll adjust accordingly. Deal?"

The twins hooted and high-fived each other as she shut the door.

Yikes. Had she just offered to shell out *thirty bucks* to get her walks shoveled? What kind of precedent was that? But as she peeked out the window at the mounds of snow — two feet deep in some places because of the wind — she decided it was worth every penny.

The city trucks finally plowed Beecham Street Thursday morning, burying parked cars that hadn't been shoveled out and moved. Grace was grateful she'd put her car in the garage before the storm — except that now she couldn't get it out. City trucks didn't plow alleys and some of the drifts were over two feet deep. What was she going to do? She had an appointment with the voice therapist that afternoon.

She called a taxi.

At least she'd been a good girl and had rested her voice the past twenty-four hours, along with drinking copious amounts of water and hot lemon-honey tea — no coffee — and running the vaporizer all night. Her voice strength was at least back to where it was when Jeff Newman showed up.

The voice therapist was a lot younger than the otolaryngologist, maybe just a few years older than herself, Grace decided. The woman had wavy light-brown hair worn shoulder-length and reading glasses perched on her nose. Looked like a librarian. She introduced herself as Dr. Erskine and seemed genuinely interested in Grace's career history. What kind of music did she sing? How many tours did she do a year? Did Grace have a CD? She'd love to hear her sing . . .

"But not today!" the therapist laughed. "Today I want to do a few more tests. I've gone over your test results from Monday, and of course the first thing to take care of is that viral infection, which you say is doing much better. But I'd like to do a fiber-optic test today to assess your larynx function, as well as do a telescopic examination, which will feel awkward, but will help identify any lesions on the vocal folds — nodules, polyps, cysts, hematomas — that kind of thing."

Grace swallowed. "You think there's a problem like that?"

Dr. Erskine smiled. "Don't worry. Most of what we do is to rule things out so we can treat you most effectively. Now, you might be more comfortable if you removed your earrings . . ."

By the time Grace got home, she felt exhausted. She'd had to make all kinds of sounds and even try to sing scales up and down her pitch range with the doctor's scopes in her mouth. The good news was no lesions on the vocal folds, but, according to the therapist, she was suffering from acute vocal fatigue and abnormal muscle tension of the larynx, resulting in the ongoing dysphonia. "Hoarseness," Erskine translated.

So now she had biweekly appointments for the next month, with exercises to strengthen her vocal chords, build better breath support, and . . . Grace wasn't sure what all. "But even if you start to feel better," the therapist had warned, "use this sabbatical to slow down, get extra rest, pay attention to your diet and exercise, do some reevaluation of the emotional stressors in your life — in short, take care of yourself. It's all related, you know."

It was almost as if the doctor knew about the emotional stressors in her life. But she couldn't . . . no. Probably just her regular spiel to all her patients. Still, Grace knew it was good advice. But how to get all that extra rest and healthy diet and exercise and de-stress her life — *that* was something else altogether. For the past week she'd just been plodding her way through each day. Only the family Sunday dinner and Jeff Newman's extended visit had broken up the monotony.

Grace tossed her coat on a chair and flopped down on the couch, which Oreo took for a personal invitation to jump into her lap. What in the world was she going to do with a whole month at home — in the dead of winter? She needed a plan . . . except she was too tired to make a plan. She'd figure that out tomorrow, after a good night's sleep. Right now she needed food.

She pulled out her phone, typed in the appointment reminders on her calendar, and was in the middle of a call to Siam Pasta ordering pad thai and jasmine rice, when a notice flashed on her cell screen that she had a new text message —

"Yes, yes, Beecham has been plowed . . . did you say forty minutes? . . . All right, thank you." Ending the phone call, she quickly switched to Messages. Oh. From Samantha Curtis. Had it been a whole week since she'd communicated with her assistant? Feeling a pang of guilt, she clicked on the message . . .

Grace! Sorry for not staying in touch better. Busy helping mom. But coming home Sat. Your voice OK? Is Roger still going 2 Sweetheart concert with U? If U need me, I could come 2. Otherwise, when do U want me to catch up fan mail & stuff? Best! Sam

Grace tossed the phone on the couch with a groan. She still hadn't told Sam she'd canceled the sweetheart gig plus the next couple concerts as well. Or that Roger was out of the picture. Or that her trip home from Memphis had been hell. Or that she had a new agent. Knowing Sam, once she had the whole story she'd be all over her like a mother hen, cluck-clucking, giving *her* opinion of Roger's desertion, checking on her every day, making sure she was taking care of herself, offering her a shoulder to cry on . . . though, to be honest, she wouldn't mind a little of Sam's motherly TLC, even if the girl was her junior by five years.

Oreo jumped off her lap and wandered off. Grace, sprawled listlessly on the couch, watched him go. Somewhere outside, she heard kids calling, laughing. Probably on the way home from school, throwing snowballs. Inside, she sat in a pocket of silence . . . except for the ticking of the schoolhouse clock, which seemed to grow louder as the minutes passed.

Tick-tock, tick-tock, tick-tock . . .

Saturday . . . the day Sam was coming home. Two days away. But for some reason, it felt like forever. Just her and Oreo and that darn ticking clock, stuck in this house like house arrest.

Tick-tock, tick-tock, tick-tock . . .

Saturday . . . the day she and Roger had been scheduled to show up at the sweetheart banquet in Milwaukee as the sweetheart poster couple.

Tick-tock, tick-tock, tick-tock . . .

Saturday . . . the day Jeff Newman would be on the slopes skiing with his blind date.

Tick-tock, tick-tock, tick-tock . . .

Suddenly grabbing for her phone, she found Sam's text and hit Reply:

Sam! Glad Ur mom doing OK. Sweetheart was canceled. Can you come to the house on Sunday? She hesitated a moment, then typed, *Really want to see you.* She signed it *Grace,* and hit Send.

And then she grabbed a throw pillow and hugged it tight.

CHAPTER 16

A text message from Jeff Newman on Friday said he was on his way back to Denver, he'd work on the cancellations first thing Monday and let her know how it went. *And thanks again for the hospitality.*

Grace stood at the front window, absently watching somebody across the street shoveling out his car, wondering how to reply. Businesslike? Chatty? Ask how his meetings went in Nashville? Tell him to have fun this weekend? Finally she just typed *Thanks* and hit Send — just as a UPS truck pulled up in front of the house and put on its hazard blinkers. Had to be her brother . . .

"Can't stay long, Sis," Mark said as she opened the door for him. "Just wanted to check on you. You doing okay?" Without waiting for an answer, Mark jerked a thumb over his shoulder. "I see you got your walks shoveled. Neighbor kid?"

"Kids plural. Twins from next door. Seems

like a nice family." She gave him a peck on the cheek. "It's twelve thirty. Want some lunch?"

"Nah, can't. Got a ton of deliveries. Hope your car isn't one of those buried by the snowplow. Aren't people supposed to move their cars so the city can plow the whole street?"

Grace shrugged. "Street signs say cars on one side are supposed to move on odd days during a snow emergency, the other side is supposed to move on even days until both sides get plowed." She shrugged. "But my car is safely tucked in my garage surrounded by snowdrifts and an unplowed alley. Going to have to shovel it out myself, I guess. Or wait till spring when it thaws."

Mark guffawed, then grinned apologetically. "Sorry. Not funny. Uh, maybe I can come back this weekend and shovel it out. Or tell you what — I'll call Roger and tell *him* to get his butt over here and dig you out. The cad owes you that much."

She gave him a *don't-you-dare* look. "Don't worry about it. Besides, I'm supposed to be taking it easy for the next few weeks till my, you know" — she pointed at her throat — "gets better, not running around." But she grimaced. "Unless I go stir-crazy first. It's been a looong week."

A series of impatient car honks outside sent Mark to the front window. "Uh-oh. I'm blocking somebody. Gotta go." He pulled open the front door. "You want to come out to the house again for Sunday dinner?"

"Oh, Mark, thanks, but —"

"I mean, if we can get your car out — or I could pick you up."

The car honks got more insistent. Her brother yanked the door open and glared at the big SUV, which was nose to nose with his UPS truck. "Who's the jerk?" he muttered.

"Uhhh, not sure." Fancy car. Might be the guy at the end of the block in the Mc-Mansion. "But about Sunday . . . Sam — Samantha Curtis, my assistant — is coming here that afternoon. She's been in Memphis ever since my last concert, her mom had a heart attack, and —"

"Okay, okay, I get it. Gotta go." Mark was already down the steps. "Call if you change your mind. See ya!" He hustled down her walk and detoured via a shoveled-out parking space in front of the house next door to reach his truck. Watching from the window, it seemed to Grace like he backed down the street a lot slower than he had to. Probably just to spite the guy in the SUV.

She snickered. Her brother was a nut —

lovable, but still a nut.

Standing at the window till the UPS truck disappeared from sight, Grace noticed the shoveled-out parking space next door had lawn chairs set up in it, no doubt to keep anyone else from parking there. She glanced up and down the block and saw three or four other shoveled parking spaces with similar barricades, interspersed between the lumps of snow-covered cars.

Couldn't really blame folks for claiming parking spots after going to all that work, though she doubted it was legal. At least she'd done her duty this time and had her walks shoveled, like most of the other neighbors up and down the street — except for the two-flat across the street. The walk was still only half-shoveled where Jeff and the lawn service guy and the twins' father had tried to make a path for the paramedics two days ago.

Grace wondered what had happened to the old lady who'd fallen down the basement stairs. Was she still in the hospital? Sign said her house was in foreclosure . . . was she coming back? Had she died? Did anybody on the street even know?

Saturday was the pits.

The temperature had fluctuated between

170

ten and twenty degrees the past few days with just enough wind to knife the cold right into her bones the few times she'd ventured outside. No new snow, but the snow from the mini-blizzard was still half frozen — not conducive to going for a walk or getting exercise.

She stayed in, trying not to think about the sweetheart banquet going on without her. Trying not to wonder what Roger was doing instead. Trying not to think about Jeff Newman's ski weekend.

And failing.

Nothing like a pity party when it's just you and the cat, who doesn't care that you haven't done your hair or put on makeup as long as you're there to open a can of cat food and provide a lap for a nap or two during the day.

At least she had Sunday to look forward to. Sam had said she'd drive up from the South Side right after church and bring some takeout for lunch.

Church . . .

Grace had a sudden craving to go to church Sunday morning. It'd been too long — way too long — since she'd been to church just to worship. On tour, she mostly went to church when she was invited to sing. On her off Sundays, she was usually too beat and justified not going anywhere by taking a much-needed day of rest. That was scriptural, wasn't it?

But when she woke up Sunday she felt restless. Tired of being cooped up in the house. And hungry too — hungry for something to soothe her soul.

She could call a cab. But not way out to County Line. Roger would be there — though a tiny part of her was tempted to show up and show *him.* But it would be too awkward, and it was just too far, way out in the western 'burbs. Surely she could find a church closer by.

She thought of the little storefront churches along Touhy Avenue or Clark Street with names like God's Battle Axe Prayer Ministries or Triumphant Saints Holiness. Ethnic churches she supposed — African American or Jamaican or Ethiopian. Most within walking distance. Ha. What would they think if she walked in, this strange white lady?

More to the point, would she have the nerve? Probably not. Not alone, anyway. Too far out of her comfort zone. She laughed at the irony. Here she was, a Christian artist boldly proclaiming God's message of love to strangers far and wide, and she couldn't gather the nerve to be the stranger two blocks from home.

She should have asked Sam if she was going to church. Perhaps she still had time to get a taxi and meet Sam there. Sam attended one of the large black churches on the South Side, but at least she'd be with Sam to help her navigate. Might be interesting.

Grace tried Sam's cell phone, but it went right to voice mail. So much for that idea. She wasn't going to just show up at a strange church on the South Side if Sam didn't know she was coming.

"Well, Oreo, guess we'll have to have our own church," she said, pushing the cat over to make room on the couch and picking up the TV remote. A quick scan through the channels turned up a couple of talking heads with thick Southern accents — she with big hair and he with fleshy jowls and a pink tie — inviting viewers to support their ministry and receive a ten-fold blessing . . . the Crystal Cathedral with its big organ pipes and sea of a thousand-plus faces . . . a black pastor pacing a red-carpeted platform whose every phrase brought forth shouts of "Amen!" and "Say it!" and "Hallelujah!" from the televised congregation.

She turned off the electric church and tossed the remote, then wandered into her bedroom looking for her Bible. Where had she put it? Had she really not read her Bible since she'd come home from her New Year, New You tour? It was still in her suitcase, which she hadn't yet completely emptied.

She flopped onto her bed with the Bible her parents had given her for high school graduation. On tour it was hard to find time for personal prayer and Bible reading, though she didn't hesitate to encourage the young people who came to her concerts to have a "quiet time with the Lord." She often quoted favorite scriptures between songs — promises like, "Seek first the kingdom of God and his righteousness, and all these things will be added unto you" and "Trust in the Lord with all your heart, and don't lean on your own understanding; in all your ways acknowledge him and he will direct your paths."

Grace flipped to the familiar verses she'd marked with tiny Post-its. *All these things will be added unto you . . .* " Did she really believe that? Seemed like a lot of things had been taken away from her lately. And *"he will direct your paths . . ."* Really? Felt more like she'd been pushed out of the boat and was treading water.

What was happening to her life? Had God abandoned her too?

She lay propped on the bed pillows, flipping to the verses she used during her concerts, trying to read some of the psalms. It all felt like so many words . . .

She must've dozed off, because the next thing she knew the doorbell was ringing and Oreo streaked out of the bedroom to check out who dared interrupt their nap. Grace followed, wishing she'd gargled or drunk some water or *something* so she didn't feel so groggy.

Turning the lock and sliding off the security chain, she opened the door. Her assistant stood on the stoop, swaddled in a black winter coat, matching brown-and-gold knit beret and neck scarf, holding a bulging plastic bag in one hand and the handle of a small suitcase-on-wheels in the other. The large dark eyes peering out from beneath the beret were looking her up and down, lips parted in consternation as if not sure she was at the right house.

"Grace? What in the world . . . Girl, what *is* the matter with you?!"

CHAPTER 17

Grace grabbed for Oreo, who looked like he might make a dash for it, left the door open and marched over to the couch. "Well, nice to see you too."

"Oh, Grace, I'm sorry. It's just . . ." Samantha hustled inside, shut the door, and shed her wraps. She stood there for a long moment in her black Sunday dress slacks and a silky white blouse under a black suit jacket, but when Grace didn't say anything, she held up the plastic bag. "Lunch. I just need a minute to warm it up." Sam's sassy twists disappeared into the kitchen, and Grace heard cupboards opening and dishes rattling.

Dumping the cat, Grace got up and peeked at her reflection in the narrow mirror that hung by the front door. When she got up that morning, she'd wound her long hair into a careless bunch on the back of her head and held it there with a clip, the shag ends falling out untidily around her face. No makeup, skin pale and blotchy, eyes red, lips chapped, clothes rumpled . . .

Guess she did look a bit the worse for wear. But she had good reasons, didn't she?

Grace glanced at the schoolhouse clock. Sam was taking longer than necessary to stick the carryout in the oven. She should probably follow her into the kitchen and start over with a real greeting — she really was glad to see her! But she took up a cross-legged position on the couch instead. Samantha deserved to know what had been going on, but Grace needed to suck up some courage to tell the whole story.

When her assistant did come back into the living room, she was carrying two steaming mugs of tea. "Food will need fifteen minutes or so to reheat. Thought you could use this."

Grace took a sip from the mug Sam handed her. Fixed just the way she liked it, with just the right amount of lemon and honey. "Thanks." Another sip. "So tell me, how is your mom?"

"All right, I guess, considering." Sam sank into the overstuffed chair, two hands wrapped around the other mug. "I was glad I could stay a few days to help out when she first came home from the hospital. But honestly! After a while, *nothing* I did was right. She kept fussin' at me, said to quit nagging her about taking her meds and all the butter she was eatin' — all the stuff the doctor said she had to do so it wouldn't happen again. Decided it was time to leave." Sam cut her eyes sideways at Grace from beneath her tiny twists. "Besides, she kept calling me Sammie Ruth. Sammie Ruth this, Sammie Ruth that. Like I was still ten years old."

"That's your middle name?"

"Yeah. What's yours?"

"Actually, Grace is my middle name." She flushed a little. She *always* went by Grace Meredith. That was her professional name, and no way did she want her full name to go public. But . . . Samantha was discreet. Part of a personal assistant's job description. "I'm named after my mother, Margaret — Margaret Grace. But of course they called me Grace, since we already had a Margaret in the family. I've dropped the Margaret, except for legal stuff. And *you* are sworn to secrecy."

Sam smiled and made an X over her heart with her forefinger. "Promise. Though I think Margaret is a beautiful name. Margaret Grace . . ."

Grace gave her a warning look.

"Okay, okay!" But Sam frowned at Grace. "But what about you? You said the sweetheart gig got canceled. What happened? Is it your voice? Is your throat still giving you trouble? Have you seen a doctor?" A *ding* went off in the kitchen. "Oh, food's hot. Be back in a sec." Sam scrambled out of the chair and disappeared into the kitchen. Two minutes later she was back with two plates heaped high with fried chicken, red beans and rice, crab cakes and —

"Fried green tomatoes!" Grace squeaked. "Where'd you get all this?"

Sam laughed. "My favorite soul-food place on the South Side. Thought I'd bring you a little taste of Memphis, since you weren't there long enough to enjoy the food."

Memphis . . . Grace winced.

"What?" Sam frowned. "You made a face. You don't like soul food?"

"No, no, food's great. It's just . . ." Taking a deep breath, Grace described what had happened at the airport after the last concert. It was the first time she'd told anyone that part, except for her doctor, and she had to reach for the tissues.

Sam listened wide-eyed, her own face crumpling by the time Grace finished. "Oh, Grace, I'm so sorry. That's horrible! Did

179

you file a complaint? Oh, if only I hadn't left you alone to —"

"Oh stop it." Grace regretted her tears. Regretted that on that horrible weekend she actually *had* felt like blaming Samantha for abandoning her. "You had to do what you had to do. Couldn't be helped. I didn't file a complaint" — she hadn't even thought of that — "but there's no way I'm going to go through that airport security again."

Samantha stared. "But . . . you have to fly. I mean, you've got that West Coast tour coming up, and several concerts before that! Surely it won't happen again — I mean, lightning doesn't strike twice, right? Those security people pick people at random — just to prove they're not profiling, you know."

Grace just kept shaking her head. How could she explain?

Samantha was quiet a few moments. Then she ventured, "That's not all, is it? You were upset even before you did your last concert. Was it the phone call with Roger? When I came back to the room after my sister and cousin left, I heard you crying . . ."

They talked. Grace told her the whole story. Their food got cold. Samantha moved over to the couch, put an arm around Grace, and let her cry.

"And on top of everything else," Grace sniffed, "my agent dumped me too, turned me over to his assistant."

"You're kidding."

"Nope. It gets better — or worse. His name is Jeff Newman. He came to Chicago to meet me last Tuesday — the day of the big storm, remember? Oh . . . you were still in Memphis. But you can still see how much snow is left. Anyway, he got stranded here. At my house. Overnight." Grace rolled her eyes.

"No!" Samantha started to giggle. "What's he like? Forty-five, balding, bit of a paunch — or maybe he's one of those music agents we sometimes see with a Mohawk, pierced nose, tattoos everywhere?"

Grace shook her head. "Neither. Actually seems like a nice guy. Maybe thirty."

Samantha raised an eyebrow.

"Forget it," Grace said. "I'm in no place to start thinking about men again." She paused. "Besides, he's spending the weekend skiing with a girlfriend as we speak."

"Oh." Samantha made a face, and then jumped up. "I'm going to warm up this food again — microwave this time. All this bad news is hard to take on an empty stomach. And say . . ." She paused in the doorway. "Would you like me to give you a facial? I do it for my cousins all the time. And you might feel better if you had a hot shower and gave that hair a good brushing. When was the last time you had it cut and conditioned? Before the New Year, New You tour, I'll bet. Tomorrow. First thing tomorrow we're going to the beauty salon. Fan mail can wait."

"Tomorrow? You're coming back?"

"Coming back nothing. I'm moving in." Sam pointed to the suitcase. "Well, not really, but I brought my jammies just in case. I had a feeling I might need to stay a few days."

Samantha was as good as her word. After they'd eaten, she padded a kitchen chair with pillows from the bedroom, made a "cape" out of a plastic garbage bag, and sat Grace down, head back on a pillow, feet up on another chair. Soaking a clean hand towel in hot water from the teakettle, she laid it gently on Grace's face to steam open her pores. From beneath the towel, Grace heard Sam raiding the bathroom down the hall, and a few minutes later she came back with a basket of creams and lotions.

"*Mmm,* feels wonderful," Grace murmured, her eyes closed as Sam followed a thorough facial cleansing with astringent,

and then a good face massage with a soothing lotion. So relaxing . . .

"Ouch!" Her eyes flew open.

"Sorry." Samantha didn't look sorry.
"Those eyebrows need a good tweezing.
Hold still."

Now that was getting a bit personal, Grace
thought. But after the facial, she obediently
took a hot shower, washed and conditioned
her hair, and put on some makeup. Watching herself in the mirror as she used the
blow dryer, she smiled, realizing the trans-
formation was having its desired effect.
When she came out of the bathroom, Samantha nodded approvingly. "Better. Much
better. Still need to get that hair shaped and
the split ends cut off tomorrow. But right
now" — she steered Grace down the hall
toward her bedroom — "we're going to get
you out of those sweatpants and into something decent."

"Why?" Grace protested as she was pro-
pelled into her bedroom. "I mean, I appreciate all the TLC, but I'm not going anywhere."

"Who says?" Samantha slid open the
closet door and pulled out a pair of black
slacks and a royal-blue brushed sweater,
holding them up against Grace. "It's February fourteenth, sweetie, and who wants to

sit home on Valentine's Day? Not me. And definitely not you. What we need, girl, is some *chocolate.*"

When Grace woke up the next morning, she felt more rested than she had since she'd come home two weeks ago. It had felt so . . . so comforting to know Samantha was in the house last night. A slow grin spread over her face remembering their foray into the frozen wasteland to find chocolate. They'd just come out the front door swaddled in coats, hats, scarves, and boots when Sam had stopped, puzzled. "Can't remember where I parked my car. Couldn't find any parking on your block. All those lawn-chair barricades and home-made signs saying, 'Don't even *think* about parking here!' are scary."

"Didn't know you had a car." Grace had always envied how easily Sam got around the city by public transportation.

Samantha had shrugged. "I didn't, until yesterday. Leased one when I got back. Trying it out for a month, see if I want to buy. It's cold standing on those El platforms."

They found the little Honda Civic parked two blocks away, drove down Lake Shore Drive to Ghirardelli's Chocolate Shop and Soda Fountain on North Michigan Avenue and ordered two of their signature chocolate brownies with double-rich vanilla-bean ice cream on top, swimming in hot fudge sauce. Ignoring all the couples getting their Valentine's Day chocolate fix, they'd giggled over high school and college antics like a couple of teenagers . . .

Grace stretched, slid out of the covers, and stuck her feet into her slippers. It had felt good to laugh and just have fun — though a tiny part of her noggin wondered if letting down her hair with her personal assistant was the wisest thing to do for their working relationship.

Sam was all business by the time Grace got out of the shower. "You have an eleven o'clock at Johnny's Beauty Salon and a two o'clock at Curves —"

"Curves!"

Sam lifted an eyebrow. "Didn't you tell me your doctor said to use this sabbatical to get healthy again? Get lots of rest, eat right, exercise —"

Grace rolled her eyes. "All right, I get it." *Curves.* Sam was getting downright bossy.

Except for the trip to the beauty salon and getting Grace signed up with a trainer at Curves, Samantha worked most of the day on answering the backlog of fan mail — both e-mail and letters. She created a form letter reporting about the New Year, New You tour they'd just finished, adding "Thanks so much for writing, your comments mean so much," and then personalized each reply in some way, especially if a fan had a question. But there was one sticking point. "What should I say to these fans who say, 'Can't wait for your upcoming concert, already have tickets'?"

Grace winced. How would Bongo handle that? "Um, put those into a Hold folder for now. Newman said he'd get back to me after he'd handled the cancellations. Guess we have to let them know something."

Sam frowned. "How many cancellations are we talking about?"

"Just two. Norfolk and Houston." For now, anyway. There was that sticky question about how she'd travel — and what to do about her concerts. She wasn't ready to talk about being "worth the wait" yet. Not after Roger's sudden departure. And not after . . . she stopped herself from going there. She couldn't look at her past. Not now. And now wasn't the time to tell Sam she was toying with giving up the whole shebang.

The e-mail from Newman arrived Tuesday morning, saying he'd negotiated the cancellations by offering to reschedule the Norfolk and Houston venues — they'd work out specific dates later. The two venues agreed to contact ticket holders and say they'd honor them at a later date, still to be determined. Grace sent an e-mail back, asking if those venues would be willing to honor those tickets at another concert or event, in case it didn't work out to reschedule.

Jeff Newman's second e-mail was short and to the point: *They don't want just anyone, Grace. They want you.*

Sam leaned over Grace's shoulder and read the e-mail. "Feels good to be wanted, doesn't it?"

It should — but right now, it felt more like pressure. What did she have to offer?

But she didn't stop Sam from replying to the fans who mentioned having tickets to those two concerts.

Samantha drove Grace to her appointment with the voice therapist and waited as Dr. Erskine put her through the exercises. "Good grief, that was some workout," Sam said as they got back in the Honda Civic an hour later. "Are you sure she's helping you? You sound wasted."

"Thanks a lot," Grace croaked. But she did feel exhausted, and was grateful Sam was driving, not her.

Back at the house, Sam said, "Look, I'm

going to finish up answering the last of the fan-mail backlog and then I'm outta here. Oh, I made up a schedule for you — Curves on Monday, Wednesday, and Friday at eight, and Dr. Erskine Tuesdays and Thursdays at two. That'll get you out of the house at least once a day. I'll be back Friday to answer any more e-mails that come in, and we'll go out to dinner or something. Okay with you? Anything else you want me to do before I head home?"

Grace tried not to show her disappointment. Of course Sam had to go home. She had barely been back from Memphis for twenty-four hours before she'd shown up at Grace's house. She'd been a big help — more than she knew.

Grace shook her head. "No. You've done enough for now. Thanks for staying over. I really appreciate it. And Friday's good — oh, wait. There is one thing you can do."

She headed for the guest room, Sam on her heels, and jerked the wedding dress from the closet. "Take this with you. Just get it out of here."

CHAPTER 18

The house felt really empty after Sam left. But at least her voice got more rest with no one to talk to except Oreo, who yawned to show his lack of interest. Grace couldn't believe Sam had signed her up for an eight o'clock with the fitness trainer, though. Eight *a.m.*! She had to leave the house the next morning by seven thirty. At least her shower and breakfast could wait till she got home, so all she had to do was pull on her sweats and make coffee before the taxi came.

The trainer was at least ten years older than Grace, a slender woman with long legs, short sporty hair, and an easy grin. Could probably run the Chicago Marathon. "I'm Susan," she said, shaking Grace's hand firmly. They sat while Susan had her fill out a Fitness Goals Assessment sheet. Grace didn't really know what to put down, so the trainer set some modest goals — aerobic exercise and strength training — and then proceeded to show her the various pieces of equipment. She had Grace warm up on the treadmill, do five minutes on the elliptical — which felt like a combination of skiing, skating, and rowing, so confusing! — and then showed her how to use a multi-station contraption with various sitting positions and graduated weights she was supposed to pull with her arms or push with her feet to work various muscles.

At the end of the hour session, Grace felt so pooped she was tempted to go home and crawl back in bed. But by the time she got home, she felt more ravenous than tired. While making hot oatmeal and toast, she heard water dripping off the bushes outside the kitchen window. Turning on the TV to the Weather Channel, she saw the forecast called for temperatures above freezing the rest of the week, and in the low forties by Friday.

"Hey, Oreo, hear that?" she said to the cat, who was begging for more breakfast. "I might be able to get my car out of the garage after all!"

Grace turned off the TV and opened the living room drapes before returning to the kitchen — which is when she noticed a small black-and-silver SUV drive slowly up the block, turn around in the cul-de-sac by the big house at the end of the block, and then park in the shoveled-out space across the street where the *Farid's Total Lawn Service* truck usually parked. Didn't think she'd seen the car before — though it could be somebody from the other end of the block. Whoever it was better hope Farid didn't show up, or he might push that car right on down the street with that big plow of his.

An older black man wearing a Chicago Bears jacket got out of the car — sixtyish, no hat, bald, like somebody's grandpa — and stood for several minutes in front of the two-flat with the For Sale sign, looking it over. She watched as he went up onto the front porch and peered into the glass door, then came back down the steps and picked his way through the snow along the walk that went around the side of the house and disappeared toward the back.

The house was in foreclosure — at least that's what the yellow sign tacked onto the For Sale sign said. Was the bank moving ahead to sell the house already? It'd only been a week since the ambulance took the old woman to the hospital. If she had to have surgery, she'd be in the hospital for a week or so, maybe have to go to rehab, but then what? Surely they wouldn't sell the house right out from under her, leaving her with no place to come home to —

A burning smell wafted from the kitchen. Ack! The oatmeal! Grace ran to the kitchen, but it was too late. She had to scrape the mess into the garbage and start over. But once the oatmeal was bubbling again and the timer set, she drifted to the kitchen window to see if she could get another glimpse of the man. Nobody. But the car was still there.

Her conscience pricked her. *Like I have a right to get all concerned now.* It wasn't as if she'd made any effort to get to know the woman, other than a wave or "Nice day!" on the rare occasions when they both happened outside at the same time. Even in good weather Grace usually went out the back door, since she kept her car in the garage and came and went through the alley.

Still. She felt bad. If that kid hadn't broken the old woman's window with the snowball, she might've died without anybody knowing about it for days. Maybe weeks. Unless she had family somewhere in the city who checked on her. Must be hard to get old and live alone.

An involuntary shudder almost made

Grace spill her coffee. She was pushing thirty and not married. Her engagement to Roger had seemed like a sure thing. Wedding dress. Wedding plans. They'd buy a house. Hopefully have babies and go to PTA meetings, show up for graduations, cry at their weddings, proudly show off pictures of the grandchildren, and grow old together . . .

Pffft. Gone overnight, just like that.

The timer dinged. Grace turned off the oatmeal, but now it didn't look that appetizing. Oreo seemed to sense her mood and rubbed against her ankles. Grace picked up the cat and hugged him close, listening to his happy motor start up. But even her beloved cat wouldn't live long enough to keep her company when she got old —

No, no, no! She was not going to mope around about growing old. Grace dumped the cat and dished up the oatmeal. The session at Curves had energized her and she wasn't going to waste it.

She'd wanted to clean out some of her closets for months. A little spring cleaning wouldn't hurt in February. While chowing down the oatmeal and toast — she really was hungry! — she made a list of chores. Number one on the list: guest room closet, especially now that the wedding dress was gone. But just before heading down the hall with a box of garbage bags, she glanced once more out the front window.

The little black SUV was gone.

By the time Grace finished cleaning out the guest room closet, she had a whole garbage bag full of clothes, old shoes, two sets of sheets, and a nonfunctioning electric blanket to take to the Salvation Army. And she was motivated to start in on her own closet the next morning since her Thursday appointment with Dr. Erskine wasn't until two. But the tomblike silence of the house was giving her the jitters, so she kept the TV on as she walked back and forth between her bedroom and the front room, making piles on the couch of stuff she no longer wore or used. Or wanted. The blue dress Roger said he liked? Out. Same with the dress she'd been wearing when he'd popped the question.

The weather report confirmed that a high of forty degrees was expected by Friday, and she could almost see the piles of snow steadily shrinking every time she glanced outside.

And the black SUV was back.

Curiosity got the best of her and she stopped what she was doing to stand where she could see but not be seen. The same man got out of the car — one of those Toyota RAV4s — but this time a woman was with him. He helped her out of the passenger side and she held onto his arm as they made their way up the slushy walk to the front porch. A plus-size black woman, but even from a distance she seemed attractive — one of those women who carried her weight well. She too looked the building up and down, giving it a good once-over, as the man — her husband? — pointed at this and that.

A few minutes later another car parked behind the RAV4, and a man in a suit and topcoat joined the couple on the porch. He led them to the front door, unlocked it, and all three disappeared inside.

Grace shook her head. Must be a real estate agent showing the house. Really too bad. She wondered if any of the neighbors knew what had happened to the old woman. Well, guess it was none of her business. If she wanted to finish this closet-cleaning business before she had to get ready for her second visit to the voice therapist, she'd better keep at it. Probably wouldn't feel like doing much of anything once Dr. Erskine put her through all those vocal paces.

The unplowed alley was such a mess with

all the melting snow — rutted ice beneath several inches of water — that Grace called another taxi to make her eight o'clock at Curves Friday morning. Didn't feel much like going, but Samantha had said she'd be back today, and Grace decided she'd rather face the trainer than Sam's disapproval if she missed.

Hopefully she could come early. With Sam's help, maybe they could take all the stuff she'd weeded out to the Salvation Army or Goodwill. And at least she'd have someone to talk to.

The workout at Curves still felt grueling, especially since the trainer added some free-standing exercises with hand weights. But Susan said, "Good job," at the end of the hour, which perked Grace up a bit. Checking her cell on the way home in the taxi, she realized she'd missed a text message from Sam saying she wouldn't be able to get there until almost noon. *Bummer.* She was about to shut off the cell when a new text message popped onto her screen. *Sent e-mail yesterday. Can you get back to me before the weekend? Jeff N.*

Grace screwed up her face. She'd gotten so involved in her spring-cleaning project she hadn't checked e-mail for two days.

Popping some frozen waffles into the

toaster — not like the ones her mom used to make from scratch, but cooking for one called for an easier option — Grace pulled up her e-mail, which took a while to download. Thirty-six new messages in her fan-mail folder. She was tempted to open that folder, but decided to check her regular e-mail first.

Spam . . . spam . . . a cute forward from her mom of a skateboard-riding dog . . . more *spam . . .* a long e-mail from her brother Tim about the soccer exploits of his oldest girl, Nanci, which he'd sent to his whole e-mail list, of course . . . oh, there was the one Jeff Newman sent yesterday. The subject line said, *Concert tour theme?*

The waffles popped up. Why was he bugging her about a theme? She was supposed to be taking a break. Plopping the waffles onto a plate, she spooned vanilla yogurt over them, poured on some maple syrup for good measure, and dug in. Maybe she'd read some of her fan mail while she ate. Why ruin a good breakfast doing business?

But once the syrupy plate had been rinsed and put into the dishwasher, Grace sighed, poured another cup of coffee, and opened Jeff's e-mail. She couldn't exactly ignore her agent . . .

Dear Grace,

Hope you're feeling much better and that wonderful voice of yours is recovering. The Bongo staff here is still teasing this California kid about getting snowbound in Chicago. I see the weather out there might be helping to clear all that snow away, though. Of course, there's always Farid's Lawn Service if you need a hurry-up job . . .

Grace had to smile. Walter Fowler would never have started an e-mail this tongue-in-cheek.

Meantime, we're getting requests for final promo material for your upcoming West Coast tour. Are you still planning to continue your purity theme? If so, we could just change the New Year, New You name and you could basically present the same sets. But if you'd like to go a whole new direction, now is the time.

Same for the two college concerts you have scheduled before the tour: at Greenville College in downstate Illinois on March 19 and Cincinnati Christian University the following week. Could be the same repertoire as the tour, or

198

something totally different. Up to you. We just need to be giving these venues a little direction as they prepare to promote the concert. Otherwise they'll make presumptions or come up with their own ideas — and believe me, you don't want that to happen. I once worked with a band that called themselves Big Bash and they just said "do whatever you want" to a promoter. When they got to the venue, all the posters said, Dig Hash — and all the potheads for miles around showed up en masse . . .

Grace couldn't help laughing — for about half a minute. But reading the last couple sentences sobered her up.

Would like to hear from you before the weekend if possible. We should get on this right away.

Best, Jeff

Before the weekend? That meant she had to send something today. But what? She had no idea.

Grace closed the laptop and wandered into the living room, but felt too restless to sit. She drifted around the room, winding the schoolhouse clock, absently arranging and rearranging photos and paper clips and notepads on the secretary desk, brushing cat hairs from the couch — and avoiding the piano. Even thinking about the upcoming concerts made her feel panicky. She only had a month — three weeks now — to get her act together so she would feel confident enough to walk out on a stage and sing her heart out. And that had nothing to do with her voice, which hopefully would be back to full strength by then. She'd really believed in her message — "I'm worth the wait" — but it all sounded so hollow now.

Maybe she should give up doing concerts, do something else with her life. If she did, would Roger come back?

Would I want him if he did?

She was still pacing when the doorbell rang, interrupting her fruitless spiral of thoughts. Samantha stood grinning on the stoop, but Grace saw the grin fade slightly as her assistant came in, and she was suddenly aware that she was still in her sweatpants and T-shirt, hadn't even showered since her workout. She threw up her hands defensively. "I can explain. Went to Curves this morning, got distracted when I got back, just haven't —"

Samantha held up a hand to stop her and

the smile was back. "It's all right, Grace. You don't have to dress up for me. But if you want to shower or whatever before we start, I can check the fan folder and see what needs to be done today, then we can get to work, okay?"

"Yeah, yeah, good. Okay." Grace escaped to the bathroom. When she came out toweling her hair, Sam was scrolling through e-mails on her laptop in the kitchen.

"Have you read these fan letters yet? Here, let me read you this one —"

"Wait." Grace sat down across from her assistant at the kitchen table. "There's something I want you to read first. Let me . . ." She pulled the laptop over, found Jeff's e-mail, and turned the laptop back to Sam. "Read that."

Sam shrugged. "Okay." She was silent a few minutes as she read and then looked up. "Sooo . . . what are you thinking?"

Grace shook her head, picking at a spot of dried food on the table. "I don't *know*. That's the problem. Newman wants to hear from me, like, today, and . . . Sam, I don't know what to do! I can't do the New Year, New You thing again. And the "worth the wait" theme? I know everyone likes that song, but . . . I don't know. I need more time . . . I — I'm all confused, you know, after Roger . . . after . . ."

Samantha reached a slim brown hand across the table and laid it on Grace's nervous fingers. "Hey. First things first. Let's pray about it, okay? It's gonna be all right."

Grace nodded and Sam plunged right in. "Father God, you are the one who gave Grace her talent and her voice and the precious theme she's been sharing with young people all over this country in the first place. You've been using her concerts, working your purpose out in the lives of her fans, so we *know* you haven't brought her this far to leave her now. So we're asking you to make it clear what's next. Put the right theme on Grace's heart so that she can sing *from* her heart, just as she's done before. And we're thanking you right now for what you're going to do, whatever that is."

A lump formed in Grace's throat as Sam prayed. *Had* God been using her? Did he still want to use her? But how? Could she really thank him for what he was going to do, even before she knew what that was? She knew the right answers to these questions, of course. She could teach a course on doing the right thing, trusting God. But she was struggling to feel God's presence in any of this. Sam had so much faith! But she didn't know Grace was tempted to just throw in the towel. Didn't know the troubled memories that threatened to undo her confidence in her calling.

God did.

Would he give her a new focus knowing she felt so ambivalent right now?

"Grace?"

Sam's voice pulled Grace out of her inner thoughts. "Um . . . what?"

"I just had an idea. Why not skip the whole theme thing for a while. Just go with 'Grace Meredith in Concert' or something. Then you could take more time to decide on the songs you want to do, the direction you want to take. It could lend itself to, oh, I don't know — a lot of possibilities!"

Grace stared at Samantha. A load seemed to slide off her shoulders. "Samantha Curtis, you're a lifesaver. I think maybe I could get used to having you around."

"Well good. 'Cause I'm not going anywhere. Now, can we talk about how you want to answer this one?" The younger woman pointed to the computer screen. "This fan says she's always dreamed of singing on stage, wants to know if you'll put in a good word for her with your agent." Samantha rolled her eyes. "Honestly! Some people!"

CHAPTER 19

The weather stayed above freezing all weekend and Grace decided it was time to get her car out of the garage. She grinned when the motor purred with the first turn of the key. So glad she'd bought a new car last year! The sporty red of the Ford Focus cheered her up too. Not to mention making it easier to find in a parking lot, sticking out like Santa's cherry-red nose among all the white, black, silver, and beige look-alike cars and SUVs.

No Curves and no vocal therapy on Saturday! Grace felt liberated as she managed to get out of the slippery alley without dinging the car or anyone's garage. She headed toward the Lincolnwood Mall, first swinging by the Salvation Army store on Devon Avenue to drop off her bags of gently used clothing. She'd never actually been inside the used-clothing store before and was impressed by how organized it was. A lot of shoppers wandered the aisles, including parents outfitting small children with everything from jeans and T-shirts to party dresses and winter coats.

Grace felt a tad guilty heading for the mall with its big department stores like Kohls and the tony Carson Pirie Scott, as well as dozens of specialty shops. But she had to laugh at some of the jeans in the store windows as she moseyed through the mall — hot brand names already pre-ripped and "distressed." The teenagers snapping them up might as well go to the Salvation Army store — except the jeans at the Salvation Army were probably in better shape.

She came home with a good pair of gym shoes, sport socks, a sports bra, and some decent workout capris and tops. No more baggy sweat pants and sweatshirt. Almost made her look forward to her next session at Curves on Monday.

Well, almost.

As she dumped her packages on the couch and picked up Oreo, she noticed the black SUV parked in front of the two-flat across the street again. A while later she caught a glimpse from the kitchen of a young boy, maybe twelve or thirteen, bounding out of the house, followed by the man helping an elderly woman down the steps. Was that . . .

could that be the Krakowski woman, home again? She scurried into the living room to get a closer look. No . . . this old woman was black, maybe the boy's grandmother.

In spite of her shopping spree, Sunday loomed long and lonesome again. Grace still didn't know where to go to church. She called her brother Mark, asked for the address of their church, and drove out to the suburbs in time for the eleven o'clock. Mark said the traditional service was at nine, but they usually went to the contemporary service at eleven.

Faith Chapel was a lot smaller than County Line Christian Fellowship, though she guessed there were at least two to three hundred at the contemporary service. She'd like something smaller than a megachurch. Maybe she should attend here for a while. It was nice being there with family, though her nephews had junior church and she didn't see them till afterward.

Most of the contemporary songs projected onto the big screen were familiar, and the worship band was decent. Good drummer. The sermon was okay, a retelling of Jesus raising Lazarus from the dead, though it didn't seem to have much personal application. Or maybe it was just her. She'd been having a hard time reading the Bible and getting anything new out of it.

But the people seemed friendly enough, greeting her along with Mark and Denise with a smile and handshake after the service. "Sorry I didn't introduce you properly, but I'm not good with names," Denise admitted as they walked out to the parking lot, trailing Marcus and Luke who ran ahead playing tag around the parked cars. Come to think of it, even though people greeted them, nobody had asked Grace her name or if this was her first time. Just "hello-nice-to-see-you." Churchy greetings. And no one had recognized her. This didn't really surprise her, though, even after the surprising success of her independent release. There were so many distractions competing for everyone's attention these days. Not like when she was young and Amy Grant was grabbing headlines.

She accepted Denise's invitation to join them at Old Country Buffet for lunch, so it was almost three thirty by the time Grace got home, feeling fuller than she'd like. Still, she was glad she'd gone. Sunday ought to be a day spent at church and with family. Maybe that's what she'd do for a while, spend Sunday with Mark and Denise and the boys.

After cleaning Oreo's litter box and putting the breakfast dishes she'd left into the dishwasher, Grace checked e-mail. A brief reply from Jeff said, *Okay, will do,* to her note suggesting "Grace Meredith in Concert" for her upcoming concert promo. And she had more fan mail. At least there'd be something for Sam to do when she came this week. If she hadn't canceled the Norfolk concert next Saturday, there'd be travel arrangements and a zillion other details.

As Grace was about to shut down her laptop, another e-mail popped in. From Barry, the band manager. Barry was *not* happy with the cancellations. The band, he said, had spent a lot of time laying down tracks for the new songs she'd planned to sing at those concerts — Norfolk and Houston being too far and too expensive to bring the live band each time — and they still hadn't been paid. But Bongo *had* hired them for the Midwest concerts, the ones within driving distance of Chicago with their van and trailer full of equipment. Could she guarantee that the two cancellations were *it?* That the two college gigs and the West Coast tour were still a go?

Grace's stomach knotted. She hadn't thought through how her cancellations would affect so many people.

But she couldn't deal with Barry. Bongo

did all the contract negotiations with the band. She clicked Forward and sent the e-mail to Jeff Newman with a brief note: *Jeff, can you take care of this? Make sure the band gets paid for the work they did, even if we don't use the tracks. Do what's right for these guys. Even if it has to come out of my pocket.*

Ouch. That was going to hurt.

Grace shut down her laptop and got up to draw the living room drapes — and saw that it was snowing. *Oh no.* Not more snow. She was really ready for the snow to go away and spring to come.

Now that her sabbatical was official, her routine fell into an easier rhythm. Grace began to feel results from the regular physical exercise, and Dr. Erskine seemed pleased with the progress she was making in her vocal-therapy sessions. Sam showed up on Monday and again on Friday. "Uhhhhh," she yawned, arching her back and stretching as she finished answering the last of the fan mail Friday afternoon. "February's almost over. Wonder what Norfolk is like this time of year? Can't imagine they get all this snow."

Grace cut her eyes at her assistant. "Sam . . . don't." She didn't want to think about the canceled concert in Virginia. Except . . . she had been thinking about it, almost wishing she and Sam were leaving for the airport that afternoon. It would've been her first concert at the large Baptist church in Norfolk, which was known for hosting big-name Christian artists. It would have been a nice boost for her career. The weekend-from-hell in Memphis was almost four weeks ago, and the painful edges of her memory had muted somewhat. Maybe she shouldn't have canceled Norfolk and Houston —

"Sorry." Sam busied herself shutting down the computer. "That was selfish."

"Selfish? What do you mean?"

Sam looked embarrassed. "Oh . . . I miss the excitement of the concerts. I love traveling with you. Dream job. Probably as close to my fantasy as I'll ever get."

Grace studied her assistant. She'd been a music major at Fisk University and her music background had certainly weighed in her favor when she'd applied as Grace's assistant. But Grace hadn't given Sam's own career much thought.

"Do you do any singing . . . now, I mean?"

Sam shrugged as she packed the laptop into its case. "Well, sure. I sing with the choir at Salem Baptist when I'm in town, sing the lead sometimes . . . but, look. Sorry I brought the whole thing up. I know you need time for your voice to recover. You'll be back on the road soon enough."

"I'd like to come hear you sometime."

Sam grinned. "Sure, if you want. Uh, you still want to go out to eat? We could try that new restaurant on Western Avenue — Belly Shack or something. Heard it was good and not too expensive."

Both of which turned out to be true. But even while laughing helplessly as she and Sam tried to figure out how to eat the messy meatball-and-rice-noodles pita sandwich, Saturday's canceled concert loomed like a black hole in Grace's consciousness. Maybe she'd overreacted to the emotional trauma. Four to six weeks of "house arrest" in the middle of winter wasn't all it was cracked up to be. She missed doing music, missed the excitement of a concert, missed feeling like her days had a purpose . . .

Those days would soon return. Greenville College was coming up in mid-March, just a few weeks away. She still needed to decide what songs she would sing and send the scores to Barry so he could line up practice times with the band.

"Definitely not too soon to prepare for the Greenville gig," Sam agreed. They doodled a to-do list on a napkin as the waiter took their plates away and brought two cups of strong Korean coffee. "I can come three days next week — more if you want. But, Grace, better check with Dr. Erskine first, ask what she thinks about practice for these concerts. You don't want to strain your voice before you're ready."

Deciding to start preparations for the Greenville College concert should have perked up Grace's spirit, but for some reason she woke up Saturday feeling depressed and anxious. Could she really pull it together in time? If all that crap hadn't happened in Memphis, she and Sam would be in Norfolk getting ready to head over to the church to practice with the band. She'd been told the auditorium could seat two thousand. She pictured the concert she was missing — the dimming lights, walking on-stage to loud applause, the hush settling like a mantle as she started to sing.

She loved that feeling — loved sharing her songs, loved knowing there were young people in the audience who needed another voice cutting through the sexual babble from the media world, who needed to hear they were worth waiting for, who came for her music and got a double dose of encour-

213

agement to become the men and women God had designed them to be. And afterward . . . the excitement of meeting her eager fans, basking in their delight as she signed autographs, shook hands, made little jokes, gave hugs . . .

It built her up. Gave her purpose. Made her feel special. And worthy.

But none of that today. Just another weekend slopping around the house with only Oreo for company.

Not even sure she'd be ready for the concert at Greenville.

But who was she if she couldn't sing?

Dragging herself out of bed, Grace plodded into the kitchen, started the coffee, and wandered back into the living room to open the drapes. A large rental truck was parked in front of the old lady's two-flat and a crew of burly guys were hauling furniture and boxes — and what looked like a whole lot of junk — out of the house. Some of the stuff disappeared around back — must have a dumpster or something back there.

The crew worked most of the day, and once when Grace looked out, she saw the same little RAV4, parked this time on her side of the street.

When the truck and little SUV were finally gone, Grace realized the For Sale sign was gone too.

Well, they'd done it. Sold the house right out from under the old lady.

CHAPTER 20

March rolled in windy and cold. Even though the temperatures were inching above freezing, the gusty winds off Lake Michigan under perpetually cloudy skies seemed to cut to the bone whenever Grace ventured outside — which she had to do at least once a day to get to the fitness center or voice therapist appointments.

But that first week of March wasn't all bad. Sam came Monday, Wednesday, *and* Friday to start work on all the details for the upcoming Greenville concert. And Jeff Newman called twice that week, just checking in.

"So I can talk to you in person now?" he joked on Friday, his call interrupting the vocal exercises she was doing at the piano while Sam "supervised" from the dining nook as she worked on hotel arrangements. "Seriously, Grace, your voice is sounding a lot better. I'm so grateful. We've been praying for you here at Bongo."

"Oh. Well, thanks." People said that all the time — *she* often said it — but that didn't mean they always did it.

But almost as if he read into her tone of voice, he said, "I mean it. We start each day in the office with a fifteen-minute prayer time, especially to pray for our clients. Your name has been at the top of the list."

"Okay." Grace squirmed on the piano bench. How much had Newman told them? "Um, well, Dr. Erskine says if things keep improving at this rate, I should be ready to sing by mid-month. Hope she moves that up, though, because I need to practice with the band before then. Practice, period. Feeling pretty rusty."

"You'll be fine. Just work back in easy. Say . . . I'm working on a couple of new opportunities for you, but nothing's definite yet. No rush. We can talk about them later. You just concentrate on the two college concerts for now. Just wanted you to know I haven't been slacking." He chuckled on the other end of the phone.

Grace definitely hadn't been worried about her agent "slacking." She was tempted to tell him *not* to work on anything new. The more gigs he lined up for her, the deeper the rut she'd be in and harder to get out of — not that she wanted to, exactly, but might be something to consider if she and Roger ever . . .

She dropped her head into her hands after the call ended, elbows making a discordant noise on the keyboard. *O God, I don't know what I want! I need some help here!* Seemed like all her prayers were "foxhole prayers" these days. But she did need help — help knowing what God wanted her to do with her life, help figuring out what songs she should sing at the upcoming concerts, even help corralling her panic over how she was going to get there —

"You okay?"

Grace looked up. Her assistant was standing in the arched doorway of the dining nook, notebook in hand. "Yeah, fine. Sorry. What's up?"

"I found a hotel near the college campus. Just need to know if you want it for one night or two. The flight from Chicago to St. Louis is only an hour, but someone at the college would need to pick us up and Greenville is another hour or so by car. You could fly in Friday morning and probably still have time to practice with the band before the concert that night . . ."

Grace's stomach knotted. She stared at the white and black piano keys, which started to blur. There it was. The Big Question. Was she willing to go through airport security again?

Sam didn't wait for her response. "You know what? Don't worry about it. We can drive and go down on Thursday. The band will be driving Barry's van and pulling a trailer, it's only a few hours — four or five at the most. I'll rent a car and we can drive back on Saturday. If I drive down, you'll be rested and have plenty of time on Friday to get set up in the auditorium and practice with the band."

Grace looked up at her gratefully. "Sounds good. Yes, let's do that."

"But . . . the next concert is Cincinnati, a bit further. Might make sense to fly. Should I — ?"

Grace quickly shook her head. "Wait on that, okay? Go ahead and book a hotel near the university for two nights. That'll give us room to decide how we travel there. The band's driving to Cincinnati, right? Must be doable."

Sam looked dubious, but shrugged. "Okay." She headed back toward the dining table where she'd been working on the laptop, then turned back. "Uh, just one more thing."

It was all Grace could do not to roll her

eyes. "What?"

Sam didn't flinch. "Look, don't shoot the messenger. But there's a new e-mail from Barry. Says he needs your song list ASAP since it's only two weeks till Greenville. He also wants to know if you plan to practice with them here in Chicago or wait to put it together at the college."

Grace sighed. "I know. I'm sorry, Sam. I shouldn't have snapped at you. Just feeling all this tension. I — I feel stuck."

Sam moved quickly over to the piano, sat down on the bench beside her, and gave Grace a hug. "Hey, that's what you have an assistant for! Look, soon as I make these hotel reservations and line up a rental car, let's come up with a set list. You've got some great songs. Honestly, I don't think it's going to be that hard."

Sitting on the living room floor an hour later, the two women sifted through Grace's song file and began making piles by category: original songs Grace had written herself . . . songs written by other artists that Bongo had gotten permission for her to use . . . new arrangements she'd done of classic hymns. "Why don't you pick a few from each category," Sam said, "some of your favorites. After all, this is just 'Grace

Meredith in Concert.' You can sing whatever you want —"

"Wait." Grace's eyes widened. "Greenville is my alma mater. I should take advantage of that, maybe do a retro thing — sing some of the songs that were popular when I was a music major there. I wrote a number of songs then too."

Sam laughed aloud. "Grace! That's a great idea! You could lighten it up by telling stories from your college days . . ."

The two women brainstormed and sorted, and finally had a set list. Grace was pretty sure the band already had scores for most of these — except the songs she'd written while still a student — but Sam said she'd drop them off that weekend.

As Sam left the house, she poked her head back inside the front door. "Hey! My sister and cousin are coming in for the weekend. You want to come have a sleepover with us tomorrow night? Do you good to just have some fun."

A *sleepover*? She hadn't done anything like that since crazy high school days. She didn't really know Sam's sister and cousin — just a brief introduction after the concert in Memphis. Would feel kinda weird. "Uhhh, thanks for the invite, but think I'll decline. Need my beauty sleep, you know."

It was supposed to be a joke, but Sam didn't smile. "What you *need,* Grace Meredith, is some *girlfriends.*"

Grace felt mildly annoyed. What did Sam know about her friends? But she couldn't let it bother her. She really did have stuff to do this weekend and she couldn't afford to stay up till all hours and risk getting sick again.

Grace spent Saturday morning rehearsing several of the songs they'd selected, accompanying herself on the piano, but keeping her voice level to about a third of her normal concert strength. "Don't want to wear out the instrument too fast too soon," she told Oreo, who'd taken up residence on the piano bench beside her, his rumbling purrs adding a steady rhythm section. But it felt good to sing some of the old songs again . . .

"I could sing of your love forever . . ."

She couldn't help smiling as the words to Martin Smith's hit came flooding back into her memory and through her fingers on the keys. Still, she was surprised how limited her range was. She should've been more faithful to do the at-home vocal exercises Dr. Erskine had given her. But . . . there was still time.

And there was the first song she'd composed at Greenville. *"You said follow me (and yes I will but . . .) First I need to see what life can offer . . . before I bend my knee (one day I will, but . . .) . . ."* Never recorded — for obvious reasons. Kind of corny, but it had reflected a real spiritual struggle she and many other students identified with back in the day. Might speak to some of today's students too.

Grace finally closed the lid on the piano, bundled up, and went for a walk in the welcome afternoon sunshine. The sun had traveled in a clear sky all day Saturday, sending temperatures into the forties again. Most of the snow was finally gone, the lawn chairs and saw-horses had disappeared, and flocks of chickadees could be heard twittering in the trees up and down the block.

Several of the neighbors were out tinkering with cars or sweeping salt off their sidewalks. She nodded hello as she passed, noting that the two-flat across the street was still empty. There was another two-flat on the block, this one two houses down on her side of the street. The family on the first floor was Hispanic, with two or three cute kids Grace saw from time to time. She'd seen several other adults of various ages too. Maybe they were related. All the other houses on the block were single-story brick bungalows similar to hers, probably with functional basements. A few had one or two garret rooms in the attic with curtains in the gable windows.

She glanced back over her shoulder. All, except for that oversized McMansion at the dead end, backing up against the cemetery. What was *his* story?

As Grace reached the end of the block and turned the corner, planning to walk around to the main gate of the cemetery, she saw the Jewish family who lived on the corner walking toward her. Of course . . . Saturday. Probably had been to synagogue. The man sported a serious beard and wore a large black hat with a flat brim and a black suit coat, the fringes of a white prayer shawl hanging beneath it. The mother wore a long black skirt beneath her winter coat, hair gathered into some kind of covering, pushing a stroller with a sleeping toddler. Two other children — a boy wearing a yarmulke and a girl in a winter coat and dress — trotted alongside, chattering away happily, noses red from the still nippy air.

Grace nodded, smiled, and said hello, and the woman smiled back. Her husband grunted absently as they passed. Must be Orthodox. Seemed to be a lot of Orthodox

Jews living in the area. Somewhere she'd heard they had to live within walking distance of a synagogue. She wondered where it was.

Reaching St. Mark's Cemetery, she stretched her legs, walking as fast as her snow boots allowed. She could tell the exercise at Curves had been helpful. She avoided a graveside service — a small huddle of people under a protective tent — choosing another wide path . . . but realized she wasn't being entirely successful stuffing down feelings that she should be in Houston that weekend, filling another large venue.

At least things were coming together for the concert at her alma mater. That helped. She and Sam were going to drive — that was a relief. And she had a song list. Once the band had had time to work on the music, they could schedule several sessions and decide on the final sets, which would be important, since most of the songs were different from the New Year, New You tour —

Things were coming together . . .

An answer to prayer?

A pair of cardinals flitted from one bare tree to another, chirping happily in the welcome sunshine. Grace stopped and turned her face upward, feeling the warmth of the sun on her skin. "Thank you," she whispered.

Maybe God hadn't turned a deaf ear to her after all.

CHAPTER 21

By the end of the next week, Barry Fox called to say the band was ready with the retro songs, and he and Sam scheduled a practice with Grace for that Saturday. Barry thought the mix was good — a sampling of songs by Steven Curtis Chapman, Michael W. Smith, Avalon, and Sonicflood, plus Grace's early original songs — but he met Grace and Sam at the practice studio with a wry grin. "Just remember, a few of these guys" — he jerked a thumb toward the band members who were setting up — "were only in middle school ten years ago. They've never heard some of these songs."

"Oh, thanks." Grace swatted his arm. "Nice way to make a girl feel old."

"Don't they go to church?" Sam asked. "We still sing some of these worship songs at my church . . . well, okay, not many. Salem is big into black gospel. But I bet County Line and those other megachurches do."

Grace thought the first practice session went well — though Sam had to remind her to hold back on volume and intensity. And even then, Grace was a little hoarse the rest of the weekend, and back on lemon-and-honey tea and frequent gargles.

But it was March — surely spring was coming, in spite of the up-and-down temperatures. Some of the days had already made it into the fifties and sixties, along with foggy mornings, cloudy skies, and the occasional soggy drizzle. "Sure would like to see the sun, though," Grace muttered to the cat the following Monday as she got ready to leave for her session at Curves. The countdown toward the Greenville concert seemed to be speeding up. Another practice with the band that evening, a third scheduled for Wednesday, and the drive to Greenville on Thursday.

Whatever happened to that long, leisurely sabbatical?

At least she'd cleaned out the bedroom closets. And the sessions with the trainer at Curves were definitely paying off — or would eventually. She felt stronger physically, actually had an appetite, and was sleeping better.

Except on those nights when she let her mind wander into that wasteland of her failed relationship with Roger.

Strange that she hadn't heard from Jeff, though, for . . . what, over a week? He'd said he'd keep in regular touch with her during her sabbatical. When he still hadn't called by Wednesday, she decided to call the office to give him an update. She eyed Oreo as the phone rang in her ear. "And, *hmm, what am I going* to do with *you* for three days?"

"Grace!" Newman said when the receptionist at the Bongo Booking Agency put her through. "Believe it or not, I had you on my to-do list to call today. Sorry I haven't been in touch, but I've been out of the office. Trying to get face time with each of the clients Fowler handed off to me. How are you feeling? How's the prep coming for the Greenville gig? — hey, that's this weekend! Can't believe it! You doing okay?"

It took Grace a moment to actually answer, "Uh, yes, I'm fine," because her mind was still dodging Jeff's pinball greeting. She was an item on his to-do list? *Good grief, Grace.* She shook off the niggling temptation to feel neglected. Talk about being oversensitive! He sounded genuinely glad to hear from her. "Thought I'd let you know I'm feeling ready for this weekend. Greenville is my alma mater, you know, so I decided to do a retro concert, putting together popular worship songs from the years I was a student there with some songs I wrote back then —"

"Grace! What a great idea."

"Yeah, well, maybe, maybe not. Half the guys in my band hadn't heard of some of the songs I chose. So it probably won't be a walk down memory lane for today's crop of Greenville students."

"Hey, shoot me the song list, will you? I still think it's a great idea. We need to keep some of these classics alive. They'll love it."

"Okay." Grace felt warmed by his support. "I'm kind of glad this first concert after my sabbatical is Greenville. The college isn't that big so it'll be a small crowd."

"Let's see . . . they've got you in the La-Due Auditorium. How large is that?"

"Mm, I'm guessing it holds four hundred, give or take. If the crowd is smaller than that" — she grinned at the thought — "they'll probably move us to the Blackroom. It's a professional performance space with great sound and lighting, mostly for campus groups, but quite a bit smaller than LaDue. I gave a few concerts there when I was a student."

"So this will be quite a homecoming."

I laughed. "I doubt it. After all, that was

almost ten years ago. Nobody there would know me personally except maybe a few of my old profs."

"But you might have a whole new crop of fans."

"Thanks, we'll see. Well . . . guess I better let you go —"

"No, no, no. Hold on. I was going to call you today, remember? Because I've got a new venue for you — a church in St. Louis. They had to cancel a band that got into some legal trouble, and called Bongo asking if we had an artist who could fill in. When I told them Grace Meredith might be available, they got very excited. Just got the official invitation this week."

Grace's mouth went dry. "When?" It came out almost in a whisper. But Jeff didn't seem to notice.

"Uhh . . . first Saturday in April, two weeks away. That's after the Cincinnati concert but still a few weeks before you leave on your West Coast tour. It's a really great opportunity for you, Grace."

She was silent for a long minute.

"Grace? Look, if this is too much, you don't have to do it. But to be honest, I've been worried about the impact the cancellations might have on other opportunities — word tends to get around. This invitation gives you a chance to say, 'I'm back!' Still . . . it's up to you. I mean it."

"Uh, when do they need to know?"

He snorted. "Yesterday. But seriously, by tomorrow or Friday if at all possible. I'm really sorry for the crunch. Wouldn't do it if it wasn't such a great opportunity."

Tomorrow! But he did say St. Louis. That was still within driving distance of Chicago. She wouldn't have to pass through an airport . . .

Samantha picked her up at nine the next morning in a rental, a comfortable road car with a CD player and a handy GPS. She'd brought a stack of gospel CDs — "To get us in the mood!" she laughed. "Hey, don't we have to take Oreo to that cat boarding place? Or did you ask a neighbor to come in and do scooper duty?"

Grace shook her head as she snapped her seat belt. "Don't really know anyone around here well enough to give them the key to my house. My brother said he could stop by this weekend — but fat lot of good that'd do since we're coming home on Saturday. Oreo will be fine for three days. I left lots of food and water."

"Ooh, living dangerously. Will your curtains survive?"

"Just drive." Grace settled into the passenger seat, enjoying the smell of new leather — like the rustic smell of the tack room in a riding stable. That took her back — back before . . . everything.

She had looked forward to the drive, but the temperature had dropped back into the forties and the forecast said strong winds. It wasn't so bad going through the city, but once they were on Route 57 heading south through midwestern flatlands, the unhindered wind shook the car relentlessly and Sam had to white-knuckle the wheel, especially after a large semi roared past and they nearly got blown off the road in its wake.

Grace chewed on a thumbnail and stared out the side window.

"All right now, God," Sam said loudly, gripping the wheel as another truck flew past, "we've got two of your daughters here in this car, and we need some of those guardian angels the Bible talks about. We're on our way to do the Father's business, so we're asking for your protection from wind, from any crazy drivers, from accidents, from flat tires, or any other thing that ol' Satan might try to throw at us to keep us from doing your will. So I'm thankin' you now for keeping us safe!"

Grace almost laughed. It was such an in-your-face prayer — but she murmured, "Amen," and then eyed Sam sideways. "Wish I could pray like you."

"Like me? What do you mean?"

"So confident that God's listening. Going to take care of it."

Sam tossed her a look. "Well, of course he's listening! That's what prayer is, talking to God, just telling him whatever's on your heart."

Grace glanced away. "I know." How could she tell Sam she felt uncertain whether she *was* on "the Father's business"? She'd thought so, fulfilling her mission to share God's purity message with a new generation of young people. But it all seemed to fall apart so quickly after her last tour. So what was she doing now? Just doing her job? Just fulfilling her commitments? Was God — *would* God still bless her concerts? Or was she still paying for the past?

She still hadn't called Jeff with an answer for the church in St. Louis. She wanted to talk it over with Sam first, ask her to pray about it with her straightforward trust that God cares and would answer. But while Sam was keeping the car on the road under highwind conditions didn't seem like the time.

They pulled off at Champaign-Urbana,

home to the University of Illinois, to get some lunch, and Grace finally brought up the St. Louis option over fish burgers and milkshakes.

Sam licked her fingers and chewed. "Pretty cheeky to expect you to show up with only two weeks' notice. Maybe you should check with the band."

Check with the band . . . of course. If they couldn't go, her only option would be tracks. Not her preferred approach. She loved the immediacy and energy of performing with a band. "What about you? Is the distance drivable?"

Sam stopped chewing, her eyes on Grace. "Okay, can I be honest here? I wasn't exactly hired to be your driver — not that I'm complaining about this weekend, mind you. I offered. But I don't know, Grace . . . I'm not really enjoying this drive."

Grace grimaced. "I know. I'm sorry, Sam —"

"Okay, look. I'm not saying no. But, talk to Barry and the band, see what they say, and . . . let's pray about it. That's the bottom line anyway. Is this the Father's business? When do you have to give an answer?"

"Today. Tomorrow latest."

"Today!" Sam snorted. "Oh, brother. No time to waste." She reached for Grace's

hand, bowed her head right there in the fast-food place, and asked God to show them the path to take.

By the time they got back on the road, the wind had died down and the traffic had lightened up. "Thank you, Jesus!" Sam laughed. "Maybe God's giving us a thumbs-up about that trip to St. Louis." She stuck a WOW Gospel CD with last year's gospel hits into the player and happily sang along with Marvin Sapp and Nicole Mullen. "I don't have to save my voice, so there," she laughed.

Understatement. Sam had a good, strong voice.

They pulled into the parking lot of the hotel around two thirty. Grace raised an eyebrow. "Super 8?"

Sam shrugged as she unloaded the luggage from the trunk. "Best I could find close to the campus. It's Greenville. Not that many options. If you'd rather try further away . . ."

"No, no, it's fine." And it was. Clean rooms side by side. Comfy bed. A couple restaurants close by. Complimentary breakfast. Had she been getting spoiled by the higher-end hotels on the New Year, New You tour in major cities? Probably. How many other ways had she let her recent success go to her head?

Sam called Barry and put the phone on speaker. The band was on the road and would be getting in later that evening. They planned to set up in the college auditorium the next morning and be ready to practice with Grace by eleven. "Great," Sam said. "But hold on. Grace wants to talk to you."

"Whoa!" Barry said after Grace outlined the invitation from the St. Louis church. "The guys were just talkin' about doin' some local gigs in Chicago before the West Coast tour. But . . . St. Louis? I've heard of that church you mentioned. Some big names have done concerts there. I think the guys would buy it. We could drive the van — don't think it's much further than Greenville, maybe another hour. The local gigs don't pay anything anyway. So . . . make up your mind and let us know. By tomorrow, though."

Grace handed the phone back and eyed Samantha. "So . . . what do you think?" She'd been half hoping the band was already booked so she'd have an excuse to say no.

Sam tossed her corkscrew twists with a grin. "Looks like the door's still standing open — and I always say, if God opens a door, walk through it unless it closes in your face. Who knows what hearts are waiting to be touched by your songs in St. Louis? I say go for it! We can figure out how to get there later. Maybe the band can squeeze us into the van this once?"

Grace looked at her, wide-eyed. "There's barely room for the guys and their Cheetos."

"We could always ride on top," said Sam with a laugh, and Grace soon joined her.

It was exactly the kind of lighthearted moment Grace needed.

Grace was nervous as she waited for the signal to come out on stage at the LaDue Auditorium the next evening. Good grief. What was she nervous for? The Greenville people she'd met that day, both staff and students, had been warm and friendly — like the weather, which had hiked back up into the mid-sixties. "It's a real encouragement for one of our own who's making it on the CCM circuit to come back," the college choral director had said.

Samantha peeked and said the auditorium was filling with "a nice crowd" — Sam-speak meaning it wasn't packed. Okay. A nice crowd. Grace was actually grateful. Not too large, not too small. Just right for getting her feet back on the ground.

She'd agonized about what to wear. This

238

was a college campus. Dress up? Dress down? She'd finally decided on casual black jeans and ankle boots, a white tunic with embroidered neck and sleeves to dress it up, and her hair down and casual in its long shag style.

Father God, she prayed silently as she waited in the wings, imitating some of Sam's prayer-isms, *I do want to be about your business. So I dedicate this evening to you, even though* — Grace hesitated — *even though I've been kind of out of touch lately.* A paraphrase of Psalm 49 seemed a good way to finish her prayer. *Let the songs of my mouth and the meditations of my heart be acceptable to you tonight, O Lord* —

"Grace, you're on," Sam whispered, giving her a little push.

Grace walked out onto the stage, momentarily blinded by the spotlights. But as her eyes adjusted, she saw big smiles on the faces of students and older adults alike, heard the warm clapping. Closing her eyes for a moment and drawing in a slow breath, she waited as Petey and the rest of the band gave her a short intro, and then she began . . .

"Over the mountains and the sea, your river runs with love for me . . ."

As the song welled up in her spirit, Grace

almost felt she was singing in a bubble. Nothing mattered but the song. But as she got to the chorus, the music seemed to swell even louder. Opening her eyes, she realized the entire auditorium was on its feet singing along. She felt lifted . . .

"I will sing of your love forever . . . !"

"You did great last night — hope you know that." It was the fifth time Sam had said something similar on the drive home the next day. "Your little stories between songs were great — that one about accidentally leaving your alarm clock in the women's dorm bathroom after 9/11 and the janitor treating it as a possible terrorist attack was hilarious. Well, not at the time, I suppose." She giggled at the wheel. "But your audience loved it."

"Mm." Grace had already said "Thanks" to Sam's compliments. She'd peppered the evening with stories about campus life "back when," both funny and serious, and the night seemed to go well. Merch sales had been decent and students had crowded around afterward getting her autograph. All good . . . except she'd been taken aback by one of the deans who cornered her. "We thought you'd bring a strong abstinence message — isn't that what you do? Even

240

students at Christian colleges need that, you know."

The comment still bothered her. Did she even have a "message" anymore? Was she going to have to publicly announce she was single again? Not that being single changed the message . . . no. It wasn't about the message. It was about her. The story no one knew. The secret that had bubbled to the surface of her heart, caused her to doubt. What right did she have to encourage others to wait?

"But can you believe this weather?" Sam slapped the steering wheel as they came off Route 57 and joined 94, heading for Lake Shore Drive. "Now it's starting to snow!"

The one-day reprieve had evaporated overnight and temperatures had dropped back into the thirties, getting colder as they headed north. By the time Sam turned onto Beecham Street, there was at least two inches of white stuff on the ground — and a U-Haul truck blocking the street. "What in the world? I can't get close to your house!"

Grace peered through the snowflakes landing on the windshield. "Remember I told you about the old lady who fell? Lost her house too. Somebody bought it."

"Oh. That's kinda sad." Sam watched the

people hauling things into the two-flat in question, then started to back up. "Guess I'll drive up the alley and drop you off in back."

Unlocking the back door five minutes later, Grace waved good-bye to Samantha as the rental car disappeared. Gusty winds on the way down . . . snow on the way back. How fair was it to ask Sam to drive to her concerts, even if they were drivable?

Did she have the courage to fly to Cincinnati next weekend?

CHAPTER 22

The drapes were still in one piece and Oreo seemed none the worse for wear from "baching it" for a couple days — except he had tipped over his food bowl and pooped outside his litter box in the basement, and his water bowl was empty. Maybe leaving him alone wasn't such a good idea. Did Grace dare ask Tavis or his sister to come over once a day to check on the cat and scoop the litter box? She'd have to give the mother a house key . . .

No, no, she didn't know the family *that* well. Not yet, anyway.

It was still spitting snow mixed with rain on Sunday — ha! So much for being the first day of spring — but Grace drove to Faith Chapel anyway, arriving a few minutes late. "Hey, should've told us you were coming!" her brother whispered as he and Denise scooted over to make room for her in the pew. "We've been invited to hang out with some friends this afternoon; they've got kids the same ages as our boys. Thought you were gone all weekend —"

"Mark, it's fine. I don't have to have dinner with you every time I come to church. Go. I'm good."

Grace stood with the rest of the congregation as the praise band launched into a lively tune. She noticed hymnbooks in the racks on the back of the pews — did they sing hymns in the traditional service? Maybe she'd come to the earlier service one of these Sundays just to check it out.

Staying just long enough after the service to hug her nephews and wave good-bye, Grace headed for home. She was glad she'd decided to attend Faith Chapel for a while. Just the routine of going to church every Sunday was in itself helpful, and sitting with her brother and his wife gave her a sense of family, of connection, in spite of everything. But Sam was right: she really didn't have close girlfriends anymore. College friends had gotten married and lost touch except for the annual Christmas missive. Add the demands of touring, becoming a public figure in the CCM world, and attaching herself to Roger as a "couple" with any time left over, and she'd pretty much flunked out of Girlfriend 102.

Parking the car in front of her house — she still needed to do some food shopping after being gone for three days — she saw the black-and-silver RAV4 come up Beecham, turn around in the cul-de-sac, and park on the other side of the street in front of the two-flat. Grace busied herself unlocking the front door, but once inside she stepped to the window to watch as four people got out of the small SUV and headed up the walk. She'd seen the older man and woman before, looking at the house — no surprise there; she'd assumed they were the ones who'd bought the house — and the boy. The man was wearing a suit and topcoat, and the woman wore a long dress that hung beneath her coat and a brightly colored something on her head — not a hat exactly, more like a fancy headwrap — as if they'd just come from church.

But who was the other man? Younger, also dark-skinned, tall, slender, not so dressed up, trailing the others. Could be the boy's father. Or a cousin or uncle — who knew? The elderly woman who'd come with the couple that one time was nowhere to be seen.

Grace turned from the window. As long as the neighborhood stayed peaceful, she didn't care who moved in. There were other extended families on the block — the Hispanic family in the two-flat a couple houses down and a family she thought might be African in the single-story brick on the corner with grandparents who didn't seem to speak English. Everyone minded their own business.

Her business of the moment was to decide whether to drive or fly to Cincinnati next weekend. Flying itself wasn't the issue, if it wasn't for all the invasive security. She wished she could talk it over with someone — but did anyone really understand why this was such a big issue for her? She might've talked it over with Roger "back when" — wasn't that what a soul mate should be, someone you could talk to about anything? Who loved you no matter what?

But even Roger hadn't known everything.

Well, Samantha was coming to work tomorrow — that would be time enough to decide. Right now she should get some lunch and do a quickie trip to the grocery store. Then she could relax.

But the thought nagged at her the rest of the day. *Drive or fly?*

At least pray about it, she told herself as she put groceries away later. She knew what the Bible said: *"If any of you lacks wisdom, . . . ask God, who gives generously to all without finding fault."* But was it wisdom she needed? She already knew that if she were going to continue touring, she would need to fly. She couldn't drive everywhere.

What she needed was courage.

After fretting about it most of the afternoon and not getting much done, she threw up her hands. "Okay, God, your Word says I can do all things through Christ who strengthens me. So . . . I need some of that strength."

She'd wasted most of the afternoon worrying about it. Time to suck it up and just do it. She'd tell Samantha to make flight arrangements tomorrow.

Stepping to the window to close the drapes as twilight deepened, she noticed the new couple was walking arm in arm down the sidewalk in front of her house. Just out for a walk? Kind of cute for people their age — but it was getting dark enough outside, she didn't need to be showing off all her business from her lighted living room. She pulled the drapes shut.

The limo pulled up alongside Terminal 3 at O'Hare Airport at ten o'clock sharp Thursday morning. "You sure you want to leave this early?" Sam had asked when she'd researched flight times from Chicago to

Cincinnati. "United has a two-thirty flight that would get us in at four-forty — that's with the time change. Band won't get in till ten or so tonight with the van 'cause they're pulling a trailer — but we'd still have the evening free and plenty of time to rehearse on Friday."

"Morning's better. And don't do it online — costs a mint to change it if we have to."

Sam had humored her, booked business class on American Airlines, and stayed overnight Wednesday so the car from Lincoln Limo Service would only have to make one stop. "That's all you're taking?" she said when Grace walked out of her bedroom the next morning pulling her teal-blue carry-on bag.

"That's all *you* bring for these short hops. Might as well avoid those nasty baggage fees. Besides —" Grace hefted her large, roomy purse. "— you'd be amazed what all I can stick in here."

Sam had given her an odd look but just shrugged. "And you're leaving Oreo again all by his lonesome?"

"My brother promised to stop in tomorrow. He'll be fine." And at least the cat would be there when she got home.

After the limo driver deposited their luggage on the curb and got his tip, Grace followed Sam into the terminal. She'd done this dozens of times with no problem, hadn't she? Other than the occasional delayed flight or annoying seatmate. Hadn't been to Cincinnati before though. What was their airport security like? No, no, she wouldn't think about that. One day at a time. She was grateful Sam was traveling with her. Grateful for Sam, period. Who raised this girl to have such a steady faith, such a calming presence? *Thank you, Jesus, for Samantha . . .*

Checking in was easy enough — no checked baggage, and the lines at the counter decent on a Thursday morning. Boarding passes in hand, they headed for security pulling their carry-on bags. Grace did a mental check. She was wearing her leather clogs, easy to slip off . . . all her liquid toiletries were in a ziplock bag in three-ounce sizes . . . no clippers or nail scissors or anything sharp that would cause suspicion . . .

Grace followed Sam through the security line as it wound back and forth, studying the people in the line next to her — business travelers, both men and women, with briefcases; parents with children wearing stuffed animal backpacks and pulling their own tiny Spider-man or Barbie carry-on bags; lots of young people with bulging backpacks. Was it spring break?

She glanced at her watch. No ruby birthstone, just the simple silver watch her parents had given her for high school graduation. Only ten thirty . . . they had plenty of time. Boarding passes and ID at the first checkpoint. "Have a nice flight," the agent said, handing back Grace's driver's license and waving the next person forward. Still more back and forth as the line moved toward the stacks of plastic bins, rows of conveyer belts, and TSA agents. Grace studied people's shoes. Everything from flip-flops to mukluks. Four people ahead of them . . . then three . . . two . . .

Grace took a deep breath and looked up. Two lines over, a middle-aged woman's purse was being searched. Beyond the metal detectors, a young man had been pulled aside and was being wanded by a TSA agent.

A sudden taste of bile caught in her throat. Her heart seemed to pound in her chest. Sam was reaching for a bin when Grace grabbed her arm. "Sam . . . wait. Wait." She stepped out of the line, her breath coming hard and fast. She felt lightheaded . . . faint.

"Grace?" Sam's voice seemed to come

from yards away.

Grace shook her head. "I can't . . . I can't do it. I . . ." She turned and began threading her way back through the line, hands gripping her carry-on and purse. *O God, O God . . .*

"Grace, wait!"

She heard Sam's voice behind her but kept moving. "I'm sorry . . . sorry," she mumbled to people as she headed the wrong way, past the first checkpoint, past the last person in line . . . and finally stopped, back in the main lobby. She bent over, hands on her knees. *You fool! You coward!* She chided herself, taking deep gulps of air as passengers heading for the security lines skirted around her.

"Grace! What happened? Are you all right?" Without waiting for an answer, Sam took her arm and steered her toward a row of steel and Naugahyde seats by the large windows at the front of the terminal. They sat. For a long time, neither of them said anything. Grace kept taking deep gulps, trying to regain her breath.

Finally she shook her head. "I'm sorry, Sam. I . . . thought I could. I wanted to. But . . ."

Sam said nothing. Was she angry? Tears welled up in Grace's eyes and she fished for a tissue but couldn't find one in the big purse she'd stuffed with all her extras. Sam handed her one, and they continued to sit in silence as Grace dabbed at her eyes and blew her nose.

A few minutes later, Grace felt Sam's slim hand take hers and give it a squeeze — gentle, kind. "It's going to be all right, Grace," her assistant murmured. "I have to admit, I don't fully understand what's going on, but it'll be okay." But a moment later she stood up. "Give me your boarding pass."

"What?" Grace looked up. "What are you going to do?"

"Turn them in. And then rent a car. We still have time to drive to Cincinnati if we get with it. It's only five or six hours."

"Oh, Sam . . ."

"Just give me the boarding pass."

They were on the road an hour later, and driving south through Indiana on Route 65 an hour after that. Grace vacillated between relief and galling disappointment in herself — an emotional cocktail that was hard to swallow. Sam had matter-of-factly canceled their flight and picked up a rental car at Hertz, and didn't seem angry. Frustrated, perhaps, but not angry. But they didn't do much talking, which Grace appreciated. How could she explain herself?

All the confidence she'd sucked up at the Greenville concert seeped out of her spirit like water disappearing into sand. Would she be able to get up on that stage at Cincinnati Christian University and sing from the heart? Tell funny stories and chat with students — she'd decided to repeat the retro concert sets since CCU was also a college with a strong music program — when she felt like such a failure?

As the cornfields flashed by, Sam finally broke the long silence. "You planned for this, didn't you?"

"Wh-what do you mean?"

"Telling me to get our tickets through the travel agent, the kind that can be changed or refunded. Bringing only a carry-on bag — you've never done that before. Both of which made it possible to walk away from the airport back there."

"No, no, I really wanted to —" Grace stopped, her face suddenly hot, her protest sticking in her throat.

Tears squeezed from her eyes. Sam was right. She'd kept a back door open, an escape hatch in case the hoped-for courage from God didn't come through.

What kind of trust was that?

CHAPTER 23

It was over. She'd made it through . . . somehow.

As the limo driver unloaded their suitcases in front of Grace's house Saturday afternoon, Sam told him, "You don't need to wait — I've got my car here this time. But thanks for rescheduling." They'd had to return the rental car to the airport anyway, so Sam had called Lincoln Limo and simply rescheduled their pickup time.

The driver, dressed in the usual black suit and tie, shrugged it off. "Happens all the time. Planes are late — you know the drill. As long as Paddock has enough drivers, we can usually handle the delays."

Grace, already halfway up her front walk, heard Sam say, "Paddock?"

"That's right. Lincoln Paddock, the owner of Lincoln Limo. He's your neighbor — you didn't know that?"

No, why would we know that? Grace muttered to herself, getting out her key. Oreo greeted her at the front door with a litany of complaints about being left alone for so long. Grace shed her coat and absently picked up the cat as if in a fog.

Sam came in a few minutes later, picking up the mail that had been pushed through the door slot the past few days. "Did you hear that? The owner of Lincoln Limo — the company we've been using for the past year — lives in that big house at the end of your street! Kind of weird."

No, she hadn't heard that part. The big house on the cul-de-sac? Guess that explained a few things. She'd seen sleek black stretch limos come and go from time to time — had just assumed he was some corporate big shot. But Grace wasn't sure if Sam meant weird-that-he-lived-on-the-same-street, or weird-that-she-didn't-know-her-neighbors-well-enough-to-know-that.

Sam stuck the mail into the living room secretary and eyed Grace with concern. "You sure you don't want me to stay? Fix supper? Order in?"

"No, no. You've done enough, Sam. Go home and get some rest. You drove both ways." Grace wondered if she'd ever stop feeling guilty about that.

"Grace, look . . . it's fine. And as for next

week, we're just going to drive to St. Louis. It's no further time-wise than Cincinnati. After that, well, we'll still have a couple weeks before the West Coast tour to decide what to do."

Grace shrugged. She never should've said okay to the St. Louis invitation. Too late to back out now.

"And Grace, I know I've already said this, but you did good at the concert last night. My Meemaw would've been proud of you."

Grace allowed a rueful grin. "Yeah, well, but you gotta find another expression besides, 'Man up, girl!' — even if that's what your Meemaw used to say to you."

Sam rolled her eyes. "She still does." She gave Grace a quick hug. "Okay, I'm off. Be back Monday. And hey, I think Barry's idea to focus on a resurrection theme next weekend in St. Louis is spot on. Can't believe it's Palm Sunday tomorrow . . . say, you wanna come to church with me? I'm going to sing."

Grace hesitated . . . but shook her head. "Thanks. Another time. I promise."

Leaning back against the door after Samantha headed out to her car, Grace shut her eyes wearily. They'd had a brainstorming session with the band that morning before leaving the hotel about the upcoming concert in St. Louis. She was supposed to look through her repertoire and send Barry a list before Monday.

Tomorrow . . . she'd think about it tomorrow. She was too exhausted to do it now.

Oreo rubbed against her ankles, meowing pitifully. Grace pushed herself away from the door and gathered up the cat. "Okay, okay, let's go see if you've demolished all that food I left you. You better not have left me any nasty surprises though."

It was Palm Sunday . . . but Grace didn't feel like making the effort to go to Faith Chapel. Mark and Denise would probably invite her to lunch, would want to hear about the concert. What if they asked how the flight went? She would feel like a fool trying to explain her actions.

Besides, she still felt exhausted. Probably more emotional than physical, though even a three-day trip sapped her energy. Why not treat this Sunday as a real day of rest — literally.

She spent the morning in her robe and slippers, drinking coffee, playing praise and worship CDs, and idly sorting through her mail — gas bill, credit card bill, a couple of catalogs, Goodman Theater ad, more junk mail . . . She put the bills in a slot in the secretary to pay on Monday and sat down on the floor with her file box of song sheets. Was her voice strong enough to hit the high notes of "Hear the Bells Ringing"? She had permission to sing the popular Second Chapter of Acts number in concerts, though not record it on any of her CDs. She also liked "A New Hallelujah" by Michael W. Smith — and what about some of the beautiful Easter hymns?

None of her own songs had a clear resurrection theme. But maybe she could use a few of her songs that focused on Jesus as Savior. Then there was the matter of her most popular song — the song everyone would want to hear, no matter what theme she chose. She just didn't want to sing that song right now . . .

By the time noon rolled around, Grace felt encouraged by her song list. And was getting hungry. After a quick shower, she pulled on a pair of jeans and her old, comfy flannel shirt, fixed herself a large green salad with tuna fish for lunch, and let Oreo clean out the tuna can. Taking the salad into the living room, she flopped on the couch and pointed the remote to see if she could find an old movie on TV. Ha! *The African Queen* — perfect. Nobody like Humphrey Bogart and Katherine Hepburn . . .

Standing in the bathroom, trying to scrub dirt off her face . . . a bell ringing . . . she'd be late for school! No, no, she couldn't be late, they'd ask why! . . .

The bell rang again. Grace opened her eyes. Oreo was standing on her chest licking her mouth and chin. "Oreo! Stop it!" She pushed the cat away. Yuck! She must've fallen asleep with tuna fish on her chin —

The doorbell rang again. *The doorbell!* Swinging her feet off the couch and punching the Off button on the TV remote, Grace shook the sleep out of her head and peeked through the security peephole. A pleasant brown face . . . a woman, not a kid . . . who in the world?

She opened the door. A middle-aged black woman wearing a red wool poncho stood on her doorstep. Straightened black hair with streaks of silver hung to her shoulders, and she held something enveloped in clear plastic wrap and tied with a red ribbon. The woman looked familiar . . . "Yes?"

"Hope I'm not botherin' you," the woman said, all smiles. "I'm your new neighbor, across the street. Name's Estelle Bentley."

Of course. She'd only seen the woman from a distance, but now recognized her full figure and attractive features. Mrs. Bentley held out the package. "Just wanted to meet my new neighbors — brought you some of my homemade cinnamon rolls."

Grace grabbed Oreo just before he tried to slip out the front door. "Oh! That's . . . that's very nice of you." She stood there awkwardly, momentarily unsure what to do. If she put Oreo down, he might run outside. But she couldn't hold the cat and take the package too — oh, this was stupid. "Uh, won't you come in a moment?"

Grace stepped back and the woman stepped in. "Oh, what a lovely home," Mrs. Bentley said, looking around as the door closed behind her. "Love that antique clock you've got . . . oh, here." She held out the package again as Grace put Oreo down and shooed him toward the basement.

"Thank you. That's very kind." Grace examined the package of plastic wrap and ribbon. "You made these cinnamon rolls? They look delicious."

Mrs. Bentley's dark eyes sparkled. "My specialty. Uh, you are . . . ?"

"I'm sorry . . . I'm Grace Meredith. I fell asleep on the couch and I'm still foggy." She held out a hand. "And you said your name is Bentley?"

The woman shook her hand with a firm clasp. "Estelle Bentley. Just Estelle is fine. Harry an' I — that's my husband — came

260

by yesterday deliverin' rolls to our new neighbors, but you weren't home. So glad I caught you today. Wanted you to have these while they're still fresh."

"Yes, well, I was out of town. Just got back late yesterday."

"Really?" Estelle Bentley's eyebrows lifted with interest. "You travel for business? What do you do?"

Grace really hadn't planned on getting into a conversation, but it seemed rude to keep the woman standing in the middle of her living room. "Please, sit down. Would you like a cup of tea or coffee?"

"Oh, I can't stay but a moment, but . . . thank you. Coffee if it's not too much trouble. With sugar." The woman slipped off her poncho and lowered herself onto the couch.

Grace took the plate of cinnamon rolls into the kitchen and started a fresh pot of coffee. She felt embarrassed by the woman's generosity. Wasn't this sort of backwards? She remembered her mother taking a casserole or a pie to new neighbors, but this new couple had been out delivering homemade cinnamon rolls to the *old* neighbors.

Well, she deserved to be embarrassed. They'd moved in a week ago, and she, for one, hadn't even gone over to say, "Welcome to the neighborhood." Had anyone? Probably not. It wasn't exactly that kind of neighborhood.

As soon as the coffee was ready, Grace poured two mugs, added the sugar bowl, napkins, and a couple of the gooey cinnamon rolls on a plate, and took the tray back into the living room. The woman had gotten up and was standing at her piano, looking at the music she'd been practicing earlier that morning. Grace set the tray on the coffee table. "Sorry to keep you waiting. Had to make a fresh pot. But cinnamon rolls definitely call for a cup of coffee!"

Estelle laughed and turned from the piano. "My sentiments exactly! But those are for you. I've had too many as it is." She chuckled as she returned to the couch and stirred two heaping spoonfuls of sugar into her cup of coffee. "I noticed your piano. Do you play? Oh . . . silly question. Of course you do."

Grace had just taken a bite of the soft, sweet cinnamon roll — *ohhh, so good* — so it was several moments before she could answer. "Well, not really. Some. Mostly I sing."

Estelle's mouth widened in a delighted smile. "You sing! Gospel music?"

Grace flushed. "Not exactly gospel. Contemporary Christian music, praise and worship, that sort of thing. I, um . . . that's what I do. Just got back from doing a concert in Cincinnati, and I have another next weekend in St. Louis." Was she telling too much? Felt like her tongue was flapping.

The woman's mouth dropped and she slapped her leg. "Praise *Jesus*! Another Christian in our new neighborhood! What did you say your name is . . . Grace — ?"

"Grace Meredith."

Mrs. Bentley shook her head. "My, my. I'm sorry to say I haven't heard of you. But that's my fault — I don't keep up with the new crop of Christian musicians. And, have to admit I listen mostly to gospel — Babbie Mason, CeCe Winans, Fred Hammond — folks like that. But I'd love to hear your songs sometime."

"That's all right." Grace smiled, trying to put the woman at ease. Oreo was back and hopped up on the couch, staring with unabashed curiosity at the visitor. "Oreo! Shoo! I'm sorry . . . are you okay with cats?"

"Oh, no problem. We've got a *dog* now." Estelle rolled her eyes. "Takes a lot more work than a cat. Now *there's* a story . . . say! Would you like to come over to our house for supper sometime this week? Harry will be so delighted that we have a Christian sister for a neighbor! And then you can meet the rest of the family — our grandson, DaShawn, you've probably seen him around, and his daddy, Rodney, who's just here temporary-like . . . well, long story there. But then we can really get acquainted." She stood up. "I should go. But please come. What evening would be good for you?"

Grace also stood, swallowing the bite of cinnamon roll she had in her mouth with difficulty. Go to *supper* at their house? She didn't even know these people! "Uh . . ."

"Now don't say no. As much as you travel, I'm sure you can use a good home-cooked meal. What about Wednesday? I get home from work about four, Harry comes in about six . . . would six thirty be okay?"

Grace licked her lips, her mind scrambling. She had to send her song list to Barry today . . . the band would practice the music tomorrow night . . . then she was supposed to practice with the band Tuesday night and Thursday, leaving for St. Louis on Friday . . .

Nothing on Wednesday.

"Well . . . all right. I think I could make it Wednesday night."

"Praise Jesus! See you at six thirty then." Estelle Bentley gave Grace a quick hug, pulled her red wool poncho over her head, and headed for the door.

When the new neighbor had left, Grace just stood in the middle of her living room. Had she really agreed to go to supper at the Bentley home that coming Wednesday? She should have excused herself, said she was too busy preparing for the upcoming concert.

Because the truth of the matter was, she had too much on her plate right now to deal with getting to know new people. Estelle Bentley was so eager to "really get acquainted." But that meant people asking you questions and having to talk about yourself. And right now, she didn't feel very confident — about herself, about her work, about . . . anything.

Sighing, Grace gathered up the coffee mugs, plate of cinnamon rolls, and her dirty lunch dishes and headed for the kitchen. Cleanup done, she stood by the kitchen window and contemplated the two-flat across the street. Her new neighbors. Okay, this was silly, but . . . she'd never had supper with a black family before. Not in their own home. She'd eaten with Samantha, sure, here at her house or in a zillion restaurants, but she'd never been to Sam's apartment. Or her church. Never had to be the minority.

What did that say about her? *Hey, diversity is fine as long as I can stay on my own turf. Just don't take me out of my comfort zone!*

How pathetic was that?

Grace turned from the window. She should go. After all, the lady seemed really nice. And they were Christians too. Wait till she told Sam — she'd probably never hear the end of it.

CHAPTER 24

Grace studied her closet. What does a person wear when you go to dinner at a stranger's house? Not too dressy — something casual but not grungy. Maybe her black slacks, a turquoise knit top, and some silver-and-turquoise jewelry — the Native American set she'd bought for herself the last time she sang in Tucson. She wouldn't need a coat — it had actually gotten up to the mid-seventies today! A perfect spring evening.

She should take a hostess gift — flowers? box of chocolates? She'd have to run out and — *wait.* Mrs. Bentley had said she'd like to hear her songs. Maybe she should take one of her CDs as a gift. Or was that too self-serving? *Hey, look at me!* Worse, what if they didn't like her music? Mrs. Bentley said she mostly listened to gospel — probably black gospel. Still, it was the thought that counted, wasn't it?

In spite of feeling as nervous as the time she'd first met Roger's parents, Grace showed up on the small porch of the Bentleys' two-flat and rang the bell. *The Bentleys' two-flat . . .* strange to think of it that way. It'd always been "the old lady's house" in her thoughts. Even that was wrong. Should've been "Mrs. Krakowski's house."

She still hadn't heard if the old woman had survived her ordeal.

The door opened. A boy about twelve or thirteen with close-cropped black hair looked at her curiously. "You Miz Meredith?" When Grace nodded, he pulled the door wider so she could step into the spacious foyer. An open stairway on the right led to the second floor. A door on the left must be to the first-floor apartment. The boy yelled up the stairs, "Yo, Pops! The lady's here!" He turned back to Grace. "Go on up. They expectin' you."

As Grace started up the carpeted stairs to the second floor, she heard the boy open the door on the left and yell, "Hey, Dad! Supper's ready! An' we got company!"

Well, at least she knew what the relationship was.

As Grace got to the top of the stairs, a black man about six feet tall with a smooth shaved head met her with a warm smile in

268

the open doorway. "You must be Grace. Estelle's been telling me all about you." Up close, she noticed a trim gray beard and moustache framed just his mouth and chin. Shave the head, grow it on the face. But it made him look distinguished.

He shook her hand, introduced himself as "Harry," and ushered her into a sparse living room facing the street. Nothing fancy — just a couch and a couple chairs, a flatscreen TV, an area rug on the floor, no pictures on the wall, but a couple large plants hung in the bay windows and several more were sitting on floor stands. The bay windows were open, letting in a light breeze.

Grace took a seat on the couch just as Estelle Bentley bustled in, wearing a large white apron and carrying a tray with several small glasses. "There she is! No, no, don't get up, young lady. Would you like some cranberry juice? It's nice and cold, feels good on a warm day like this."

Grace took a glass and smiled her thanks. Her hostess was wearing her hair pulled back from her face and gathered on top of her head in a loose topknot, which seemed to enhance her large eyes and generous mouth.

"Mercy! We're so glad you came," Estelle beamed. "Supper will be ready quicker'n water runnin' downhill . . . now where did that boy slip off to? *DaShawn!* Come finish settin' the table! An' Harry, call Rodney. Don't want my food coolin' its heels on the table while we hunt everybody down."

Estelle bustled back toward the kitchen, while Harry excused himself and disappeared down the stairs toward the first floor, leaving Grace alone in the living room, sipping her cranberry juice and wondering just what she was doing there.

But the boy came running up the stairs a moment later, threw her a grin, and headed for the kitchen, followed by Harry Bentley at a more moderate pace, and a younger man she presumed was the boy's father. She stood up as Harry said, "Miss Meredith, this is my son, Rodney . . . Rodney, Grace Meredith, one of our new neighbors."

"How ya doin'?" Rodney mumbled, giving her hand a quick shake. He sat down on the edge of one of the chairs, as if not planning to stay long. He was taller than his father, slender, with muscular arms and tattoos peeking out from his short shirtsleeves, hair an inch or so long worn in a short, careless afro, and eyes that didn't quite look you in the eye. Maybe thirty-five?

"Y'all can come on to the table now," Estelle called from the other room. Grace followed Harry into the dining room, where a wooden table surrounded by five chairs — only three of which matched — had been set with bamboo placemats and blue-rimmed ceramic dishes. Harry pulled out one of the chairs for Grace and she sat down, eyeing the table, which seemed piled with food — a platter of pungent fried chicken, another with thick slices of ham, a creamy yellow casserole that looked like macaroni and cheese, and a bowl of steaming green beans dripping butter. As the rest of them sat, Estelle came in carrying a basket covered by a red-checked cloth. DaShawn licked his lips and made a grab for the basket, but she slapped his hand away. "That cornbread just came outta th' oven, young man. Gonna burn your fingers." She sat down with an *oomph*. "Now I know this here's a high-yeller meal" — Grace heard Rodney snicker — "but them green beans an' ham oughta color up the plate. Harry, ya gonna do the honors?"

A "high-yeller meal"? Must be all the yellow food dishes, but what was so funny? Grace realized the Bentleys were reaching out their hands to make a circle around the table, so she held the hands of Estelle and DaShawn, who were sitting on either side of her, and bowed her head as Harry began

271

his prayer.

"Lord God" — he cleared his throat — "for food in a world where many walk in hunger, for faith in a world where many walk in fear, and for friends in a world where many walk alone, we give you thanks . . ."

Goosebumps prickled on Grace's skin as Harry said, "Amen." *What a beautiful prayer.* She blinked rapidly before looking up, hoping she wouldn't get all teary in front of these people. But she wasn't the only one who was touched. Estelle said, "Harry Bentley, where'd you get that prayer? Never heard you pray like that!"

Harry just grunted as he reached for the platter of fried chicken. "Don't you remember? Last Thanksgiving, at the Manna House dinner, that Canadian pastor prayed it. When I looked around at all those women at the shelter, I thought, *That says it all.* Been bouncin' around in my head ever since. But maybe you were still back in the kitchen, might not've heard it . . . Rodney, pass this on down to our guest. DaShawn, you wait."

The Bentleys made sure Grace got served first, and soon her plate was full. "This all tastes wonderful," she said to Estelle, after spending several minutes sampling every-

272

thing. "You shouldn't have gone to so much trouble on my account. I'm used to cooking for one, so it's usually pretty simple."

"Trouble?" Estelle's husband chuckled, waving a forkful of ham and green beans. "My wife lives to cook! She cooks for the Manna House Women's Shelter, you know."

"Is that why you married Miz Estelle, Grandpa?" DaShawn piped up. "So's you could eat good?"

"Now there's a smart young man." Harry pointed the fork at his grandson and grinned before popping the food into his mouth.

Miz Estelle? Odd thing to call his grandmother . . . unless she wasn't. Grace smiled at their teasing, but turned back to Estelle. "You cook for a women's shelter? I'd like to hear more about that." This gave her a chance to eat more of the yummy macaroni and cheese on her plate. It was nothing like the box kind!

Estelle shrugged. "Not much to tell. Stayed there myself for a time, till it burned down. Bunch of good sisters at SouledOut Community Church helped me get back on my feet, so I decided one way to give back was volunteer at the shelter when it got up an' runnin' again, which turned into a job —"

" 'Cause they liked her cookin'." Harry

winked at his wife.

"You . . . just eat," Estelle scolded. "What I want to hear about is Grace's singin'. I'm just sorry we don't have a piano, 'cause I sure would love to hear you sing."

Grace flushed. "Well, I did bring one of my CDs as a gift for you. Mostly songs I've written. Contemporary praise and worship music."

DaShawn's eyes got big. "You got a CD? Can I listen to it? I got my own CD player. An' I already got fifteen CDs. But Grandpa won't let me listen to —"

"DaShawn! You're interrupting." Harry gave his grandson a warning eye. "That's real nice of you, Miss Meredith. We'd love to hear it. My wife tells me you travel 'round the country givin' concerts, said you just got back from someplace and got another trip comin' up this weekend . . . Now, you go ahead an' eat that chicken with your fingers," he added, picking up his own piece. "We got plenty napkins."

Grace gratefully picked up her chicken and took a bite. Ohhh, so crispy on the outside, juicy on the inside. But Estelle asked, "Do you travel every weekend?"

Grace took a moment to chew and swallow. She felt flattered by their interest in her concerts. "Well," she said, wiping her mouth

274

and fingers with a paper napkin, "when I'm on tour, it's several weeks at a time, actually." She briefly described her New Year, New You tour in January, and told about the ten-day West Coast tour coming up. "But the last few weekends I've had a couple college concerts, and I'll be going to St. Louis on Friday. Some of these large churches have wonderful auditoriums with state-of-the-art sound systems, everything." She paused for a breath, suddenly feeling as if she'd said too much.

"All those concerts . . . Lord, have mercy! You must be flyin' here, there, an' everywhere." Estelle shook her head, her topknot flopping loosely. "Don't think I'd like that — but if that's how the Lord's usin' you to bless others, why, I just say praise the Lord!"

Estelle's comment seemed to stick in Grace's throat. She coughed, reached for her glass, and took a sip of water. "Sorry . . . I've been doing all the talking. Think I better eat before my food gets cold. It's all so good." She lifted a bite of macaroni and cheese. "Uh, what about you, Mr. Bentley? What kind of work do you do?"

Harry Bentley chuckled self-consciously. "Well, believe it or not, I'm supposed to be retired. Used to be a Chicago cop — but I just got pulled back workin' for Amtrak police. Only been on the job a week."

"Yeah, an' now we got a dog — ow!" DaShawn glared at his father and grandfather, as if one of them had kicked him under the table. Well, Grace thought, at least they were training him not to interrupt — though she hadn't seen any sign of a dog.

"Rodney, you and DaShawn done?" Estelle said. "Why don't you two go in the living room and watch some TV. I'll call you back when it's time for dessert."

Rodney hadn't said a word during the meal, and he and the boy had indeed polished off their plates. The two disappeared into the next room, and a moment later she heard the TV leap to life.

"Keep it down!" Estelle called after them. The TV sound was muffled.

"Must be nice having a two-flat so your son and grandson can live so close to you," Grace said, returning to her meal. But out of the corner of her eye she saw Estelle and her husband exchange a quick glance.

Harry cleared his throat. "Actually, DaShawn lives with us. And we're lookin' to rent out the first-floor apartment. Rodney's just stayin' down there temporary-like, helpin' with the renovations. Been a big help . . . but he's lookin' for a job."

"That's right," Estelle nodded. "Something you can help us pray for. Also the poor woman who used to live here needs our prayers. Did you know Mattie Krakowski?"

Grace shook her head. "Not really." *Not at all, really.* So that was her full name — Mattie Krakowski. "I know she had an accident, but I haven't heard —"

"Poor soul." Estelle wagged her head. "Guess she broke her hip, had to have surgery, and her son put her into a nursin' home. My heart just goes out to her."

So. Mrs. Krakowski hadn't died after all. But then why had her house been sold right out from under her? Had these people taken advantage of her bad fortune? No, no, she shouldn't think like that. There'd been that foreclosure sign out front even before the old lady fell. She must've been losing the house already. And there was just something about the Bentleys. Something solid, something real.

Grace laid down her fork and wiped her mouth with her napkin. "Wonderful dinner, Mrs. Bentley. Can I help clear the table?"

"Now that's what I'm talkin' about!" Estelle chuckled as she got up. "Somebody trained you right, young lady. I'm still trainin' the young men in this family, though this ol' man" — she gave Harry a playful poke as he passed her on the way to the kitchen carrying a couple dishes — "he came already trained, 'cause he'd been bachin' for so long."

Grace smiled to herself. It was fun to see a couple their age still joking with each other. Sounded like they hadn't been married long. For the next few minutes, Grace helped Harry clear dishes from the table and load the dishwasher as Estelle put away leftovers.

"So . . . tell us about this upcoming concert," Estelle said, starting a pot of coffee. "Somethin' like that must take a lot of preparation. How can we pray for you?"

Grace was startled. The gentle request brought tears to her eyes and she had to grab a paper napkin. "I — I'm sorry . . . thank you," she whispered. "I do need some prayer." Why did she feel as if these people, whom she'd barely met, were people who might actually understand?

"Now, now," Estelle clucked, "nothin' to be sorry about. You sit down there at the kitchen table, honey . . . that's it. Harry, hand me that tissue box. Now, tell us what needs some prayer."

Grace traded the paper napkin for a tissue. "Well, I — I haven't had much time to prepare for this one . . ." Grace found herself telling the Bentleys about coming home from her last tour with a virus, dealing with a lot of stress, losing her voice, and having to cancel some concerts. "My agent added the St. Louis concert kind of last minute as a way to make up for the ones I had to cancel. But I'm having a hard time getting my confidence back. Was supposed to fly last weekend, but . . ." Darn! The tears welled up again. How could she explain her panic attack?

"It's all right, baby, it's all right." Estelle patted her hand and handed her another tissue.

Grace shook her head, frustrated at herself. *Baby* was right. But she felt like she needed to justify herself. "Okay, see, I . . . I had a pretty awful experience with airport security back in January coming home from the tour, and last weekend . . . well, guess the memory of my last experience was too fresh. I backed out at the last minute. So my assistant had to rent a car and drive us to Ohio. We're going to drive to St. Louis too."

"Well, now, that seems wise," Estelle said kindly.

Grace just stared down at the tissue she was twisting into a little ball in her hands, afraid to look up at the two faces listening to her spill her guts. "Except the West Coast tour is coming up. Once the tour starts in Seattle, I'll have a tour bus. But I've got to get there first. I just" — she spit out the words more fiercely than she intended — "just *don't* want to deal with airports anymore." She rolled her eyes apologetically and blew out a long breath. "So guess I could really use some prayer about that."

Estelle patted her hand again. "Well, we can sure pray about —"

"Why don't you take the train?" Harry said.

Now Grace did look up. "What?"

"The train. They handle security a lot different on the trains. You hardly know they're there. Like I said, I just started workin' for Amtrak, and they've got trains goin' everywhere. Yeah, yeah, we think everybody flies these days, but that ain't the only way to get from here to there. In fact, they got trains runnin' several times a day to St. Louis. You could try it this weekend, see if you like it."

Grace just stared at her host. She had never considered traveling by train.

"Well, now. That's somethin' to think about," Estelle said. "So how 'bout we pray about it, and then top it off with that banana cream pie I made that's just beggin' to be eaten!"

CHAPTER 25

The moment she got in the door, Grace pulled out her phone. *Nine forty-five . . .* was it too late to call Samantha? But if they were going to take the train this weekend, they had to get on it.

Sam's phone rang once and went straight to voice mail. Grace left a message: "Call me tonight if you can."

A few minutes later a text message pinged on her phone: *"Still in prayer mtg. Will call in 30 min. U okay?"*

Thirty minutes. Might as well check it out before Sam called. Grace booted up her laptop and Googled the Amtrak site. She clicked on Schedules and typed in "From Chicago, To St. Louis" . . . Mr. Bentley was right. There were five trains to St. Louis every day, two in the morning, three in the afternoon. And return trip . . . another five options.

By the time Sam called, Grace felt giddy.

She gave her assistant a quick rundown of her evening with the Bentleys and Mr. Bentley's idea to take the train. "Look, I figured it out. Actual travel time is practically the same as driving, might even be close to the same as flying if you add in all the time we waste getting there an hour or two early to check bags and go through security, blah, blah, blah." Grace laughed. "It's win-win! I won't have to fly and you won't have to drive."

"Well . . . sure," Sam said. "I like the train. I've taken the City of New Orleans to Memphis a couple times — runs overnight, but I always took coach. Anyway, I should probably call Amtrak directly to make reservations since it's such short notice. You said the trains run five times a day? What time do you want to go?"

They decided on the nine thirty morning train, getting in at three, to allow for any delays. "Uh, Grace, one more thing . . . if I can get tickets, do you want me to cancel the rental car, or hold on to it just in case?"

Ouch. Guess she deserved that after her behavior at the airport last weekend. But no back doors this time. "Cancel it. Mr. Bentley said they handle security much more unobtrusively at train stations. I think it'll be fine."

Grace woke up the next morning with snatches of words dancing to a new tune in her mind. *One born to die . . . Only one Way . . . One life for mine . . . One empty grave . . .* Could she work this into a new song? She hadn't written anything since before the New Year, New You tour. Excited, she was at the piano before breakfast, sounding out the tune tumbling in her head, when her phone rang.

It was Sam. "Okay, here's the deal. We forgot it's Easter weekend. The nine-thirty train on Friday is totally sold out, same with all three afternoon trains. However, I was able to get two business-class seats on the early train — seven o'clock. Means we'd need to get to the station by six thirty at the latest to pick up our tickets — six would be even better given the holiday crowds. Still up for it?"

Grace considered. If they drove, they could leave whenever. But this was her chance to test whether train travel would work for the trip to the West Coast. "I am if you are. We could meet at the station."

"Okay. You're the boss. Gotta get on it, so talk to you later — oh. Better call Newman at Bongo, tell him about the change in plans. He should let the folks at the church know when we're coming in."

"Okay. See you tonight at practice. I might have a new song —"

But Sam had already hung up.

Grace worked on the song a while longer, and then glanced at the schoolhouse clock. Ten after nine . . . it was an hour earlier in Denver. Did Jeff come in at eight?

"Grace! You're up and about early." Jeff's warm voice on the phone made her smile. "Everything still good for the St. Louis concert this weekend?"

"Yeah, great. That's why I'm calling. Wanted to let you know that Sam and I are going to take the train to St. Louis on Friday. Sam's working on getting tickets now. She'll e-mail you the itinerary as soon as we get it."

"The train? I just assumed you'd fly. Wouldn't it be faster? Look, if it's money, you shouldn't worry. This church has a fat budget and will cover all expenses for you and the band, plus your honorarium. They've reserved your hotel — I'll send you the confirmation."

"Oh, it's not that." Suddenly Grace felt confused. Hadn't she told Jeff about what happened at the Memphis airport? She'd told Samantha . . . and now the Bentleys, for heaven's sake. She'd told Jeff about her broken engagement, but hadn't said anything to the Bentleys about Roger . . . and what had she told her folks? They knew about Roger, but not about . . .

Grace pressed fingers to her forehead, trying to think. She couldn't remember who knew what. When Jeff had called her early in the week to ask how the Cincinnati concert went, she hadn't said anything about the failed attempt at flying. She'd been too embarrassed by her panic attack.

"Grace? What is it? Is everything all right?"

She took a deep breath. "Yes, yes, fine. I'll, uh, explain later. Don't worry, we're allowing plenty of time. Can you let them know Sam and I are coming in by train, and ask do they want to pick us up, or should we arrange for a limo or taxi? The band is still driving down. We'll need the church most of the day on Saturday to set up and do a run-through."

Grace noticed a brief pause before Jeff said, "All right. Have Sam send me the itinerary and I'll take care of everything on this end and get back to you. Is there anything else I can do, Grace, to make this weekend easier? I know we scheduled this last minute — so sorry about that."

"It's . . . it's all right. I think everything's coming together. I'll let you know if there's anything else. Just, you know, could use more of those prayers you said the Bongo staff does every morning."

As they said good-bye and hung up, Grace realized she meant it too.

Practice with the band that night ran late, and Grace had to be up at four thirty Friday morning — limo was coming at five thirty to get her to Union Station by six. But she figured she could catch a nap on the train, and she'd make sure she got to bed early at the hotel that night. It was smart to go a day early.

It was a good thing they'd decided to arrive at six to pick up their tickets because boarding the early morning commuter began at six thirty. Sam, a little bleary-eyed herself, helped Grace stow their suitcases in the luggage area over their reserved seats in the club-dinette car, and then said, "I'm going to get us some coffee."

Grace watched, amused, as her assistant moved to the snack bar in the middle of the car, and then she sank down into the wide burgundy Naugahyde seat by the window. This Amfleet club car was nice . . . very nice. Wide seats — two on one side, just

286

one on the other — spacious legroom, snack bar handy, six tables at the other end. She wondered what the regular coach cars were like.

Sam brought back coffee, two yogurt cups, and two cinnamon bagels with cream cheese. "Breakfast!" she grinned. "Want to eat here or back there at one of the tables?"

"Here's fine." But even with the coffee, Grace managed to doze off before the train passed Joliet . . . and woke an hour later as the train pulled into the station at Bloomington-Normal.

"Hey, sleepyhead." Sam had on her reading light and was leafing through a magazine she'd brought along. "Figured out one good thing about taking this early train — fewer stops. It's only been a couple hours, about three to go. But we should get there about noon."

Grace got up to use the restroom, then made her way back to their seats. The car was full, but didn't feel crowded. Several people were playing cards at the tables in the back, laughing and talking, or just drinking coffee and reading the newspaper. Others were in their seats, working on their laptops or reading. Or zonked, legs stretched out on the retractable footrest.

This really was a great way to travel. And

she didn't have to feel guilty about Sam doing all that driving just so she could be rested.

Cornfields of yellow stubble and pastures just beginning to turn a hopeful green flashed by the window. A few farmers were turning over their fields with monster tractors, getting ready for planting. The mournful train whistle sounded its warning at every rural crossing, and once she saw a horse pulling an Amish buggy down a road at a real clip. Things she'd never hear or see thousands of feet in the sky. Nice.

But . . . would it be feasible to take the train all the way to Seattle? It might take a few days to get there, but once the tour started, they'd have a tour bus from Seattle to LA, and then a few days back by train.

It was her time, after all. Well, Sam's too. Grace really didn't want to travel alone. But maybe she should give the girl the option.

Grace opened her notebook and worked a little more on the song she'd been playing with that she'd titled "One." Would the band be able to pick it up on such short notice? Except . . . some of the lyrics just weren't coming together. Maybe trying to do a new song was a bad idea.

A young man sporting a grin, a two-day

288

growth of beard, jeans, and a T-shirt, and a blonde woman dressed in a modest navy suit were holding up an eight-by-ten-inch sign saying "Welcome Grace Meredith" when Grace and Sam made their way into the St. Louis Gateway Station among hundreds of travelers coming or going.

"Hello!" Beaming, the woman reached out to shake Grace's hand. "I'm Willa Baker, this is Doug Swarthmore. We are so thrilled you were able to come. We've been blanketing the city with radio promo and sending invitations to all the churches, so hopefully we'll have a good crowd tomorrow night. Is this all your luggage, or did you check some bags?" She seemed to notice Samantha for the first time. "And this is . . . ?"

Grace introduced Sam as "Samantha Curtis, without whom the world might stand still," which earned her a smirky glance from Sam. Once in the church van that proclaimed Hawthorn Christian Fellowship along both sides in large letters, Willa chatted on. They learned that Doug was part of the sound team at Hawthorn and would be working with the band for the concert tomorrow night. And Willa was the event coordinator.

"We didn't expect you quite this early —

just got the call from Bongo yesterday that you were arriving by train. But it's all good," the woman giggled. "The hotel should let us check you in early. We don't have any dinner plans for tonight, but the hotel has a fine restaurant. Of course, you're welcome to join us for our Good Friday service — starts at eight o'clock."

Grace felt torn. It was Easter weekend, after all. But there was probably no way she could just slip in and slip out, and both she and Sam had been up since before sunup. "Sounds tempting," she murmured. "but we, uh, have prep to do for tomorrow." And she'd like more time to work on that new song. "But I have a question . . . I'd love a meet and greet time after the concert tomorrow night. Would that work out?"

"Oooo. Great idea. We'll make sure to reserve a room for that. How many people should we invite? I'm sure the ministry team and pastoral team — if they're at the concert — would love a chance to chat with you."

Grace glanced at Sam, giving her a *Say something!* look.

"I think what Miss Meredith means is, she'd like to meet some of the concertgoers, especially some of the young people — teens, college age."

"Oh. Yes, of course . . ." she said. "We'll

work out something."

The auditorium of Hawthorn Christian Fellowship was beautiful — and immense. "Going to be a bit embarrassing if we don't fill it," Grace murmured to Sam as they walked in the next morning, taking in the rows upon rows of plush, red theater-type seats.

"Don't worry about it. God'll bring whoever's supposed to be here tonight. Just pick one person and sing to that person — oh, there's Barry. Gotta talk to him about the changes you want to make in the first set." Sam waved at the band manager, who was testing microphones and set off toward the stage.

Grace felt slightly chided by her assistant — but of course Sam was right. *This isn't about me,* she told herself — but she still hoped they had a decent crowd.

The practice sessions went well — except for the new song. The poetry just wasn't clicking. Petey said he'd like to work more on the melody. "Give it some time," Barry said. "Maybe you can do it on tour."

Grace was disappointed. It took her down a peg or two. Would she ever be able to write her own songs again?

As she and Sam waited offstage that

evening for her cue to begin, she caught a glimpse of the auditorium. The balconies were sparse, but the lower level was nearly full, which, she'd been told, held at least a thousand. *Thank you, Lord!* A good crowd after all. Mostly a sea of white faces, though, which was often the case at her concerts. How did Sam feel about that, or Zach in the band, always playing to mostly white audiences?

She'd never really thought about that before. Somehow meeting the Bentleys in their home, wondering if they'd like to come to one of her concerts . . . She'd love to draw a more multicultural crowd, but how? Could she sing gospel — the kind Estelle Bentley listened to? Probably not, though she'd heard the band cut loose on some gospel songs a few times, just jamming. Maybe —

"You're on," Sam murmured, giving her a nudge.

". . . our special guest, straight from Chicago — Grace Meredith!" The dramatic announcement by Hawthorn's minister of music brought a burst of applause from the audience.

Grace took a deep breath, put on a smile, and sailed over the red carpeting of the large stage into the spotlights, carried by the applause. As they'd planned, the band began a soulful introduction to "Rock of Ages," a hymn that bridged Good Friday and Easter. As she waited for the applause to die and her eyes to adjust to the bright lights, she remembered what Sam had said earlier: "Pick one person and just sing to that person." Might help her focus . . . ah, there was her musical cue.

"Rock of Ages, cleft for me . . ." Her start was strong, low and steady. "Let me hide myself in thee!" Faces were beginning to emerge from the bright lights. Her eyes swept the first row as she sang the next line: "Let the water and the blood, from thy wounded side which flowed . . ."

There. A young teenager in a red sweater caught her eye, face enraptured. She'd focus on her.

"Be of sin the double cure, save from wrath and make me pure . . ."

The band repeated the melody of the last line before starting in on the second verse. A man sitting next to the girl had a big smile on his face. Must be her father —

Wait. No . . . it couldn't be!

But it was.

Her agent. Jeff Newman.

CHAPTER 26

Willa Baker found Grace at intermission and told her they'd picked twenty people at random to get "backstage passes" for the meet and greet time. Grace told her to be sure to include the girl in the red sweater in the front row and anyone she was with. "And that's my agent sitting next to her. Bring him back too."

"That's Jeff Newman?" Willa Baker peeked into the sanctuary. "Of course! He arranged this whole concert. We spent hours on the phone — he was so helpful." She peeked again and tittered. "Gosh, he's hot. Is he single?"

Grace stopped short of rolling her eyes.

But she had to hand it to the event coordinator: there was even coffee and lemonade in the church lounge for the meet and greet after the concert. Grace hugged the girl in the red sweater — "I'm Becky," the girl said, giggling with two of her friends —

and told her she was her inspiration that evening. "I was?" Becky's eyes went wide, setting off another round of giggles and embarrassed hands covering her face.

But Grace kept looking for Jeff — and finally saw him as the crowd thinned, leaning against the wall with a paper cup of coffee, still grinning. She'd almost forgotten how attractive he was — all that dark curly hair and a dark shadow where a beard would be if he let it grow. She made her way over to him and spouted, "Jeff Newman! Don't ever do that again! At least warn me next time you decide to spy on my concert. I nearly forgot a verse!"

The lopsided grin got wider. "Sorry about that. Though it was kind of fun to catch your eye and watch you flounder for a second or two. Nice recovery though." He nodded approvingly. "Good concert. Your voice sounds really great."

That was sweet to hear. She'd tanked up on lozenges and hot tea during the short intermission while the Hawthorn emcee took an offering for something or other, but personally she'd felt her voice had stayed clear and strong. "But what are you doing here? I just talked to you in Colorado on Thursday!"

He shrugged. "Felt kinda bad, arranging

this venue so last minute. Realized you were making a major effort to get here and had to come up with a whole new song set on top of it. Thought the least I could do was show up and give you some support. Besides, I haven't ever heard you in live concert. Decided this weekend was as good as any — well, except for the holiday. Yesterday was a madhouse at the airport, but I was able to get a flight this afternoon, and . . . here I am." The grin again.

Grace hardly knew what to say. She was glad to see him — but she also felt awkward. Before she could respond, he waggled his paper cup. "This coffee doesn't quite make it. Any chance you'd be up for a real cup of joe or something? I saw a coffee bar on the next block. But if you're wiped and need to crash . . ."

"No, no, that'd be great. Takes me a couple hours to wind down after a concert, anyway. But I should tell Sam — oh, speaking of Sam . . ."

Grace waved Sam over, feeling slightly giddy with adrenaline and fatigue. "Sam, this is Jeff Newman, my new agent, who showed up tonight unannounced and had the bad manners to sit in the front row." She deliberately kept a straight face. "And Jeff, this is Samantha Curtis, my assistant

— in name only. She's actually She Who Must Be Obeyed. You two have talked on the phone, right?" Ignoring the face Sam made, Grace added, "Anyway, Sam, we're going out for coffee to take care of some business, won't be long." *Business* . . . why did she say that? Jeff hadn't said anything about "taking care of business."

But Jeff just greeted Sam warmly — "About time we met in person!" — and said he'd get Grace back to the hotel in an hour. Sam tossed her twists and looked him over with a critical eye. "You better. We have to be at the train station in the morning by seven thirty. Bum way to spend Easter Sunday, but had to take what we could get. Anyway, go . . . go." She fluttered a hand at Grace. "I'll pack up your stuff in the dressing room. But don't be late!" She scurried off with her clipboard.

Chuckling, Jeff escorted Grace out of the church. "So that fire-cracker is Samantha Curtis. How old is she?"

"Twenty-five, I think." Grace pulled her soft pashmina shawl around her shoulders against the cool April air. "Yeah, she's bossy — that's what I pay her for — but she's a jewel. Don't know what I'd do without her. Ethnic food and chocolate are her cure for everything, I think — though I drew the line

297

at the pajama party she tried to cook up a couple weeks ago."

"Pajama party!" He thought that was pretty funny. Grace didn't mention she kind of wished she'd gone. But a few minutes later they slid into a booth at the coffee bar a block away and ordered two decaf lattes. Grace felt herself relaxing. "So tell me what you thought of the concert."

Jeff laid an arm along the back of the padded booth and seemed to be studying her. "As I already said, it was a nice concert. And your voice is sounding great."

Nice. For the first time, Grace heard a qualification in the word. Not "great," not "awesome."

She sighed. "Okay. I need to know. What did you really think? To be honest, I've been struggling with getting my confidence back, so I know I wasn't at a hundred percent."

He didn't answer right away, again seemed to be studying her. She felt a bit flustered. Was her hair a mess? Had she chewed off all her lipstick?

The lattes came and he leaned forward, wrapping both hands around his tall mug. "What I said was true. It was a nice concert — very nice. Good theme for Easter weekend, some real good song choices. But . . ."

She winced. "Uh-huh. I knew it." *Don't*

cry, you big baby, she told herself. She took a sip of her latte and realized her hand was shaking.

"Something was missing. Your passion." Jeff leaned forward. "Grace, I've seen the video from your New Year, New You tour, and you had a *passion* in those concerts. Your songs, your stories, the way you talked to the audience — it all came from your heart. Maybe . . ." He frowned thoughtfully. "Have you thought about returning to that theme — encouraging young people to stay pure sexually, to believe they're 'worth waiting for,' as you so often said?"

Grace stared into her mug, slowly shaking her head. She couldn't. Not now. Not yet. She just wasn't ready to be that vulnerable. Not just because of the recent breakup and what that implied. But because she felt like such an imposter . . .

A lump formed in her throat and she couldn't speak.

Jeff sighed. "I'm sorry, Grace. You asked, and I wanted to be honest with you." He leaned forward. "Because I believe in you! You have the makings of a star — not the unreachable kind, but the sort of artist that everyone can relate to. And I know that passion for life is still there. It doesn't have to be the purity theme, or whatever you want to call it. You've had a setback, but you still have a lot to give. If the real Grace can crawl out of that hole where you've locked her away, your music will go off the charts."

Grace still shook her head, the lump in her throat growing larger. Her eyes blurred . . . but just then she felt Jeff's hand cover hers on the table. His touch sent little shivers up her arm. He spoke again. "Look deep inside, Grace. Tap into that passion, the truth that sets you free. I know it's there. You just have to know it too."

Sam took one look at Grace in the morning and said, "You okay? Didn't you sleep well last night?"

Grace grimaced. "Not the best. Just thinking about a lot of stuff. I'll be okay." She stifled a yawn. "But I definitely need coffee. Maybe a bagel. Is the hotel café open yet?"

"Mm-hm." Sam arched an eyebrow at her knowingly. "You didn't tell me he was so good-looking."

"Oh, come on! He's my agent. We talked about my voice, the concert, stuff like that." She colored slightly. But it was true, wasn't it?

They managed to get to the train station by seven thirty, and once on board, Grace got an Amtrak pillow and pretended to be

300

asleep most of the way back to Chicago. But she kept thinking about what Jeff had said about tapping into something she felt passionately about . . . and knew it was true. Something was missing from her music. "Look deep inside . . ." he had said.

That was the problem.

She was scared to look too deep. Scared to poke at old wounds. Afraid of what she might find. Afraid of how people would see her. Or maybe afraid of how she would see herself.

Grace dozed on and off as the train whistled its way through the Illinois countryside at every country crossing, her conversation with Jeff weaving in and out of her semiconsciousness, along with the memory of his touch when he laid his hand over hers . . .

"Grace? Grace . . . we're pulling into Union Station." Sam's gentle shaking pulled Grace out of her stupor. She shook the sleep from her head and helped gather their suitcases and various bags.

"I feel sorry for the band," Sam said, as the train eased to a stop with a slight bump and they made their way to the exit. "They're probably still on the road — and here we are, fresh as a daisy."

The Amtrak station was full of travelers,

301

even though it was the middle of the day on Easter Sunday. "Oh, forgot to tell you," Sam said as they threaded their way through the crowd. "Couldn't get a limo for the ride home. Lincoln said all their drivers were booked this weekend — the holiday, I guess. Hopefully we can get a couple of taxis."

"That's all right. Just sorry you had to miss Easter services." Grace gave her assistant a hug after Sam hailed two separate taxis. "But thanks for everything. Don't come to work tomorrow — we both need to take a day or two off."

"You still thinking about taking the train to Seattle?"

Grace nodded. "Thinking about it. I know we have to decide. I'll call you tomorrow, maybe we can talk about it then."

"Okay. I might go ahead and check train schedules, see what's available. Sleeper car, right?"

Grace grinned as she climbed into the back seat of the Yellow Cab. "Definitely. But not today! Go home. Go to church. Do something besides thinking about that West Coast tour."

"Somebody has to think about it."

At least that's what Grace thought Sam said as her assistant shut the back door of the taxi, waving from the curb as the cab driver pulled away.

As Grace was letting herself into the house, she saw the Bentleys' RAV4 pass by and do a turnaround in the cul-de-sac. *Wonder where they go to church . . .*

She waved as the small SUV parked in front of the old lady's two-flat — in front of the *Bentleys'* two-flat, she reminded herself — but went on into the house and closed the door behind her. Grace didn't feel like chatting right now, but maybe later she'd go over and thank Mr. Bentley for suggesting the train. He was right. She hadn't even thought much about security going either way, though she'd seen some Amtrak police here and there, even one officer with a dog strolling among the passengers in the station.

That alone was enough to make her decide to take the train next time.

Her cell phone rang, muted somewhere in her purse, just as she picked up Oreo, who'd been meowing insistently ever since she walked in the door. "Let it ring," she murmured to the cat, holding him close and rubbing her face in his soft neck fur. "How've you been, baby? Yeah, yeah, I know, three days is a long time, but I'm home now . . ." But she couldn't leave the cat alone when she went on tour in a few weeks. She'd have to board him at Meeow Chicago again.

Only later, as she fixed herself a cheese omelet and popped Estelle Bentley's last cinnamon roll into the toaster oven to warm up, did she bother to get out her cell phone to see who called. She had a new voice mail . . . from Roger.

Grace caught her breath. *O Lord, now what?* Did she even want to listen to his message? She'd already given his ring back — what more did he want? But she tapped the Play button and held the phone to her ear, her heart rate speeding up a little . . .

"Hi, Grace, it's Roger. Was hoping to talk to you — just wanted to hear your voice, been wondering how you are. Call me back, okay? Or . . . I can try again later. Take care." And the message clicked off.

Chapter 27

Grace stood in the middle of the kitchen, stunned. Roger's voice — it was soft, almost tender. She pushed the Play button again. *". . . just wanted to hear your voice, been wondering how you are . . ."* Her neck prickled. Was he playing games with her? . . . No. He wouldn't be that cruel. But what did it mean?

A scorching smell pulled her out of her trance and she jerked the frying pan off the stove. So much for her "brunch." She dumped the burned omelet in the trash and started over. The cinnamon roll had cooled again in the toaster oven, but she ate it anyway, hardly noticing what she ate. Should she call him back? Wait for another call?

She decided to wait. Why not run across the street to thank Mr. Bentley for his suggestion to take the train to St. Louis. Maybe he'd have advice about the longer trip to Seattle.

The day was warm for April — in the seventies. *Nice.* The sky was clouding over, could be rain by evening. But she didn't need even a sweater to run across the street and ring the doorbell for the second floor of the two-flat. She didn't see the black car, but maybe they just put it in the garage —

The front door pulled open. The Bentleys' gangly grandson grinned at her. "Hey, Miz Grace. Happy Easter."

She returned his smile. "Happy Easter to you, DaShawn. Say, is your grandfather home?"

"Nah. He an' Miz Estelle went to the hospital to see my great-grandma. She had another stroke last night, but they thinkin' she might get better."

"Oh. I'm sorry to hear that — I mean, sorry to hear she had a stroke."

"DaShawn!" A male voice yelled from somewhere inside. "Who's at the door?"

A moment later, Rodney Bentley came striding out of the first-floor apartment, then slowed when he saw Grace.

"Oh, it's you . . . uh, Miss Meredith, right? Thought it might be someone else. You lookin' for my pop an' Estelle?"

Grace nodded. "DaShawn says they're at the hospital with his great-grandmother."

306

What *was* the relationship? Mrs. Bentley — Estelle — clearly wasn't the boy's natural grandmother, so probably not Rodney's mother either. How did the great-grandmother fit in here? Was she the elderly woman she'd seen with the Bentleys that time looking at the house before they bought it?

Rodney was saying, "Yeah, ya just missed 'em. But they oughta be back this evening. Don't think they'll stay overnight again."

"Yeah," DaShawn butted in, "they stayed all night last night and *still* went to church this mornin'!" He rolled his eyes. "Me, I'da crawled in the bed an' stayed there, Easter or no Easter."

Rodney seemed to give his son a *shut up* look and Grace realized she should go. "Well, I'll catch up with them later. Sorry to hear about your great-grandma, DaShawn. I hope she gets better."

She had started down the steps when she heard Rodney say, "Uh, Miss Meredith? If you hear about any job openings, I'd appreciate you lettin' me know. I'm lookin' for a job, any kind of job, the sooner the better."

Grace turned back. "Of course. I don't know of any offhand, but if I do hear of anything, I'll let you know." It was a lame thing to say, she decided, walking back across the street. She had no idea what jobs were available, blue collar or white collar. What kind of skills did he have, anyway? Why in the world did he ask *her*? There wasn't anything she could do about it —

"That's something you can pray about for us." That's what Mrs. Bentley had said when they were loading the dishwasher the other night.

Once in the house, Grace sank onto the couch — which Oreo considered a personal invitation to hop onto her lap. So at least she could pray. "Lord . . ." she murmured, and then paused. What should she pray? She started again. "Lord, the Bentleys' son needs a job, and they asked me to pray. So I'm asking you on Rodney's behalf that he'd find a job soon. And Lord, while I'm at it, be with the great-grandmother who's had a stroke. I don't know how bad it is, but it must be hard on . . . on . . ." *Hmm, whose mother was she?* ". . . hard on Harry and the rest of the family. Comfort them and help her to recover and may your will be done. Amen."

Oreo rubbed his head against her chest as if she'd been talking to him. Hopefully her prayers went further than *that* — though Grace sometimes still felt as if she was on probation with God.

Sudden tears welled up and Grace curled up in a ball on the couch, hugging the cat, who finally decided enough was enough and squeezed out of her grip. What was she going to do? Jeff Newman had told her to dig deep, to find her passion . . .

But she was afraid.

She must've dozed off, because she woke with a start. What was all that screaming and yelling . . . had she left the TV on? No, the screen was black. Rolling off the couch, she stumbled half-awake to the front window and peeked out. At first she didn't see anything — it was starting to rain, big fat drops sweeping across the street and pinging on her window. But then a movement caught her eye and she saw a skinny black woman in tight pink pants stomping down the opposite sidewalk, holding on to her hat or wig or whatever she had on her head. Across the street, Mr. Bentley and his grandson were heading into the house, followed by a black dog. Rodney stayed out on the porch of the two-flat watching the woman go, but before long he too disappeared into the house.

What was *that* all about?

■ ■ ■ ■

Pushing herself on the treadmill at Curves the next morning, Grace cranked up her walking speed from 3.5 to 3.7 . . . and up to 4.0. After ten minutes she pushed the speed even further, up to 4.5, and then 5.0, which made her jog. Sweat ran in little rivulets between her breasts. She couldn't keep up the pace for longer than ten minutes and slowed down to walking speed — but it felt good. She'd come a long way in two months. Maybe she'd start jogging for real, build up her strength.

Yesterday's tears had snuck up on her, but that was yesterday. She determined not to blubber about things she couldn't do anything about. On the treadmill she decided to call Roger back. Not during the day though. She didn't want to catch him at work or have to leave a message. She'd wait till tonight — if he didn't call first. After all, she was stronger now, and not just physically either. She didn't feel desperate. Yes, she was still sad, still disappointed about the broken engagement, but she and Roger had to make peace if she was going to move forward, right?

Once showered, breakfasted, and dressed,

Grace started to call Sam about travel arrangements for the West Coast tour, but glancing out the front window, she noticed the Bentleys' car out front. Maybe she should catch Harry.

This time when she rang the doorbell, a buzzer buzzed back and she pushed the door open. "Come on up!" called Estelle's voice from above.

Grace mounted the open stairs on the right. "It's me, Mrs. Bentley — Grace Meredith."

Estelle appeared in the open doorway as Grace turned the corner at the top. "Well, well," the older woman beamed. "Come on in, young lady. An' you can call me Estelle, all right? I'm glad to see you — though I've only got time for a quick cup of coffee, because I'm needin' to go to work soon. But come in, come in!"

"Oh, I can't stay," Grace hastened to say. "I just wanted to thank Mr. Bentley for encouraging me to try the train for my trip to St. Louis. I saw the car . . . is he here?"

Estelle laughed as she led the way back to the kitchen. "The Toyota? Don't go by the car — he's got an Amtrak car now." She grabbed two mugs from the cupboard and poured coffee. "Now sit, sit. Sorry, Harry's not home. He's already gone to work, won't be home till tomorrow. Somethin' they call doin' a short run . . . milk and sugar?"

Grace shook her head. "Just black. Thanks." She watched as Estelle stirred two heaping teaspoons of sugar into her own coffee before sinking down into a chair at the small kitchen table. "I came by yesterday, but DaShawn said you were at the hospital with his great-grandma, that she'd had a stroke. I'm sorry to hear that."

Estelle nodded soberly. "That's right, Lord have mercy! It's been a few weeks now since Mother Bentley had her first stroke. We were hoping she could move into the first-floor apartment — that's the reason we bought this place. Then she had another stroke over the weekend, an' they told us she was in a coma. But, praise Jesus! She woke up on Easter mornin', alert as you please, and we think she's gonna come through! Now you tell me, is God good or is God *good!*"

Grace nodded with a polite smile. She was curious about the woman who'd been yelling outside their house yesterday late afternoon, but she didn't want to ask.

"Now tell me how that concert went!" Estelle went on. "I was prayin' for you — well, have to admit, once we got word about Mother Bentley, that sort of took over my prayers. But I did pray for you. How did everything work out?"

"It was great. The train was restful, there was a good crowd Saturday night, and my voice held up. Thank you for the prayers. Since it was Easter weekend, I did a resurrection theme and I think it, um, went, um, well . . ." Grace suddenly faltered and looked away. Jeff's words echoed in her head: *The concert was "nice," but lacked passion.* She took a sip of her coffee to recover her composure.

Estelle eyed her carefully. "But . . . ?"

Grace slowly set her coffee mug down. The woman was too perceptive. "It's just . . . well, I need a focus for the West Coast tour and time is getting short. Now that the St. Louis concert is over, I need to start practice sessions with the band, but —" She shook her head. If she wasn't careful, she'd get blubbery again. Why did this woman *do* that to her?

"Hmm. You said your last tour went really well . . . what did you call it? 'New' somethin'."

"New Year, New You."

"Which meant . . . ?"

Grace squirmed inside. "You know how we all make New Year's resolutions. Well, I encouraged young people to make a very important resolution, to wait till marriage for physical intimacy. Kind of a purity theme. Trusting God to bring them the mate he has for them, that they're worth waiting for . . . that kind of thing."

"Lord knows that's needed." Estelle got up and refilled their mugs. "Why don't you just use the same theme? Seems like your West Coast fans need that message as much as your fans down south."

"Well, it's not the New Year anymore, and —"

"Goodness sakes!" Estelle chuckled. "Just give it a new name."

Grace shook her head. "It's . . . it's awkward for me right now. You see, I, uh, was engaged this past year, and I made it public at all my concerts, but my fiancé, he, uh, recently broke it off and . . ." Darn it! She reached for a napkin and pressed it to her eyes.

"Ah. I see."

Grace took a deep breath and blew it out, quickly recovering. "I'm sorry. Really, I'm over it, pretty much anyway. But it . . . it just feels complicated, and I . . . I need a different focus right now. Guess I could use prayer about that."

"So you need a new name for this tour?"

"Well, I can always use 'Grace Meredith

314

in Concert.' That's what I'm doing now. It's just . . . I like having a theme in my head to help me choose the right songs to sing. And sometimes it helps with promotion — gives the promoters something to advertise besides me."

"Mm-hm. I see . . ." Estelle glanced at the kitchen clock as she hefted herself out of her chair and took their half-full mugs to the sink. "I've gotta go to work in a few minutes — Manna House ladies depending on me for somethin' to eat come lunchtime. An' I teach a sewing class after lunch on Mondays till three, but I should be home no later than four." She walked Grace toward the stairs. "Tell you what, I'll drop over to your house around four to pray about that new theme you need. Don't you worry now. God is faithful! He's gonna give you just what you need."

The next thing Grace knew, Estelle had enveloped her in a warm hug and sent her off down the stairs, calling after her, "See you at four!"

Standing on the Bentleys' front porch a moment later, Grace blinked in dismay. She hadn't expected Estelle Bentley to take her *that* seriously when she said she needed prayer.

CHAPTER 28

The mail had come while she was across the street, but Grace just tossed it on the coffee table and grabbed up the cell phone she'd left sitting there. Three voice mail messages were blinking on the screen — all from Sam. She called back.

"There you are!" her assistant said after the first ring. "I got worried when you didn't answer after trying three times. I thought you'd be back from Curves ages ago."

"I was. But I ended up having coffee with my new neighbor across the street and forgot to take my phone. But, hey, I pumped it up to five miles an hour jogging on the treadmill today for about ten minutes — how about that?"

"Coffee with your neighbor? Hey, that's great. I'd like to meet her sometime. But do you have a couple minutes? I've got some information about taking the train to Seattle. Do you want to do this over the phone, or do you want me to drive up?"

Sam hadn't even heard what she'd said about her new milestone at Curves. "Let's do what we can by phone. What's the deal?"

As it turned out, Sam said, there was only one train a day leaving for Seattle, the Empire Builder, which left each day at two fifteen.

"So how long does it take from here to there?"

"Two nights, but gets in around ten in the morning on the third day. Since your first concert is Friday night, I figure we'd have to leave on Tuesday afternoon, which would get us in on Thursday morning, giving us plenty of flex time if the train is late. *Or* we could fly to Seattle on Thursday, which takes about four hours. I talked to Barry — the band is planning to fly. They're taking some equipment and renting the rest on the other end. We could all fly together, but . . . it's up to you. You're the boss."

Why was Sam talking this way? She'd seemed really open to taking the train when Grace had brought it up before.

"You said two nights . . ."

"Right. If we take the train, we should definitely take a sleeping car. The roomettes hold two people, but those seem kinda small. They also have larger bedrooms, and I checked — there're still a few available on that Tuesday. Those have their own toilet and sink and even a shower, I think. Oh, meals are included in the sleeping car ticket too, that's kinda nice. But the Amtrak lady said if we want a bedroom, we should make our reservations, like, today, 'cause that's just two weeks from tomorrow and she can't hold them."

"Sam, I want to go by train. But . . ." Grace hesitated. "But if you'd rather fly, you could travel with the band —"

"Are you kidding?" Samantha laughed on the other end. "The train sounds like a blast. I just didn't want to sway you one way or the other. If *you're* game, I'm in."

Grace sighed with relief. A two-day trip by train would be a lot more enjoyable traveling with Sam. They talked about a few other details — luggage limits, one bedroom or two. They decided on one, since Sam was willing to sleep on the top berth that folded down.

"Oh, one more thing," Sam said. "I got a call from Barry. The band needs the song list for the West Coast tour. I told him you're working on it — you are, right? — and we'd get back to him as soon as possible."

"I *know.* I get it." Grace heard the sharp note in her voice. She tried to soften her tone. "Maybe we can brainstorm when you come to work — is tomorrow good for you?"

Oreo was down to his last can of cat food — not to mention that "Mother Hubbard's cupboards" and the refrigerator were pretty bare too. Grace made a run after lunch to the grocery store, plus did a couple other errands she'd put off. But she kept a wary eye on the time just in case Estelle Bentley made good on her declaration to come over after work. Sure enough, Grace had no sooner put the groceries away than the doorbell rang.

Six minutes after four.

"Sorry to be late," Estelle puffed, sinking down onto the couch. "But I'm still gettin' used to Harry workin' again — he was always the one who got DaShawn started on his homework after school. I had to make sure the boy applied the seat of his pants to the seat of the chair before I could leave — not easy after he got used to lazin' around all last week durin' spring break." She waved a hand in front of her face. "Would've asked his dad to supervise, but Rodney's out too — lookin' for work, hopefully."

"Would you —" Grace started, intending

to offer some tea, but was taken aback when Estelle started to laugh.

"Would you look at me?" The laugh grew louder. "I forgot to take off my apron when I left Manna House and not a soul said anything to me about it!" She patted the large white apron. "An' I had seven women sewin' tote bags an' learnin' to read patterns for two hours. Even DaShawn said nary a word when he got home from school." Her dark eyes crinkled. "An' how long were *you* gonna sit there with me all decked out in this here apron without telling me?"

Grace grinned. "I don't know. I didn't really think anything of it. My mom used to wear an apron all day around the house."

Estelle rolled her eyes upward and patted the top of her head. "Well, at least I took off that ugly net cap I gotta wear when I'm cookin' at the shelter. Now, you better tell me first thing if you ever see me comin' home wearin' *that.*"

Her new neighbor followed Grace into the kitchen, chatting away as Grace made a pot of herbal tea and prepared a tray with a plate of almond-and-chocolate biscotti. Once they'd settled back into the living room with their teacups, Estelle said, "Well, I came to pray and I don't want to take too much of your time." She set her cup down and pulled a worn Bible out of her tote bag. "Came across this prayer the apostle Paul prayed for his friends in Colossae, and it seemed a good place to start. Do you mind?"

"No, no, of course not." Well, this was different than what she'd expected.

"Well, Lord," Estelle began, her eyes scanning the open page in her Bible, "I want to thank God, the Father of our Lord Jesus Christ, as we pray for my dear sister here, ever since I heard of her faith in Christ Jesus and of her love for all the saints — especially her love for the young people who attend her concerts. Her faith and love spring from the hope stored up for her in heaven, ever since she first heard the truth of the Good News. This same Good News is going out all over the world and bearing fruit everywhere by changing lives, just as it changed her life from the day she first heard and understood the truth about God's wonderful grace . . ."

She was reading from her Bible, but paraphrasing it as a personal prayer — for her. Grace felt a little uncomfortable about all the spiritual things Estelle was saying about her, but she closed her eyes and listened to the rich voice, which was becoming more passionate.

". . . For this reason we want to keep on prayin' for her, askin' that she would be filled with the knowledge of your will in all wisdom and spiritual understanding — especially, Lord, as she seeks the focus you want for this upcoming concert tour. And we pray that she would walk worthy of the Lord, fully pleasing you, bein' fruitful in every good work and growin' in the knowledge of God, strengthened with all might" — Estelle's voice rose, almost as if she was pleading with the Almighty — "accordin' to your glorious power. Give her great endurance and patience, joyfully giving thanks to the Father who has qualified her to share in the inheritance of the saints . . ."

Estelle's voice dropped and the powerful words hung in the quiet room. Grace hardly dared to breathe. The silence stretched for a long moment and she opened her eyes. But Estelle's eyes were now closed, her face tilted upward, glistening with perspiration, and she was moving her lips as if praying silently.

Grace waited, the words of the prayer still ringing in her ears. *". . . that she would be filled with the knowledge of your will in all wisdom and spiritual understanding . . ."*

Finally Estelle opened her eyes and

smiled. "Amen!"

Grace blew out the breath she'd been holding in. "Whew. Where did you find that prayer?" Her question came out in a squeak.

"First chapter of Colossians. Look it up and pray it over yourself!" Estelle reached for her tea and munched on another biscotti. "*Mmm, these are good.*"

But a rumble of thunder in the distance caused her to rise. "Better get myself home before that thunder chases rain this way. You know spring is really here when these late-afternoon showers roll through most every day." Giving Grace a warm hug, she opened the door, and then paused. "Bible says to 'pray without ceasing.' I'm going to go see Mother Bentley tomorrow after work, but . . . how 'bout Wednesday, same time? I'm excited to see what God's gonna do for this tour of yours." She laughed and waved a hand in the air as she headed out the door. "Halle*lu*jah!"

Grace wasn't sure she deserved most of what her neighbor had prayed. Thanking God for her "love for the saints"? Implying that she was "bearing fruit" and "changing lives"? But she did want to read the last part of the prayer — the part about asking God for "wisdom and spiritual understanding."

She needed that for sure! And the part about endurance and patience . . . she needed that, too.

She got out her old King James Bible and read Colossians, chapter one, and then compared it to her modern English translation. Did she dare pray this prayer for herself?

A guitar strum interrupted her musing. She picked up her cell and looked at the caller ID. *Roger.* She was glad she'd waited. "Hello?"

"Grace? So glad I got you! Do you have a few minutes to talk?

She felt wary. "Maybe a few. Depends."

"Actually, I called to see if I could take you to dinner. Are you in town this weekend?"

Dinner? "Roger, I don't think that's appro—"

"I know, I know how it sounds. But please, just give me a chance here. I actually called to apologize for ending the engagement so abruptly without giving us time to talk — you know, really talk — about the stresses in our relationship. I'd . . . I'd like to make that up to you."

She sighed audibly. "It's a little late, Roger. What's done is done. Time for us both to move on, don't you think?"

"Well, that's, uh, that's what I'd like to talk about. I never gave you a chance — never gave *us* a chance — to even see if we could work on the problems we were experiencing."

Oreo jumped on her lap, but Grace pushed him off. "Not 'we,' Roger. You. I didn't know we were having any problems." She felt her throat go tight.

"I know. I . . . I wasn't forthright with you. But I'd like to back up and do things right. I was hasty and I see that now. Maybe . . . maybe things didn't have to end up this way. But even if they do, I'd like to make amends for how I handled things. At the very least, I'd really like to remain friends. We could go out to dinner just as friends, couldn't we?"

Grace was silent. She was tempted to hang up. Let it go. Let *him* go.

But was that the right thing to do? Even if their relationship was over, if he wanted to apologize for how he'd ended it, shouldn't she give him a chance? If she was going to move on, it might be good to lay it all to rest, not hold on to any anger and bitterness . . .

"Grace? I know I'm asking a lot. But I don't really want to do this over the phone. That was my mistake in the first place.

Please . . . let me take you to dinner. Are you free Friday or Saturday?"

She hesitated. He sounded genuinely contrite. But no way was she going to let this hang over her head for five days. She'd be a basket case by the time the weekend rolled around.

"Wednesday," she said. "You can pick me up at seven."

Chapter 29

"You agreed to do . . . what?" Samantha's mouth hung open, staring at Grace as if she'd sprouted pointy ears and announced she'd just arrived from the planet Vulcan. "Dinner with Roger?!"

Grace's assistant had shown up at nine o'clock the next day, looking rejuvenated after her day off — wearing a tunic in a black, red, and tan African print over tan slacks, her perky twists redone, sporting a fresh manicure of deep red polish with white feathery designs on her middle fingernails — but "ready to work," she'd said. Pouring a cup of coffee, Sam said she was waiting for a callback confirming the tour bus from Seattle to LA she'd lined up months ago, and she'd asked Bongo Booking to e-mail her any updated info for the ten-day tour schedule.

"So, do you want me to answer fan mail first, or do you want help putting together a song list for the upcoming tour? Using 'Grace Meredith in Concert' as your promo title leaves you lots of room — you could even have several different sets with a different focus. Whatever we do, just keep in mind the band needs —"

"Stop."

Sam had blinked in surprise. "Okay. Sorry. I was just wanting to know —"

"Just stop a minute. I need to tell you something. But you should probably sit down." Sam sat. Taking a deep breath, Grace told her about Roger's call last night, and that she'd agreed to go out to dinner with him Wednesday night.

"Dinner. With Roger," Sam said again, plopping back against the couch cushions bowled over. "You're kidding, right?"

Grace shook her head.

"Okaaay, not kidding." Sam sat forward again, elbows on the knees of her slacks. "Grace, I know it isn't any of my business, but . . . do you know what you're doing? I don't want you to get hurt again. Why is he doing this? Did he give you a reason?"

Grace, sitting in the opposite chair, nodded. "He said he wanted to apologize for how he ended the engagement, without even giving us a chance to work on the problems in the relationship."

"But —"

"I know. I told him that was all very nice — well, I didn't say it like that — but what's done is done, it's over, we both needed to move on."

"Exactly. Good for you."

"But he said he wanted to back up and do things right. Said he wanted to make amends, apologize for how he'd handled things, and be able to talk about what went wrong in the relationship —"

Sam snorted. "He probably had his eye on somebody else while you were gone, but it didn't work out, so now he's crawling back to you."

"Sam! You don't know that!" Though the thought had flitted through Grace's mind a time or two.

Sam put up her hands, palms out. "Sorry. I'm just sayin'."

"Well, don't say. Unless you know. I don't think he'd do that." Grace took a deep breath. "Anyway, he said at the very least he wants us to be able to be friends. And to be honest, Sam, I've wished that too. At least wished I didn't still feel so mad at him for how it happened. Maybe if he apologizes — he did seem very sincere, contrite even — I could forgive him and move on. That'd be better than just stuffing it down, like I've been doing. Right?"

Sam looked at her for a long moment. "Does he want you to give him another chance?"

"I —" Grace hesitated. Roger *had* said maybe things didn't have to end up this way. She licked her dry lips. "I'm not sure."

"Ohhh, Grace." Sam's response sounded almost like a groan.

Grace felt a little miffed. "What would be so wrong with that? I mean, I don't have *any* expectations, don't know if I'd even be able to take him back — but would that be so horrible? Good grief, we were in love, you know. Engaged for almost a year. Planning to get married. You don't throw all that away without some serious thought."

"*He* did." Sam's hands went up again. "Okay, okay, I need to shut up. Maybe you're right. Go to dinner, see what happens. Give the man a chance to apologize. Just . . . be wise, Grace. Don't rush back into anything. Pray about it — a lot, okay?"

Pray about it . . .

She would ask Estelle Bentley to pray about it with her when she came over Wednesday afternoon. She wouldn't have to share all the details. The woman did seem to have a special connection with God.

After spending Tuesday coming up with a solid song list for the tour and e-mailing it to Barry, Grace had told Sam she could work from home on Wednesday and Thursday, since "work" for the next few days mostly involved e-mails and phone calls double-checking arrangements at each of the ten venues along the Pacific coast.

"I'll schedule practices with you and the band for next week," Sam promised when she left on Tuesday. "Meantime, be good. Don't do anything tomorrow night I wouldn't do."

Grace snickered. "Ha. In that case I should probably clock him one. If I do, I'll tell Roger it's from you." She shut the door behind Sam with a sigh of relief. She didn't really want her assistant hovering over her all day tomorrow, making her more nervous than she already was about her date with Roger.

But where the time went on Wednesday, she had no idea. The temperature had dropped again and the day turned to drizzle. She'd planned to spend most of the day doing voice exercises and practicing the songs she and Sam had chosen for the tour, with an appointment at the beauty salon to get a manicure and pedicure before her dinner with Roger.

But she no sooner got home from Curves than Jeff called. He'd gotten a call from Samantha about sticking with Grace Meredith in Concert for the tour title, and wanted to double-check with her. "It's fine, really. Your name alone will draw plenty of your fans. And I know you'll do a great job with the concerts. But I just wanted to hear from you, you know, to see if you had any more thoughts about what we talked about in St. Louis."

Grace flushed, remembering the touch of his hand over hers in the coffee shop. She quickly shook off the memory. What was she *doing*? Here she was, going out to dinner that evening with her fiancé — okay, ex-fiancé — and having fleeting fantasies about her agent.

"I . . ." she stumbled, realizing she hadn't responded to his question. "I haven't forgotten. But I don't know . . ."

"It's okay. And I mean that." Jeff's voice was kind, reassuring. "We're praying for you and the tour here at Bongo, and if God has a new focus for you, he's going to show you. So don't stress about it. I mean that too. In fact, one of the other Bongo agents read a couple verses in Proverbs this morning during our staff time, which made me think about you. Look 'em up — chapter three, verses five and six. Hold on to that last phrase . . . Hey, gotta go. I'll check in with you in a few days."

Grace knew those verses. *"Trust in the LORD with all your heart; do not depend on your own understanding. Seek his will in all you do, and he will show you which path to take."* They were some of the scriptures she often shared with her fans during her concerts. Hold on to the last phrase, Jeff had said: *"Seek his will . . . and he will show you . . ."* The words were comforting.

But it felt kind of strange, getting spiritual advice from her agent. Not what one normally expected from an agent — but then, her relationship with Jeff Newman hadn't been "normal" from the beginning. She had to snicker remembering the snowstorm when they'd met . . .

She mentioned Jeff's call and the verses from Proverbs when Estelle came over at four, after telling her about the surprise invitation from her ex. Her neighbor nodded. "That's right, honey. You don't have to stress. In fact, I think those verses would be a very good prayer to pray about this dinner you're having tonight with your fiancé —"

"Ex-fiancé," Grace corrected. But Estelle went right on.

"— as well as for your upcoming concert

tour. Now, Jesus, halle*lu*jah, we praise your name . . ." Holding one of Grace's hands, the older woman moved right into a prayer, asking God that Grace would trust him with all her heart, even if she didn't understand what he was doing, and have the confidence that God would indeed show her the path to take. "And for this, we *thank* you, for all you've done and for all you're gonna do! In your precious name . . . Amen."

Estelle rose from the couch. "All right now, gonna get myself on home, since I know you got that date tonight. My men are gonna be hungry too." She gave Grace a warm hug. "But, there's somethin' I been meanin' to ask you and don't want to take your time now. An' I should go see Mother Bentley at the hospital after work tomorrow afternoon, but . . . any chance we could get together in the mornin'? Besides . . ." She winked. "I'll be curious how your dinner date goes tonight. I'll be prayin'!"

The doorbell rang at five minutes to seven that evening. Grace shut Oreo in the base-ment so the cat wouldn't try to escape like he had the last time Roger showed up, let the doorbell ring a second time, and then opened the door. She smiled pleasantly. "Hi." She held the door open so he could come in.

"Hi, yourself." Roger smiled back, blue-gray eyes taking her in. "You look great."

She knew she did. She'd added a wash, trim, and blow-dry at the beauty salon when she got her nails done, and her hair hung casually below her shoulders in a fresh, layered fall. She'd taken extra care with her makeup, highlighting her amber eyes with a soft brown eyeliner and eye shadow, picking up the warmth of her berry blush and lipstick. Her dress — a three-quarter-sleeved wrap style in the same berry tones with a tie belt that hung softly to just above her knees — was one she was sure he hadn't seen before.

"I'll get my coat." The drizzle had stopped, but she still opted for her dark-gray London Fog and a small umbrella in her bag. He ushered her out to his car, a sporty, silver, two-door Acura. She wondered if Estelle Bentley was peeking out her front window, but didn't see anyone. Beecham Street was empty.

Roger glanced at her as he pulled away from the curb and turned around in the cul-de-sac at the end. "Is Thai food okay? There's a nice restaurant in the River North area, not too far."

"Mm-hm." At least he remembered what

she liked.

The ride to the restaurant felt awkward, but somehow they managed with short chats about the weather, the Cubs, a movie he'd seen. But the Star of Siam took her by surprise — a converted warehouse with exposed pipes, done in deep shades of red and burgundy. Guests could either sit at small tables with a padded bench along one side up against a curved brick wall, or at low tables on a raised platform, sitting on cushions with one's legs in a well beneath a low table. They chose a low table.

Grace ordered chicken satay and pad thai, Roger ordered the crab rangoon and cashew chicken. As he ordered their food, she had a chance to look him over. The familiar dark-blond hair brushed slightly to the side, blue-gray eyes, the always clean-shaven, strong jaw. He was dressed impeccably in an open-necked light-gray silk shirt with almost imperceptible stripes, and a dark, charcoal-gray suit. The good looks that used to set her heart tripping. Not that her heart wasn't tripping a little even now.

The waiter brought hot green tea and poured, and finally they were alone. Grace drew in a breath and looked him in the eyes. "Well, here we are. You wanted to talk?"

He seemed to study her for a moment,

but she determined not to look away. Then he nodded, toying with his red napkin. "Yes. I've been thinking a lot about us in the past few weeks. I made a mistake, ending our engagement so abruptly. It wasn't fair to do that, least of all on the phone, without even giving us a chance to talk about the problems in our relationship. You were right, I should have given us a chance to work on the issues that troubled me. That wasn't right, and I . . . I want to apologize."

A hundred nasty retorts sprang to her tongue. She felt like yelling at him, releasing all the pent-up hurt and anger she'd buried deep down in her gut. In spite of the other diners chatting at the tables around them, the clink of dishes, the smell of spicy food wafting from the kitchen. She didn't care — it'd be soul cleansing.

Except . . . she wasn't brave enough to make a scene. And, oddly, she didn't want to embarrass Roger. He sounded contrite, sincere, just like he had on the phone. At the moment, all she could do was not be too quick to let him off the hook. Picking up her teacup in both hands, she sipped the hot green tea, trying to keep her fingers from shaking.

The appetizers came. Roger said a brief prayer of thanks for the food, and they ate in silence for several minutes, broken only by small comments of appreciation for the tasty food. Finally he wiped his mouth, took a sip of water, and cleared his throat.

"I know I don't have any right to ask this after the way I handled things, but . . . would you be willing to give our relationship another chance? I do care about you, Grace — I care a lot."

"Was there someone else?"

Roger looked startled.

He shook his head. "No . . . not someone in particular. I did date a couple women in the past few months — not while we were engaged, though, I promise you that. But frankly, it made me realize how much I still cared about you."

Grace pursed her lips and thought about that. Gratefully, the waiter brought their entrees and she didn't have to answer immediately. So. Taking her to dinner wasn't just about apologizing for the way he'd handled ending their engagement. But what did he mean? Start over? Pick up where they left off? Was it even possible?

Swallowing a bite of pad thai, she laid down her fork. "You said, give us a chance to work on the problems in our relationship. What issues, exactly?"

"Well, as I told you, the amount of travel

involved in your concert tours has been a problem for me — we would definitely need to face the impact of our careers on a marriage. My mistake was not even talking about it, seeing what we could work out."

"*Our* careers."

"Well, yes. Obviously, getting married changes things. We . . . well, I confess, we didn't talk very much about a lot of important things. I take responsibility for that."

They finished their entrees, let the waiter take their dishes away, and ordered another pot of tea. Roger was saying things she never thought she'd hear him say. *"I made a mistake . . . You were right . . . I apologize . . . I care about you, Grace, I care a lot . . ."*

Part of her wanted to just say, *"Yes, I forgive you! Of course I'm willing to give us another chance!"* She'd be crazy not to, wouldn't she? After all, every marriage — and engagement — had rocky places to navigate. That was a reality too. She wouldn't have to tell her fans that the engagement had been called off. Roger would be back in her life, maybe she could rediscover that passion in her message Jeff had talked about.

Jeff . . .

She could also hear Sam's voice in her head. *"Don't rush back into anything."* And she was pretty sure her new friend Estelle would say, *"Take time to pray about it, young lady."*

She finally sucked in a breath and blew it out. "Roger," she said, "I appreciate your apology. That means a lot to me. But, to be honest, I've spent a lot of emotional energy getting over you the past couple of months. It's not as easy as just saying, okay, I forgive you, let's give our relationship another chance. Frankly, I'm a little numb. I . . . I need time to even know what I feel. Give me some time to think and pray about it, and then we can talk some more."

"Of course. I understand. Do you want to, uh, get together again this weekend? Or next week some time?"

Grace shook her head. "No. I'm heading to the West Coast pretty soon for a ten-day concert tour. Taking the train, so it'll be a little more than two weeks when I add travel on either end." She saw his jaw muscles tighten. Disappointment? Frustration?

Reaching out her hand, she touched his and smiled ruefully. "I know that's not what you want to hear, Roger, but I promise you this — I promise to use the time I'm away to seriously consider what you've said."

CHAPTER 30

The gentle patter of a spring rain greeted Grace when she woke up the next morning. She stretched and then cuddled deeper under her comforter. A heavy lump at the foot of the bed moved, and a moment later a rumbling purr preceded Oreo's cool nose exploring the exposed part of her face.

"Go 'way, Oreo," she mumbled, pushing the cat off the bed. But she couldn't help smiling. *Dinner with Roger . . .* a week ago she never could've imagined such a thing. But after finishing their meal — in spite of the seriousness of their "talk" — they'd walked the few blocks to the Chicago River in the foggy evening, meandering along the riverwalk for half an hour. The city was dazzling, liquid lights reflecting and rippling in the dark waters of the river that cut through the city. It had almost seemed like old times.

Almost. But not quite.

He'd offered his arm when they crossed

streets and skirted puddles, and they'd chatted about the new buildings populating the city skyline and shaken their heads at the lighted boats full of tourists plying the river in spite of the chill. But he hadn't tried to kiss her when he walked her up to her door, and she didn't invite him in.

Too much water under their bridge for that — at this point, anyway.

She sat up in the bed, hugging her knees. Was it possible that the confusing and painful breakdown in their relationship could turn around? If so, why had God put her through all that pain in the first place? What was he up to?

Well. The dinner might be a glimmer of hope, but she couldn't figure it out in one day. Grace threw off the comforter and stuck her feet in her slippers. She'd made no promises, except to think about it for the next few weeks.

But a few minutes later, staring into the bathroom mirror, Grace suddenly grabbed two fistfuls of her hair, her face crumpling as old memories started to surface — memories she'd pushed deep in order to be who she was today. Even if she and Roger did get back together, things would be different. There was no way she could pretend the breakup never happened. No way to jump right back into the purity theme in her concerts. Taking several gulps of air, Grace backed away from the mirror and fumbled with the shower handles. She needed to get a grip . . . a hot shower would help.

Grace browsed her e-mail during breakfast — *ah.* Samantha said Barry was suggesting a practice session with the band at the studio Saturday afternoon, then at least three more evening sessions the following week. Could she put those on her calendar? *Got it,* she wrote back and hit Send.

An hour later Grace was sitting at her piano, humming through one of the songs she'd written and chosen for the upcoming tour, when the doorbell rang.

Estelle Bentley was standing on her stoop under a large black umbrella.

"Oh, uh, hi! Come in." Good grief. She'd totally forgotten that Estelle mentioned coming over this morning.

"Don't really need this ol' thing," the woman chuckled, shaking the umbrella and hooking the handle on the iron railing. "Rain is supposed to stop soon anyway. Am I interrupting something?"

"Just practicing, but I can use a break.

Would you like some coffee? I still have half a pot."

"Coffee sounds good. But I don't want to stay too long if you're practicin'."

Estelle followed Grace into the kitchen. "Say, I like those café curtains in the window. Lets you look out without everybody lookin' in." She took the mug of coffee Grace handed her, spooned sugar into it from the bowl on the small kitchen table, and lowered herself into a chair. Resting her elbows on the table and sipping from the mug, she peered up at Grace over the rim. "Can't help askin' . . . how did your dinner date go?"

Grace shrugged as she filled a second mug and joined Estelle at the table. "A bit awkward, but all right, I guess. He apologized for how he ended our relationship —"

"Good! More men need to know it ain't gonna kill 'em to say they're sorry!"

"Yeah, well, that wasn't all. He said he'd like to back up and 'do it right.' " She made a face. "Which I think means talk about what he thinks is wrong with our relationship. Or me."

Estelle cocked an eyebrow. "Hmm."

Grace added hastily, "I shouldn't have said it like that. To be fair, Roger did say he should've given us a chance to work on our relationship."

"And you said . . . ?"

Grace shrugged. "Said I appreciated his apology, but I needed time to think about it."

"Glad to hear it, girl." Estelle reached out and laid a hand on Grace's arm. "You've been through some mighty tough things the last few months, just from the little bit you've shared with Harry an' me. Give God some time to show you the path he wants you to take — like that verse from Proverbs we prayed yesterday."

Grace nodded. "Thanks. Um, is that what you wanted to ask me — about going out with Roger last night, I mean?"

Estelle shook her head. "Not really. Has more to do with what you asked me to pray about in the first place — needin' a new theme for your concert tour comin' up. I'm tryin' to understand, so I know how to pray. Just wanted to ask, if you don't mind sayin', *why* you were focusing on a purity message in your past concerts?"

"Why?" Grace felt a little taken aback. "Well, uh . . . because, you know, there's so much sexual pressure on kids today. Kids are confused, they think everybody's 'doing it.' It seemed important to let young people know that *not* everyone's doing it — you

know, using the platform God has given me to let kids know it's a good thing to wait until marriage for sexual intimacy . . ." Her voice trailed off. For some reason, her explanation sounded flat, even in her own ears, as if she was just saying *blah, blah, blah.*

Estelle nodded slowly. "Yes, but . . ." She tipped her head slightly to the side, her graying topknot bobbing, dark eyes full of concern. "What I meant is, why was it so important to *you*?"

The question pierced Grace. She stared at Estelle. Who *was* this woman sitting in her kitchen? This woman who took casual Christian-y comments like, "Pray for me," so *seriously*? This woman who seemed to see right into the deepest part of her soul?

Grace avoided Estelle's gaze. "I don't know . . . I mean, guess it had to do with some things I struggled with back in high school. You know, I was a typical good girl, grew up in a churchgoing, Christian family. People had all these high expectations of me — my parents, the church people, even other kids in my youth group — so hard to live up to." She swallowed. "But I was just a teenager, trying to be liked, and there was this guy . . ."

Grace gripped her mug, staring into the black liquid. *No, no . . . I can't go there. What business is it of Estelle's, anyway?* But it was as if she'd poked a hole in a bulging water bag, and the water couldn't be held back — first a trickle, then a stream . . .

"He — he sat next to me in assembly, last name was Metcalf — we all sat alphabetically, you know — and he was really cute, but I never thought he'd pay any attention to *me*. He was really popular, a jock, played soccer, and I was, you know, a dud — couldn't go to dances, couldn't date until I was sixteen, stuff like that."

Estelle chuckled, nodding, and Grace glanced at her gratefully.

"But Darin — that was his name — broke up with this other really popular girl and started flirting with me. At first I just ignored him — my folks would never approve. He wasn't a Christian or anything, not that I knew of, but . . . I was flattered by the attention and started flirting back. He seemed to really like me, started hanging out with me after school, and . . . it felt great! All his friends accepted me, the other girls were pretty jealous, but started inviting me to parties and stuff — which had never happened before. Suddenly all the Christian 'rules' I'd been trying to live by just seemed so old-fashioned. So one weekend when my parents were away visiting one of

347

my brothers for parents weekend or something — both my brothers were in college by then — Darin asked me to go out, and I said sure!" Grace shrugged, fiddling with her mug of coffee. "I was barely sixteen, and it felt so exciting to be driving around in a car with a good-looking guy, going on a real date. We went to a movie, don't even remember what it was, but the one he picked was R-rated and made me very uncomfortable, and I kinda wanted to go home. But afterwards he —"

Grace stopped. Getting up suddenly, she mumbled, "Uh, sorry. Gotta go . . ." and stumbled toward the bathroom. Sinking onto the closed toilet seat, she dropped her head into her hands. Estelle was going to think she was so rude, leaving the table like that! But . . . she couldn't go on.

After a few minutes, Grace flushed the toilet, ran water in the sink, and then tentatively came out of the bathroom. Estelle looked up from the couch as she came into the living room and patted the cushion beside her. "It's all right, honey. I've been around the block a few times myself. Nothin' you can say will surprise me. And nothin' you say will leave this house. But sometimes it helps to say it, 'specially if you been keepin' it locked away

348

down in your belly, where it's been eatin' you alive."

Grace sank down onto the other end of the couch but just shook her head, fighting back the tears. After a few long moments, Estelle said gently, "So Darin got aggressive, pushed you to have sex, right?"

The tears that had been threatening finally spilled over. "I . . . I didn't want to, nothing like that! I just wanted to be liked, to have fun like other girls, but he . . . he parked the car and was suddenly all over me, pushing me down, running his hands up under my skirt, grabbing at my breasts, even laughing when I started to struggle . . ."

Grace began to shake all over. The next thing she knew, Estelle had moved over beside her on the couch and was pulling her into a comforting embrace. "It's all right, baby," Estelle crooned, rocking her like a child. "Go ahead an' cry, get it all out . . ." Grace leaned deeper into Estelle's cushiony bosom and wept. Oh, how she wept as the pent-up secrets started to unravel like barbwire come loose, whipping about in the wind.

Finally the well of tears slowed and Grace sat back, taking the tissues Estelle handed her. She blew her nose and mopped her face, which was probably a raccoony mess by now. So much for putting on her makeup this morning.

"I'm guessin' you didn't tell your parents," Estelle said kindly, handing her yet another tissue.

Grace shook her head. "I — I felt so dirty. And it was all my fault, going out with that boy behind their backs. I couldn't face telling them. Spent years trying to forget his rough hands under my clothes, and I pretty much did — until that incident at the Memphis airport after my last tour, when that security agent groped me in full view of a long line of other passengers . . ." She shuddered.

"Oh, honey," Estelle murmured, patting her hand. "Oh, baby. No wonder you don't want to fly anymore. But you can't blame yourself. That was date rape, pure and simple, and you —"

"No. Not that simple." Grace pulled her hand away. "That's not all," she said dully. The bag of secrets had been punctured, and there was no stopping it now. She lifted stricken eyes to Estelle's kind face. "A couple months later I discovered I was" — She swallowed with difficulty — "that I was pregnant. Estelle, I . . . I didn't know what to do! I was terrified. And that very next Sunday, some woman at church says to my mom, right in front of me, 'You must be so proud of your daughter — such a sweet Christian. We're so glad the younger girls in this church have someone like her to look up to.' "

"Lord, have mercy." Now it was Estelle who wagged her head.

"How could I tell my parents after that?" Grace's voice rose. Her eyes flashed. "Have a baby out of wedlock? Become a teenage mother? My reputation would be ruined forever! I thought I'd never get married — no decent Christian man would want me. So I —" Grace drew in a long, shuddering breath, and her voice dropped almost to a whisper. "I had an abortion. Went by myself. Didn't tell anyone."

There. She'd said it. Words she'd never spoken aloud. Words pushed deep into the crevices of her mind and her spirit. She glanced at Estelle. What would the woman think of her now? Estelle's eyes were closed and she was humming softly, some tune that sounded vaguely familiar, but Grace couldn't pinpoint what it was exactly.

Finally Estelle spoke. "I think I understand it now. Your purity message . . ."

Grace stared at the tissue she was absently shredding in her lap. "Yeah. I told God over and over I was so sorry. Thought maybe I

351

could make amends for my sin by preaching a purity message to other teens, keep them from making the same mistake I had — though I didn't dare tell anyone about my 'mistake.' So I started encouraging other kids in my youth group to take the biblical view of sex seriously, to wait until marriage. My parents seemed really proud of me for being so outspoken, so later when my singing career took off" — Grace shrugged — "it just seemed natural to tell young people they were 'worth the wait.' And I thought it was true until . . ."

Grace stared at the empty place on the lamp table where the framed photo of her and Roger, taken at their engagement party, had stood.

"Until?" Estelle prodded gently.

"Until Roger dumped me." Kicking off her shoes and pulling her feet up onto the couch, Grace hugged her legs, resting her chin on her knees.

"Oh honey, just because Roger broke your engagement doesn't mean you're not worth the wait. Those're two separate things."

Grace just hugged her knees for a long moment. Then she sighed. "Guess I know that, logically. But it doesn't feel that way. Sometimes I think God is punishing me for that abortion by dangling the promise of marriage in my face, then snatching it away again." She turned her head slightly to look at Estelle. "What do you think about all this?"

Estelle seemed to be studying her. For several long moments she didn't say anything. And then, gently, "What do I think? I think that if you're looking for a new theme, you might start by meditating on the meaning of your name."

CHAPTER 31

Grace shut the door behind Estelle, then stepped over to the window to watch her neighbor walk across the street and disappear into the two-flat. *Meditate on the meaning of my name?* Odd thing to say after she'd just spilled her guts about the painful memories that'd been haunting her recently.

Frankly, after scraping her insides raw and bawling like a baby for the past hour, she felt exhausted. She didn't even have the energy to go back to the piano, much less "meditate." Maybe after a nap she'd feel like practicing again . . .

But even though she stretched out on her bed and turned on a fan to create a soothing white noise, Grace couldn't fall asleep. Estelle's words kept tumbling through her thoughts. *"Meditate on the meaning of your name . . ."*

Wasn't like it was all that complicated. Her name was Grace. "We're saved by grace" — she'd heard that a lot growing up. Salvation was God's work, not ours, wasn't that it? That was the thing about Christianity — salvation was a gift we accepted by faith, not a list of things we had to do to earn it.

She hadn't especially liked her name as a teenager. Grace . . . It had seemed *too* religious, like waving "I'm a Christian" in people's faces, especially when she wanted to just blend in with the other kids at school. Too old-fashioned too, when other girls in her class had cool names like Nicole and Tiffany and Amber. At least she hadn't been named Faith or Hope like two of her friends in the music program at Greenville College. The girls had joked that she should change her name to Charity — "Then the three of us could go on the road as a gospel trio!"

By comparison, the name Grace felt pretty harmless.

But Faith and Hope had married college sweethearts and she'd lost touch. Of the three, she was the only one who'd moved professionally into the contemporary music scene. The name Grace actually worked for her in that context. It created a subtle "respectability" and spiritual tone that helped build her reputation as a solid Christian artist — at least that's what her first agent at Bongo had told her. "Don't make up some crazy stage name," he'd warned. "Stick with Grace Meredith. It's a good name."

In spite of her meandering thoughts, she finally fell asleep until the familiar throb of the guitar-strum ringtone woke her. A heavy weight on her stomach seemed to pin her down as her hand groped for the phone — "Uhh, Oreo, get *off* me!" — but she finally found it and yawned, "Hello?"

"Grace? That you?"

Grace sat up, pushing the cat off the bed. She could barely hear the caller because of the background racket on the other end. "Yes, this is Grace. Who's this?"

"Estelle Bentley! Sorry for the noise. I'm at work and it's the middle of lunch . . . 'scuse me a sec." Estelle's voice dropped into the background. "I already *said,* no seconds till everybody's been served . . . Yes, that's the rule!" Then she was back. "Sorry 'bout that. Here, let me find a quiet corner . . ."

Phone to her ear, Grace turned off the fan and wandered toward the kitchen to make some coffee.

"Okay, I'm back," Estelle said. "You still there?"

The background chatter and banging dishes in Grace's ear had muted. "I'm here." She filled the carafe with cold water, spooned coffee grounds into the filter basket, and turned the coffee maker on.

"I've been thinkin' about our talk this mornin', and I wondered if you'd like to come to work with me tomorrow."

Grace blinked. "Excuse me?"

"Come to work with me tomorrow — visit the Manna House Shelter, I mean." Grace heard a deep-throated chuckle on the other end. "I know, I know, it's last minute an' all that, but a while back you said you'd like to hear more about what I do. Hearin's one thing, but seein's a lot better, an' Friday's always a special day. There's a young lady I'd like you to meet, 'bout your age, she leads a Bible study here Friday mornings. Powerful good stuff. Anyway, God dropped it into my spirit to ask if you'd like to visit tomorrow, might be a real pick-me-up for you right now . . ."

Grace rolled her eyes. She had a natural suspicion of anything that smacked of *"God told me . . ."* "Uh, I don't know, Estelle. My assistant is coming tomorrow, we've got some work to do, and I —"

"Well, bring her too! Been wantin' to meet her, anyway. It's just a few hours, 'cause all

I gotta do tomorrow is make lunch, don't have any classes to teach in the afternoon. Rain's s'posed to let up tonight, be a beautiful day tomorrow. It'd do you some good to get out and about — oh. Speakin' of rain . . . did I leave my umbrella hangin' on the railing outside your front door?"

In spite of the fact that Estelle's call felt like being swept along by a tsunami, Grace actually liked the idea of getting out of the house and visiting the shelter where her neighbor worked — though it took two cups of coffee to unfog her brain and think about it. She called Sam to see if she'd like to come with her — "Or if not, you could come to work later, say around two?"

"No, no, I'd love to come with! What time do you get back from Curves . . . nine? And she wants to leave at ten? Tell you what, I'll be there at nine, get a bunch of fan mail answered for an hour, and then do whatever else we need to do when we get back. I've heard of Manna House before, but never been there."

True to her word, Sam was waiting on her front steps at nine the next morning dressed in jeans, white tee, and a skinny jean jacket when Grace pulled up in front of the house after her stint at Curves. Sam hefted the big black umbrella still hanging from the railing as Grace came up the walk. "Yours?"

At ten o'clock, when Estelle yoo-hooed outside where she was waiting in the RAV4 with the motor running, Grace locked up the house and headed for the Bentleys' car. She knocked on the driver's side window with the handle of the black umbrella. "It's sunny today," she grinned, "but you're going to need this again one of these days — it's April after all."

"Thanks." Estelle chuckled, hauled the folded umbrella through the window as Grace and Sam climbed in from the other side, and a minute later headed east toward Lake Shore Drive.

"Thanks for inviting me too," Sam said from the back seat. "I've often heard about Manna House but don't know anything about it. Who are the women you serve?"

Estelle practically hooted. "Who *aren't* the women we serve! We got our share of drug addicts who've hit bottom, prostitutes who're trying to get away from their pimps, some single moms who just couldn't make ends meet, and others whose circumstances took a nose dive in this economy through no fault of their own. Even one woman who used to live in one of these fancy high-rises" — She pointed out the window at the luxury towers they were passing along Lake Shore Drive — "who got kicked out by her husband and ended up with blocked credit cards and no place to go. She also happened to be our program director. Now *that's* a story." Estelle chuckled to herself, and Grace wondered what the rest of the story was, but the Manna House cook was already on to other stories of women who'd been in and out of the shelter.

To Grace's surprise, they'd been on Lake Shore Drive only a few minutes when the little black SUV took the Irving Park Road exit into the Wrigleyville North neighborhood, jogged a few streets, and pulled up in front of a brick church crunched between a Laundromat and an apartment building.

"A church?" Sam said, gawking at the fairly new building as they got out. But several women were lounging on the stone steps, a couple of them smoking, as Grace and Sam followed Estelle toward the building.

"Hey, Miz Estelle! What's fer lunch?" a weathered-looking white woman of indeterminate age hollered.

"Menu's posted in the kitchen!" Estelle said mildly, pushing a doorbell.

"See ya got some new helpers," another snickered. "Guess I don't need ta show up for lunch duty today."

"Mm-hm. No lunch duty, no lunch," Estelle shot back, her grin taking out any sting. "These are my guests, Grace and Samantha."

To Grace's surprise, three of the stepsitters stood up to shake their hands, and the others gave a nod or "Nice ta meetcha."

A buzzer allowed Estelle to pull the solid oak door open, leading into a pleasant vestibule. She introduced them to the receptionist sitting in a glass cubicle — a pretty, young Asian woman — signed them all in, then led them through two swinging doors into a large room. "Hey, Precious!" Estelle called to a thirtysomething black woman who was pushing an odd assortment of overstuffed chairs, loveseats, and folding chairs into a semicircle facing a large mural on the wall opposite the doors. "Mind giving my guests a tour? We have some time before the Bible study, unless you've got kids to look after."

"Nah, they're all home with Sabrina . . . Hi! Name's Precious." The thin, wiry woman pumped their hands with a firm grip. "C'mon, I'll show you around."

As Grace and Sam tromped after their guide — starting with the main floor, which contained the big lounging area, and behind

it a schoolroom, a small playroom with toddler toys, a tiny prayer chapel, and a TV
room — they learned that Precious had
once been a "guest" at Manna House, but
now lived with her daughter and grandson
at the House of Hope, a six-unit building
designated as second-stage housing for
single moms with kids. "But I volunteer
here at the shelter whenever they need me
— and they *always* need me for somethin'!"
The wiry woman laughed. "Usually come
Friday mornin's to give Edesa a hand an'
take care of her babies so she can teach the
Bible study, 'cept my Sabrina kept 'em
today. You two stayin' for the Bible study?"

Grace followed Precious up a flight of narrow stairs to the second floor. "I guess so.
Whatever's going on today." She was surprised to see how neat everything was in
the bunkrooms — six rooms, four bunk
beds in each, beds made up, with a central
lounge and bathrooms and showers off to
one side. A few of the bunks were occupied
by women napping or reading or doing their
nails, which made her feel like an intruder.
Grace was relieved when Precious led them
back down the stairs, past the main floor,
and down to the lower level, which housed
the dining room and kitchen, where Estelle
was bustling around behind a steel counter.

They only had time for a quick glance at the side rooms — a rec room with a Ping-Pong table, a laundry room, and somebody's office — when Estelle hollered, "Almost eleven! Edesa's ready to start. I'll be up in a minute."

A smattering of women of different ages had settled into the semicircle, though several others were still scattered around the room reading magazines or playing cards or snoozing. "Guess attending the Bible study isn't mandatory," Sam murmured to Grace as they settled into two folding chairs in the second row.

"Buenos días, mis amigas!" beamed a pretty black woman standing in front of the semicircle, taking Grace by surprise. She was definitely dark-skinned, with tiny braids similar to Sam's twists pulled back from her broad forehead, but her accent was heavily Spanish. "Welcome everyone. I am Edesa Baxter — and I see we have some visitors with us today . . . Oh, there you are, Estelle. Do you want to introduce your guests?"

Grace squirmed, wishing they hadn't been singled out. She already felt awkward, like tourists come to gawk at the homeless. But Estelle, wearing her big white apron and funny net cap over her topknot, just said, "This is one of my neighbors, Grace, and her friend, Samantha. Came by to see where I work. I been tellin' 'em how well I feed y'all, so don't make me a liar!" Everybody guffawed, and Grace relaxed.

"Does everybody have a Bible? Precious, could you . . ."

Precious was already passing out a stack of hardcover Bibles, asking, "Spanish or English?"

Grace and Sam each took an English Bible.

"We're starting a new study on the Gospel of John," Edesa said. "Does someone want to read the first eighteen verses of the first chapter?"

As the verses were read by a woman with a raspy smoker's voice, Grace noticed the painted mural on the wall behind Edesa for the first time. A shepherd — the biblical kind, in robe and beard and sandals — was surrounded by a flock of sheep. But unlike the pictures of the Good Shepherd she'd often seen in Sunday school growing up, these weren't a flock of white wooly sheep, but a ragtag flock. They were all shades of black and brown and not-so-white, and their wooly coats looked the worse for wear — all matted and mangy and bloody.

Grace glanced surreptitiously around the semicircle at the women frowning at the pages in front of them as the scripture passage was read. A strange feeling crept down her spine. A few of the women were dressed neatly, their hair combed or braided, but many looked hard beyond their years. Scars on arms and faces. Faces lined by weather or worry. Clothes mismatched or the wrong size. A few with too much makeup. A fairly ragtag bunch. Like the sheep in the mural.

She looked back up at the painting. All the sheep had their faces turned up toward the Shepherd, and the Shepherd was looking at them, smiling, love shining from his eyes. Just love. And maybe gladness too. Like he was thinking, *These are my sheep, and I love them no matter who they are!"*

The reader had stopped and Edesa was talking again. Grace realized she hadn't been paying attention and tried to focus. "Look at verse seventeen again. 'The law was given through Moses . . . but grace and truth came through Jesus Christ.' Can anyone tell me what you think this means?"

A hand waved. "Well, wasn't it the Moses dude what brought down them Ten Commandments from God?"

"Yeah, an' you probably done broke ever' one of 'em," someone snickered. Laughter swept the group.

"Exactly!" Edesa said, beaming like a

teacher who just got the right answer. "The Old Testament is full of 'the law' — but scripture also says that if we break even one of the laws, we've broken them all. Because it's impossible to keep God's laws in our own strength. And there's a verse in the third chapter of Romans that says, '*All* of us have sinned and fall short of the glory of God.' "

"Yeah, well," a steely-eyed woman muttered, "I may've done some drugs in my time, but at least I didn't go hookin' an' thievin' like some people I know."

The woman next to her backhanded her on the arm. "Girl, you better watch your mouth! Whatchu know about it? You don't know nothin'!"

Grace eyed Sam beside her. This was definitely not like any Bible study she'd been to at County Line, or any other church for that matter. She wondered what Sam was thinking.

"That's just it!" Edesa said, acting as if this was exactly the discussion she'd been hoping for. "It doesn't matter who you are or what you've done — or who I am, or what I've done — the law that came through Moses can't save us. Even so-called good people don't measure up. Check out Isaiah 64, verse 6." She first read from her Bible in Spanish, then translated in English, 'All our goodness is like a pile of filthy rags.'" She wrinkled her nose. "*Trapos apestosos* — like stinky rags. But what does the first chapter of John say came through Jesus?"

"Grace an' truth," the raspy voice read again.

"*Sí,* that's right. And, *mis amigas,* let me tell you something. People talk about getting justice — getting what we think we deserve. But if *some* of us got what we deserve . . . uh-uh. I'd rather have mercy — *not* getting what I deserve."

"Ain't *that* the truth" . . . "Now you're talkin'." Several women wagged their heads.

"But *grace,*" Edesa went on, closing her eyes and lifting a hand in the air, almost as if talking to herself, "*grace* is something else. Grace means there is nothing we can do to make God love us more — and grace also means there is nothing we can do to make God love us less."

A silence settled over the room. Even the women who hadn't come into the semicircle seemed to stop what they were doing and take in what she'd just said. The words echoed inside Grace's head. *"Grace means there is nothing we can do to make God love us more — and grace also means there is nothing we can do to make God love us less."*

"O, gracias, Señor," Edesa began to pray . . . but tears were slipping down Grace's cheeks. *"Think about the meaning of your name,"* Estelle had said. And there it was. She'd carried her secret for so long, so afraid people would think less of her, and yes, even afraid that God was still angry with her for having that abortion. And ever since, she'd been trying to make up for it, trying to be that "good girl" she knew she wasn't, trying to be "good enough" to deserve God's love again.

She'd never really understood the meaning of her name.

Grace.

CHAPTER 32

Grace was quiet on the ride home, letting Sam, and Estelle, in the front seat, chat like old friends.

The rest of their time at Manna House had been interesting, beginning with Estelle's lunch, something she called Mexican lasagna consisting of layers of corn tortillas, rice, black beans, hamburger, corn, cheese, and who knew what all. Delicious. They'd sat at a table with Precious and several of the shelter guests, but didn't get to talk much because a heated argument erupted about who was to blame for a mine disaster in West Virginia that'd been in the news the past few days. "*Somebody* oughta go ta jail for all them safety violations," groused a middle-aged woman with frowzy brown hair. "Lookit all them widows an' orphans what lost their husbands an' daddies. Gonna end up in a shelter just like this."

After lunch, however, they'd met a few of

the staff and volunteers, including the program director Estelle had mentioned — Gabby Somebody — a woman with a head full of curly red hair.

But though Grace had enjoyed the rest of their time at the shelter — even joining the cleanup crew after lunch, which felt a bit like the time she'd worked kitchen crew as a teenager at summer camp — her mind was still mulling over the Bible study. Had Estelle known what the topic was going to be? Was that the reason she'd invited them to come today?

It didn't matter. What mattered is that Grace felt like God was lancing a festering sore in her spirit. It had even started with Estelle's gentle probing yesterday, dredging up the secret she'd been so afraid to tell anyone. But the older woman hadn't seemed blown away, hadn't lectured her about what a phony she'd been, traveling all over the country talking about *purity.* No, she'd just said Grace should meditate on the meaning of her name.

She hadn't realized it so much yesterday, but hanging out with Estelle today, meeting the people she worked with, and being introduced to everyone as one of her new neighbors, Grace realized she felt a powerful connection with this woman. Estelle knew the worst about her and still . . . still *liked* her. And Estelle was taking her request to pray for the upcoming concert tour seriously, as though she still believed in her.

Grace watched as her assistant talked, with lively gestures and laughter. Had holding tight to the secrets of her past even kept people like Samantha Curtis at arm's length? Sam was more than an assistant really, a person so loyal, so fun to be around, a sister in spirit, who could be a close friend . . .

Estelle did a turnaround in the cul-de-sac at the end of Beecham Street and pulled up in front of the Bentleys' house. "Thanks for comin' with me today," she said as they all piled out. "Hope I didn't take up too much of your workday."

"Don't worry," Sam laughed. "Grace'll just keep me working till nine tonight — but that usually means we get to eat out." The young woman gave Estelle a hug. "I'm so glad to meet you, Miss Estelle. Thanks for letting me come today."

Grace gave Estelle a hug too. "Yes, thanks," she whispered. "More than I can say."

They waved good-bye and walked across the street to Grace's bungalow. "You were kinda quiet on the ride home," Sam said as she followed Grace into the house. "You okay?"

"Uh-huh. Just thinking." Grace picked up Oreo, who'd lost no time doing circle eights around her ankles, and nuzzled his soft black fur.

"Well." Sam threw her shoulder bag on the couch. "Time to get to work. I'll tackle the fan mail unless there's something else you want me to do first."

Grace hesitated a moment, then said, "There is." She sat down on the couch and patted the cushion beside her. "Come sit. There's something I want to share with you — something I should've told you a long time ago . . ."

Sam was in tears by the time Grace finished telling her about her rebellion as a teenager that had led to such disastrous consequences, and how the recent humiliating experience with airport security and Roger breaking their engagement had combined to form a perfect storm that shook her to the core, dredging up all her buried secrets to haunt her again.

"Oh, Grace," Sam sniffled, scooting over on the couch and giving her a tight squeeze. "Thank you so much for telling me. I . . . it really means a lot that you trust me enough to confide in me."

The younger woman grabbed a tissue and made a sour face. "Believe me, you're not the only one who ever messed up. I ran with a bunch of real wildcats in high school, turned my mama's hair gray, until God slapped me upside the head and I got right with Jesus. See? There's stuff I never told you either. Wanna hear it?"

Grace shook her head, a wry smile tipping a corner of her mouth. "Maybe sometime. But there's more I need to tell you . . ." Taking a deep breath, she told Sam about the revelation she'd had after her talk with Estelle yesterday about her motives for her message — trying to make it up to God for having the abortion. "But the Bible study at the shelter today really got to me, all the things Edesa said about grace. After I spilled my guts to Estelle yesterday, all she said was, if I need a theme for my upcoming tour, I should meditate on the meaning of my name."

Sam just stared at her for a long moment. "Wow. That's kinda deep."

"I know."

"But, uh, we already gave Barry and the band a song list."

"I know."

"And we have a practice scheduled with

the band tomorrow down at the studio."

"I know."

The two women sat quietly on the couch for several minutes. Then Grace said, "But I want to come up with a new list for the last set — about grace. I'd like to try writing at least one new song, but for the rest . . . well, I could use some help choosing those. I need the weekend at least to work on a song and search out the possibilities." She cast a guilty glance at Sam. "So would you, uh, call Barry and cancel the practice tomorrow?"

Sam rolled her eyes, then grabbed a small accent pillow and threw it at Grace. "Me?! He'll kill me! That's gotta be above my pay grade."

Grace threw the pillow back. "Then I'll give you a raise," she giggled, and before she knew it, they were both laughing hysterically and whacking each other with the throw pillows, sending Oreo flying from the room to safety in the basement.

Barry had a fit when Sam called him that afternoon — Grace could hear him yelling even though Sam didn't have her phone on speaker — but after a few minutes of sputtering about last-minute changes, with the tour less than two weeks away, there was a long pause . . . And then all Grace heard was Sam saying, "Uh-huh . . . Uh-huh . . . Really? . . . Okay, I'll tell her."

Grace grimaced as Sam pocketed her cell phone. "Tell me what?"

A slow smile spread across Sam's face. "He likes your idea for the last set."

Grace screeched. *"Yes!"*

"He's going to send you a few suggestions of his own. But he wants a new song list no later than Sunday night, and wants you to commit to practices *every* evening next week if he can get the rehearsal space."

"Yes, yes, I'll do it!" Grace started dancing around the room. "I know this is right! Thank you, Lord! Hallelujah!"

"Ahem!" Sam said, arms crossed, tapping her foot. "Maybe we should save the hallelujahs till we see whether we can actually get *permissions* for these songs on such short notice."

Grace stopped dancing, chagrined. "Oh. You're right. That's a lot of extra work for you. Are you . . . do you . . . I mean —"

Sam dropped her phony fuss and laughed. "Of course, silly! Whatever it takes! We're gonna do this thing!"

While Grace was brushing her teeth the next morning, something Edesa had said yesterday popped into her head — something about mercy is *not getting* what we deserve, and grace is *getting* what we *don't* deserve. She frowned at her reflection in the mirror, toothbrush sticking out of her mouth. What did that really mean?

Fifteen minutes later she curled up on the couch with a cup of coffee, the cat, and her Bible. She'd been anxious to get to work on a new song, but . . . it was all too easy to let "urgent" stuff crowd out the important — like taking time to get into the Word and pray. This didn't seem like the right time to skip it.

She read through the first chapter of John's gospel again — and stopped at verse sixteen. "From his abundance we have all received one gracious blessing after another." Wow. *Blessing upon blessing . . .*

Blessings weren't earned. Or rewards. They were gifts.

Blessing upon blessing . . .

She had heard this before. Probably nodded assent during a sermon or two as if she really understood it. But she hadn't. Not until now. Grace stared out the window absently, thinking about the blessings God had poured out on her over the years. Being able to sing, doing something she loved . . . rising success as a contemporary Christian music artist . . . a family who loved her, even her two rascally brothers . . . the greatest assistant she could ever hope for . . .

And Roger? Was Roger's change of heart part of God's grace for her, redeeming a relationship she thought was lost? She hadn't thought of it that way till now, but . . . She'd thought getting dumped by Fowler at Bongo was bad news, but that turned out to be a blessing too, getting a new agent who —

Ohmygoodness. Her agent! She really needed to call Jeff about her idea for the West Coast tour! She almost reached for the phone, and then remembered it was Saturday. The Bongo office would be closed. Well, she'd call him first thing Monday. That'd be better anyway, because by then she'd have her song list — she'd better have, anyway — and maybe even a new name for the tour.

Yikes. Would giving this tour a focused theme upset the apple cart? Most of the scheduled venues had probably already done their promo for the tour. She could still use "Grace Meredith in Concert," of course, but she'd like something stronger, something passionate.

Something bigger than her.

Her meandering thoughts were interrupted by a movement outside the window. The Bentleys' grandson was running across the street. He passed her house and ran up the Jaspers' walk next door. A minute later she saw him running back toward the two-flat with Tavis and his older brother hot on his heels. She grinned. The boys were excited about something.

That was another blessing — getting to know her new neighbors, the Bentleys. And even the Jaspers next door, though she hadn't seen much of the twins since the snow melted. She should make more of an effort to be neighborly.

But right now she needed to get busy. She had a song to write. Hopping off the couch, Grace headed for the kitchen to make breakfast, her heart full. *Thank you, Lord, for blessing upon blessings you've given me, blessings I don't deserve . . . pure gifts.* And then she laughed out loud. That was it! Her new song . . . "Blessing upon Blessing"!

A while later, sitting at the piano with her laptop on the bench beside her, Grace moved hands and thoughts back and forth between the two keyboards, first playing with the words, then teasing a tune from the piano. Time slowed as she worked, writing and deleting, trying another phrase, rearranging things. After a while, an incoming e-mail pinged, interrupting her concentration. She almost ignored it, but saw it was from Sam, forwarding some song suggestions from Barry.

She skimmed through the e-mail. These were great! "Grace" by Michael W. Smith . . . "If Not for Grace" by Clint Brown — she loved that one . . . and "Grace Like Rain" by Todd Agnew, for starters. Sam had attached a few suggestions of her own and added, *Wouldn't hurt to include a few hymns. Most of them are older than dirt and we don't need permission to use them. Just saying!*

Grace spent the rest of the day listening to the suggested songs, printing out song sheets when she could find them, and even thumbing through an old hymnbook, then returning to the half-finished song at the piano. She wasn't satisfied with the new song, not yet . . . but by Sunday morning she'd chosen several songs for a meaningful set, maybe adding a hymn or two if some permissions were hard to get.

The new song would come in time; somehow she knew it.

Glancing at the clock, she saw it was still early. Why not go to the traditional service at Mark and Denise's church? She'd wanted to try it. She might even stay for the contemporary service at eleven. After all, she'd missed Easter Sunday last weekend, and had skipped church on Palm Sunday.

She slipped into the sanctuary at Faith Chapel a few minutes after the first service had started and took a seat toward the back. She smiled — no words were being projected on a screen in this service. Everyone was using a hymnbook as the congregation sang the opening hymn.

As the song leader announced the next hymn, Grace took a hymnal from the rack in front of her and turned to the page number as the organ and piano played the last few measures as an intro. She started to sing, and then stopped as the words focused on the page . . .

Marvelous grace of our loving Lord,
grace that exceeds our sin and our
    guilt! . . .

Goosebumps crawled down her arms, and her mouth suddenly went dry even as her eyes filled with sudden tears. *Grace that exceeds my sin and my guilt . . .* Had God brought her here this morning to remind her one more time what his grace for her was all about? Blinking back the tears and licking her lips, she was finally able to join in on the last phrase of the chorus . . .

Grace, grace, God's grace,
grace that is greater than all our sin!

Grace sat with Mark and Denise at the eleven o'clock. They seemed delighted to see her, but she declined their lunch invitation. "I leave for the West Coast a week from Tuesday and I'm still working on a new song. Gotta get a song list to Barry by this afternoon too." She edged toward the door. "Can I take a rain check?"

Her brother made her promise to stay for lunch the following Sunday, before the tour — "Cross your heart and hope to die, Sis!" — but they finally hugged and let her go. She waved as she headed out of the church parking lot. She wasn't quite ready to share with her brother and Denise the revolution God had been doing in her spirit this past week — but it did feel strange to have shared so intimately with Estelle Bentley and Sam things she'd never shared with her own family.

In some ways, that was going to be a lot harder. She had more to lose if they were deeply disappointed in her.

And Roger . . . *O God.* Should she tell Roger about the abortion? How would he

381

react? Would he still want to give their relationship another chance? Thinking about telling Roger was the scariest of all.

By four o'clock Sunday afternoon, Grace had a song list. She sent it by e-mail to Sam to look over first before sending it on to Barry, and half an hour later Sam called back. "Wow, this looks great. And you have a new song? That's great! 'Blessing upon Blessing' . . . can I hear it?"

"Not yet. Still tweaking the tune." Grace was excited. The words had come on the drive home from church, had fallen into place, had fallen right out of her heart. Like a prayer.

"*Hmm,* okay. See you took my suggestion about including a hymn. Not sure I'm familiar with this one though. Tell me about it."

Grace got her hymnbook and read the words of all three verses and chorus. "I don't know . . . it really moved me this morning. It says what I want to say. Might end the set with this. Even the tune supports the words — kind and tender. God's grace is greater than all my sin. Bottom line, what God offers us is . . . just grace."

There was silence on the other end of the call for a long moment. And then Sam must've had the exact thought that hit Grace like a thunderbolt in the same instant, because her assistant suddenly screeched. "That's it! What you just said! *That's* your new title for your tour! *Just Grace!*"

CHAPTER 33

Grace was just crawling into bed that night — still so excited about her new theme and concert title that she wasn't sure she could fall asleep — when her cell phone rang. She glanced at the caller ID. *Roger Baldwin . . .* A warm feeling spread through her body. Almost like old times, Roger calling just before she went to sleep.

"Hey, there," he said. "Didn't wake you, I hope."

"No, no, I'm still awake."

"You doing okay? Kind of thought you'd call this weekend, just to stay in touch, you know, even if you still need time to consider how we're going to move forward in our relationship."

"I'm fine." Grace didn't know whether she felt pleased or annoyed that he'd expected her to call. "I did tell you I needed some space to consider what we talked about. It's only been a few days, Roger, not even a week."

"I know, but . . . I'm thinking about you. Just thought I'd call. But I'll hang up if you —"

"No, it's okay, Roger." Her mind scrambled. What would be safe to talk about? "Actually, I'm kind of excited, because God has given me a new theme for my upcoming concert tour — but I'm going to have to practice like mad this week with the band, since it's kind of late in the game."

There was a slight pause on the other end. "A new theme?"

"Uh-huh. We're calling it Just Grace."

"Ah. That's clever. Just Grace . . . just you in concert."

"Well, yes, but it has double meaning, because I'm focusing on songs about God's grace."

"Oh. Of course. Well, that's good. But kind of a departure from your previous theme isn't it? What brought this about?"

Grace hesitated. "Just . . . a lot has happened since my last tour, Roger — you know that. I think this theme reflects my spiritual journey right now. But just to assure you" — she made an instant decision — "I heard you when you said you didn't like me talking about you publicly. So don't worry. I didn't say anything about our broken engagement at the few concerts I've done recently and won't say anything on the tour about where we are right now. If someone asks me directly, I'll try to be appropriately vague and discreet."

"Well . . . that's good. I appreciate that."

Time to change the subject. "So, what's up with you? You didn't have to work this weekend I hope."

Grace listened as Roger chatted easily, told her he was starting to run, was hoping to work up to a half-marathon by next year, and, oh yes, he'd been asked to teach a young adult Sunday school class on "The Christian in the Workplace" at County Line Community Church. But when they finally said goodnight and hung up, some of the excitement about her new theme had dissipated. Would Roger understand?

Grace had planned to call Jeff first thing Monday morning, but the call with Roger the night before made her hesitate. How could she talk about her new theme without telling the whole story? The thought of telling a man — even a kind, caring man like Jeff — about her past made her feel all . . . all exposed and naked. But toweling her hair after her workout at Curves, she knew she had to call — Jeff was her agent and needed to know her plans. Would he be willing to get on the phone with the multiple venues and ask them to refocus their promotion efforts?

Taking a deep breath, she hit the speed-dial number for Bongo Booking Agency. The receptionist put her through . . .

"Grace! Uh-oh. You caught me sneaking my second cup of coffee — and it's not coffee break yet. What's up?"

"I've got a new direction for the West Coast tour. All your fault, you know."

He laughed, but she heard him close a door. "Great. I'm all ears."

She told him as briefly as she could, making sure to mention that her prayer partner — well, that's what Estelle was, wasn't she? — had suggested she meditate on the meaning of her name. "And then it all fell into place — the theme, the songs, a new title."

Jeff whistled softly on the other end. " 'Just Grace' . . . wow. I really love it. Venues have been promoting 'Grace Meredith in Concert,' but I think we can ask them to start talking about this new theme. Posters have been up for a while, but we can target radio. It will cost a little money, but if you think it's worth it, we can cross that bridge when we come to it."

"I do — think it's worth it, I mean. I'm

willing to pay to make it happen. Could we do new posters? Maybe that's asking too much for this tour. But could you think about it? Let me know?" *Willing to pay . . . but able?* She'd have to trust God for that.

"I'll make it happen. God's grace is such a powerful theme. If you don't mind my asking, I sense there's more to the story. You care to share it?"

Grace had to blink back sudden tears. "I . . . there is, but not just now, okay?"

"You bet. I trust you. Sounds like you've tapped into that passion we were talking about — which makes me want to tap-dance on my desk." He chuckled in her ear, and then got all businesslike. "Look, have Sam shoot me the song list you've come up with — you said you've put together a mix of contemporary songs and hymns? If she has any trouble getting permissions, have her call me. Maybe I can help."

Relief flowed through her tense muscles. He liked her ideas. "Thanks so much, Jeff. And I just wanted you to know . . . I've written a new song for the tour. I've got the words and the tune, but I'll need the band to fill it out."

"I'm really glad to hear this, Grace. You have real talent in that area, you know. I had a feeling God might drop a new song

388

into your heart. He has a way of doing that when the time and the theme and the soul passion is right."

"Thanks, Jeff. I really appreciate the encouragement." Grace's doorbell rang. "I better go. I think that's Sam. I'll have her send you the song list . . . Oh, Jeff? One more thing. Just thought you ought to know that my fiancé is asking for us to work on patching up our relationship. I — I haven't given him an answer, but I thought you'd like to know since we'd sort of talked about that."

There was a momentary silence on his end. Then he said, "Thanks for letting me know. I'm glad you're taking some time to think about it." His voice softened. "Take care, Grace."

Sam spent most of the day on the phone, chasing down copyrights and agents. "Wish I could talk directly to the artists," she grumbled at one point, sticking her head into the living room where Grace was at the piano working on a hymn arrangement. "I should think they'd be delighted to have their songs getting more exposure. You always give the original artist credit when you use a song — seems like a win-win to me! It's these blankety-blank third-party legal eagles who are a pain in the neck. Oh, and those annoying phone menus they make you wade through." She pinched her nose and got tinny. " 'If you want to speak to the janitor, dial extension 0000 . . .' "

Grace laughed in spite of the interruption. "Jeff Newman might be able to help with the sticky ones. Now if you don't mind, I'm trying to work on some music here." She leaned over the keys, sounding out a new arrangement for the chorus of "He Giveth More Grace" as Sam once again holed herself up in the kitchen.

They'd just decided to wrap it up for the day and take a break before leaving for the studio that evening, when the doorbell rang. Sam got to the door first. "Miss Estelle! Come in!"

With a start, Grace realized she hadn't talked with her neighbor since their trip to the women's shelter on Friday — and hadn't told her the good news.

Estelle hesitated on the doorstep. "Am I interrupting? Just got home from work and thought I'd come by for a few minutes. Wanted to pray with you about your upcoming concert tour. But if you're busy —"

"No, please, come in!" Grinning, Grace grabbed Estelle by the hand and pulled the woman over to the couch. "We've got an answer to one of your prayers!" It all came out in bits and pieces: meditating on her name . . . the Bible study at Manna House . . . deciding to open her heart to Sam . . . the growing realization that "grace" was her theme . . . the songs that were starting to come together . . . and the concert title that had dropped into their hearts at the same time.

Estelle began to laugh and raised her hands. "Halle*lu*jah! Thank you, Jesus! *Ha-ha-ha.* 'Just Grace' . . . Oh, Lord, you are such a *good* God! *Mmm-hmmm . . .*" Then with a sudden clap, she said, "Well, now, let's pray that God will smooth all the rough places — you say you've got practices every evening this week? Well then, Lord, we're asking you to give Grace and Samantha, these two dear sisters, as well as the band, extra strength and grace and good tempers as they prepare to serve you on the concert tour that's just around the corner . . ."

Grace eyed Sam with a grin, and then bowed her head. Estelle was already off and praying.

". . . and prepare the hearts of young people all up and down the West Coast to receive your message of love and mercy and grace through our sister's beautiful music and testimony . . ."

Hmm. Grace wasn't sure about the testimony part.

". . . And, Lord, while we're at it, I want to pray for dear Mrs. Krakowski, the former owner of our two-flat, who's lost a box of precious mementos. Lord, you know where that box is, and it would mean so much to her if it could be found. She's lost so much, Lord — her home, her neighborhood, her familiar friends . . ."

Grace squirmed. She didn't think Mrs. Krakowski had had many friends in this neighborhood. Everyone seemed too busy with their own little worlds . . . *Like me, Lord.* Her heart wrenched. *O God, please forgive me for not reaching out to that lonely old woman.* She'd missed her chance, and now it was too late.

Too late for Mrs. Krakowski. But maybe not too late for her other neighbors. Once she was back from this tour, she'd definitely try to reach out more to —

". . . And for Harry's dear mother, Lord, who's lost her ability to speak with that stroke, but we're askin' you, Lord, to bring her home to us, so we can make her comfortable in these last years of her life . . ."

"Yes, Jesus, yes!" Sam murmured on the other side of Estelle.

". . . but you also know we need to get

Harry's boy on up out of that apartment, so, Lord, we're askin' you for that job you're preparin' for Rodney Bentley right now. He needs the satisfaction of honest work to keep him out of trouble, to help him turn his life around, to help him provide for his own son . . ."

Somewhere in the middle of her prayer, Estelle had reached for one of Grace's hands — one of Sam's too — and was gripping them hard as she prayed. And then suddenly she released their hands, sweaty now, and sat back against the couch cushions with a *whoosh.* "Amen, thank you, Jesus, *mm-hm.*" She picked up a magazine from the coffee table and fanned herself.

Sam was looking at her strangely. "Rodney . . . he's your husband's son? And he's living with you?"

Estelle nodded and kept fanning. "Just came up from Atlanta a while back, been lookin' for a job. He's stayin' in one of the rooms on the first floor, but we need to get that apartment ready for Mother Bentley. And . . . well, there are other reasons he needs to get his own place. But the good Lord knows."

Sam started to laugh. "Did you know that the owner of Lincoln Limo lives right on this block? That big house at the end of the street. We've used them a bunch of times for transport to and from the airport — and I know for a fact that they're hiring. They need more drivers. Do you think Rodney would be interested?"

CHAPTER 34

Grace couldn't help mulling over what had happened in her living room just half an hour ago, even while she tried to keep Sam's leased Honda Civic in sight as they threaded their way through rush-hour traffic. No sooner had she closed the door behind Estelle Bentley than she'd realized they needed to leave *now* if they were going to get to the address in time to make the six o'clock practice with the band. No time for supper first — they'd have to eat after. Just as well. Grace knew she didn't sing as well on a full stomach.

They'd decided to drive their own cars so Sam wouldn't have to come back to the house later, leaving Grace alone with her thoughts behind the wheel. Estelle Bentley just happened to drop in while Sam was there, just happened to throw out a prayer about Harry's son needing a job, it just happened that Sam knew Lincoln Limo was hiring *and* that the owner lived right up the street? It was like some cosmic jigsaw puzzle, where only God had the box cover and knew what the final picture would look like.

"*If* they hire him," Grace murmured to herself. From what Estelle said, it sounded as if Rodney Bentley had been in some kind of trouble — which might explain why he'd been having a difficult time getting a job. But Estelle had started thanking God for this answer to prayer even before she'd hustled home to tell Rodney. Well, as Estelle would probably say, "God knows." It wasn't her worry.

Her worry reared its face as Grace pulled into the small parking lot alongside Sam's car at the rehearsal space Barry had found. It was little more than a warehouse, really. Barry's van and cars belonging to other band members were already there. Barry had grudgingly forgiven her for changing half the song list for the West Coast tour — but what about the guys in the band? Were they mad at her for canceling Saturday's practice and changing the song list on them? After all, it meant extra practices for all of them. She'd have to make it up to them somehow. Show them how much she appreciated them. She definitely didn't want them to feel taken advantage of.

Then there was the matter of the brand-new song, one that would take some work on the band's part to come up with an arrangement. At least she'd written out the words and the melody and faxed them to Barry to give him a heads-up.

She locked the car and met her assistant at the front door of the building. "We're only two minutes late," Sam assured her as they made their way up a flight of stairs to the second floor. Grace wished they'd been ten minutes early. She hesitated as they came into the room full of mikes, amps, and other sound equipment, being careful not to trip over long wires snaking here and there. All five members of the band were busy setting up their instruments. Barry was standing at the soundboard, doing sound checks with first one, then another.

Reno was the first one to notice them, stopping mid-chord at the keyboard. Then Nigel looked up and put down his drumsticks. Petey, saxophone strapped around his neck and shaved head glistening under the fluorescent lights, stared in her direction. Like synchronized swimmers, the two guitarists — freckle-faced, redheaded Alex and Zach, still sporting his African knots —

turned toward them, instruments gone silent.

Grace's mouth went dry. *Oh, God* . . . It was worse than she thought. She needed to say something, apologize, do something —

And then Reno began to clap his hands together — *thwop, thwop, thwop* — as a slow grin spread over his face. One by one the others joined in. Clapping. Grinning. Laughing.

"Good on ya, Grace!" Petey called out in his fake Australian accent.

Alex did a loud *wah-wah-wah* trill on his guitar. "Yeah! Gonna be the best tour yet."

"All ya need now is a good black gospel song!" Zach's skilled fingers added a rhythmic beat on his bass guitar, picked up in an instant by Nigel's snare drums, and a moment later all five musicians were jamming something that sounded vaguely like "Amazing Grace" as Grace just stood there, not sure whether to laugh or cry.

Barry walked over to them, a big grin plastered on his bearded face. "Grace . . . Sam . . . good to see you." He handed a pair of large, padded earphones to Grace. "You ready?"

They only got through three songs Monday night, including "Blessing upon Blessing," and then they all went out for Giordano's pizza afterward — the first time Grace had actually just hung out with the guys. Why hadn't she ever done this before? She sat back in the large padded booth and just listened as they laughed and joshed each other, making wisecracks about Nigel's tattoos and Barry's latest gray hairs. Grace felt overwhelmed by the support of Barry and the band — one more "gift of grace," she thought, knowing they'd had every reason to be upset with the last-minute changes.

A black gospel song, Zach had said . . . could she do it? That would show respect for the band — for Zach in particular. And add a nice variety to the theme.

By the time they got together again Tuesday night, she'd found the song: "Your Grace and Mercy" by the Mississippi Mass Choir. Zach was so happy he gave her a big kiss. "Now that's what I'm talkin' about, sister!"

"I might need some help," she admitted. Black gospel wasn't really her style. The only other gospel song she'd done was an old spiritual she'd recorded for her CD.

Zach shook his head. "Just think about the words and sing 'em like you mean it, nice an' slow."

Your grace and mercy brought me

through . . . Yes, she could sing that song and mean it.

Sam was at the house every day, still working on getting permissions while Grace practiced her songs, but it was Wednesday before Grace realized they hadn't heard anything from Estelle Bentley about whether she still planned to drop in again to pray that afternoon. Grace was curious — had Rodney followed up with the job possibility at Lincoln Limo? Probably too soon to know anything. They'd find out in good time.

But when they stopped for lunch, Sam went to the front window and pulled back the thin curtains that let in light but kept out prying eyes. "Doesn't Miss Estelle cook for the women's shelter every day?"

"I think so. Why?"

"Just asking. I noticed her car is still sitting in front of the house, been there all morning. Hope she's okay."

Grace peeked out the window. The little black SUV was there all right. "Maybe she just had the day off."

"I think we oughta call."

"Call? Whatever for?"

Sam turned. "Duh. Because that's what neighbors do when they notice something might not be right."

"Sounds like being nosy to me."

"Just . . . call, Grace. Miss Estelle won't mind. If everything's okay, she'll still appreciate that you cared. Or if you won't, I will."

"Okay, okay, I'll call." Besides, it would be nice to know if Estelle planned to drop over again to pray, and if so, what time. She needed to let her know they had to leave by five to get to practice.

Sam stuck her head in the refrigerator to rustle up some lunch while Grace dialed Estelle's number. The voice that answered was breathless. "Grace? That you? Lord, Lord, . . . I'm so sorry I didn't call to let you know."

Grace made a frantic motion at Sam and pointed to the phone as she switched to speaker. "Let me know what? Has something happened?"

"Yes, yes. O sweet Jesus! Mother Bentley passed yesterday. Just like that, another stroke! We've been all up in a tizzy, makin' arrangements an' plannin' her homegoin' service. But, oh dear, I should've called earlier."

Sam hovered at Grace's elbow, dark eyes widened, hand over her mouth.

"No, no, it's all right," Grace said. "But I'm so sorry to hear that Mr. Bentley's mother died. Sam is too. She's right here. Uh, is there anything we can do?"

"Fact is, yes, there is . . . look, can I run over in about half an hour? I've got some more calls to make, but I need to talk to you. Would you have a few minutes?"

Grace and Sam ate a quick lunch of tuna sandwiches. Sam kept shaking her head. "That's so sad. Didn't Miss Estelle say they were fixing up the first-floor apartment for Mother Bentley? Wonder what they'll do with it now."

The doorbell rang. Estelle came in, wearing a loose caftan and sloppy slip-ons that had seen better days, her straightened salt-and-pepper hair caught up in a careless topknot. Both Grace and Sam gave her a hug, once again expressing their sympathy for the Bentleys' loss.

Estelle got right to the point. "Can't stay . . . sorry about our prayer time today, but I'm workin' on the repast. Harry should be the one to ask you this, but . . . oh, you know, he's got a dozen different things on his mind, dealin' with the funeral home, the cemetery, his mother's apartment."

"Of course. But, um . . . ask me what?"

"We could bring something to the repast," Sam jumped in helpfully.

"Oh, no. that's all right. My Yada Yada

prayer group sisters have got that covered now, thank you, Jesus. But Harry wanted to ask you for a special favor, Grace. Wanted to ask if you'd sing at his mother's home-goin'."

"Sing?" Grace was startled. She'd never even met the woman, and barely knew Harry. In fact, she'd never sung at anyone's funeral before.

Estelle nodded. "He wants that song on your CD. Harry plays it over an' over. Has come to mean a lot to him, he says. You know the one, that old spiritual . . . 'Give Me Jesus.' "

Which is how Grace came to be sitting in the strangest church she'd ever been in the following Saturday, a large storefront in the Howard Street Shopping Center, its big glass windows looking out over the parking lot with *SouledOut Community Church — All Are Welcome* in big red script across the glass. The large room with its rows of padded folding chairs set in a semicircle was filling with a diverse crowd of young and old, mostly African Americans and whites, but a good number of Hispanics as well. The room almost looked festive. Colorful handmade banners hanging on the wall behind a low platform seemed to shout,

GOD IS GOOD . . . ALL THE TIME and THE JOY OF THE LORD IS OUR STRENGTH.

When she and Sam first arrived, someone was playing gentle music on a keyboard as people slowly filed past an open casket flanked by two large flower arrangements, but they'd simply found seats toward the back. When the service started, the casket was closed, and then Harry and Estelle Bentley, followed by Rodney Bentley, his son DaShawn, and a few other people who must be relatives walked up the middle aisle and took their seats in the front row.

Grace looked at her program, wondering where she was scheduled to sing. A sweet picture of a smiling black woman filled the front page. *Wanda M. Bentley, 1922–2010.* Wow, almost ninety years old. The inside page had a biography on the left and an order of service — called a "Homegoing Celebration" — on the right: *Prelude . . . Processional of Family Members . . . Praise and Worship . . . Remarks . . . Resolutions of Condolence . . . Reading of the Obituary . . .*

Oh, there it was. *"Give Me Jesus" by Grace Meredith, Soloist,* just before the eulogy.

The praise and worship time was so exuberant and joyous — not like any funeral service Grace had ever been to — that by the time the pastor leading the service finally called on her, she felt wrung out. But with an encouraging squeeze on her arm from Sam, Grace walked to the front of the room, took the cordless mike that was handed to her, and nodded at the man standing at the soundboard in the back of the room. Glancing at the Bentley family in the front row, she got an encouraging smile from Estelle, dressed in lovely black and white, but her husband's eyes were closed, as if waiting expectantly. As the instrumental track began to play, Grace focused her gaze on the family, took a deep breath, and began to sing the rich old spiritual.

Give me Jesus,
Give me Jesus
You may have all the world,
Give me Jesus.

She sang first one verse, and then another, and saw tears sliding down Harry's face.

And when I come to die,
And when I come to die,
And when I come to die,
Give me Jesus.

But not only tears glistened on his face. A smile of perfect peace.

As Grace sat down, the words of the song were still echoing in her spirit. *You may have all the world . . . Give me Jesus*. Would she be willing to give up all *her* world for Jesus? Her singing career? The concert tours? The admiration of her fans?

Easy to say. She didn't think Jesus was asking her to give it up.

But . . . would she be willing to give it up for Roger?

CHAPTER 35

The burial was going to be a private affair later that day, so after the service, tables were set up and mountains of food appeared for the repast. Grace and Sam stayed for a little while, but soon had to excuse themselves as Barry had scheduled yet another practice with the band that afternoon.

"When you leavin' for the tour?" Estelle asked as they hugged good-bye.

"Tuesday. We're taking the train, you know. The first concert is in Seattle on Friday, but we have to allow three days for travel."

Estelle wagged her head. "*Mm-mm,* hope Harry doesn't get assigned to one of those long-distance routes, but . . . I shouldn't complain. Just glad he has a job."

Grace was tempted to ask whether Rodney had gotten a job, but decided this wasn't the time.

"So you'll still be here on Monday?"

Estelle was saying. "Good. I'll come over to pray for your tour — and will keep you covered each day you're on the road. God's got your back, you know." The older woman wrapped Grace in another big hug. "Thanks for singin' that song," she murmured. "Meant a great deal to my Harry."

The homegoing service for Mother Bentley — which Sam said was pretty traditional for black folks — stayed with Grace the rest of the weekend. The Resolutions of Condolence from various churches and organizations, as well as the remarks of family and friends, made Grace wish she'd known Harry's mother. It was so easy to think of the elderly as just . . . *old,* forgetting that they too had once been rambunctious kids with big dreams, had worked hard to support their families, had suffered disappointments and sorrows along the way with dignity and courage, and had influenced their worlds, big or small. Once again Grace felt a pang that she'd never taken the time to get to know old Mrs. Krakowski across the street.

Monday night's practice with the band would be the last one before the tour, but Grace felt Saturday's had gone so well, she honored her promise to have Sunday lunch with her brother and his family after church. Her nephews had gone gaga at the prospect of spending *days* on a train and peppered her with questions. Where was she going to sleep? Could she get off? Did they show movies? What if bandits robbed the train? Laughing, Grace said it was her first cross-country train trip, but promised to regale them with her adventures when she got back.

But once Marcus and Luke left the table to play video games, Grace took a deep breath to bring Mark and Denise up to speed about her new focus on Just Grace — and why. Denise got teary when she told them about her teenage abortion and reached out to hold Grace's hand, but Mark looked positively stricken. "Have you . . . have you told Mom and Dad?"

She shook her head. "I . . . I mean to, just not sure when. Or how. I know they'll be so disappointed in me." A tear slid down her cheek.

Her brother pushed back from the table and came around to Grace's chair, leaning over her from behind and wrapping his arms around her. "I'm so sorry you went through that alone, Sis," he said, his voice husky. "At sixteen! We should've been there for you. But at least I can be there for you now. Why don't you wait to tell Mom and Dad until we're together, and I can be with you too?"

She nodded, unable to speak past the lump in her throat. Another gift of God's grace . . .

But her brother's mood changed when, in the interest of full disclosure, Grace told them Roger had admitted he was wrong to end their engagement so suddenly, and wanted to back up and give them a chance to work things out. "You gotta be kidding," Mark growled. "You aren't actually going to give him another chance, are you?"

"I . . . I haven't said yes or no. But I did promise I'd think about it. He seemed very sincere when he apologized. After all, people make mistakes — I should know, right? So maybe Roger needs some grace too."

"Now, Mark," chided Denise as her husband snorted, eyes rolling. "Don't make your sister fight you too." She squeezed Grace's hand. "We just don't want to see you hurt again, sweetie. So just . . . be sure, okay?"

Grace felt a little unsettled by her brother's reaction to the news that she was considering a reconciliation with Roger. If she and Roger did get married, she'd want him to be a welcome member of the family. If she could forgive him, maybe Mark could too.

Well, it had been a lot to dump on her brother and sister-in-law. He was just being a protective big brother. He'd come around.

Sam decided to work from home on Monday, since she also had laundry and packing to do. Most of the permissions had come in, and she'd been on the phone with Jeff Newman at Bongo Booking about the few holdouts.

As much as Grace enjoyed Sam's easygoing presence, she was grateful for a quiet day at home before leaving on her trip. She skipped her session at Curves to get her laundry started, spent the morning doing voice exercises and running through several of the songs she'd be doing on the tour, and then took Oreo to Meeow Chicago right after lunch so she'd have time to start packing before the evening session at the studio.

"Good-bye, buddy," she murmured, nuzzling the cat before reluctantly releasing him to one of the attendants. "Gonna miss you." For a brief moment she wondered if she could've arranged to bring the cat along — after all, didn't some of the big secular music stars travel with pets on their tour bus?

Yeah, right. Now you're getting nuts, she

told herself, watching Oreo disappear in the attendant's arms behind swinging doors.

Later, folding laundry on the couch, Grace saw Estelle Bentley pull up and get out of the car. But instead of going into the house, she waved at someone, and a moment later Grace saw her come across the street and stand on the sidewalk talking to the twins' mother from next door. Grace glanced at the clock . . . almost three thirty. If her neighbor was going to come over to pray one more time about the West Coast tour, Grace hoped she'd come soon, so she wouldn't be late to rehearsal.

The doorbell rang fifteen minutes later. Grace jumped up — good, they still had time. But when she opened the door, she was startled to see that Estelle wasn't alone. The twins' mother smiled self-consciously as Estelle said, "I ran into your next-door neighbor here comin' home from work — you're a caseworker with DCFS, right, Sister Michelle? — and she looked mighty troubled so . . . uh, may we come in?"

"Oh, yes, of course!" Grace stepped back, flustered. "Please, sit down . . . just let me move this stuff." She grabbed a pile of folded laundry off the couch and ran it into her bedroom. Returning to the living room, where the two black women had settled on the couch, she said, "I'm sorry, just trying to get my laundry done before I leave on a trip tomorrow."

"Which is what I was telling Sister Michelle," Estelle beamed. "Told her I was comin' over to pray with you about your trip, and she said . . . well, why don't you tell Grace here what you said, honey."

Michelle Jasper, still in her trench coat and holding a purse and bulging briefcase on her lap, shook her head as if embarrassed. "I just asked Miss Estelle here to send up a prayer or two for me, because I sure need it, and next thing I know, she's inviting me to join you. Feel like I'm barging in though . . . are you sure you don't mind?"

Grace did mind, a little bit. Not that she had anything against Michelle Jasper, but her prayer times with Estelle had been very personal and adding someone else at the last moment, someone she hardly knew, put a damper on that. "No, of course not," she said, then cast a questioning glance at Estelle as if to ask, *What's this about?*

Estelle saw the glance and nodded. "See, the Bible says where two or three are gathered together 'in my name' — that's Jesus talkin' — he says he's right there in their midst. And anything they ask *in his name* — meanin' anything that lines up with God's purpose an' the Word of God — well, he's gonna do it! So I thought, since we all have things that need prayer, let's pray for each other in the name of Jesus an' claim that promise!" She reached out and patted Michelle's hand. "How can we pray for you, sister?"

Michelle Jasper shook her head. "Hardly know where to start. I had to come home early from work for a parent meeting with Tavis's teacher — he got in a fight today over . . . honestly, I can hardly remember! This kid at school has picked on Tavis all year and I guess Tavis had had it. The other parent didn't show — just as well. Last time Tavis got in a fight with this boy, the mother blamed everybody *except* her kid."

Estelle nodded. "Mm-hm. I know the type."

"I want Tavis to take responsibility for his actions, but it's hard when this other boy is such a bully. Unfortunately, it also meant I had to reschedule an important home visit where we've gotten complaints from some neighbors about children home alone. I hated to put it off. If only my husband . . ." Her voice drifted off.

Estelle and Grace waited a long moment. Then Estelle said, "If only?"

"Oh, nothing. Just wish Jared was more available to handle this boy stuff. But his work schedule at O'Hare puts a lot of stress on the family. Even if this had been one of his early days when he'd get off at two, he needs to get some sleep before going back." Michelle heaved a sigh. "I'm sorry. Don't mean to dump my woes on the two of you. It's just . . . on days like today I seriously consider quitting my job."

"Well, that's what sisters in Christ are for, to carry each other's burdens!" Estelle reached for their hands and wasted no time moving right into a prayer. "*Mmm,* Father God, you are *worthy* to be praised! Thank you for your promise to pour out strength when we feel overwhelmed, and you said when we need wisdom, all we need to do is ask . . ."

As she listened, Grace felt a familiar pang. She lived next door to the Jaspers and knew next to nothing about them. Estelle had called Michelle a sister in Christ — which made it even worse. Fellow believers, and she didn't even know it. Still, she couldn't help sneaking a peek at the wall clock . . . 4:05. She still had more laundry to fold and had hoped to start packing . . .

"Thank you," Michelle whispered as Estelle said amen. "I really needed that prayer." She fished in her coat pocket for a tissue and blew her nose.

Grace looked at Estelle, wondering how to move things along under the circumstances, just as a phone rang from somewhere on Michelle's lap. "I'm so sorry!" Michelle rummaged in her purse and pulled out the offending cell phone. "It's one of my kids. I better take it." She rose, causing her briefcase to fall off her lap, and with a frustrated glance at the case on the floor, stepped into the dining alcove off the living room. Moving to pick up the briefcase and a wad of brochures that had fallen out of a front pocket, Grace heard Michelle say, "*All right.* I'm just next door. I'll be there in a minute."

Returning, her neighbor shook her head. "Wouldn't you know. Destin forgot to get his permission slip signed for driver's ed and of course it's due by five o'clock *today.* Teenagers! I wish I could stay but . . . I need to get home. Please forgive me for running off."

"That's all right. We understand." Grace handed her the briefcase and a handful of brochures.

"Thank you. That was clumsy of me . . . oh!" She looked at the brochures in her hand, then at Grace and Estelle. "I volunteer

416

at the crisis pregnancy center. If you know anyone who can use these, please send them to us." She laid a few brochures on the coffee table, and smiled at Grace. "Will you be gone long on your trip? If there's anything we can do while you're gone . . ."

Grace thanked her but said no, her brother was going to stop in and check on things. A moment later Michelle Jasper was gone.

"Well," Estelle said as Grace shut the door behind their guest. "Thanks for bein' flexible. I could tell that sister needed some prayer and it's always good to pray *with* someone, not just *for* them. But I'm glad we can have a few minutes alone. I have something for you." Estelle reached into her large purse and pulled out a small, leather-look notebook with gilt-edged pages and a fold-over clasp. "I got you a journal for your trip — don't know about you, but sometimes when life gets hectic, it helps to write down my thoughts and prayers." She handed the book to Grace with a warm smile. "Took the liberty of writing down some scriptures to read when you have time."

"Oh, Estelle." Grace opened the clasp and peeked into the book. On the front flyleaf, Estelle had written: *To Grace with love ~ "His grace and mercy will carry you through"*

~ *Your sister in Christ, Estelle.* And the first page had several scripture references printed neatly in a list. "Thank you so much. I . . . I'm not real good at having a regular prayer time. And when I'm touring, it's even harder! But I promise to use this — every day."

"Good! Now, I know you've got to skedaddle out of here real quick, so . . . Lord, your precious lamb here an' your other daughter, Sam, are heading out tomorrow for the West Coast . . ."

Grace couldn't help but smile, even as Estelle's passionate prayer filled the room. Like usual, it was hard to tell when her neighbor stopped talking to her and started talking to God.

CHAPTER 36

The last rehearsal. They went through all the songs one last time. As the final notes of "Your Grace and Mercy" died away, the room fell quiet, as if holding its breath. And then Samantha and Barry began to clap. "You're gonna sing like a soul sister yet, girl!" Sam called over to Grace.

The band laughed and high-fived each other. It'd been an intense week. But good.

Grace begged off going out to eat, though, saying she really needed to get to bed. Still had packing to do in the morning. "But thanks, guys. You're the best. We'll keep in touch on the road —"

"On the rails, you mean," Zach snickered, packing up his electric bass.

"Right." She grinned at the crew. "So, guess we'll see you in Seattle. First concert is Friday."

Sam stayed to work on some logistics with Barry about the tour, so Petey walked Grace out to the parking lot. She wished she'd worn a heavier jacket. The temperature had dropped into the forties, the lights of the tallest city buildings were shrouded by clouds, and the wind had picked up. "Not too late to change your mind about flyin'," the saxophonist teased as Grace unlocked her car. "Just think. It's gonna take you and Sam three days by train and it's gonna take us four hours."

Grace shivered — and it wasn't just the wind chill. "Not a chance. I'm done with airports. Good luck with security, though." She got into the car, but lowered the window a few inches. "Thanks for walking me to the car. Everything okay with you and your girlfriend?" She'd met the girl once. Nice. Studying to be a lawyer or something.

"Yeah, we're good. She's not happy when I'm gone on tour but . . . another reason to fly, I guess." He slapped the roof of her car. "Drive safe. It's kinda foggy."

Not happy when I'm gone on tour . . .

Well, that was Roger too. Must be hard on all significant others left behind. Maybe she should call him, show some understanding. Besides, she really should touch base with him before she left town, even though she hadn't promised an answer until she returned. She wanted him to know she was still taking his request seriously.

Snuggling under her blankets an hour later, she hit the familiar speed-dial. What would it be like to resume these nightly "visits"? She'd always looked forward to them, the sweet nothings, sharing his day . . . her day . . .

"You've reached Roger Baldwin. I'm not here right now, but I'll return your call as soon as I'm able."

Figured. Grace hit the End button, plugged the phone into its charger, and turned out the light. She missed Oreo's familiar weight on her feet at the end of the bed.

The phone rang. She groped in the dark till she found it.

"Grace? So sorry! I wasn't expecting your call so I didn't have my phone handy. I'm so glad you called."

She plumped up her pillows so she was half-sitting in the dark. "Just wanted to call you before I leave for Seattle tomorrow. I'm taking the train so Sam and I have to leave a few days early."

"That's right. I forgot you were taking the train . . ." A long, silent moment hung between them. "Wish you weren't. It'll make the time you're gone longer."

"I know. I'm sorry about that. But . . . flying isn't an option right now. At least this is only a ten-day tour, not a whole month like last January." *Stop it, Grace. You're being defensive. You were going to show understanding for those left behind.* "Um, still, I know it feels long, especially since you're waiting for an answer from me. But . . ." She floundered. "Anyway, how are you? How's your new Sunday school class going?"

They talked for ten minutes. Roger said the class was good, thirty-five people were attending. Grace told about visiting Faith Chapel with her brother and family, also that a neighbor had asked her to sing at his mother's funeral. "They called it a 'homegoing' — different, but I really enjoyed it."

"Uh-huh. That's good."

Their conversation felt forced with The Question still hanging over their heads. "Well, I better get some sleep. Take care, Roger. I'll be in touch, okay? Goodnight." She clicked Off and scooched down under the quilt, tucking it up around her chin. But she lay awake a long time, wondering what was wrong with her. Why didn't she know how to respond to Roger's apology and willingness to work on their relationship? If they were going to be married, they certainly needed to know how to talk through problems.

She wished they could *really* back up and start all over again, forget the engagement, just date each other for a while, get to know each other by doing things together, having fun, rather than plunging into "issues." See if they still liked each other enough to tackle the hard stuff.

Maybe that's what she'd suggest when she got back from the tour.

The 2:15 departure time gave Grace the morning to finish packing, call her folks, and tidy up the house before the limo was supposed to arrive. Setting her suitcases by the front door, she noticed the brochures Michelle Jasper had left on the coffee table. She grabbed one and stuffed it in her tote bag.

The black town car pulled up in front of the house at half past noon. Sam had ordered a car from Lincoln Limo, but said she was going early to pick up their tickets and boarding passes, and would meet her at the station. Grace opened the door as the driver hustled up the walk to retrieve her luggage.

"Afternoon, Miss Meredith. Just these two bags?"

Grace laughed when she saw who it was. "Rodney Bentley. You got the job!"

Harry's son grinned. "Yes, ma'am. Thanks to you and your friend. Miss Estelle told me you were the ones who told her the company was hirin'." He hauled the bags down the walk, set them into the trunk, and opened the back door of the town car for her. Settling into the driver's seat, Rodney did a turnaround in the cul-de-sac and headed south toward the city.

"So you 'just happened' to pick me up today?"

He grinned at her in the rearview mirror. "Not exactly. I saw your name and address on the dispatcher's list and asked if I could take this run. My way of sayin' thank you."

They chatted about this and that on the half-hour drive to the Loop — nothing much. Grace realized she'd never actually had a conversation with Rodney before, and thought it wise not to get too personal. It felt a little awkward having her limo driver live right across the street.

But he did everything by the book and seemed to know the city, pulling up at the main entrance to Union Station right at one o'clock. "Can you manage?" he asked, setting her bags on the sidewalk. "I'd take them in for you, but I can't park here."

"I'm fine. Thanks, Rodney. And please, just call me Grace." *Tip, Grace, tip!* she reminded herself, finding a ten in her purse.

The man held up his hand. "Thanks, but tips are added to the bill. They told me it's all taken care of. And sorry, I have to call all my customers by last name. Company rule."

"All right then, *Mr. Bentley.*" She smiled as she tucked the bill back in her purse. "We shall both remain businesslike as long as you're wearing that uniform. By the way, I'm returning on May fourth. I'll tell Sam — my assistant — to request you as our driver. Again."

Rodney grinned. "Thanks. Have a good trip."

Inside the station, Grace took the escalator down to ticketing — though it was a bit of a crunch juggling two suitcases, her purse, and a large tote bag — and saw Sam waving a handful of tickets at her by the e-ticket kiosks. "Grace! You should've let me know you were here! I have Red Cap service waiting to help with luggage." Sam motioned to an Amtrak employee, who loaded their bags on a cart and headed off. "Follow them. Sleeping car passengers get to use the Metropolitan Lounge."

Checking in at the desk inside the lounge,

they were told the Empire Builder would begin loading at 1:45, but in the meantime to help themselves to complimentary coffee and refreshments. Grace sank down into a comfortable padded chair with a hot cup of Starbucks and smirked at Sam. "Ahhh, the airport was never like this."

An hour later, the Red Cap was stowing their larger bags in a luggage area on the lower level of sleeping car 327 and took their smaller suitcases to the upper level. "Room D . . . that's us," Sam chirped, handing the man a tip.

Curious, Grace explored the long, narrow room that took up the width of the train car except for the passageway running along the far side of the car. Besides the long couch seat that made up into a single bed, and an upper berth that got lowered at night, the room had its own toilet, shower — in the same tiny space as the toilet — and separate sink and vanity. "Not exactly a hotel suite, but kinda cute. Like a motor home." She looked at Sam, who was already curled up in the single padded coach seat beside the window facing the two berths. "Sure you don't mind sleeping on the upper bunk?"

Sam made a face. "I'll let you know after two nights on the train."

Their sleeping car attendant appeared in the open doorway, a middle-aged man with laugh wrinkles around his gray eyes, his uniform jacket unbuttoned over a white shirt. He introduced himself as Ernie and cracked, "Do you want the good news or bad news first?"

"Uhh, good news."

"Smart move." He chuckled. "The dining car steward will be along shortly to get your dinner reservation — all meals are complimentary for sleeping car passengers. Also, hot coffee, bottled water, and juice are available in the middle of the car. Coffee's made fresh at 6:00 a.m. Would either of you like an extra pillow tonight?"

Grace smiled. "Please. Thanks. Now the bad news."

"We're supposed to leave at 2:15, but one of the trains coming through Ohio and Indiana got delayed — some mechanical problem — and they have connecting passengers. So we'll be waiting for them to arrive before we can leave. Hopefully just fifteen minutes or so."

It was three o'clock before the Empire Builder pulled out of Union Station. And later, as Grace looked up from the magazine she was reading, she noticed the train was stopped on the tracks with just the Wisconsin countryside stretching into the distance, no station in sight.

"Oh — Ernie?" she called as the attendant passed by. "Why are we stopped?"

Ernie poked his head in. "Waiting for a freight train to pass. Unfortunately, by starting late, we got out of our time slot, so other trains have the right of way. But we can sometimes make up the time on the longer stretches." He waggled his eyebrows. "The joys of training."

Grace woke up the next morning to hear Sam slide open their compartment door, slip out, and slide it shut again. Daylight peeked along the edges of the room-darkening curtains. She'd managed to get a fairly decent night's sleep in spite of waking when they pulled into Minneapolis around midnight, and again a few hours later in Fargo, North Dakota, as new passengers got on and got settled. The train whistle during the night had been oddly comforting, lulling her back to sleep again.

Stretching, Grace got up, used the toilet in the cubby, and splashed water on her face. *Mmm,* Ernie had said there'd be fresh coffee just around the corner . . .

A few minutes later, curled up on the unmade lower berth with a cup of hot coffee, watching fields of winter wheat, grazing lands full of sagebrush, and occasional clusters of farm buildings slide by her window, Grace realized she would've missed all this if she'd flown to Seattle. Hop on a plane, plug into your iPad or watch the in-flight movie, get off in another state . . . and totally miss the changing landscape rolling across the country.

Grace pulled the journal Estelle had given her out of her tote — and Michelle Jasper's brochure fell out too. She picked it up. Wait . . . what was this? It said, "Hope and Healing for those suffering from PAS — Post Abortion Syndrome." This wasn't just a brochure about the services offered by a crisis pregnancy center, but reaching out to women who'd already had an abortion.

Heart beating faster, Grace read through the brochure. *Symptoms of PAS — guilt, depression, sadness, lack of self-worth . . .* O Lord, so true. At least she hadn't numbed herself with alcohol or drugs, thank God. She'd coped by passionately preaching purity on her tours — covering up her own guilt and shame. But the brochure talked about support groups that could help teens and other women who'd aborted to talk about grief, anger, guilt, and forgiveness . . . "all in a safe and confidential environment pointing to the hope and healing found in Christ."

If only she'd known something like this existed when she was sixteen and so alone. Only now had she been given the courage to shine a light on the secrets she'd been carrying for more than a decade. All because Estelle Bentley had encouraged her to think about the meaning of her name. *Grace . . .*

Tucking the brochure back into her bag and opening the journal, Grace looked at the first scripture Estelle had written in the front. *"There is now no condemnation for those who are in Christ Jesus, because through Christ Jesus the law of the Spirit of life set me free from the law of sin and death . . ." (Romans 8:1–2).* Grace stared out the window again. *No condemnation . . .* She'd been a Christian most of her life. Why had it taken her so long to believe this? She'd gotten so used to being a "good Christian girl," that when she'd blown it, all she could think of to make things right again was to try even harder to be that girl.

Grace Meredith, the singer with the "purity message."

She read the next one in Estelle's neat handwriting: *"If by grace, then it is no longer by works; if it were, grace would no longer be grace" (Romans 11:6).* Huh. *Works.* That's exactly what she'd been doing these past few years. Trying to make up for her failings. She'd skipped right over grace. No wonder she thought God was punishing her for her past sins, slamming the door of happiness in her face when Roger ended their engagement. She'd still felt condemned. Still believed Satan's lie whispering in her ear: *"You're* not *worth it."*

A tear slid down her cheek. *Thank you, Estelle . . . thank you, Jesus . . .*

She started writing in the journal, trying to put into words all that God had been teaching her the past few weeks about mercy and grace. A short while later, the compartment door slid open. "Hey, you're up." Sam came in, dressed in jeans and a jersey top, carrying her overnight kit. "I showered downstairs — there's a bigger shower and dressing room down there — and then went to the observation car for a while, trying to let you get some beauty sleep. I see it didn't work. You've still got bed head."

"Ha-ha." Grace threw a pillow at her assistant. Missed.

"I'm hungry. Want to go to breakfast?"

Grace stowed her journal. "Yes. Just let me get a quick shower." She peeked into the multi-purpose cubby that held toilet and

showerhead. "Hmm. How does this work?"
Sam snickered. "Good luck with that."

CHAPTER 37

The Empire Builder was only twenty minutes late pulling into King Street Station in Seattle Thursday morning. "Best wishes, Miss Meredith!" Ernie said as he helped Grace and Samantha step off the sleeping car onto the platform. "Wish I could come to your concert tomorrow, but this train heads back to Chicago later this afternoon."

"Thanks, Ernie. You made the trip really enjoyable." Grace handed him the tip she and Sam had agreed he definitely deserved. The man had been full of interesting facts about various sights along the way, had stopped by frequently to see if they needed anything, and had even left a gold-wrapped Hershey's Kiss on their pillows when he made up their berths each night. "*Shhh,* don't tell anyone about those Kisses," he'd winked. "Those are just for my favorite customers."

Outside the station they caught a Yellow

Cab to the Grand Hyatt Hotel in downtown Seattle. "Is the band staying here too?" Grace asked, drinking in the beautiful marbled lobby as Sam checked them in for three nights. Bongo had booked two concerts, Friday night at a popular megachurch and Saturday at one of Seattle's major theaters.

"Yeah. Newman thought we all might as well get a good night's sleep while we're here." Sam handed Grace her room key and headed for the elevators behind a bellhop with their luggage on a cart.

"I'm glad." Once they left Seattle, the band would sleep on the tour bus until they hit LA. She and Sam had lucked out — most of the travel down the coast between tour cities took just a morning or less, so Sam had booked hotel rooms for them most of the way. All except the trip between Portland and Redding — that'd be an overnight for everyone. "Maybe we can meet up for supper tonight."

The bellhop punched the button for their floor and the doors closed.

Sam shrugged. "Don't know about that. Their plane gets in this afternoon, but they've got a lot of running around to do — outfitting the bus and getting set up at the church. Barry had a long list. We have a practice scheduled for ten tomorrow morning at the church, though."

Their suite was on the twenty-ninth floor and Grace's eyes popped at the view, which gave them a panorama of Puget Sound. Across the Sound she could see the Olympic Peninsula and ferries crossing both ways. The sky was mostly cloudy, but every now and then sunshine broke through. At least it wasn't raining.

"Grace? Did you see the flowers?" Sam picked a small card out of a gorgeous bouquet of Stargazer lilies and white and pink roses sitting on the desk and handed it to Grace. "If they're from Roger, I may have to upgrade my opinion of the man."

Grace took the card. Flowers from Roger? That was sweet, though maybe a bit premature. But when she pulled out the card, it read: *"Grace — Praying for the tour. We believe in you!"* It was signed, *"All of us at Bongo Booking."*

Sam peeked over her shoulder. "Aww, look at that. You really lucked out getting such a sweet guy for your agent."

Grace felt flustered. Flowers from Jeff? Well, from the whole Bongo staff. But still . . . She turned away from Sam, feeling her face flush. "Yeah, that was thoughtful." She pulled out her cell phone and sent a text to Jeff: *Flowers are lovely. Means a lot. Thank everybody.* And then, with a twinge of guilt, she also sent a text to Roger: *Arrived safely. Seattle is beautiful! Wish you were here.* She hesitated, and then erased the last sentence before hitting Send.

Sam was already busy hanging up clothes in the spacious closet. Grace busied herself unpacking her toiletries, arranging them on one side of the vanity in the bathroom, and laying neat piles of underthings and accessories in one of the deep empty drawers of the dresser. Shoes in a row.

Not knowing what else to do, Grace picked up the city guide from the desk and flopped into a padded armchair, mesmerized by the scenic photos and inviting tourist destinations. "Sam?"

"Yeah?" Her assistant still had her head inside the closet.

"We don't have to be anywhere today, right? Why don't we go to Pike Place Market down on the waterfront or up the Space Needle or something?"

Sam poked her head around the closet door. "You sure? Tomorrow's going to be really busy with sound checks and practice, even before the concert. We came a day early so you can be rested."

"I *am* rested." Grace grinned. "The train

was great! Well . . . okay, not exactly the best sleep I've ever had, but still. It's only noonish. We could sightsee around the city for a few hours and still get back in time for an early night. What do you say?"

In spite of good-natured grumbling from the band that Grace and Sam had "played" all Thursday afternoon while they had to do setup, the rehearsal had gone well Friday morning, and everyone from Samantha to Barry to the guys in the band seemed psyched about that night's concert. But Grace still felt nervous as she waited in the side room she was using as a dressing room while the local band that was headlining for her played their set.

She absently smoothed the soft folds of the rich rose-colored dress that set off her long brunette hair so well, and retouched her lipstick. This was the first concert with her new theme . . . *grace.* She'd done the other theme for so long, her folksy comments between songs had become familiar and routine. But tonight? She'd tried to think of things she wanted to say, but wasn't sure how personal to get. She'd promised Roger she wouldn't be talking about him or their relationship publicly anymore. But it wasn't just Roger. Only a few people knew her real story — Estelle, Samantha, and her brother Mark and his wife. Going public about her teenage pregnancy and abortion before she'd told her parents . . . no, no, that'd be totally unfair.

She felt relieved to have good reasons for not getting too personal. Except . . . how could she fully communicate God's grace and mercy to fans at these concerts — young men and women who might be hurting from hidden secrets, just like she'd been — without sharing the healing God was doing in her own life?

"Grace?" Sam broke into her thoughts. "Can the band come in? Barry is suggesting we all pray before you're up. We have about five minutes."

Yes, yes, she desperately needed prayer — they all did. Barry and the guys in the band filed into the side room and perched wherever they could. As the band manager led out with a prayer for this first concert on the tour, Grace's eyes swept over the bowed heads around the circle. Barry's salt-and-pepper hair and beard . . . Alex's red hair . . . Nigel's ponytail . . . Zach's African knots . . . Petey's glistening shaved head . . . Reno's unruly black thatch. What a bunch of great guys. And Sam, her head full of tiny twists framing her smooth caramel skin, eyes closed, face peaceful and lifted.

She couldn't do this without any of them.

". . . and help us to remember this concert isn't about us," Barry was praying. "It's not about Grace, it's not about the band, it's not even about this concert or this tour. It's about you, Jesus. We just want to be instruments you can use to encourage somebody out there in the audience tonight. Each one of us has experienced your grace in amazing ways, and we want to share the good news with someone who needs that same grace and mercy. To God be all the glory . . ." The guys responded with a resounding "Amen!"

Relief flooded through Grace's spirit as she hugged the band members and Sam, accepting their murmurs of encouragement. This wasn't about her. She could give it all to God, ask him to not only give her the voice to sing, but the words to say.

A sound guy poked his head into the room. "Grace, you're on in two."

Grace couldn't believe it. She hadn't written out what she wanted to say. Hadn't practiced in front of a mirror. But somehow the songs she'd chosen flowed, one into the other, not really needing comments between most of them. After singing, ". . . they will dance with joy" from "I Could Sing of Your Love Forever," she twirled with sheer joy herself even as fans were on their feet, dancing in the aisles.

But before singing the quiet hymn "He Giveth More Grace" just before intermission, she'd felt an inner prompting. Looking out over the packed auditorium of young faces, she took a deep breath. "Listen carefully to the words of this next hymn. God's love has no limit! We can't measure his grace! If you're like me, you may feel you don't deserve his grace — and that's true. We don't deserve it! But no matter how much you've messed up, God wants to pour out his grace and mercy and forgiveness into your life. Like the chorus says, 'He giveth, and giveth, and giveth again!'" Then she nodded at the band, and Nigel clicked his drumsticks together. *One, two, three, four . . .*

As she came off stage, Sam gave her a quick squeeze. "Oh, Grace!" she whispered. "That was perfect."

Grace didn't know about perfect. She was overwhelmed herself by the experience of feeling the nudging of the Holy Spirit, giving her words to say.

It happened again in the second set.

As she sang the words to "Your Grace and

Mercy," the lights dimmed, the spotlight shining on the silvery chiffon dress she'd changed into. For a moment, Grace wished the house lights had stayed up so she could look into the faces in the rows in front of her. But as she sang in the darkened room, she realized afresh that the song was a prayer: "I'm living this moment because of you . . ." Closing her own eyes, she sang, not to the audience but to Jesus. And as the notes died away, she murmured into the mike, "Yes, thank you, Jesus! I *am* living this moment because of you! It's your grace and mercy that has brought me through. In spite of my own failures, you continue to pour out blessing upon blessing. And so I dedicate this next song to you as my prayer of thanks."

Petey's sax moved right into the new song as Grace lifted her voice . . .

For blessing upon blessing
For every gift you've given
From the fullness of your grace
For all you have forgiven
I thank you, oh! I thank you . . .

She sang the simple prayer song through once, twice, then let it go. The auditorium was absolutely still. And then she heard the

441

sound of muffled sobs here . . . and there . . . and there around the big room. She waited a long moment before giving the band the signal to begin the last hymn: "Marvelous grace . . . God's grace . . . grace that is greater than all our sin."

Grace was so drained by the emotion of the concert, it took her thirty minutes to pull herself together before she could go to the meet and greet. The room was packed — more than the usual twenty. Grace tried to speak at least a word or two to each person who'd come and autographed their programs or the CDs they'd bought. Several of the fans — mostly young women — gave her a hug and whispered, "Thank you. I really needed to hear that."

But as the room thinned, Grace noticed a young woman — maybe nineteen or twenty — who'd held back. She looked as if she'd been crying. Grace went to her and put an arm around her. "Are you okay?"

The young woman started to nod — and then shook her head. Fresh tears spilled down her face. "I . . . I don't know if God can forgive me. I've done something . . . something . . ." She couldn't finish. Sam appeared right at that moment and slipped the girl a wad of tissues.

Grace led the young woman to a set of chairs and they sat down. "What's your name?" she asked kindly.

Several sniffs. "Ashley."

"Ashley, why don't you think God can forgive you?"

"Because I . . . I did something terrible. And I can't undo it."

Grace's stomach clinched. She'd had that same awful feeling after she'd left the clinic. *It's done . . . I can't undo it now.* "Did you have an abortion?" she asked softly.

The girl's eyes flew open. "How . . . how did you know?"

"Because when I was even younger than you, I did too. And I couldn't undo it. No way did I deserve God's grace." She took the girl's hands. "Have you told anyone? Your parents or . . . ?"

Ashley shook her head and started to cry again.

"Oh, Ashley . . ." Grace's heart ached. The girl was carrying her burden alone. Just as Grace had done.

She talked to Ashley earnestly for another twenty minutes, sharing some of the things God had been teaching her. If only she knew someone who could really help this girl . . . *wait.* The brochure Michelle Jasper had given her! She motioned to Sam who was waiting discreetly at a distance, then sent her to her dressing room for her tote bag. When Sam returned, she dug out the brochure and gave it to Ashley. "Call that number. This ministry is located in Chicago, but I'm guessing they could tell you someone to call and talk to here in Seattle. Promise me you'll do that?"

Ashley nodded, and before she left, Grace prayed with this young woman who so needed to experience the gift of God's grace.

Finally the room emptied. "Whoa." Sam sank into a padded chair. "Do you think this is going to happen at every concert?"

Grace shook her head. She hardly knew what to think! If only she'd brought more of those brochures. There must be a half dozen sitting back on her coffee table. But even that might not be enough . . .

"Sam. What time is it?" She didn't usually wear her high school watch onstage.

"Uh . . . ten thirty. Why?"

"Ouch. That's already twelve thirty back in Chicago." Too late to call the Bentleys for the Jaspers' phone number. Pulling out her cell phone, she dialed 4-1-1.

Sam stared at her. "What are you doing?"

"Calling information. I need my next-door neighbor's number. I'm going to call Michelle Jasper first thing tomorrow morning and ask her to overnight a hundred of those brochures to me at our next stop."

CHAPTER 38

Even though it was late when she got to bed, Grace set her alarm for six thirty the next morning — eight thirty Chicago time — and called Michelle Jasper.

Her neighbor was surprised to hear from her. Michelle didn't even know why Grace was traveling, so Grace briefly filled her in about the concert tour.

"Oh my! I had no idea!"

Grace knew that was more her fault than her neighbor's. "But the reason I'm calling . . ." Without going into a lot of detail, Grace told her young people were coming to her concerts who needed services like the ones in the brochures she'd left at Grace's house — including the postabortion counseling. "But we're moving from city to city each day, and I don't know who to refer them to. I thought if I gave them a copy of your brochure, maybe they could call and get a referral."

"Of course! In fact, I think there's a directory of crisis pregnancy centers around the US on the Web — I'll have to look it up, though." But in the meantime, Michelle promised to overnight a couple hundred brochures to Grace. "Except tomorrow's Sunday," she noted. "Where will you be on Monday?"

Monday! That was two days away! "Can you hold on a moment?" Putting the call on hold, Grace ran into the bathroom to consult with Sam who was staring bleary-eyed into the mirror.

Sam shook her head, as if trying to wake up. "Uh . . . I think USPS Express Mail delivers 365 days a year — including Sunday. Tell her to check it out. Here . . . I'll give her the address of our contact people in Portland."

Grace handed off the phone to Sam, who arranged with Michelle Jasper where to send the brochures. When the call was finally over, the two women looked at each other. "Okay, which is it?" Sam yawned. "Do we go back to bed — or go to the pool and get in some laps?"

They went back to bed. After all, they wouldn't be able to sleep in tomorrow, because they'd need to check out early and get on the road.

But that night at the theater, another girl — this one looked about fifteen — came to the meet and greet all distraught. Gave her name as Janeece. She'd just taken an at-home pregnancy test and it was positive. She was afraid to tell anyone, even her boyfriend. She knew he'd pressure her to get an abortion.

Grace felt so helpless! She wished she had a copy of the directory Michelle Jasper had mentioned. But she had Sam take Janeece's phone number and promised they'd have someone contact her who knew where she could get help.

As Grace fell into her bed that night, she prayed for Ashley and Janeece. Why were these girls coming out of the woodwork on *this* tour? The theme of her previous tours had touched on the culture of premature sex — except her upbeat message had been to save sexual intimacy for marriage. They were "worth the wait."

But . . . it didn't take into account that many young people had already messed up. What then?

The package from Michelle Jasper arrived at the big church in Portland while they were setting up Sunday afternoon for that night's concert. Sam suggested putting the brochures out on the merch table, along with a little sign that said, "Take one. To find a crisis pregnancy center or postabortion ministry close to you, call this number."

Grace grimaced. "I hope Michelle knew what she was doing when she gave me permission to give out their number. I think she's just a volunteer."

"Why don't you call her again, see if she found that directory. Maybe we could print it out and make it available . . . never mind, I'll do it. Barry's waving at you. You need to do a sound check with the band."

How Sam managed it, Grace didn't know, but her assistant had copies of a CPC directory stacked on the table alongside the brochures before the concert. "Your neighbor said it's not complete, but she included a Pregnancy Helpline number."

No one spilled their hearts to Grace after the concert the way Ashley and Janeece had in Seattle, though she noticed that several of the fans who came to the meet and greet afterward to give her hugs and get her autograph were clutching copies of the brochure or the directory — or both. Later, as they were packing up, Sam said at least a quarter of the brochures were already gone, and almost all of the photocopies. "At this rate, our supply isn't going to last the whole tour."

Grace tried to think as she followed Sam out to the enormous tour bus idling in the parking lot. No hotel tonight. The trip to Redding, California — her next concert — would take at least seven or eight hours. "Guess we need to call Michelle Jasper again in the morning. We did tell her we'll reimburse her for the Express Mail postage, didn't we?"

Barry tried to keep the postconcert wind-down on the bus to a dull roar so Grace could get some sleep in the back bedroom. But it wasn't the laughter and good-natured fights over the last few pieces of pizza that kept Grace awake till after midnight. Wrapped in the comforter on the big bed that took up nearly the width of the bus, she stared at the tiny blips of light sneaking past the room-darkening shades as the tour bus headed down Interstate 5. She was a singer — not a social worker or a trained counselor. Yes, God had given her a message — a message that was still at work in her own heart. But when it touched the lives of the young people who came to her concerts . . . what then?

O God, I'm still working on understanding your grace myself! What do I have to offer

450

these kids?

She hadn't even had a chance to talk to her folks yet . . . or her fiancé. Or ex-fiancé. Whatever Roger was at this point.

Or her agent. Didn't Jeff Newman deserve to know the story behind her new theme?

But as the noises quieted on the bus, Grace seemed to hear a Voice in her spirit. *"Just do what you've been given to do, Grace. Sing about my grace. Love on the hurting fans who turn to you. Tell them you understand. Point them to people who can help. And point them to me."*

Redding . . . Oakland . . . San Francisco . . . Fresno . . .

The concerts seemed to be going well. Michelle had sent more brochures. But even with hotel nights on the shorter runs, Grace was tiring fast. So was everyone else. Barry always took time before a show to get Grace and Sam and the band together to pray, and that helped to ease the familiar frustrations and irritations that arose from having to deal with a new venue each night.

Grace was no longer surprised when one or two or three young people would hang back at the meet and greet, and then share a sadly similar story. Pressure to have sex. Or they'd bought into the "no big deal" myth themselves. But afterward, struggling with guilt. For some, an unplanned pregnancy. Feeling scared. Alone. Overwhelmed. An abortion. Secrets. Depression. Even thoughts of suicide. One girl had cut herself and had scars on her arms to prove it.

Grace had told Sam about the inner Voice that told her to "just do what you've been given to do," and they'd prayed about that together at least once a day.

But there was one other thing that worried them both: Grace's voice was starting to weaken and she often woke up with a sore throat. By the time the bus drove into the parking lot of the Embassy Suites Hotel in Los Angeles at noon on Friday, where they would all stay for two nights, Grace was drinking hot honey-lemon tea and sucking Slippery Elm Lozenges nonstop.

Sam made Grace crawl into the hotel bed as soon as they got checked in while she unpacked and sent some of Grace's clothes out to be cleaned, pressed, and back by four o'clock. Grace didn't protest. The comfy bed and pillows felt sooo good. At least the tour was almost over. Bongo Booking had scheduled her at Azusa Pacific University that night . . . a large church on Saturday night . . . and a reprise of one of her songs at the worship service — same church —

Sunday morning.

And then . . . home. The Southwest Chief left Sunday evening from downtown LA, and they'd be home by Tuesday afternoon.

Though at this point, Grace almost wished she could fly home.

No. She still had a lot of thinking and praying to do. The train ride would give her time to unwind.

Grace dozed on and off all afternoon, skipping the usual afternoon sound check, which Barry agreed to as long as she got there an hour before the show. Eating a light supper at four, she felt good, ready to go when she and Sam showed up at the auditorium at six. And Barry's prayers for her voice and her general health when they did their preconcert prayer circle strengthened her spirit too.

The concert went well. Her voice held out — though Sam nearly drowned her with hot tea during the break. "You're gonna make me have to pee during the last set," Grace complained — which set them both off laughing.

Yeah, they were tired, even when they didn't feel tired.

But Grace was somewhat taken aback when two college-age guys came to the meet and greet after the concert and asked if they could talk. One senior admitted he'd slept with his girlfriend in spite of the university's expectations that students would abide by biblical standards of sexual behavior. But since she hadn't gotten pregnant, he hadn't worried too much about it — until tonight. Another had done the same thing, but his girl had broken up with him and later left school. He didn't know if he'd gotten her pregnant, or if she had a baby, or had gotten an abortion, because she'd cut off all contact. But he was living with a lot of guilt, even felt like he didn't deserve to graduate.

Grace's heart ached. Behind every young woman who'd talked to her, there was also a guy — maybe like one of these young men. She sent Sam to ask Barry and Petey if they'd talk with them — guy to guy — and when she'd finished meeting the last of her fans, the guys were still praying together in a corner of the room.

"I've never been on a tour like this," Grace confessed as she and Sam got ready for bed a while later in their hotel suite. "I mean, all I keep thinking about as I'm singing is, who out there in the audience is hurting right now? I imagine her in my mind — someone like Ashley or Janeece — and I find myself singing to that person."

Sam nodded soberly. "The other tours

were great, Grace — really. But this one feels especially anointed. God is really using you." She handed Grace a steaming cup of honey-lemon tea. "But I'm gonna be honest with you. Your voice did not sound as strong tonight, and we still have two — well, one and a half — concerts to go. You still need to take care of your throat."

"Yes, Mama Sam." Grace obediently drank her tea . . . but woke up Saturday morning with a flaming sore throat. She'd hoped they could get to the beach — after all, it was the first day of May! In California! — and soak up a few rays before practice that afternoon, but Sam talked her into soaking up those rays by the hotel pool instead. Grace needed to take it easy if she wanted to make it through the concert tonight.

Sam even intercepted her phone calls — including one from Jeff, who'd called to wish Grace the best on her last night. "Sorry, she can't talk right now. Actually, Jeff, you might want to get the Bongo staff together and pray. She's got a really sore throat and we've still got tonight's concert."

Grace rolled her eyes. She wished Sam wouldn't be so dramatic. Her assistant listened, nodded, said "Uh-huh" and "Uh-uh" a few times, then clicked the phone off.

"Your *agent* —" She overemphasized the word with a little smile. "— is really concerned. Asked if you'd seen a doctor. Asked if there was anything he could do. Personally, I wouldn't be surprised if he showed up tonight."

Grace managed a snort. "Yeah, and if he did he'd wonder what all the fuss was about if the concert goes off without a hitch." But she couldn't help grinning. It was just the kind of thing Jeff would do.

Thanks to Sam's nursing, Grace was feeling much better by the time she walked on-stage that night. She'd chosen a simple black crepe V-neck dress that skimmed her knees, her long hair falling softly in layered strands around her shoulders, and she knew she looked good in spite of the slight scratchiness in her throat.

The church was packed. To keep each evening fresh, she and the band sometimes rearranged the order of the songs, and she continued to depend on that nudge from the Holy Spirit for what to say. The first set seemed to go well, and at the break, she obediently drank lots of water and sucked on her lozenges. *One more set tonight . . . and just a short set in the morning. I can do this.* "Be strong," Sam whispered as the emcee brought down the lights after the break and boomed into the mike, "Once again, we bring you Just Grace!"

Waves of loud applause greeted her as she moved into the spotlight wearing the silver chiffon dress — her favorite. *Just Grace.* Her heart was full as she nodded to the band and they swung into Todd Agnew's "Grace Like Rain." The song was slow and easy, in a comfortable range, and she sang it confidently. "Hallelujah, grace like rain falls down on me . . ."

But she had a little trouble on the next song — failing to hit one of the high notes, but recovering and coming in again on the next phrase. Giving herself a little break, she talked to the audience with words of encouragement, sharing one of the truths God was teaching her: "You feel as if you don't deserve God's grace? Well, you're right! You don't. Neither do I. But that's what grace is all about — God longs to pour out his love and mercy, no matter what mistakes we've made, even though we *don't* deserve it. And that's what brings us through . . ."

With those key words, the band moved into the song made popular by the Mississippi Mass Choir: "Your grace and mercy brought me through . . ."

Grace made it through the first chorus,

but realized she was struggling with the first verse. The volume wasn't there, and her voice sounded ragged, even to her. Pulling the mike aside while she cleared her throat, she brought it back again but hummed through the rest of the verse — hoping it might seem something planned — and then came back in on the chorus.

But it wasn't happening. She couldn't hit the notes. A small bubble of panic started to rise in her chest — but just at that moment Sam appeared at her side with a hand-held mike in her hand, smiling at Grace, mouthing, *"Sing alto"* . . .

It only took a nanosecond for Grace to realize what was happening. Sam was going to make this a duet! — letting her drop her voice into the alto range while Sam picked up the soprano. Grace smiled back . . . and opened her mouth to sing again. Together they finished the chorus and moved on to the second verse.

Their voices blended beautifully, and together they sang the final chorus through to the last line: "Your grace and mercy . . . brought me through!"

As the last notes died away, Grace slipped an arm around Sam's waist and held her close as she raised her other arm high. The audience was on its feet, hooting and hollering, clapping and clapping.

They'd loved it.

Sam started to slip away, but Grace grabbed her hand and held her there. Trying to find a break in the applause, Grace spoke into the mike. "As you can see, it wasn't 'Just Grace' tonight" —

Laughter swept the room.

— "it was God's grace, all the way."

CHAPTER 39

Grace sank down into one of the big leather seats in the cavernous waiting room of Los Angeles Union Station Sunday evening, glad to get off her feet. It'd been a long day — singing at the worship service in the same church that had hosted Saturday night's concert, packing, checking out of the hotel, saying good-bye to Barry and the band, and waiting for a car to take them to the train station. She was looking forward to getting on the Southwest Chief and kicking back with nothing to do for two days except rest and watch the scenery.

Sam propped their suitcases against a couple of the other leather seats but didn't sit down. "Did you see all the police and security guards? Even some K-9 dogs. Wonder what's up?"

Grace flinched. It was a bit unsettling to see so much security. Did it mean they'd be searched before they could board? Mr.

Bentley had practically promised that didn't happen on the train. She shuddered. She didn't want to think about it.

Sam looked around. "I'm hungry. Wonder if they've got any restaurants or concessions around here. We've still got half an hour till we can board."

"Won't they serve dinner when we get on the train?"

"Yeah, but I need something to tide me over. You?"

"Sure. Nothing sweet though."

As Sam disappeared, Grace took a good look around her — and almost had to laugh. The rows of wide leather seats for waiting passengers had old-fashioned high backs and wide wooden arms, making her feel a bit like Goldilocks trying out Papa Bear's "too big" chair. But the seats did seem to fit the waiting room's personality: high arched doorways, large ceiling beams, intricate inlaid wall tiles, and highly polished floors. Beautiful.

Grace closed her eyes, alone for the first time that day — if one could be alone surrounded by hundreds of other passengers. Her voice had recovered somewhat overnight with lots of gargling and a steam treatment. But when they'd arrived at the church that morning, the event coordinator —

who'd been at the concert the previous night — asked if she and Sam could do a reprise of their duet. "And," he added, "we were wondering if the two of you would also sing 'Amazing Grace'? That would be very poignant, you know — black and white together — given the history of that song."

History of that song . . . Yes, written by a former slave trader, his confession of God's amazing grace, that God would "save a wretch like me." And it had been moving. Zach was practically in tears afterward.

So why did she feel conflicted? Samantha had come to her rescue, had saved her song, and the audience had loved it. And Grace *was* grateful . . . but what did that mean for the future? Would Sam expect to do duets with her at every concert? Was she being selfish to even wonder about that? Prideful?

Samantha Curtis did have a beautiful voice. Maybe she should talk to Jeff about her one of these days, see what he thought about getting her an agent —

"*Hola.* May I sit here?"

Grace's eyes flew open at the unfamiliar voice. A young girl, maybe seventeen or eighteen, stood a few feet away, pointing at the high-back chair next to Grace. Skinny jeans, a tan suede jacket. Thick, dark hair fell over one side of her face. Very pretty really — large brown eyes with long lashes, bow-shaped lips, creamy tan skin.

"Sure." Grace smiled politely. Odd, though. It wasn't like there weren't other empty seats around the waiting room.

The girl sank down into the seat, looking even more lost in the big chair than Grace had felt. "*Gracias.* I'm going to Chicago, first time." She eyed Grace curiously. "You are from Chicago?"

Grace nodded. "Yes. On my way home."

"Nice." The girl smiled shyly. "Do you like Chicago? . . . Oh, I'm Ramona." She extended a slender hand.

Hmm. Super friendly. Grace shook her hand and smiled back. "I'm Grace. Yes, I like Chicago."

Ramona tipped her chin toward their luggage. "You have a lot of bags. You did not want to check them?"

Okay. Now she was getting nosy. "Not all mine. I'm traveling with a friend."

"Ah. I see."

The girl seemed about to ask another question, but just then Sam walked up holding two bags of luscious-smelling popcorn. "Oh . . . hi. Hope I'm not interrupting something." She nodded at the girl, then held out the two bags of popcorn toward Grace. "Parmesan or Spicy Paprika?"

"*Mmm.* Parmesan. Thanks."

Sam shoved Grace's suitcase aside and sank into the seat on the other side of her. "The only thing open on Sunday in the whole place is the Traxx Bar. Hope this is okay."

"Dee-lish. Oh — Sam, this is Ramona. She's going to Chicago too."

Sam gave the girl a smile and a little wave. "Hi." She leaned across Grace and held out her bag of popcorn. "Would you like some?"

"Oh, no, no . . . that's okay." The girl glanced across the big room. "Oh. There's my man. I have to go." Ramona bounced up. "Have a good trip."

Grace watched as the girl scurried away, pulling her small bag. A tall, blond guy was waving at her. He looked at least in his late twenties, much older than Ramona. Did her parents know she was off to Chicago with this guy?

Sam looked at her watch. "I thought they said we'd be boarding by now. I'm gonna check." She hurried off, and a few moments later came hurrying back. "First class passengers are gathering around the corner. Huh! You'd think they'd make an announcement on the intercom or something."

Ten minutes later, Grace and Sam climbed on an electric cart with two other first class passengers and held on tight as the driver scooted through the station, up a ramp, and out onto the platform before braking to a stop and unloading their luggage. The Southwest Chief stretched out before them on the track, Amtrak attendants standing at the open car doors. Pulling their suitcases, Sam stopped at the first sleeper behind the engines and baggage car and showed her ticket. "Car 433?"

The attendant smiled and pointed down the track. "Two cars down."

A sturdy African American woman in uniform stood by the door of Car 433. "Let me help you with those." She swung their big suitcases aboard and checked their tickets. "Bedroom E is on the second level. Up the stairs, turn left. Welcome aboard!"

Grace and Sam stowed their big suitcases on the luggage rack on the lower level, then made their way to the second level and into E. Collapsing on the long padded seat that turned into a lower berth, Grace laughed. "Ah! Home sweet home for the next two days!"

Sylvia, their sleeping car attendant, came by as the train pulled out of the station to let them know the dining car steward would be by shortly to get their dinner reservation and to ask if they had any questions. But after the two days on the Empire Builder, both Grace and Sam figured they knew the drill. By seven o'clock they were seated in the dining car perusing the menu and introducing themselves to their tablemates, a middle-aged white couple.

"Tim Crawford, my wife Patty. Just came out to visit our son at the navy base in San Diego. You?" Grace felt a little embarrassed to introduce herself as a concert artist, but Sam had no qualms and chatted freely about the recent West Coast tour. Patty seemed especially interested.

Their salmon and chicken dinners arrived along with salads, rolls, hot tea, and soft drinks — Tim and Patty had wine with their salmon dinners — and the foursome chatted amiably as the wait staff bustled back and forth, not missing a step in spite of the sometimes swaying car. Grace, sitting by the window just beyond the galley in the middle of the dining car, was riding backward, watching as drainage ditches and large concrete walls hiding housing developments slid past her view. Not exactly great scenery coming out of Los Angeles.

A man coming through the galley and passing their table caught her attention — a middle-aged African American wearing a plaid flat hat and dark glasses . . . *wait.* Could it be — ?

"Mr. Bentley?" Grace called out. "Mr. Bentley, is that you?"

But the man just kept moving down the middle aisle. And then she saw he was holding the handle of a black guide dog pressed close to his leg. *Duh.* The man was blind.

"Someone you know?" Tim Crawford asked, twisting his head to look after the man and his dog as they made their way to the door at the end and disappeared into the lounge car.

Grace shook her head, embarrassed. "No. He looked like one of my neighbors back home, but I was obviously mistaken."

Sam gave her a teasing poke. "I guess so. Not all black people look alike, you know."

Grace ignored her and flagged one of the wait staff. "What do you have for dessert?" After all, it was the end of the tour and she was ready to celebrate.

As they got ready to leave the diner, Sam said, "Think I'll go to the lounge car — should be nice watching the sunset over the desert. Wanna come?"

Grace shook her head. "No, think I'll go back. But you go on. I'll be fine." She really needed some time alone to think about what she would tell Roger when she got home.

Back in their compartment, Grace drew the curtain over the glass in the door, and curled up in the corner by the window. The backyards of Los Angeles had disappeared into the twilight and they were out in the desert. A waning full moon cast an eerie glow over the landscape.

Grace leaned her cheek against the cool window. *O God . . . I truly did love Roger. I was so happy, so looking forward to being married. But I felt so burned, so rejected when he broke our engagement, I just don't know how to trust him again. And yet . . . he really seems to be sorry for how abruptly he ended things, seems to want to give our relationship another chance. Shouldn't I at least give us a chance? See if we can learn how to work out problems in a healthy way?*

All couples had problems. She'd obviously been too starry-eyed to see them creep up. How immature was that? She needed to grow up. Be willing to face her faults like an adult, make changes if need be.

But exactly what changes did Roger want to make in their relationship? Changes for their good as a couple — or changes because she wasn't the person he imagined her to be?

Grace sighed as the darkness outside deepened. They definitely needed to work on their communication. Learn how to be open and honest with each other. Which meant she had to be honest with Roger about her past —

A tapping on the glass door of the compartment broke into her thoughts. "Yes, who is it?" A few more light taps on the door. Grace got up, slid back the curtain — and had a start. The blind man she'd seen in the dining car stood at her door. What — ?

As she slid open the door, the man removed his glasses and said in a low voice, "May I come in, Miss Meredith?"

There stood Estelle Bentley's husband, big as life. "It *was* you!" she gasped.

Harry Bentley put a finger to his lips and raised his eyebrows as if repeating his request.

She lowered her own voice. "Of course! Come in. What in the world are you doing here?"

Her neighbor stepped in, the sweet-faced black Lab with its handle and leather harness that said "Guide Dog" right at his side, and slid the door closed behind him. "May I?" He pointed to the long couch.

"Yes, yes. Take a seat." Grace could hardly get over her surprise.

"Sorry I had to ignore you in the dining car, Miss Grace, but you almost gave away my cover." Harry sat. "You know I do security for Amtrak. I'm riding some of the trains as an Amtrak detective, and — I know this get-up may seem silly — but I needed a cover so I could bring the dog. I need to ask you not to speak to me or acknowledge me in any way. Or your friend either. She . . . doesn't know who I am, does she?"

Grace shook her head. "She knows your wife, but I don't think she's ever seen you. And she thinks I was totally off thinking you were on the train."

Harry nodded. "Good. Keep it that way. Wish I could stay and talk, but I should move on. I'm two cars ahead in the handicapped compartment."

His dog had been sniffing around the compartment and now came over to Grace. "Do you mind?" Harry said.

"Not at all. Such a sweet dog." Grace reached out her hand and the black dog licked it.

"Yeah. Corky's my partner. But please don't interact with her out in the train."

The man rose and replaced his dark glasses once more. "Well, I'll be seeing you around." He emphasized the word *seeing* with a grin. "Just don't be offended if I ignore you the rest of the trip."

"Of course."

"C'mon, Corky." He slipped out, sliding the heavy door shut behind him.

Of all things! Harry Bentley working undercover on the trains as a blind man with a guide dog! Wait till she told — oh, no. She couldn't tell Sam. That would have been so fun.

Had they had undercover detectives on the Empire Builder too? Ordinary-looking passengers just riding the rails to keep the other passengers safe?

She smiled. She liked that.

Harry Bentley's surprise visit made it hard to get her mind back on her dilemma with Roger. She decided to join Sam in the lounge car. But as she made her way into the domed car, she saw the girl from the station, Ramona, and the guy she was with sitting in one of the double seats facing the observation windows. Up close, she took in his casual J. Crew look — faded jeans, tight black tee, black sport coat. His face was pale, accentuating his blond hair, cut short on the sides and in back, with a spiky thatch on top. He had earphones plugged into his ears and was listening to an iPod, his arm on the back of the girl's chair as she flipped through a magazine.

Grace stopped. "Hi, Ramona. Nice to see you again." She waited for a response.

"Grace, in the station . . . remember?"

Ramona looked up. "Oh. Yes! *Hola.*"

Grace tipped her head, looking past the girl to the guy, her eyebrows raised, silently asking to meet him too.

"Oh, uh . . ." Ramona glanced at her companion, but the young man turned away ever so slightly. The girl just shrugged at Grace.

Grace felt awkward. "Well . . . maybe I'll see you around." She moved on, still looking for Sam.

A voice behind her said, "Wait." She turned to see Ramona half rise out of her seat, but in the next moment the boyfriend — or whatever he was — yanked on her arm and pulled her back down.

Grace stared. It was all she could do not to march back and get in the guy's face. But then he put his arm around the girl again and pulled her close, nuzzling her neck. Ramona seemed to resist for a moment, then shrugged and leaned back against him.

"Grace?" Sam's voice called her. Her assistant waved at her from a seat beyond the stairway that went down to the café on the lower level. Grace joined her and dropped into an adjoining seat. But anger boiled up inside her gut. She didn't like what she'd just seen. What was a kid like Ramona doing traveling all the way to Chicago with a guy his age, anyway? He had to be at least ten years older. Young girls could so easily be manipulated by older guys — or even charming guys their own age.

She ought to know.

CHAPTER 40

Grace slid on the brocade wedding dress and turned slowly in the mirror. The curved sweetheart neckline delicately framed her breasts just above the empire waistline. Soft folds of ivory brocade fell to the floor and trailed behind her in a lovely train. A wreath of ivory rosebuds in her hair . . . a bouquet of ivory roses and green ivy in her hands . . .

"Grace, it's time," someone said. She floated down the long church aisle with its red carpet, the pews filled with smiling faces. A man in a black tux — her husband-to-be — stood at the front waiting. But his back was turned. Wait . . . why was he turned away from her? A feeling of panic stopped her mid-aisle. She was getting married, but she didn't know to whom. She —

A slight jerk made Grace's eyes fly open. Daylight peeked in at the sides of the thick curtains covering the wide window. The tour bus? . . . No. The train. Their bedroom compartment on the Southwest Chief.

She'd been dreaming.

Grace sat up, careful not to bump her head on the berth above her, and glanced at her cell phone — 6:10. Still early, but no way did she want to fall back asleep. The dream disturbed her.

She listened. Given the steady breathing above her head, Sam was still asleep. Quietly gathering her toiletries, fresh undies, and the change of clothes she'd laid out last night, she slipped out of the compartment in her dark-green velour pants and top and made her way down the stairs in the middle of the car. On the landing she stood on tiptoe and peeked out the window. Where were they? Arizona somewhere, she guessed, by the rugged sandstone formations and desert vegetation sliding past. A small cluster of homes and trailers, a one-pump gas station, even a tepee — probably for tourists — huddled at the base of one of the formations. So isolated! As the train headed toward the sun, she saw several crumbling adobe houses standing a couple hundred feet from the tracks, just yards away from frame or cement-block houses that had replaced them.

She continued down to the lower level . . . good. No one else seemed to be about. But making her way past the luggage rack and vestibule, she'd just reached for the handle of the door marked "Shower" when she heard a voice say, "Hello? Who's there?" To her surprise, the door to the handicapped accessible bedroom slid open and Harry Bentley stood in the doorway, dark glasses and all. What was he doing in their car? She thought he'd said he was in a sleeper two cars forward.

She almost said, "Good morning, Mr. Bentley!" but remembered what he'd said about not acknowledging him. "It's Grace Meredith from Room E."

"Uh, miss, would you mind getting me a cup of coffee? I'd ask the attendant but I don't know where she is."

Grace smiled. She could play along. "Of course. Give me a minute."

Setting her shower things on the shelf of the luggage compartment, she scurried back up the stairs, following the smell of fresh coffee to the urn in the cubby at the top of the stairs. How did he like his coffee? She poured two cups, snapped on plastic lids, and stuck a few packets of sweetener and creamer in the pocket of her leisure top. Downstairs he was waiting at his door. As she handed him a coffee, he motioned her inside, slid the door shut, and smiled. "We can talk now."

She grinned. "This is nice. Didn't think we'd get a chance to visit anymore." He waved aside her offer of sweetener and creamer and invited her to sit down. She sat down opposite him in one of the two seats facing each other beside the window, ducking under the upper berth that was still made up, though it didn't look as if it'd been slept in. The seats beside the window probably slid together and lay flat to make into a lower berth, like the ones in the roomettes. Harry's guide dog rested on the floor, muzzle on her front paws. "You caught me by surprise," she said quietly, sipping her hot coffee. "I thought you were in a different car."

He grinned sheepishly. "Asked if I could move. The whistle was just too loud in that first sleeper." But he looked at her somewhat quizzically. "My son said he gave you a ride to the train. Did you ask for him?"

She shook her head. "I think he saw my name on that day's list of pickups and asked for the assignment. Nice of him. Said he'd pick us up when we got back too."

Harry Bentley frowned slightly. Maybe he and his son didn't get along all that well. She decided to change the subject. "I'm so glad you and your wife moved into the neighborhood, Mr. Bentley. Your wife . . ." Grace hesitated. How much had Estelle told her husband about the personal things Grace had shared in their prayer times? " . . . has really helped me face some things spiritually."

The man chuckled. "Yeah. That sounds like Estelle. She's a rock, that woman."

She's a rock, that woman. Would Roger ever say something like that about her?

"Mr. Bentley," she said suddenly, "how did you know Estelle was the one — you know, the person you were supposed to marry? The two of you seem to have a very special relationship."

The dog got up, walked over to Harry, and then sat down, leaning against his leg. He absently stroked her head as he stared out the window, pondering. Then he looked back at Grace, a shy smile on his friendly face. "Because when I'm with Estelle, she makes me feel like a complete person. Like I can be who God wants me to be. She believes in me, even when I don't believe in myself."

She believes in me . . .

Grace blinked back sudden tears, drained her coffee, and stood up. "Well, I should probably get my shower. Thanks, Mr. Bentley."

He got up in a hurry, slid the door open a crack — probably to see if the coast was clear — and then let her slip out.

But darn it! Someone else was in the shower.

Breakfast in the dining car that morning was fun. Grace and Sam were seated with two young Amish women on their way home from Mexico, where they'd been teaching school to a group of Mennonite children who'd lost their teacher a few months ago. A new teacher had been found, so they were returning to their community in Indiana. Grace was fascinated — what a different world they lived in. But the two young women — Rachel and Elizabeth — seemed just as fascinated by Grace and Sam, asking lots of questions about what it was like to tour the country singing popular Christian songs.

As the dining steward cleared their dishes, Grace told Sam she'd like to go to the lounge car, see if she could find Ramona again and talk to her. "Okay," Sam said. "Think I'll go back to our compartment. The beds should be made up by now." She grinned. "My book is getting to the good part."

Sam had been spending hours with her

nose in a well-worn paperback. Something by Toni Morrison. Grace hadn't realized Sam was such a reader. Maybe she'd ask to read it when Sam was done.

Grace walked the length of the lounge car, but didn't see the girl. Should she walk through the coaches? That might seem awfully obvious. On a whim, Grace decided to check the café below the lounge — and there she was, sitting at one of the booths chowing down on a hamburger. The lower area seemed unusually warm and the girl had taken off the suede jacket and laid it on the table along with her shoulder bag.

"Hi again!" Grace smiled, indicating the opposite padded bench of the booth. "May I sit — or are you expecting your friend?"

Ramona stopped mid-chew and stared at Grace, then her dark eyes flickered anxiously toward the stairs and back again. But she shook her head. Grace decided that meant she wasn't expecting him and slid into the booth with a smile. "That's an unusual breakfast." It was only nine thirty.

Ramona put down the hamburger and wiped catsup and mustard off her mouth with a napkin as she swallowed. "Max was still asleep," she said defensively, "but I got hungry." She eyed Grace. "Did you come down here to get something to eat too?"

"Oh." Grace thought fast. "No, just wanted to get a cup of coffee." She stood up. "Please, go ahead and eat. I'll be back in a minute."

She ordered a decaf coffee from the café counter — she'd already had enough caffeine for one morning — and came back to the booth. "So you're on your way to Chicago. How long will you be staying?"

Again the girl's eyes darted toward the stairs. "Uh, not sure. Max wants to see some friends. Stuff like that."

At the station in Los Angeles, Ramona had been outgoing and friendly. Overly so. Now she seemed like a timid rabbit. But Grace had an idea why.

Grace took off the plastic lid from her disposable hot cup and peeled the top off a couple tiny creamers even though she usually drank her coffee black. She decided to press. "You said it's your first visit to Chicago. How about Max? His too?"

The girl shook her head. "No. He's . . . from there." She took another bite of her hamburger — just as the train gave a lurch rounding a corner around a large sandstone formation. But before Grace could grab her coffee cup, it tipped, and hot liquid sloshed all over the suede jacket.

"Oh, no!" she cried, grabbing the empty

cup, even as the plastic bottles of catsup and mustard also fell over and rolled across the table toward the window. With her free hand, Grace grabbed the mustard, but the cap was loose and mustard squirted every which way.

In horror, Grace stared at the jacket, a large coffee stain darkening the beautiful tan suede. And as if that wasn't bad enough, splashes of yellow mustard had landed on the jacket too.

"My jacket!" screeched Ramona. She looked absolutely stricken. "Max will kill me! He bought that for me for the trip!"

"Oh, Ramona." Grace picked up the jacket, but knew better than to start dabbing at the stains with a napkin. "I am *so* sorry. Look — I'll have it cleaned and get it back to you."

Ramona glared at her. "What do you mean?"

"This is my fault. I should pay to get it cleaned. If you give me the address of the place you're staying, I'll get it cleaned and bring it to you myself. I promise."

But the girl shook her head. "No, no, you can't . . . I don't . . . I'm not sure where we'll be staying. Don't know the address."

"Do you have a cell phone? I'll call you."

Again Ramona shook her head, her eyes

brimming with tears.

"Oh, Ramona. Please don't cry. I'm sure I can make this right. Here." Grace dug in her purse for the small notebook she carried and a pen. "Here's my cell phone number. As soon as you get to Chicago and find out where you're staying, you call me and let me know. I'll bring your jacket as soon as it's cleaned."

Grace stood up, jacket in hand, then reached out and touched the girl on the shoulder. "Again, I am so sorry. Please forgive me."

Ramona grabbed her hand. "Just don't . . . just don't tell Max about this. I'll think of something, I'll say I put it away. He'd kill me if he knew I didn't have it."

Grace nodded. "All right. But don't worry. I'm sure a dry cleaner can get these stains out if we do it as soon as possible. I'll get it back to you good as new or . . . or I'll buy you a new one." She gave the girl a reassuring smile. "Just hang on to my number, okay?"

Sam gaped wide-eyed as Grace spilled the whole story. She held up the jacket. "You're right. It's one awful mess. I'll go find something to wrap it in so that mustard doesn't get over any of *our* clothes." She slipped out the door to go look for the attendant.

Grace leaned back against the headrest of her seat with a sigh. Hopefully the jacket would come clean. But it bothered her that the girl had said, *"Max will kill me!"* two different times. Of course people often said that when they knew someone would be upset, but she'd seemed really afraid. Made her even more suspicious that the guy —

Grace's cell phone rang. Fishing it out of her bag, she smiled at the caller ID. *Bongo Booking Agency.* "Hello, Jeff. Checking up on me again?"

"You bet." Her agent's voice sounded warm, almost excited. "I've been getting some great reports from the tour . . . but first of all, are you okay? Barry said he was afraid you'd really hurt your voice again by the end of the tour."

"I think I'm going to be all right. But glad it's over."

"I hear your meet and greet times practically turned into counseling sessions . . . that's just amazing, Grace."

She chuckled at his choice of words. "It was pretty overwhelming at times, I have to admit. But to be honest, Jeff, I've never had a tour like this one, never felt the Spirit of God so present. There are a lot of hurting young people out there and . . . and somehow they just opened up."

"Look, I want to hear all about it. I mean that. In fact, I'm actually calling because I have this really crazy idea. Are you sitting down?"

Grace listened as Jeff spilled his idea, her eyes widening. She swallowed. It *was* crazy. Absolutely crazy! "But . . . do you think it's even possible?"

"Yes. I've checked with Amtrak. But you'll have to get off at Albuquerque and talk to the ticket office there to get your tickets changed."

Sam came in with a large, empty trash bag, saying, "Look what I found." But Grace put up her hand for silence as she listened to Jeff's instructions.

"Okay," she said finally. "I'll see what we can do and let you know." She closed her phone and eyed Sam cautiously. "Um, you're never going to believe this, but that was Jeff Newman. He's, uh, proposing that we get off at Raton, New Mexico, later this afternoon and take an Amtrak Bus to Denver to spend a day at Bongo Booking. He . . . he thought it'd be a good chance to meet the staff there and give us a chance to debrief about the tour in person."

"But —"

"Jeff says we could pick up the California Zephyr in Denver tomorrow night, which would get us home the next day. Only one day later. But we'd have to get our tickets changed in Albuquerque — there's a short layover there. What do you think?"

Sam looked flustered. "Are you serious? I mean, I was really looking forward to getting home tomorrow. You should too, don't you think? I'm tired, you're tired. And you need to take care of your voice, give it a good rest."

Grace studied the young woman who'd been her assistant for over a year now. Good ol' Sam . . . loyal, smart, funny, practical, helpful in a zillion ways. And so pretty with those sassy twists she wore, creamy caramel skin, and delightful grin. But the Samantha Curtis who'd rescued her at Saturday's concert had something else — a lovely voice. A voice that deserved a chance to be heard. And Jeff's whole nutty idea suddenly made sense in another way.

"I know it sounds crazy," she admitted. "But I was just thinking. If we take this chance to visit Bongo Booking, maybe we could ask Jeff to set up an appointment for you to talk to someone there about your own career. Would you like to do that?"

Sam's hand flew to her mouth, her large,

dark eyes bugging. "You're kidding! Oh, Grace . . . oh, Grace! Really? *Really?*" She started hopping around their little compartment saying, "Thank you, Jesus! Oh, hallelujah!"

Grace smiled. Well, why not? On top of everything else, it *would* be a good chance for Sam to meet the people at Bongo Booking in person. But it wasn't just the opportunity to meet the Bongo staff that had intrigued Grace. It was something else Jeff had said — something she hadn't shared with Sam. "To be honest, Grace, I got this crazy idea because . . . because I really want to see you. No, I *need* to see you."

CHAPTER 41

"This *is* crazy you know," Sam giggled, standing in the lower vestibule of the sleeper with their suitcases and bags as the Southwest Chief pulled into the station at Raton, New Mexico.

"I know." Grace smiled absently at another passenger who was determined to get off at this stop for a quick smoke, in spite of announcements over the intercom that Raton was *not* a smoking stop, and would only be in the station long enough for passengers to board or — in their case — make a connection with the Amtrak Thruway Bus to Colorado Springs and Denver. She stepped back deliberately, allowing the nervous man to get between her and Sam and the car attendant, who was waiting till the train totally stopped before opening the door.

This was her chance to slip the note she'd written under Harry Bentley's compartment door just beyond the shower and toilets.

Ever since they got their tickets changed in Albuquerque, Grace had been hoping to get a chance to let her neighbor-in-disguise know about their change in plans. She'd come down to the lower level a couple of times, hoping to catch him alone — but each time there had been someone using one of the toilets or a couple of passengers sitting in the lower-level roomettes with their doors open talking to each other across the passageway.

So she'd written a brief note telling him about their change of plans, along with her cell phone number, asking him to call her if he got a chance and she'd explain more. Then she'd added a PS: *If you can, please keep an eye on a young couple in the first coach behind the lounge car. He's tall, blond hair, late twenties, name is Max. Ramona's just a teenager, has dark hair. Speaks Spanish. Something doesn't feel right. She seems scared. He seems too controlling.*

She didn't have much to go on. Harry might think she was sticking her nose into other people's business where it didn't belong. But she felt led to say something.

"Grace! Come on!"

The train had stopped. Sam and the smoker had already gotten off. Grace stepped out onto the step stool and then onto the platform as the sleeping car attendant grabbed her teal-blue suitcases and pulled up the handles for her. "Sorry you're leavin' us," Sylvia said straight-faced. "Hope it wasn't because I short-sheeted your bunks."

Grace laughed. "No, everything was great. Thanks."

"Thank *you*." Sylvia gave them a wink as Sam pressed a twenty into her hand. "Better get on over there to that bus. It won't wait long."

A sleek new Greyhound bus stood in the lot beside the station, motor running. And sure enough, the driver had no sooner stowed the luggage of the transfer passengers into the belly of the beast than he was back in his seat and pulling the bus out of the tiny parking lot.

Grace twisted in her seat by the window and looked back. The Southwest Chief was already picking up speed and disappearing in the distance. How she'd wanted to find Ramona again and assure her she wasn't running off with her suede jacket! She'd wandered into the coach cars and found the pair in the first coach, but Max was sitting next to the aisle, iPod plugged into his ears, and Ramona was curled up next to the window with a blanket and pillow, sleeping.

No way could she say anything to Max about the jacket. She'd moved past and walked through the other coaches before turning back. But Ramona had still been asleep.

She'd just have to wait for the girl to call when she got back to Chicago. Surely she would, wouldn't she? Ramona had seemed anxious to get the jacket back. And it'd be a good excuse for Grace to see her again. For some reason, the pretty teenager had pricked her heart.

Sam pulled out her book and stuck her nose in it. Grace stared out the window, watching the changing scenery. The landscape was rockier, dotted with scrubby trees, and the horizon was rising into hills and low mountains.

"Grace." She felt a poke in her side from Sam. "Your cell phone."

"Oh." Sure enough, Grace's cell phone was doing its guitar-strum thing somewhere in her purse. Digging it out, she checked the caller ID . . . hmm, no name, unfamiliar number. But she answered it anyway. "Hello, this is Grace."

"Grace?" The voice in her ear sounded high-pitched, panicky, accusing — but with a familiar Spanish lilt. "You got off the train!

With my jacket! But you promised to return it!"

"Ramona?" Grace flagged Sam's attention and pointed at the phone. "Ramona, I'm so glad you called. I wanted to tell you that we had a slight change in plans, but please don't worry! My friend and I are catching the California Zephyr tomorrow night from Denver and we'll be back in Chicago on Wednesday afternoon. I promise I'll still get your jacket cleaned and —" Grace's mind scrambled. "— in fact, I might be able to get it cleaned in Denver, and then won't even lose a day. Do you want me to call you as soon as I —"

"No! Don't call this number. I'll — I'll call you. Okay, thanks . . ." The girl's voice seemed to be calming down. "Okay." And the phone went dead.

Grace eyed Sam. "That was odd. Ramona told me she didn't have a cell phone."

Sam shrugged. "Maybe it was the guy's."

"Maybe. She still didn't want me to call her."

Sam returned to her book. Grace noticed a crossword puzzle magazine someone had left in the seatback pocket in front of her and fished it out. But she'd only been working on a puzzle for five or ten minutes when the cell phone rang again. "Aren't you popular," Sam smirked without looking up from her book. But this time the caller ID said *Harry Bentley.*

Grace answered cautiously. "Hello . . . oh, can you hold on a minute?" She climbed over Sam and made her way to the back of the bus, where she found an empty seat next to an elderly man who had nodded off. "Uh, Mr. Bentley? Sorry about that. Had to get somewhere private. I was sitting right next to Sam." *Huh.* About as private as a phone booth crammed with college students. "So you found my note?"

"I did. What happened? Is everything all right?"

"Yes, fine! We decided last minute to, um, detour to Denver to see my agent. Just adding an extra day to our trip. Got our ticket changed in Albuquerque to the California Zephyr for the last leg. I wanted to tell you but didn't want to, you know, spoil your cover."

"Appreciate that. Tell me more about this couple you mentioned."

"Well, maybe it's nothing, but . . ." Grace briefly told him about the girl being all friendly at the LA station, then backing off when she was with the guy. ". . . who's at least ten years older than she is. I don't know, just seemed funny — and I didn't

493

like how he was treating her, all cozy one minute, then snapping at her, making her sit down when she wanted to get up, stuff like that."

"Can you describe them a little bit more?"

Grace gave a few more details — Max's spiky hair, what Ramona was wearing that day. She even told him about the suede jacket fiasco and her offer to get it cleaned and returned. "I feel really bad about it, but I'm going to make sure it happens. The girl called me just a few minutes ago, guess she saw us get off the train, she sounded upset. I assured her we'd be back just one day later, coming in from Denver, and I'd —"

"She called you?" Harry Bentley's voice perked up. "What number did she call from?"

"Oh, I don't think it's hers. She didn't want me to call her back — it might be the guy's phone and she didn't want him to know about the jacket."

There was a moment's silence on the other end. "Grace, is that number still in your phone? Might be useful to have it just in case . . . you know, the concern you raised. Might be nothing we can do, but if something did happen, we might need to get in touch with her."

"Oh, well, sure, I guess . . ." Grace was

able to access Recent Calls without losing his call and read off the number. "Well, thanks, Mr. Bentley. Guess I'll see you back in the neighborhood later this week. Tell your wife hello for me . . . 'Bye."

Sam looked up curiously as Grace climbed over her into the window seat. "Sorry about that . . . a personal call." Maybe she'd think it was from Roger. She was glad Sam just nodded and turned back to her book.

It was dark when the bus pulled into the Denver Amtrak station shortly after nine. A grinning Jeff Newman was there to meet them, grabbing their two largest suitcases as the driver pulled them out of the undercarriage. "Welcome to the Mile High City! How was the bus?"

"Not bad. But ooo, it's chilly here." Grace shivered at the drop in temperature from Raton, wishing she'd kept out a sweater.

"And we totally missed supper," Sam added. "Need food." She feigned a swoon.

Jeff laughed as he piled their suitcases into the trunk of his car. "Then the least I can do is buy you a hot meal. Hotel first? Or my favorite Italian bistro?"

"Food!" Grace and Sam chorused together.

Half an hour later, they were seated in a

booth at a cozy restaurant with a late-night crowd. In spite of how hungry she was, Grace decided to go light with a poached pear salad boasting Gorgonzola cheese and candied walnuts, adding strips of rotisserie chicken to make it a main dish. Sam had a pesto and mozzarella pizza with roasted red peppers, while Jeff ordered veal scaloppini. "And some hot tea with honey and lemon, please," Grace added. She hadn't been paying enough attention to her throat.

"So." Jeff leaned forward after the waiter took their order. "I want to hear all about the tour."

Grace let Sam tell most of it, while she watched Jeff. She'd almost forgotten how good-looking he was — all that dark curly hair, the laughing gray eyes, the five o'clock shadow that always made him look as if he'd forgotten to shave. What had Jeff meant when he said he *needed* to see her? She caught him glancing at her with that boyish grin from time to time, but then he'd turn his full attention back to Sam as she recounted the tour.

". . . and the brochures and flyers we put out about postabortion ministries and crisis pregnancy centers disappeared faster than we could replace them. Makes you wonder, doesn't it?" Sam shook her head. "I mean, most of Grace's fans come from churches and Christian colleges — but a lot of them are wounded. They really needed to hear about God's grace."

Jeff nodded soberly and turned his gray eyes on Grace. "Ever since you told me about your new focus, I've been excited. It just seemed so right. The whole staff was praying for the tour."

Grace flushed. Jeff was so encouraging. She knew Sam wouldn't make a big deal of coming to her rescue, probably wouldn't even mention it, so she picked up the story, telling Jeff how Sam had invented a duet on the spot that had saved the song *and* her voice.

Jeff slapped the table and wagged his head in amazement. "You two are something else! I've asked for audios of the concerts — I'd like to hear that."

They talked and ate and laughed as the time inched toward eleven, but finally Jeff paid the bill and dropped them off at an Embassy Suites Hotel not too far from the Bongo office. "Can I pick you up at nine? The other agents and staff are eager to meet you both. But, ah, Grace . . . do you have a moment? I know you're tired, won't keep you long."

Sam gave a wave and followed the bellhop

with their luggage to the elevators. Grace noticed her assistant didn't even give her the usual lecture about "don't be late" and "you need your rest."

Jeff led the way to a comfy sitting area in the lobby. Grace gave him a weary grin. "Actually, I need to ask you something too, so thanks."

He raised his eyebrows curiously. "Okay. You first."

"It's about Sam . . ." She told him that Sam had majored in music at Fisk, had a strong voice herself, the audience had absolutely loved the duet, she'd even been asked if they'd do it again the next morning, and would it be possible for Bongo to consider representing her?

Jeff pursed his lips. "Well, sure, we could certainly get her an interview with one of the agents, though it'd be helpful if we had some demos, or could hear her sing. Once we get the CD of that concert, that'd be a start. Though, Grace . . ." He looked at her curiously. ". . . what are you thinking? Asking Sam to sing with you at your concerts? Encouraging Sam to pursue her own career?"

Grace swallowed. "I don't know. I —" What *was* she doing? "I think I'm learning that things don't happen by accident. That duet was a God-thing and . . . I'd hate to stand in the way. Maybe it's Sam's time to shine."

Jeff leaned forward, forearms resting on his knees, a slow smile spreading over his face. "You're amazing, you know that? And actually, uh, this is perfect. Because I was going to ask if we could get some time together tomorrow, just you and me. Selfish of me, but . . . I need to talk to you. If I can set something up for Sam, maybe we could go out for coffee, or lunch, or just go for a walk in Riverfront Park." He seemed a bit flustered. "Would that be okay with you?"

Grace suddenly felt tongue-tied, heat rising in her face. All she could do was nod.

"Good!" Jeff stood up. "I should go, let you get to bed. Tomorrow at nine, right?"

He started to leave, but Grace suddenly called after him. "Jeff, wait. I have a huge favor to ask you. If I run up to the room and get a jacket that has coffee and mustard stains on it — uh, long story, tell you later — could you by any chance drop it off at a good quality dry cleaner early, like before you come to pick us up? One that could do it before our train leaves tomorrow night?"

CHAPTER 42

Their twenty-four-hour stopover in Denver was over much too soon. Grace tried to busy herself settling into their new sleeping compartment on the California Zephyr the next evening, but kept looking out the window to see if Jeff was still on the platform. Had he left already? . . . No, there he was, over by the main doors, shoulders hunched inside his leather jacket, hands in the pockets, looking their way.

"Really cool that Jeff was able to get the jacket cleaned." Sam hung the hanger with the suede jacket swathed in dry-cleaner plastic on a hook, took out her toiletries and set them by the small sink and vanity, then flopped into a seat. "You want to go to the dining car? Billy said it's first come, first served now, since the train was late." Billy was their new car attendant, younger than most of the sleeping car attendants they'd seen so far. "I'm starved . . . oh, here we go."

With a slight jerk, the train slowly moved out of the station, swaying its way through Denver's backyards. From her seat by the window Grace watched until the figure on the platform disappeared from sight. Her heart was still beating faster than usual.

She needed another day here in Denver — or maybe a week, or a month! — to process her time with Jeff. Or at least a few hours by herself . . .

"Sam, would you mind if I stayed here while you go to the diner? I — I just don't feel like making small talk with total strangers tonight. If you see our car attendant, would you ask if he'd bring me a plate? Chicken's fine."

Sam crossed her arms and raised her eyebrows beneath the little twists that hung over her forehead. "Grace Meredith. Is there something going on with you and a certain Bongo agent whose name we shall not mention? You guys were gone from the office a long time this afternoon."

"Not that you suffered," Grace shot back with a teasing grin. Sam's interview with another Bongo agent — Terry Schroeder, mid-thirties — had taken place at one of Denver's high-end Asian restaurants. "All *we* had was Chinese takeout in the park."

"Uh-huh. That's what I'm talking about.

Sounds *very* businesslike."

Grace felt her face color. "Tell you when I figure it out myself."

"Okay." Sam's voice softened. "Just want you to know I care." The door to their compartment slid shut behind her.

Grace curled up in the corner of the long couch by the window. The setting sun off to the west outlined the sharp peaks of the Rocky Mountains into inky silhouettes against a rosy sky. But even though the sunset was beautiful, she closed her eyes, wanting to relive everything that had happened that day . . .

The Riverfront Park along the Platte River not far from downtown Denver was a pleasant oasis from the bustling city, and the midday temperatures had risen into the low seventies. "Nice," Grace murmured as she and Jeff found a stone bench to sit on.

They ate their egg rolls in silence for a few minutes, muted sounds of traffic behind them, while the narrow river — fuller at this time of year, Jeff said, from melting snows in the mountains — splashed over boulders and rocks and under street bridges in front of them.

Jeff cleared his throat. "Grace, if you don't mind, I need to ask you a question. But before I do, I need to warn you that this might seem to come out of left field. Just hang in here with me, okay?"

"Okay . . ."

"Just before the tour, you said your fiancé —"

"Ex-fiancé," Grace corrected.

"Well, that's the thing. You said Roger asked if you'd consider giving the two of you another chance, and my question is, uh . . . have you decided to get back together with him?"

Grace didn't dare look at him. She just shook her head.

"Does that mean, no, you're not getting back together with him, or no, you haven't decided?"

She swallowed the mouthful of egg roll she'd been chewing. "Haven't decided."

"I see." Jeff was quiet for a long moment, his Chinese takeout seemingly forgotten on the bench beside him. "Well, if you're still thinking about it, what I'm about to say might complicate things."

Now she did look at him. His gray eyes were fixed on her, the five o'clock shadow outlining his jawline in a sexy way, his dark curls kept neat by a recent haircut. She felt like she couldn't breathe.

He took a deep breath. "I think I've fallen

in love with you, Grace Meredith."

She white-knuckled the stone bench, as if holding on for dear life. She knew it might be something like this — and yet she hadn't dared put the actual thought into words in her own mind. Or heart.

Jeff put up his hands defensively. "I know it sounds crazy. We haven't spent that much time together. But ever since our first meeting — at your house, remember? You'd just gotten back from your New Year, New You tour. Your voice was shot, you could hardly talk. Roger had just dumped you —"

Grace found her voice, though it came out in a croak. "Just say it. I was a mess."

He grinned at her. "Well . . . yes. Wasn't going to say that, though. What I was going to say is how mesmerized I was by you, in spite of all that. And then that freaky snowstorm . . . I was never so glad to get snowbound in my life. Me, totally unprepared for snow. You, drying my clothes and feeding me, in spite of the fact that we'd just met. But the real clincher? Playing Scrabble till after midnight."

"And I won."

He laughed. "Yes, you won. Twice." His face sobered. "You won my heart too."

Grace gulped. "I can't understand why. You said it yourself. I was a mess."

Jeff reached out and tucked a stray strand of hair behind her ear. "All I knew was, I'd just met a beautiful, incredible woman, and couldn't understand how her fiancé could just kick her to the curb like that. I think I started to love you then. Wanted to protect you, or punch the guy out. But it scared me. At first I denied it. I was your new agent, after all. Not supposed to fall in love with a client. But . . . the feeling wouldn't go away. I'd already listened to every CD Bongo had of your concerts. And every time I heard your voice, scratchy as it was, my feelings grew. I watched you fight to overcome some pretty big obstacles and I fell in love with your toughness, your passion —"

"Thought you said I'd lost it. Down in St. Louis, remember?"

"No, I knew that passion was still there. You just had to dig deep to find it again. And . . . and you did, Grace. Everything about this last tour has just confirmed what I knew all along about the amazing woman I met in Chicago."

She believes in me, even when I don't believe in myself . . . Harry Bentley's words echoed in her head. Grace's eyes teared up, and she fished in the pocket of her jacket for a tissue.

Jeff looked alarmed. "I'm sorry, Grace. I

don't mean to upset you. If you tell me to stop, I will. But I couldn't stay silent any longer. When you told me Roger had asked you to patch up your relationship, and you were thinking about it, I thought I'd lost you. Then I realized I'd never told you how I feel. So . . . here I am, doing that very thing. I know it's crazy, and I'm probably way over the line here, but . . . I just want to know if there's any chance for us."

Grace looked away, staring at the river rippling through the city, at the large buildings rising on the other side. "You don't really know me," she whispered.

"But I love what I do know. And I'd like a chance to get to know you more."

Grace gripped the stone bench again, afraid to look at him. Afraid she'd melt into his arms without thinking. But his gentle words felt like cool water spilling over her spirit. Was this what love felt like? Was it real — or just a fragile bubble that would burst if he knew the truth . . .

He had to know. She had to tell him. She turned and met his eyes searching hers. "There's . . . there's something I need to tell you. About me." She drew in a deep breath, her voice tremulous. "You wanted to know why I chose this new theme about grace, and I said I'd tell you later — but I think you need to know. You might change your mind . . ."

Taking a deep breath, she managed to get it out in fits and starts — about being raised "a good Christian girl," and how everyone had so many high expectations of her, expectations that felt impossible to live up to. How much she wanted to fit in at school, to be liked. How naïve she'd been, dating a popular guy behind her parents' backs and ending up in the backseat of a car — and pregnant. "I couldn't face it. Couldn't face letting everybody down. So I . . ." Her eyes fell to her lap. "I had an abortion. And I never told anyone. But I hated myself. Thought God hated me too."

"Oh, Grace. I'm so sorry. That must have been so hard to face alone."

"I tried to make it up to God, to make myself worthy again — that's why I got so passionate about my purity theme. Huh. Traveling all over the country, people thinking I'm this great role model, telling kids they're 'worth the wait.' But . . ." She lifted anguished eyes to his face, once again fighting back tears. "That woman you say you fell in love with? She was a fraud. A fake. Worth the wait? She didn't wait herself. All those years, living with secrets, afraid I'd be found out."

507

Jeff seemed about to say something, but she lifted a hand to stop him. "I'm . . . I'm only now beginning to understand that God's grace is so much bigger than my sin. That's why I wanted to rename this tour, why I wanted to sing about God's gift of grace. But . . . I still didn't have the courage to tell my own story from the stage. I — I still haven't told my parents. Or Roger." She paused, sobered by a sudden realization. "I haven't told Roger, but I've told you . . ."

Grace's shoulders began to shake with regret . . . and relief. Regret that she hadn't told her parents or Roger. Regret that she had to burst Jeff's bubble of the "wonderful woman" he thought she was. But also relief that she'd been honest with him. She never wanted to live with secrets and fear, ever again. Even if the truth pushed away a truly wonderful man who'd just said he loved her. Who believed in her. Who —

But then she felt Jeff's arms go around her, and he pulled her close, holding her, his lips on her hair, whispering in her ear. "Oh, Grace. I'm so glad. So glad you trusted me enough to tell me, to let me know what you've been struggling with. None of us are perfect. You are who God made you to be. And I love the whole Grace even more than the Grace I knew before . . ."

A loud rap on the door of the sleeper bedroom shook Grace out of her memory of those precious moments in the park. Reluctantly she got up and slid back the door. There stood Billy, red-headed, owlish glasses perched on his rather short nose, holding a tray with a covered dish. "Your dinnah, madam!" he announced playfully. Did they call him Billy the Kid?

"Thank you so much." She took the tray. She should give him a tip. But before she could get to her purse, he'd already disappeared down the hallway, whistling. Well, they'd take care of him later.

Grace sat back down. Jeff's words still echoed in her ears. What was it Mr. Bentley had also said about Estelle? . . . *She makes me feel like a complete person. Like I can be who God wants me to be.*

Jeff had always been totally supportive. Well, of course, he had to be. He was her agent. That was his job. And yet . . . it'd been more than that. Jeff sincerely believed her voice was a gift from God, and that she should use it to glorify him. But he was also sensitive to her needing time to recover, time to regroup, time to rebuild her confidence — and he'd done everything he could to build up her confidence too. Not just to sing again, but her confidence to be . . . herself.

Had she ever felt that kind of support from Roger?

Grace sighed. Maybe it wasn't fair to compare the two. Jeff had been thinking about her career. Roger had been thinking about their life together. She couldn't totally dismiss his concern about how much she traveled and its impact on him . . . uh, she meant, on them.

Grace blinked. No. She was right the first time. He'd never once worried about the impact of her travel on *her*. It was always, "I don't like it."

The door of the compartment slid open. "Grace Meredith!" Sam scolded. "You haven't touched your food! Bet it's all cold now. Good thing I brought you something to warm you up." She handed Grace a disposable cup with a plastic lid. "Hot tea with lemon and honey. The café guy made it special."

Grace took it gratefully, suddenly realizing she was hungry after all. "Don't worry, I'll still eat it. Just been thinking . . ."

"Mm. Let me know when you feel like talking."

Grace nodded. She did want to talk to

510

Sam. But not yet. She didn't need opinions. She needed . . . prayer.

As she lay in the dark later that evening, she turned her thoughts and her heart toward God. *God, I confess I . . . I think I love Jeff. But I don't want to rush into something I don't fully understand. I loved Roger once — if I gave our relationship a chance, would I love him again? I need your guidance! What is my next step? I need to talk to Roger — I owe him that much. But what do I say?*

She'd been honest with Jeff. Before she and Roger could move forward, she needed to be honest with him too, about the Grace he didn't know. About the secrets of her past. About the spiritual crisis that had launched her new theme of God's undeserved grace. The truth about herself that she couldn't promise to keep private forever — not if God wanted her to share her story with the young men and women who came to her concerts, who thought they were the only ones who'd messed up.

How would Roger react to that?

The whistle at the front of the train hooted once . . . twice . . . three times. Passing some lonely country crossing in the middle of the night. Taking her home — where she'd need to face the music.

CHAPTER 43

Even though the California Zephyr had been late arriving in Denver, it managed to make up most of the time during the night and early morning hours and pulled into Chicago's Union Station only ten minutes late the next afternoon.

"Three o'clock — not bad," crowed Sam, as the sleeping car attendant helped set their luggage on the platform. "Thanks, Billy." She pressed a twenty into his hand.

"And thank *you*!" The Kid beamed. "Would you like assistance into the station? An electric cart will be coming shortly."

"Thanks, but we're fine." Grace gave him a smile, balanced her tote bag, her purse, and the plastic cleaner bag with the tan suede jacket to ride on the top of both her suitcases, and wheeled them down the platform toward the station. She was more interested in getting home than waiting for a cart. Threading their way past slower pas-

512

sengers, they followed the barked instructions of Amtrak employees, who were directing foot traffic past the departure doors and toward a large open entryway marked Arrivals.

"Grace! Hold up a minute." Sam stopped, fumbled for her phone, and held it up to her ear. A moment later she pocketed the phone and caught up with Grace, who'd stopped to wait. "That was Rodney Bentley. The limo's waiting up on Canal Street. Told him we'd be up in a few minutes. *Uh,* let's see . . . there. The escalator's straight ahead."

Grace nodded and let Sam lead the way. Sam had called Lincoln Limo about their change in plans, but Grace decided to call Rodney directly to apologize for canceling on such short notice, and said she hoped it wouldn't jeopardize anything about his job. He'd said no problem, he'd work it out — in fact, he'd insisted on picking them up today and seeing them safely home.

But she was tired. Hard to believe she'd left home fifteen days ago from this station. So many miles covered — fifty-five hundred at least. And so much had happened! She couldn't wait to pick up Oreo, get home to her own little nest on Beecham Street, stop living out of a suitcase, sleep in her own bed . . . and have time to sort through all the jumbled thoughts and feelings that had kept her awake most of the night.

Feelings she needed to sort out *before* she called Roger — or before he called her. "Grace, look. Isn't that the girl you met on the train?"

Sam's sudden question startled Grace out of her private thoughts. "Where? . . . Oh! You're right."

Ramona was standing at the bottom of the escalators, hands in the pockets of her skinny jeans and shoulders hunched, looking this way and that as if waiting for someone. What was she doing at the station? Hadn't she and Max gotten into Chicago yesterday? Grace had promised to get the jacket to her if Ramona called and gave her an address. Whatever the reason, Grace felt a stab of relief. She'd wondered if she'd ever see the girl again. As they got closer, she called out, "Ramona! Over here!"

The girl's eyes lit with recognition and she hurried toward them. The three met and stopped, making other passengers flow around them in the busy passageway. Ramona eyed Grace soberly. "You got my jacket?"

She smiled. "Matter of fact, I do." She unhooked the cleaner bag from the handle of her large suitcase and handed it to Ramona. "Here it is, good as new I hope."

The girl took it, and to Grace's surprise, slipped the plastic up, held the jacket up, and inspected it closely. "It came clean. Cool." Taking the jacket off the hanger, she put it on, running her hands up and down the soft suede. *"Gracias."* She finally smiled. "So . . . how was your time in Denver?"

Grace wanted to laugh. "It was great. Not long enough, though." She caught Sam giving her a smug smile. She'd told Sam that morning about her walk in the park with Jeff, asking her to please just listen for now. She knew Sam was highly amused at the romantic bind she was in, and no doubt had an opinion or two on what she should do.

But she ignored Sam's knowing glance and kept her attention on the girl. "How about you? Have you had a chance to do any sight-seeing yet?" Okay, that was dumb. If they were going to chat, they should get out of the way. "Actually, do you have a few minutes? We could . . . uh, Ramona? Are you okay?"

The girl suddenly seemed to sway and her eyelids fluttered. "Not . . . feeling so good. I — I need to sit down. Can we . . . over there, by the fountain?"

"Yes, of course . . . go." Grace anxiously

hustled after Sam and Ramona, threading her way through the throng with suitcases and bags — but just before they reached the square fountain, Ramona stopped . . . swayed again . . . and suddenly sank in a listless heap to the floor.

"Ramona!" Grace and Sam fell to their knees beside the inert girl, whose thick fall of black hair splayed out around her. *O God, O God, what do we do?* Grace gripped one of Ramona's hands and felt her wrist for a pulse, even as Sam took off her light jacket, quickly folded it, and slipped it under the girl's head.

A small crowd gathered around the figures on the floor in the narrow area between the fountain and the back of the escalators. "Does she need a doctor?" "What happened?" "Want me to call 9-1-1?"

Grace started to say a panicked yes, but just then she heard Ramona groan, "No, no . . ." To her relief, the girl's eyes fluttered open and she struggled to sit up. "Don't need a doctor . . . just got dizzy." She hunched over and hugged her legs, resting her head on her knees.

Grace sat down and put her arm around Ramona and held her. She glanced at Sam crouching on the other side of the girl and shaking her head as if to say, *"I don't know what to do either."*

"I'll . . . I'll be all right. Just give me a minute." Ramona's voice was muffled as she cradled her face between her knees and tentatively touched the back of her head, which she'd probably banged when she fell. The crowd lost interest and started to disperse.

Grace's heart went out to the girl. Ramona was so young, couldn't be more than seventeen or eighteen, in Chicago for the first time, probably didn't know anyone except her "man," who didn't seem to be anywhere around at the moment. What if Ramona had fainted with no one around who knew her? At least it happened while she and Sam were here — and no way would Grace leave her alone until she knew the girl was going to be all right.

Ramona raised her head and blew out a breath. "I'm . . . I'm okay now, I think." Grace and Sam got to their feet and helped her stand up.

"You okay? Here, sit down." Grace and Sam led the girl to the flat marble bench that surrounded the square fountain, then turned back to retrieve their luggage. Grace picked up her tote bag from the floor where it had fallen and slipped the strap over the handle of her wheeled carry-on case while

Sam gathered her luggage. Okay, that was two . . . but where was her larger case? "Sam? Where's my big suitcase? I thought it was right here with the other one."

"Huh, don't see it. Maybe somebody moved it — it was probably in the way."

Grace and Sam swiveled about, looking for the teal-blue suitcase. The lobby was a five-way junction, with the escalators coming down from Canal Street, the splashing fountain tucked behind the moving stairs, the row of kiosks on one side of the fountain where online tickets could be printed out, plus the row of standard ticket counters and lines of waiting passengers.

Sam said, "Wait a sec," and walked clear around the escalators while Grace circled the fountain. But both came back shaking their heads.

Grace felt a growing worry in the pit of her stomach. "You don't think . . . could someone have stolen it?" Then she remembered the girl. "Oh, Ramona, I'm sorry." She turned back to where Ramona had been sitting.

But the girl was gone.

Scrunched into a small cubicle office with Sam and an Amtrak security agent, Grace finished filling out the police report about her missing bag and laid down the pen. Her eyes felt tight, as if holding back tears. All the courage she'd built up taking the train instead of having to submit to the intense security at airports had drained out of her spirit. Her luggage had been stolen, of all things, right behind her back! Wasn't there any safe way to travel?

She glanced at Sam, sitting patiently in a folding chair off to the side, and mouthed, *"Sorry to make you wait. Did we lose our ride?"*

Sam shook her head and mouthed back, *"Rodney said he'd wait. Are you okay?"*

Grace shrugged. It wasn't just the suitcase. Ramona had disappeared too. It felt like two losses, just minutes apart. She was worried about the girl. Perhaps Ramona would still call her. But she had no reason to call now.

Somewhere in her purse, her cell phone rang, but she was distracted by a frustrated voice saying, "I'm sorry, Bentley. Your dog won't come."

Bentley? Was that Harry? Grace half stood and looked over the partition of the cubicle toward the reception area, but only saw the door leading out into the station wheeze shut. Did Mr. Bentley know her suitcase had been stolen? She wished she could talk to him before they left. She wanted to tell him about Ramona. Maybe he could —

But first she had to finish filling out the police report. Reading through it once more, she finally handed it to the security agent, who also looked it over and nodded. "Guess that's it. So sorry about this, Ms. Meredith. We'll do our best to recover your property. Glad you filled out the estimated cost of the suitcase and its contents — in case you need it for your insurance."

Grace nodded, not trusting herself to speak. It wasn't the cost that bothered her as much as the sense of being *violated*. Not to mention pretty darn inconvenient too. That case had most of her concert dresses! She didn't even want to think about it.

"Ah. You're still here."

Grace turned at the familiar voice. "Mr. Bentley!" The last time she'd seen him, he'd been wearing wraparound shades, a plaid flat hat tipped rakishly on his shaved head. Now he was leaning against the opening to the cubicle wearing ordinary black slacks, a white shirt, a tweedy sport coat, and a big grin, Corky at his side — minus the guide-dog harness.

"You lose something?"

Grace grimaced. "My suitcase was stolen."

"Uh-huh." The grin widened. "Got news for you. We caught the perp red-handed before he got out of the station and got your

suitcase back."

Grace and Sam gasped. *"What?"* Grace stared at the man, her emotions doing somersaults between relief and confusion. "How . . . oh, my. I can't believe it."

"That's the good news." Harry Bentley's face sobered. "The bad news is, Amtrak police will need to keep your suitcase for a little while until the, uh . . . thief has been booked and we've completed all the paperwork. A list of the contents would be helpful to make sure everything's still there. I'll see that you get it back as soon as they release it. Hopefully it won't be too long."

"Oh, Harry! Thank you!" Grace jumped up and gave her neighbor a hug. "I'm going to tell Estelle to cook you one of her famous dinners tonight. You deserve it!"

"Uh, it's Detective Bentley here at the station." He laughed self-consciously.

"Oh!" Grace was just about to tell him about Ramona, but he suddenly clapped his hands. "Sorry, ladies, gotta go. C'mon, Corky." He winked at Grace. "Told you Amtrak security was on the job — even when you didn't know it."

CHAPTER 44

It was five thirty by the time the limo drew up in front of Grace's bungalow on Beecham Street. Even though Rodney Bentley had said he didn't have another client till that evening and would be glad to drive both of them, Sam had elected to get a cab and go straight home. "Girl, I *know* you want to stop by Meeow Chicago and pick up Oreo," she'd teased, giving Grace a good-bye hug, "but right now *my* priority is soaking in a long bubble bath." And she'd waved good-bye as the limo pulled away.

After being together in close quarters 24/7 for the past fifteen days, Grace already missed the young woman who'd become so much more than an assistant. More like a best friend — or the sister she'd never had.

"I owe you big time, Rodney," she said, as he opened her door, took the cat carrier from her, and then helped her out. "So sorry you had to wait while I filled out that police report, but I do appreciate it."

"Not a problem, Ms. Meredith. Least I can do as thanks for you and Ms. Curtis getting me this job."

"Rodney, you can 'Ms. Meredith' me all you want at Lincoln Limo's office, but it feels really silly for neighbors to be so formal. Please, call me Grace."

He grinned, and Grace noted how much he looked like his dad just then. "All right," he said. "But we aren't neighbors anymore. I moved to my grandmother's old apartment now, took over her lease."

"Oh." Grace was surprised. She'd assumed that since the grandmother had passed maybe Rodney would live in the first-floor apartment. "Uh, is DaShawn — ?"

Rodney shook his head. "Still with my dad." He suddenly busied himself getting her luggage out of the trunk — minus the big case — and took it up to her door.

She had no idea what that was about, but decided it wasn't any of her business. This time she had a generous tip ready before waving good-bye. "For going the extra mile and letting me pick up my cat."

Once inside, and after stepping over the pile of mail and magazines on the floor under the mail slot, Grace opened the cat carrier door and lifted a meowing Oreo into her arms. "You have no idea how much I missed you, buddy," she murmured, nuzzling the black-and-white cat's soft neck fur. She giggled as his rough tongue licked her chin and his purr motor started up. "Yeah, you missed me too."

She collapsed on the couch, put her feet up on the coffee table, and laid her head back against the couch cushions. Sam's idea of a good, long soak in a bubble bath sounded like heaven . . . but should she unpack first? Get something to eat? Pick up all that mail and get it out of the way? Call Jeff and let him know she got home safely? He'd asked her to call . . . or should she call Roger first? Who did she owe her allegiance to?

Locating her purse where she'd dumped it beside the cat carrier, Grace dug out her phone and saw she had a new voice mail. *Roger.* She was just about to hit the Play button when her doorbell rang. She opened the door, ready to send whoever it was packing . . . and then grinned. "Estelle!"

Estelle Bentley stood on the stoop, her longish black-and-gray-streaked hair piled up in a loose bun on top of her head, holding a covered dish with hands shoved inside big oven mitts. "Grace! Praise God you're all right. Harry called me, said you got robbed at the train station, you poor baby." She stepped inside and headed straight for the kitchen. "I brought you some supper. I *know* you don't have anything in the house after being gone so long — and Harry might not make it home till late anyway. Said he had a case that got complicated."

Grace followed her. "Oh, Estelle, you didn't have to do that." But she was glad she had. The pungent warm smell wafting from the dish made her realize just how hungry she really was.

"Honey, you sit down and eat. Lord, Lord, having your suitcase stolen like that! You must be all worn to a frazzle." Estelle was already dishing up what looked like shepherd's pie from the hot casserole onto a plate from the cupboard.

Grace sat down at the kitchen table. "Um, did Harry tell you they caught the thief, and I'm going to get my suitcase back?"

"Yes, he did. Hallelujah! But he's worried about you, told me to check on you, make sure you're okay." Estelle put the plate and a fork in front of her, then sat down in the other chair, propped her elbows and folded hands on the table, and closed her eyes. "Lord, bless this food and we're grateful your guardian angels were on the ball at the train station this afternoon, amen . . . now eat."

Grace was salivating, but hesitated. "If Harry's not going to be home till later, why don't you dish up some of this for yourself? Hate to eat in front of you."

"Oh, maybe just a bite or two. I want to eat with Harry when he gets home." Estelle grabbed a plate from the cabinet and dished up a small portion. "But I'm not gonna stay long, 'cause I know you gotta be tired. But, land sakes, tell me what happened."

Between bites of the savory meat and vegetables hiding under a flaky crust, Grace told about the girl from the train who'd fainted, then discovering someone had taken off with her suitcase while she and Sam were helping her. "What I can't figure out is, who'd want to steal my suitcase? All it had in it was clothes and stuff."

Estelle shrugged. "Who knows. Maybe the thief thought you had some expensive jewelry. But . . . you say the girl disappeared too? That's odd."

Grace nodded. "I'm really worried about her." She told Estelle about meeting the teenager in LA, how she was traveling with a guy at least ten years older, and something just didn't feel right. "I mean, I was a vulnerable teenager once, and look what happened to me. And Ramona was traveling cross-country with this guy! But . . . I doubt I'll ever see her again. Wish there was something I could do."

Estelle was frowning. "*Hmm.* What about the guy she was with, this Max? Did you see him at the station? I wonder . . ." She tapped her fingers on the table as if thinking — then shook her head. "Oh, never mind. But you know what? I can tell God has put this Ramona girl on your heart and there *is* something you can do. You can pray for her. We'll add her to the list for when we get together to pray, how about that? But now, I better go and let you get settled back home. Keep the dish for now — there's enough for tomorrow too."

Grace saw her to the door and watched as Estelle hustled across the street. Sounded like the prayer time was going to be a regular thing. Well, she could use it. She almost wished Estelle had stayed longer so she could've told her about the new wrinkle in her life. She surely needed some prayer to know what to do about Jeff and Roger.

Roger. Picking up her phone again, she pressed Play and put it to her ear . . .

"Grace? It's Roger. Welcome back. Eager to see you. Hope you've had a day to recover. Now that the tour's out of the way, hopefully

we can spend some quality time working on our relationship. Any chance we can get together this weekend? Call me, okay?"

A day to recover? Well, of course. She'd told him she'd be back yesterday, hadn't told him yet they'd added an extra day to the trip. How was she going to explain that? *O Lord, I need more time to think — and pray!* But she had to respond to his voice mail or he'd call again before she was ready — or think she was ignoring him, which had problems of its own.

She sent a text. *Roger, thanks for the call. Yes, I'm back, but very bushed. Will call you tomorrow, OK?*

Tomorrow . . .

But right now, she was going to "settle in," as Estelle had said. The yummy shepherd's pie gave her the necessary energy to unpack and start a small load of laundry. Most of her clothes were in the other suitcase anyway. Then she ran a tub full of hot soapy water, undressed, and sank beneath the foamy bubbles. *Ahhhhhhhh . . .*

Oreo wandered into the bathroom and settled down on the rug, tucking his white paws under his chest like a Sphinx, purring happily. Yes, they were both glad to be home. The thoughts tumbling in her mind slowed and seemed to relax.

What was it Estelle had said in her prayer? That guardian angels had been "on the ball" at the train station, protecting her *and* her suitcase. And she'd been serious. Well, the Bible was serious about angels too, protecting God's people, fighting their battles. When the theft had first happened, a familiar old anxiety had elbowed its way back into her spirit. But as her muscles and spirit relaxed in the hot water, she had a new thought . . . maybe it was actually the other way around. Maybe it didn't really matter what way she traveled because, bottom line . . . her protection was in God's hands. Wherever.

Hadn't God been freeing her from her fears, from needing to hide the secrets of her past? Estelle, Samantha, her brother, Jeff . . . hadn't they all loved on her anyway, even knowing the sins of her youth? Hadn't they showed her God's grace? She no longer felt as if God was "out to get her," but instead knew God had been there all along, wanting to give her the gift of unconditional love and forgiveness.

A few months ago she'd thought her life was falling apart. Yes, she'd fallen . . . but had landed on solid ground.

Grounded in God's grace.

Tears slid down her face and mingled with

the bubbles sloshing her neck and chin. Happy, grateful tears.

The bathwater was getting cool. Grace leaned forward and ran more hot water into the tub, then slid down under the bubbles again, thoughts still roaming. Nice of Roger to call — but there was something about his message that bothered her. What did he say? Once she'd stepped out of the tub, dried off, and bundled up in her bathrobe, she picked up her phone and listened to Roger's voice mail again . . .

There. That was it. *"Now that the tour's out of the way . . ."*

Out of the way. That's what he thought of her singing, her concerts, her tours. Something to get "out of the way."

Her eyes widened. So different than Jeff's whole-hearted support of how God was using her. She thought again of what Mr. Bentley had said: *"She makes me feel like I can be who God wants me to be. She believes in me, even when I don't believe in myself."*

Roger had never made her feel like that.

A smile played on Grace's face as she crawled into bed. Oreo curled up on the foot of the bed and she picked up the phone again. She would call Roger tomorrow. But right now . . .

She dialed and waited for the cell number

to ring. Once, twice —

Her heart beat faster when she heard the hello on the other end.

"Jeff? It's me, Grace . . ."

The guitar strum ringtone woke Grace from a sound sleep. Daylight was streaming through the half-closed blinds. She peered at the ringing phone with bleary eyes. What? Almost nine? Who was it? She didn't recognize the number.

But she couldn't help a lazy smile as she pushed the Talk button. She must've been sleeping like a baby. A very, very happy baby.

"Grace? Harry Bentley here. I'm down at the station and just wanted to let you know I'll probably be able to bring the suitcase to your house by tonight. Sorry for the inconvenience, but it's just, you know, security procedure."

"Thanks, Mr. Bentley. I understand." A well of gratitude bubbled in her spirit. Funny how the Bentleys — the newest people in the neighborhood — had impacted her life so profoundly. It was high time she made more of an effort to get to know the other people around her. "That's the second time you saved me, you know."

"Saved you? Just doin' my job. . . . Uh, what do you mean 'second time'?"

Grace laughed and said, " 'Bye, Mr. Bentley. See you tonight." She ended the call.

Maybe tonight she'd tell him how his simple description of the woman he loved had saved her from making a big mistake.

BOOK CLUB DISCUSSION QUESTIONS FOR *GROUNDED*

1. Has anyone ever walked out of your life . . . or said something hurtful . . . or given you upsetting news out of the blue that left you feeling as if you'd just been hit by a truck? Who did you blame — that person? Yourself? God? Why?

2. After Grace's meltdown at the airport on the way home from her New Year, New You tour, what did you think about her vow to never fly again? (immature? unreasonable? understandable? or _____?) Why? Did your reaction to that incident change as you learned more about her past? Why or why not?

3. Grace coped with her secret by becoming passionate about purity and a message of "you're worth the wait." What was positive about the way she coped? What was negative? How did it affect her spiritually?

4. Why do you think Grace was so nervous when she was invited to her new neighbors' home for supper? Have you ever been invited into the home of someone from a different racial group or cultural background? Have you ever invited someone from another racial group or culture to share your dinner table? Why does "breaking bread" in someone's home have special significance in bridging cultural and racial barriers?

5. Think about your own neighborhood; do you know your neighbors? How well? What are the qualities that make "neighborhood" a reality? What was missing from the Beecham Street neighborhood? What happened that gave a spark of hope that one day Beecham Street might become a warm and welcoming neighborhood? What do you think Grace might do to fan that spark? In what way might she need to change?

6. Why do you think Estelle Bentley was the first person Grace felt safe enough with to tell her secret? What qualities in Estelle made Grace feel safe? What other qualities did Estelle bring to the relationship that impacted Grace in a positive way?

7. Why do hidden secrets — things that have happened in the past, things we've done, who we "really are" inside — have such a powerful grip on our lives? Why does bringing things into the light help diminish their power? What are some cautions about dredging up stuff from the past? In Grace's case, how did "owning" her secret past bring her freedom?

8. What did you think when Roger admitted he'd made a mistake and wanted to give their relationship another chance? What do you think about his reasons for ending the engagement in the first place? What do you think he was hoping would make a difference? What were *you* hoping would happen?

9. Why was what Harry Bentley said about how he knew Estelle was "the one" so important to Grace? How did it help Grace make her decision? Do you think she made the right choice? What challenges might she still have to face?

10. Did the events on the train coming home from the Just Grace tour feel like a distraction to you? Are you left feeling, "What was *that* all about?" What are some

of the questions you're left with? How would you feel if we hinted that there's more to the story involving Ramona and Max happening at the same time as Grace's story . . . coming up in the parallel novel, *Derailed,* in the Windy City Neighbors series?